"Kearney is a master storyteller."
—Virginia Henley, *New York Times* bestselling author

"Looking for something different? A futuristic romance: Susan Kearney's *The Challenge* gave me a new perspective . . . [on] love and sex in the future!"
— Carly Phillips, *New York Times* bestselling author of the Chandler Brothers series

"Out-of-this-world love scenes, pulse-pounding action, and characters who come right off the page."
—Suzanne Forster, *USA Today* bestselling author on *The Dare*

"A desperate gamble leads to high voltage action and sensuality in Ms. Kearney's newest page turner. One of Ms. Kearney's strengths is her deft use of characterization which instantly vests readers in the perilous quest."
—*Romantic Times BookClub* on *The Dare*

"From the first page, Kearney captures the reader."
—*Affaire de Coeur*

"Susan Kearney is a gifted storyteller with carefully woven plots and refreshing characterization. Her style is crisp, and keeps her readers hungrily turning the pages."
—*Tampa Tribune*

The Quest

SUSAN KEARNEY

tor romance

A TOM DOHERTY ASSOCIATES BOOK
NEW YORK

This is a work of fiction. All the characters and events portrayed in this book are either products of the author's imagination or are used fictitiously.

THE QUEST

Edited by Anna Genoese

A Tor Book
Published by Tom Doherty Associates, LLC
175 Fifth Avenue
New York, NY 10010

www.tor.com

Tor® is a registered trademark of Tom Doherty Associates, LLC.

ISBN 0-765-35449-7
EAN 978-0-765-35449-5

First edition: July 2006

Printed in the United States of America

0 9 8 7 6 5 4 3 2 1

This is for all my readers who have supported me
and kept me going. Thank you all.

Acknowledgments:

FIRST AND FOREMOST I want to thank my editor Anna Genoese for always being in my corner. I appreciate you. A lot. And I'd also like to thank the rest of the Tor team, Anthony Schiavino for another eye-catching cover, as well as production, sales, marketing, and PR. So many people work behind the scenes to take my book to market and your efforts on my behalf have been wonderful and made this feel like a team effort.

Chapter One

"CAPTAIN, WE AREN'T alone."

Angel Taylor peered at the *Raven*'s viewscreen and frowned. Another starship had just exited hyperspace, heading straight toward the Vogan ship Angel was after. Apparently, the *Raven* wasn't the only scavenger ship on a salvage foray. "Raise engine speed ten percent."

"We're already redlining," Petroy, her first officer, informed her, but just as she knew he would, he increased their speed. The *Raven*'s engines vibrated up from engineering, pulsed through the deck of the bridge beneath Angel's feet, reverberated through her bones.

Ignoring the assorted rattles and moans of her equipment, Angel gritted her teeth and peered at the viewport where a panorama of stars served as a backdrop for the asteroid belt that had trapped the abandoned ship she intended to salvage. "Just once, I wish the information we purchased could be both accurate and *confidential.*"

Despite the competition, she had to secure the Vogan ship first. Losing the salvage to a rival wasn't an option. Due to lack of funds, her ship's safety inspection was five months overdue. In fact, the *Raven*'s engines needed a complete overhaul, and if Angel failed to procure the derelict ship, she faced the humiliation of being grounded—a fate she'd avoided for the last eight years, ever since she'd won the *Raven* in a gambling joint back on Earth.

When she'd first acquired the *Raven,* it hadn't been safe to fly out of orbit, but Angel had patched the holes in the hull and reprogrammed the computer systems herself. She'd lucked out on her first run, finding and securing the salvage rights to a wrecked Venus-to-Earth transport ship, which she'd sold back to the mining company that had built her, earning enough profit to take on a crew and enough fuel to leave the solar system. Since then, Angel had never looked back, roaming the galaxy in search of abandoned space vessels in hopes of one day finding the mother lode, a haul so rich she could afford to buy a ship that wasn't older than Petroy. Meanwhile, she enjoyed the hunt. The freedom of space and being her own boss suited her—even when her ship's system was falling apart around her.

Leaning eagerly over the computer vidscreen, Angel increased the magnification. The abandoned ship ahead tumbled like a glinting piece of quartz among lumps of coal. She wasn't the mother lode, but was still a prize all right, rotating end-over-end in space, her once shiny hull now pitted and partially charred at the stern. The bow appeared undamaged and perfect for salvage. Angel could scrap the hull for metal and the tonnage alone would keep the *Raven* in fuel for several months. If she was lucky, the hulk would still possess its old engine intact, and there would be electronics in the bow section that might bring enough to pay her small crew their back wages too.

But her competition surged forward across the starscape in a streaming ribbon of light, making a beeline for her prize. Space laws were clear, albeit not always obeyed in the vast reaches between civilized worlds where enforcement tended to be sketchy. Yet, according to Federation law, the first salvage operator who attached their clutch beam to the hull possessed retrieval rights.

"Turn on recorders to verify the clutch and grab." Angel was too experienced to risk arriving first on the scene, only to later lose a court battle.

"Recorders activated."

The *Raven* had to secure the other ship—or Angel and her crew might end up dirtside slinging hash to keep their bellies full. If only she could have afforded to purchase those new hyperdrive engines she'd seen on Starbase Ten. But due to her perennial lack of funds, she'd had to settle for a retrofitting instead of a complete overhaul.

"They still have the edge, Captain." Petroy spoke crisply. "At current speed, they'll beat us to the Vogan ship."

"No, they won't. Inject the booster fuel into the engines."

Petroy's squat body shuddered and his sturdy shoulders shrugged. "Captain—"

"You want to spend the next year dirtside?"

"Better to live on a planet than blast ourselves into the ever after."

"That's where we disagree." She'd spent the first twenty years of life on Earth and had had enough of their perfect society to last a lifetime. Angel's father had abandoned her mother before she'd been born, and her mother had been too sick to work, leaving them at the mercy of her mother's family. She'd learned early that charity from her aunts and uncles came attached with strings, like obeying every societal rule. Not only had the necessity of depending on others depleted her mother's self esteem, it had sapped her will to live. After her death, Angel felt as though she couldn't breathe on Earth without violating some ordinance or other. Stars, she couldn't even listen to the music she liked without some botcop knocking on her door and handing her a ticket for violation of noise control.

"I'd prefer to live another five hundred years," Petroy spoke dryly.

She ignored his sarcasm. During her childhood on Earth, Angel had learned that money could be made from what she'd found tossed in the garbage. Over the years she'd retrieved books, restored furniture, and repaired a bicycle. Broken toys often needed just a bit of glue to fix and those she couldn't sell, she'd donated to a nearby orphanage—the scary facility where her relatives had threatened to send her if she'd caused trouble. As much as she'd hated obeying rules and depending on the charity of family, she'd seen firsthand that life in the orphanage was to be avoided. Space salvage had been a natural extension of her childhood scavenging, and now her fingers danced over the console to check on the condition of a volatile mixture of fuel she'd found on a dead space station last year and had saved for an emergency. "The booster fuel should get us there first."

"But its chemical formula has destabilized. Will we still be in one piece after you—"

She didn't have time to argue. With a quick flick of her hand, she coded in the sequence that would open a valve to mix the dangerous propellant with their normal fuel.

"Captain, I must protest."

"Sorry, Petroy." She spoke cheerfully, thoroughly enjoying the race. "If you don't want to stay, eject in the shuttle pod and I'll pick you up on the return."

Petroy showed all his teeth, the Juvanian attempt at a smile. "I wouldn't miss the ride, Captain. I only felt it my duty to—"

With the booster fuel in her tanks, the *Raven* burst forward like a junkie with a fix, her renewed energy increasing their speed to a level that would have flattened Angel if she hadn't been wearing her suit. Every Federation citizen wore a suit, made by machinery left by an ancient race called the Perceptive Ones. Directed by psi power, the suit protected her from high acceleration, filtered her air, clothed her, bathed her, took care of all her wastes, and translated the many different Federation languages. Her suit allowed her to move, in short bursts, at the speed of thought and could induce a state of null grav.

When the *Raven* accelerated, Angel automatically used her psi to adjust her suit. The soles of her boots locked onto the deck. She also strengthened the shielding against the tremendous g-forces.

The *Raven*'s hull rumbled in protest. The deck plating arched below her feet until she feared it might buckle. The viewports moaned and vibrated.

She held her breath and clenched the console. "We're gaining on them."

"Preparing to engage clutch beam." Petroy laughed a high-pitched sound that had once grated on her nerves but now she'd learned to enjoy. Petroy was an acquired taste—he usually appeared all staid and severe, but at heart he loved taking risks, although he'd never admit it.

She tensed. "On my mark."

It was going to be close. But in her heart, she knew this salvage was hers. The abandoned ship was calling to her like a first lover bent on a reunion.

Timing would be critical. If she waited too long to activate the beam, the delay could cost her the prize and the other ship would beat them to it. But if she deployed too soon, the beam would disperse, lose power, and fail to grab the spinning hull.

Her computer could calculate the particle density of the asteroid belt, the ship's speed, and the vectors, but no computer could estimate her competitor's accuracy without knowing the individual captain, the make and model of the other starship, or how much risk they were willing to take to capture the hulk themselves. Angel used her instincts, instincts that had won her the *Raven* with a pair of fours when she sensed her opponent across the card table was bluffing, instincts that had told her to help a stowaway Terran singer instead of turning her over to the men hunting her during her last run, instincts that told her that the Vogan ship was meant to be hers.

"Captain?" Petroy prodded.

"Not yet. The Vogan ship is heavy. She's spinning. And we're still at the outermost reach of the clutch beam."

"The other ship just deployed their beam. They locked on target."

Angel bit back a curse. Her competitor's beam flashed across space like skimmer headlights in a foggy storm. But just like in fog that dimmed, distance scattered the clutch beam's power. The derelict ship kept tumbling.

"Stay ready. They don't have her locked in, yet."

Angel held her breath, searching for signs the spin was slowing. But like an out-of-control top, the hulk kept tumbling. "They're losing her."

"Now?"

"Wait." Her competitor would have to recharge their beam, which would buy the *Raven* extra time. And at their speed, every extra second narrowed the distance by thousands of miles. "Load the beam."

"Beam loaded."

"Lock on target."

"Locked."

"Steady. Steady. Now."

Their clutch beam shined through space, a bright beacon of good timing and skill. The *Raven*'s force field captured the spinning ship and slowed the wild rotations.

"Got her. She's locked and latched."

As her competition jumped into hyperspace and departed, leaving the prize to Angel, satisfaction flowed through her like sweet *frelle,* the rare spice manufactured on only one world in the galaxy. And now she looked forward to her favorite part of her work, boarding her prize to see exactly what she'd taken.

"YOU SHOULD WAIT to make sure our competition has truly left for good before venturing out of the *Raven*."

"Keep watch, in case they return." Petroy's warning had come over the com system as she'd headed to the shuttle bay, but she could hear the excitement in his tone and knew he'd trade places with her in a heartbeat if given the chance. As captain, she sometimes allowed him the first right of inspection. But this time, she wanted to go herself. The tight race had fired her imagination, and the urge to board her prize was so strong that her blood hummed with excitement. She climbed into the shuttle and ignited her engine, shooting away from the *Raven*, pleased to see the Vogan ship caught in their clutch beam like a macro fly in a Debubian spider web.

Her second team, Frie and Leval, still slept, but would awaken soon and take over for her and Petroy on the next shift. But first she intended to take an inventory of their catch. Angel loved the adventure of space. She adored not knowing what waited around the next bend, or on the next planet. As a child at her mother's sickbed, she'd read many books about space and had always dreamed of escape. Life on the *Raven* suited her.

"How's she looking?" Petroy pretended to be worried, but his tone of impatience told her he was as eager to hear good news as she was to give it.

"Good. The metal alone should keep the *Raven* flying for a few more months." Even better, when Angel hauled the salvaged ship into Dakmar, a moon orbiting a gaseous planet with no life forms, she doubted the former owners would quibble over ownership and she would be able to sell it immediately. Back in the Central Federation, she'd have to fill out endless computer forms and wait for the authorities to track down the original owners to ensure she hadn't attacked the ship just to gain salvage rights. But Dakmar existed in a less-traveled region of the Federation, where the laws encouraged free enterprise. The strongest and the fittest and the smartest ran Dakmar—an efficient system that would allow Angel to turn a tidy profit without a long wait for authentication of salvage rights. She might eventually earn more on a Federation world, but the downtime would erode the extra profit.

"And?" he prodded.

She flew a slow perimeter check. "From the char marks, it looks as if an explosion took out the stern. Perhaps they lost shielding and collided with an asteroid."

"What's wrong?" Petroy asked, perhaps sensing her tone wasn't as jubilant as he'd expected. Or perhaps he just knew how to read her better than she wanted to acknowledge.

Although the evidence showed the disaster had occurred a long time ago and likely the ship had been tumbling for years, she still hoped the Vogans had escaped unharmed. The ship had obviously been abandoned, yet the hair on her arms prickled, as if in warning of danger.

"Any sign of our competition?" she asked.

"None. But it's possible a small ship could be hiding from our sensors behind some of the local asteroids."

"Are sensors picking up any contaminants on board?"

"She's as clean as a hyperdrive engine."

"Re-check."

"Nothing. There's not so much as a nano enzyme clinging to the food processors. Why?"

She tried to shrug away the tightness between her shoulder blades. "I don't know. But I feel . . ."

"Go on."

". . . As if something's waiting for me in there."

"Then don't go in."

She appreciated his concern, but they both knew she wouldn't turn back now. And luckily she was the captain and no one could order her to turn back. Even though adrenaline had kicked in and she could taste sweet success, she remained wary. "I'm armed. And the sensors are well calibrated."

"Machines can make mistakes."

"My instincts might be wrong," she countered.

"And when was the last time you were wrong?"

"Point taken." Angel was rarely incorrect about recognizing trouble, except when it came in the form of the opposite sex. Twice married, twice divorced, of late, she'd kept her relationships short, her expectations confined to sating her physical appetites. She now looked for men who fit her lifestyle, those who wanted no more than good company for a short time and who didn't mind when she left without a backward glance.

Angel flew under the belly, taking extra care to look for any details that appeared out of place. Giant mawing holes in the hull and ports gaped where the crew had popped safety pods to abandon ship, a sign they'd safely escaped.

Most damage had probably occurred after they'd left when tiny asteroids had collided with the hull.

While inspecting every exterior inch, she tried to calm her racing pulse. Her instincts were extraordinary. She had a knack for finding trouble, of being in the exact right place at the right time—where things happened. If she'd been into sports, she would have been the star player, the one who always seemed to be around the ball during a critical play. If she'd been in the military, she would have been the general on the front, in the exact location where the enemy attacked. And as a scavenger, her success rate was phenomenal, considering the equipment she had to work with.

However, when her scalp prickled and anticipation rolled in her gut, when her fingers itched on her blaster trigger for no damn reason that she could discern—like right now—she'd learned to be extra careful. Angel had even read up on the phenomena. Supposedly, her subconscious picked up signals her brain couldn't interpret—tiny signals that her conscious mind didn't see or hear or notice, but ones that could still broadcast loud and clear to her subconscious.

"Talk to me." Petroy's voice pulled her from her thoughts.

"I'm taking the flitter through a blast hole in the fuselage." She came through the damaged hull in a cloud of dust. Her exterior landing lights revealed an empty dock and she set down with no problems.

"I've landed and the shuttle bay is full of wreckage."

She'd expected no less. Still, she couldn't keep the disappointment from her tone. It would have been wonderful to find a stash of cargo, starfire gemstones from Kenderon IV or ice crystals from Ellas Prime or even a case of Zenonite brandy. But the bay had either been picked clean a long time ago or the Vogan ship had flown empty.

Angel kept her blaster handy and popped her hatch. "I'm going for a look," she said. "Engaging vidcamera."

Now Petroy could see what she saw, which wasn't much. Lots of twisted gray *bendar,* a metal manufactured to protect starships against hyperdrive forces. She placed a portable light on her head, another on her wrist.

As well as clothing her, her suit allowed her to breathe in space, kept her boots on the deck with artificial gravity, and encased her body in normal pressure. She didn't have to worry about solar radiation, but the possibility of her competitors returning was always a concern. While Petroy would notify her if they reappeared and she should have plenty of time to fly back to the *Raven,* she sensed the danger was coming from within, not outside.

Straining to listen for any strange noises, she forced air into her lungs. Absolute silence closed around her like a tomb. She couldn't open her suit to sniff the air, but from the charred hull, she imagined the odor of old dust and the lingering scent of burnt metal.

Reaching an interior hatch, she popped the handle. The massive door creaked open. She shined her light into a corridor, expecting more wreckage. But it was empty, the only sign of problems a buckled floor.

Advancing with care, she passed by the empty galley and crew quarters and, in search of electronics, turned toward where she estimated the bridge to be. Along the way she admired the heavy metal plating of the interior walls, which would bring a tidy profit on Dakmar. The cargo ship had been built like a fortress, and she suspected only a total systems failure could have left her so vulnerable to disaster.

A flicker of movement in the corner of her eye, a shade or shape that didn't belong, caught her attention. Instantly, she shined her light, raised her blaster, and peered into the gloom, but saw nothing, not even a shadow.

Her mouth went dry as moon dust. "Who's there?"

Petroy's tone lowered in concern. "No one's on the vidscreen. Sensors aren't picking up any sign of life, but be careful."

She appreciated that he didn't think she'd lost her mind and that he'd fed her data that should be useful. Although Angel had boarded dozens of ships, never before had she felt as though she was being watched and judged.

Angel squinted past the reach of her lights and saw a dark gray shadow move in the blackness beyond. A very large, very humanoid shadow.

"Come out. Now. Or I'll shoot." She assumed the intruder's suit would translate her words.

The shadow moved and advanced into her light.

"Keep your hands where I can see them."

He was tall, very tall, broad-shouldered and bronze-skinned with bright blue eyes and dark hair. But it was his carved cheekbones and full lips that curved into a confident and easy smile that made her think of a Viking warrior, one of Earth's ancient races. No, not Viking—a Rystani. She hadn't ever met any Rystani, the infamous battle-driven warriors from the planet Rystan, but she'd seen holopics. However, the holopics couldn't convey this man's massive size or his casual, self-assured attitude that would have been sexy under different circumstances.

"How did you know I was here?" he asked, ignoring the blaster that she aimed at his chest.

"Captain," Petroy spoke over the com, "a Rystani just showed up on our sensors."

"No kidding." She scowled at the man standing before her. "Since this is my ship, I'll be the one asking the questions. Why didn't our sensors pick you up?"

He shrugged his broad shoulders. "Perhaps your systems are faulty."

The stranger's deep voice matched his powerful chest

and the sound lapped against her like waves on a white sand beach—solid, gentle, all encompassing. He wore his masculinity with the same ease as he wore his smile, as if it were so much a part of him that he had nothing to prove.

He intrigued her, but she wasn't taking his word, especially when their sensors had been working perfectly when she'd left the *Raven*. She invoked privacy mode in the com so the stranger couldn't hear her or Petroy's replies. "Petroy, have the computer run a self-diagnostic."

"Already did, Captain. And we have one hundred percent efficiency."

She kept the Rystani in her blaster sights. "There are no computer malfunctions. So, what's your story? Why are you here?"

Just because he didn't appear to have a weapon didn't mean he wasn't dangerous. On muscle size alone, he could overpower her. Since one generally had to work out regularly to sport such a toned physique, she assumed he could also best her in a hand-to-hand fight. Her advantage was her drawn weapon and she kept it front and centered.

"I'm Kirek of Rystan. Take me to your captain," he demanded.

Kirek hadn't tried to lie about his planet and every word sounded sincere, though aristocratically arrogant, but he also evaded her questions about how he'd avoided their sensors and why he was here. Instead, he was acting as if he hadn't expected her to find him. Interesting.

"I'm Angel Taylor, *captain* of the *Raven*. From Earth. Now, what are you doing here?"

At her announcement of her rank, Kirek's facial muscles didn't move, but flickers of purple darkened his eyes. "I'm looking for transport to Dakmar."

She arched a brow and kept her trigger finger poised to shoot. Obviously, he didn't think the derelict ship would take him to Dakmar, so he knew her plans. "Who said I was going to Dakmar?"

"Any salvager worth their oxygen would sell this wreck of a ship on Dakmar." His tone remained confident and easy, just short of charming. But she noted he kept his hands away from his body and didn't make any sudden moves that would risk drawing her blaster fire.

"The *Raven* is not a civilian transport ship."

"I will stay right here." Kirek's tone remained patient, confident, as if he were very accustomed to giving orders. "You should pretend you do not know of my existence—"

"—Like you planned?" she guessed. If she'd depended only on her sensors, she wouldn't have found him stowing away on the derelict. But no way in hell was she sneaking Kirek onto Dakmar. Those folks were quite particular about who boarded their moon. She did too much business there to risk bringing in a stranger and being banned because he wanted a free ride.

"I do not wish to cause trouble." Kirek's casual tone implied truth. Yet, his bold stance suggested that he was a man accustomed to handling whatever came his way.

"You've already caused trouble. And I want answers. Who dropped you off? How did you know—"

"Captain," Petroy interrupted. "The other ship has returned and the captain is demanding that we turn over Kirek or prepare to be blasted from space."

The other captain had asked for Kirek by name.

She narrowed her eyes on the Rystani. "Who are they? Why do they want you? How do they know your name?"

Kirek rubbed his square jaw. "My calculations seem to have gone awry. I'll have to think about . . ."

He seemed genuinely puzzled, but she wasn't buying his innocent act. Yet she didn't have time to interrogate him, nor did she bother using privacy mode, allowing

Kirek to hear her conversation. "Petroy, is the other ship in weapons range?"

"Not yet."

"Do we have time to return to the *Raven* before they can shoot us?"

"Maybe."

"Stall negotiations until I return. Tell them I haven't found anyone named Kirek. Yet."

"And then?"

"Ask what they're willing to pay for this Kirek, if I find him."

"Aye, Captain."

Kirek's eyes flared with a heat that burned hotter than a solar flare. "You trade in slaves?"

Her instruction to Petroy had been automatic. But she'd obviously touched a sore point, and maybe it would make Kirek more agreeable to answering her questions. While she'd never deal in the slave trade, he needn't know that right away.

She intended to drop the Rystani off on the nearest habitable planet—but she also wanted to know how he'd avoided her sensors and how he'd learned her destination. She told herself she would have made the same decision not to turn him over to her competition if she'd found a slimy, eight-tentacled Osarian aboard, instead of the finest male specimen she'd seen this side of a holovid screen.

"You." She waved her blaster at Kirek. "Come with me."

He planted his feet, crossed his arms over his massive chest, and spoke with calm contempt. "I will never again be a slave."

Kirek presented one awesome picture of Rystani stubbornness, and she realized he'd called her bluff. This proud warrior would clearly rather die than give up his freedom. She couldn't imagine him ever having been anyone's slave and regretted her threat since she could most definitely sympathize with his principles.

From the rock-hard tension in his muscles, from the angry heat in his glaring eyes, she knew he was a man bent on dying before he yielded his will to anyone. Oddly, she didn't feel threatened, but sympathetic. "I do not buy, sell, or keep slaves. Not ever." She cocked her head to one side. "But if you want to live, I suggest you answer my questions. Who's after you?"

Chapter Two

"IF YOU DON'T sell slaves, why did you ask what price I'd bring?" Kirek didn't budge from his stance or his determination to remain free.

Some issues weren't debatable and slavery was one of them. Seven years ago, at the mention of anyone selling him he wouldn't have been able to restrain his seething temper. But after a good part of a decade spent traveling through the galaxy, he'd healed from his time spent on Endeki, where he'd been a hostage and suffered at the hands of a woman with an unusual taste for cruelty.

While Captain Angel Taylor might be space-hardened, she didn't emit a cruel psi, at least from what his own blast-damaged one could pick up. Kirek found his new handicap tiresome and limiting, but reminded himself that until the last century, most of humanity never had more to go on than he did right now—his instincts.

Angel stared hard at him, and while her tone had an edge, it was cut with understanding. "I asked what they would pay for you to learn your value to them. And," she continued, grinning, "to see if my threat would make you answer my question."

He couldn't help admiring the way she thought. A good brain always attracted him as much as a pleasing face and a toned body. Angel seemed to have both. Taller than Tessa, a Terran woman who lived with his family on Mystique, their new home world, Angel's slender frame still showed enough curves in her dark green suit to make him appreciate that he was back in his body, even if he was damaged.

Eight years ago, while astral projecting, Kirek had been caught in a wormhole explosion. His mind had been blasted out the far end of the wormhole, all the way into the Zin Galaxy. It had taken him seven years to return—eight, if he counted the reintegration of his mind with the body machines had meticulously kept alive, thanks to huge efforts from family and friends.

After his reintegration, doctors had warned repeatedly that his psi remained fragile and told him that his body couldn't handle astral extension again anytime soon without risking his life. So his injured psi, which had once been one of the most powerful in the Federation, had been reduced to what others considered a normal level. While he still had the unique ability to prevent scans of his body from registering on machines, he hadn't been able to hide from Angel and he didn't know why. She shouldn't have known he was there, waiting for her or another scavenger ship to transport him to Dakmar undercover.

Her finding him necessitated a change in plans. During

Kirek's astral extension into the Andromeda Galaxy, he'd found the Zin home world, the beings who had tried to wipe out the Federation with a virus. With his powerful psi, Kirek had learned the Zin still planned to invade. Unfortunately, his psi touch had made the Zin aware of his presence. So he'd stayed away from Mystique and those who could help him in fear that the Zin would find him.

But the Zin were probably now hunting him through another race. His cover was blown. In order to continue his mission, he needed to meet his contact on Dakmar and disappear again.

But Angel had found him. Without his extraordinary powers, he had to rely on his eyes and his ears and his intellect to convince her not to turn him over to the enemy.

What he'd seen so far of Captain Angel Taylor pleased him. He liked her risk-taking attitude mixed with a cautious practicality. He liked that after she'd realized she'd touched a nerve, she'd admitted her threat to sell him had been a bluff. He liked her smarts. And he most decidedly liked her wide-set, intelligent green eyes that set off her straight nose and full lips to perfection. She also attracted him, which was not unusual for a man who hadn't had sex in almost a decade.

"I don't know who is after me." He told her the truth.

"Captain, the other ship is closing," her officer informed her.

Angel eyed Kirek warily. "Start walking. Why do they want you? Why are you valuable?"

"Good questions. I can only guess at the answers." Since Kirek could no longer steal into Dakmar without her help, he assessed his options with hyperdrive efficiency. He could make up a cover on the spot, but any decent computer would poke credibility holes in his story and if she caught him in a lie, it would be difficult to regain her trust.

He could refuse to speak, but sensed that wouldn't win him her assistance, either. And he did require help. It would be useful to have an ally on Dakmar. The moon housed the thickest base of thieves, murderers, traders, and blackmailers this side of the galaxy, intermixed with legitimate businesses. As a salvage captain, Angel likely knew her way around and could introduce him to the right beings, putting him on a fast warp in the right direction—if he could gain her cooperation.

So the truth not only might work best, the truth worked with his morals. Kirek didn't like lying. Although, for the greater good, he could override his inbred Rystani morality, but he preferred to operate on the sunny side of the truth.

"What's your best guess?" she asked.

He scratched his cheek and gazed over his shoulder at her, but kept his feet moving. "You won't believe me."

"Start talking." Gesturing with the blaster toward the shuttle bay, she scowled as if expecting lies.

He could probably take away her weapon before she fired a shot, but he wouldn't risk losing whatever goodwill she might have. But his story was long and complex and the best place to start was at the beginning.

"Twenty-eight years ago," he began, speaking as if telling a story to a favorite child as he headed toward the shuttle bay, "I was born in hyperspace."

"Stars," she swore without rancor. "I'm beyond the age of fairy tales. Birth in hyperspace is impossible."

"There's no point telling you all my secrets," he teased, "if you refuse to keep an open mind."

"Fine." Sarcasm dripped from her tone. "You were born in hyperspace. Do you think we could skip to the present?"

He refused to let her skepticism throw him. Instead, he

enjoyed pushing her over the edge of incredulity. "When I was four, I traveled to a planet halfway to the galaxy's rim and the Kwadii proclaimed me their Oracle."

"Right." She snorted and he turned to catch her rolling her eyes in a Terran gesture so like Tessa's he had to restrain a chuckle. "Forgive me if I don't think you look holy." She eyed him with wary cynicism. "Perhaps you've spent too much alone-time on this abandoned ship."

"Actually, I'm in a mood to enjoy the right kind of company," he flirted back. "And you arrived right on time. It's only been a few days since I put out word about the Vogan ship."

"You set me up? You were expecting me?"

"You or another salvage ship. I needed a ride to Dakmar."

"Undercover?" she guessed.

He nodded.

"And the other ship out there wants to stop you from going to Dakmar because . . . ?"

He shrugged. That others seemed to know his mission was of great concern, but Kirek had lived through many dangerous situations. When he'd been a child, he'd been alone on Kwadii, totally separated from the adults who'd been captured. Even though he'd been terrified, he'd still managed to make new friends. He'd found other children and played computer games to earn credits to buy what he'd needed. And later, as a sexual hostage on Endeki, he'd often managed to enjoy himself under dire conditions. So even under the most trying circumstances, he'd learned to enjoy life. "My years have been eventful."

"Whose haven't? Get to the point." When Kirek didn't immediately respond, Angel prodded him lightly with the blaster. "Now."

"When I was eighteen, the Endekian leader's wife took me into her confidence and—"

"Even I know the Rystani and Endekians are enemies." She gestured again with the blaster, urging him through the shuttle bay.

Petroy interrupted. "Captain, the other ship is Kraj. Ever heard of them?"

"No."

"I have," Kirek admitted. "A most unpleasant race. Narrow-minded, intense, warlike."

"Several Kraj just showed up on our sensors." Petroy's tone turned sharp. "They are inside the Vogan ship."

"Stars. How close?" Angel asked.

"Right above you."

Kirek craned his head back. The Kraj must have hidden behind the warp engine's shielding. If his psi had been healed, he would have known they were there. But he hadn't felt their presence and obviously the *Raven's* sensors were antiquated or malfunctioning.

Without hesitation he snagged the weapon he had hidden in the fold of his suit, and reached out to grab Angel to pull her behind the cover of a column. But she'd already dived, rolled, and hidden behind twisted *bendar* hull–plating right before four Kraj dropped through the ceiling panels.

Kirek swore under his breath. Did she have to pick the worst spot in the entire cargo bay to hide? The Kraj practically descended right on top of her. Big, ugly, gray creatures, twice Angel's mass, they attacked at the speed of thought, using their psi suits to strike in formation. But as Angel fell to her back and fired her weapon into their midst, taking out one Kraj almost immediately, Kirek noted she also had the perfect counterattack spot.

From his position, he didn't have a direct shot. Hampered by his injured psi, he couldn't move faster than his opponents. Kirek lunged toward Angel, firing his weapon, but his blaster shot had no effect.

"They have a jamming device," he warned Angel, but she had figured it out as quickly as he had, and holstered her blaster and pulled another weapon. Using her psi, she lunged at a forty-five-degree angle to avoid being crushed between two oncoming Kraj.

At his words, two Kraj turned on him. But he fretted about the one still after Angel.

Before he could come to her aid, he first had to dispatch his own attackers. The two Kraj attacked together, coming in fast and hard. One punched his face—the other slammed a foot into his kidney. Despite strengthening his shield, part of the force came through. Pain radiated down his back and across his jaw.

Countering with a swift round kick to the head, Kirek knocked out one Kraj. But the other took the opportunity to choke him from behind, wrapping an arm about his throat.

Kirek shifted his hips, twisted a wrist, and flung the Kraj into a bulkhead. Out of the corner of his eye, he saw Angel duck behind a crate, then bash the metal cage into her opponent's face. The Kraj let out a roar and came after her with such force and speed that Kirek's heart marched up his throat.

He lost sight of her again as his own opponent attacked with a metal bar. The Kraj swung at Kirek, and he jerked back, watching the Kraj's eyes for an opening. The two danced forward, back, to the side, each searching for a weakness. When they edged toward a bulkhead, Kirek used his suit's null grav to kick against the wall, come in at an angle.

The Kraj raised the metal bar, but Kirek slammed the knife-edge of his hand against the other's throat. Letting out a pained croak, the Kraj dropped to the deck.

Angel cursed. And Kirek turned in time to see her take a blow to the shoulder, shift, and ram a knife into the Kraj's chest. He slumped, unconscious, maybe dead.

"You okay?" he asked, breathing hard, more out of fear for her than the exercise.

"Yes. You?" She placed her foot on the Kraj's chest, jerked out her knife, wiped off the blood on his suit, then stuffed it back up her sleeve.

"Let's get out of here." He motioned toward the shuttle.

"I want that jammer." She used null grav to lift herself through the ceiling panels.

Frustrated that she was wasting time, he tried to hide his irritation. "You can retrieve it later."

"When we tow the ship, the jammer might come loose and float out the damaged hull."

"The Kraj ship is coming," he reminded her.

She didn't stop, stubbornly lifting into the ceiling, giving him no choice but to follow. "It will only take a sec—"

Without air to convey sound, he could hear nothing except through the com. And she'd gone silent.

"Angel?" When she didn't answer, Kirek's mouth went dry. Instead of entering through one of the open panels, he chose an unbroken one to burst through, hoping to take whoever was up there by surprise.

Obviously another Kraj had been working the jammer and he'd silenced Angel. The shielding in this section was so thick, Kirek's damaged psi hadn't felt him and neither had the sensors on Angel's ship. And now the Kraj had Angel.

Praying she wasn't dead, Kirek rocketed through the panel and into the ceiling.

A Kraj turned, holding Angel across his chest and in front of him like a shield. Angel slumped in the man's arms, her head drooping, shoulders sagging, limp and either unconscious or dead.

"Move on me and I'll snap her neck," the Kraj warned, his words giving Kirek hope that she still breathed.

"If you want this ship, you can have it," Kirek replied,

stalling, knowing full well the Kraj didn't want the ship, but him. If the Kraj had had a weapon in his hand, Kirek and Angel would both be dead. But with his mothership bearing down, he need only hold out until help arrived.

"Let her go and I can make you a wealthy man," spoke Kirek, edging his feet slowly, changing his angle to attack.

The Kraj's eyes narrowed as if considering Kirek's words.

Angel chose that moment to slam her head back against the bridge of his nose.

Roaring in pain, the Kraj loosened his grip, but didn't let her go. Angel kicked her heel into his shin, and Kirek launched his body into them. The three collided, lifting them into empty space. Kirek used the collision to hammer his fist against the Kraj's temple. The big gray alien flew one way, Kirek and Angel the other.

They landed against a wall and he took the brunt of the crash, twisting to absorb the shock. She slammed into him and he cradled her. For one second her body pressed against his, her soft curves, her toned flesh, her fresh-scented hair reminding him that she might fight like a warrior but was very female. Then she shoved back, pulled the jammer that she'd somehow wrested from the Kraj from her pocket and turned it off.

She gestured to Kirek's holstered blaster and the Kraj. "Shoot him."

Kirek nudged the unconscious man with his boot. "There's no need. He can't harm us now. Let's go before his ship arrives."

Angel scowled at him. Kirek suspected if she still had her weapons, she wouldn't have hesitated to shoot. However, he never killed unless in self-defense or to save a life.

Angel raised an eyebrow at his reluctance but said no more as they hurried back to the shuttle. To protect himself during the upcoming hyper jump Kirek webbed in, pleased to learn Angel was not only intelligent but could defend herself so well. But he wished she had better equipment. The pared-down shuttle gave him a bit of trepidation and he wished he had the former use of his psi that would have spotted faulty circuits, a weak hull, or the enemy that had been hiding in the shuttle bay ceiling.

"Captain." Petroy's voice crackled over the com.

"Go ahead."

"The Kraj captain says he is done negotiating. They say that if we don't hand over the Rystani warrior, Kirek, they'll fire upon us, and from their ferocity of tone, I tend to believe them."

"Understood. Are they in clutch beam range?"

"Not yet."

"Tell them we left several Kraj alive. They are free to retrieve them. That should slow them down."

"Aye, Captain."

With Angel away from the *Raven*, Petroy appeared comfortable in charge. He remained calm in spite of the crisis.

Impressed that she didn't give many specific orders to Petroy but just the main plan, trusting her officer to handle the crisis, Kirek focused his gaze on Angel. She flew the ship as if it were second nature, her only concession to the fight they'd just been through or the warning just given a flick of a switch to raise their shields.

Outdated, with limited computerization, the bare-wired but functional shuttle had been an antique before he'd been born. Reminding himself that not everyone in the galaxy had the credits to buy the latest technological engineering, he refrained from commenting about her superior flying or the ancient gear. Instead, he peered out the spotless screen for her mothership.

As they neared, he scrutinized her lines. Above and to

starboard the *Raven*'s hull, shimmering gray *bendar* against the blackness of space, looked like a winged beast of prey. The silhouette jarred Kirek's memory, a faint vision in a long-forgotten dream suddenly sharpened.

His psi might be damaged but he still had memories of when it had worked. And he'd had a vision of this moment, this ship, this woman.

Stars. He understood he was exactly where he was supposed to be. The *Raven* and Angel were his fate.

During his lifetime, Kirek had always been haunted by flashes, visions of what should be. As a fetus in Miri's womb, he'd reached out with his psi in a healing circle, already aware that destiny would set him apart. Those instincts hadn't left him during his stays on Kwadii and Endeki or even during the long years of astral travel. Never had he envisioned a partner in his quest, but at the sight of the *Raven*, he understood that Angel would be important to his future.

If he'd had access to his psi, he might have known exactly how she was important. But now, he figured that the only way he had to find out what role they were supposed to fulfill in each other's lives was to spend time with her, to develop a relationship with her.

And so he tried to explain his quest, a course that had driven him almost since his first moment of consciousness. "Perhaps you've heard of a wormhole that opened between Earth and invaders from another galaxy?"

"The Zin? Of course, I've heard of the Zin." She slammed into overdrive and the engine purred. "Every Federation child learns in school how the Zin want to invade our galaxy, but the ancient Sentinels keep us safe."

The Sentinels were fantastic machines built by The Perceptive Ones, the same race that had left behind the machinery that manufactured Federation citizens' suits. Kirek had once been inside a Sentinel and had met two

Perceptive Ones, but Angel wasn't ready to hear that story yet.

"Captain," said Petroy, injecting himself into the conversation, "the Kraj are closing fast. If they lock a clutch beam on your shuttle—"

"Feel free to fire on them if they attack but I'm hoping that if they stop to pick up their injured it will delay them long enough for our return. We're almost in. Open bay doors."

"Doors open."

Kirek took heart that although her stripped-down shuttle was ancient, she kept it spotless and the engine hummed with well-maintained efficiency. Deciding to come clean about his mission, he leaned forward to peer around her lovely neck to catch her expression and placed absolute conviction into his tone. "The Zin are planning another attack."

"Really?" Her tone remained skeptical as she dodged an asteroid with smooth skill, flew around debris as if it were second nature, and simultaneously carried on the conversation. "No one has ever even seen the Zin and yet you proclaim to know their plans."

"It's my quest to stop the Zin invasion."

Her tone challenged him. "Because you were born in hyperspace? Because you're an Oracle?"

His soul might be older than his years, but he still enjoyed interacting with a woman like Angel Taylor. She could handle herself and her ship, and her independent spirit radiated through her conversation with the brightness of a star gone nova. Already he relished her banter, her skill, and her feminine profile. He'd carried on alone for so long, for so many years as he'd made his way back to the Milky Way Galaxy, that he'd forgotten how uplifting it could be to converse with a woman with such an individualistic spirit. But even as he recognized his attraction to Angel, he understood that preventing the Zin invasion came before any personal considerations. "I will stop the Zin . . . because I can."

"THE KRAJ HAVE recovered their people and are warming up their weapons, Captain." Petroy greeted Angel on the bridge, gave up the command seat, and moved to his copilot's position.

"Ready the hyperdrive engines," she ordered, slipping behind her console with the ease of long practice.

"Done."

She nodded thanks at the ever-efficient Petroy and frowned at the vidscreen, fully aware Kirek had trailed behind her onto the bridge and was looking around with keen interest. Although all four of the crew could fit in here at one time, it only took two to run all the systems and her tiny bridge seemed crowded with the big Rystani aboard.

He'd told her one unusual story. And she'd heard enough rumors to know it could be true . . . or a total fabrication. She hadn't decided yet whether he was trustworthy. Although he'd helped save her during the Kraj attack, saving her had saved himself.

But damn, the man could fight. He'd moved like some kind of vidscreen hero, his skill evident in his fearless attacks that took down his enemies almost faster than the eye could follow. He'd proved he was dangerous—but to whom?

Even if she'd been so inclined, locking him up on the *Raven* wasn't an option, unless she wanted to give up her quarters, and she didn't. She figured as long as the Kraj were after Kirek and she protected him, he likely wouldn't interfere with the *Raven*'s operations.

Angel drummed her fingers on her console and glared

at Kirek. What secret was he keeping? She thought it odd he'd admitted knowledge of the aliens, but then refused to admit why they wanted him. She hoped she wasn't harboring a murderer, but despite Kirek's muscles, despite his fight with the Kraj and his words about taking out the Zin, he seemed contradictorily . . . non-violent. His refusal to kill the Kraj was most unlike a Rystani warrior.

Although advanced computers could have given her a complete rundown on Kirek's background, her antiquated system didn't have enough memory to carry extraneous data about Federation history. So she had no way to check out his story until they reached Dakmar. She just prayed that he hadn't refused to kill the Kraj because they were working together in an elaborate ruse to steal her prize and the *Raven*.

So while she appeared to give the Rystani free rein of her ship, she keyed in a command code that locked out any orders that came from anyone other than her and her crew. Since she'd been careful to keep her body between his gaze and her fingers, Kirek couldn't possibly have seen her fingers move over the console, yet when she caught his amused gaze on her, she could have sworn he *knew*.

Impossible. She shook off her wild imagination and hailed the Kraj through the com. "This is Captain Angel Taylor of the *Raven*. According to Federation laws, our salvage is locked and loaded in our clutch beam. We have lawful possession and any attempt to take—"

"We have no interest in salvage." The Kraj's voice was rough and hostile. His sallow gray skin hung in loose folds over a flat, humanoid face devoid of expression, with a dominating brow and a bulbous nose. The Kraj's mouth parted to reveal sharp, pointy teeth. "We have held our fire, showing our good intentions."

"Now that's a matter of opinion," Angel muttered, her voice too low for the Kraj to hear. To the aliens, she remained polite, but she hadn't forgotten or forgiven their attack on the Vogan ship. "Perhaps we can do business on Landolin. Angel out."

"Now?" Petroy asked.

"Now," Angel agreed, and jumped into hyperspace.

At her command, webbing dropped from the ceiling to protect them during the high acceleration. Kirek started as if surprised, then accepted the web-in like a pro. While his adjustment revealed he was accustomed to space travel, he apparently hadn't seen antiquated equipment like hers. Interesting. Apparently he'd only traveled on the Federation's newest ships, the expensive ones that only the wealthiest citizens on the central planets could afford.

Angel didn't know what to think about Kirek. She was beginning to wonder if she'd ever know more than he wanted her to know. If even half the entire story he'd told her was true, he was one of the ten wonders of the Federation. Yet, he was far too real, far too male, for her to think of him as some holy oracle.

Kirek had the demeanor of a commander and muscle to match. And with a face like his, women would dream of having him in their arms. Herself included. If she'd met him during other circumstances, Angel wouldn't mind enjoying his magnificent body herself. But right now, she didn't trust him.

He carried himself with an easy self-control and poise, as if he'd been battle-tested and had come out the victor many times. What was he? Who was he, really? And was she risking her ship and possibly the lives of her crew by refusing to hand him over to the Kraj?

Hyperspace always enhanced her senses. Lights brightened. Sounds sharpened. Kirek's gaze drilled her with curiosity as the webbing retracted.

"Landolin?" Kirek's tone remained mild but a muscle in his jaw clenched. "I thought we were going to Dakmar?"

She shrugged and allowed herself a pleased grin. "I saw no reason to advertise our destination."

"Thank you." He nodded, his sincere gaze showering her with approval.

She didn't need his damn approval.

Angel turned to navigation, but she couldn't stop the glow of warmth he'd set off from making her stomach tighten—or from preventing her curiosity about the Rystani from escalating.

Chapter Three

FREE OF THE webbing, Kirek leaned over the console, peered at the vidscreen, and rubbed tightness from the back of his neck. Although Angel's cleverness at misdirecting the Kraj appeared to have worked, he sensed . . . danger. However, nothing menacing showed on the computer's systems.

"What?" Angel spun and confronted him, one hand fisted on a slender cocked hip, her eyes cool and assessing.

Kirek usually preferred to remain silent about his hunches until he could back them with factual data. But with his neck twitching and the mission so important, he made an exception. "The Kraj—"

"The Kraj," Petroy spoke at the same moment, "just exited hyperspace. Distance less than one light year and closing."

"Evasive tactics. Prepare to hyperjump again." Angel leveled a piercing stare at Kirek. "How in hell did you know the Kraj would return?"

"I didn't *know*."

His intuition came often and was abnormally accurate. And in the near future, he might need for her to accept his ability on faith. Besides, he liked showing off. It had been a long time since a woman had appreciated him for his unique abilities.

She raised her brow. "You just happened to guess they'd reappear in this quadrant of the galaxy . . . on a hunch?"

"Recalibrating hyperdrive." Petroy's hands waved over the console. The Kraj ship bore down on them with tremendous speed. "Kraj are loading weapons."

"Jump to sector seven," she ordered.

Kirek shook his head. "We don't have time to hide in the dust clouds."

Angel ignored his comment, but she tightened her lips in clear annoyance that he would question her decision. "On my mark. Jump."

The webbing dropped again and the hyperdrive engine engaged. Normal space disappeared and the sensitivity of hyperspace returned. Kirek watched Angel tamp down her annoyance before she faced him once more. "I won't tolerate command interference. If you ever again question my orders, you cannot remain on my bridge."

"I apologize, Captain." Kirek threaded his fingers through his hair and didn't point out he'd only been making a suggestion. Apparently, questioning her command was a touchy subject. "I don't believe we can lose ourselves in the cloud dust and outwit the Kraj."

"Another hunch?" She lifted her chin, as if daring him to admit it.

"Partial hunch. Partial estimate from known facts."

"What facts?" she snapped, drawing her body so taut her breasts lifted. Round breasts that appeared the perfect size to fill his palms. He imagined them swelling into his touch, the skin soft and smooth. Kirek knew enough about women to hide his admiration of her curves. Right about now, he didn't need one of his hunches to realize that a show of interest in her very delicious-looking body would irritate her so much that she probably wouldn't listen to a word he said.

Damn, his response to her was totally inappropriate, the timing ridiculous. He should be thinking about escaping the Kraj, but he couldn't help himself, and he wondered if, along with his damaged psi, his judgment had been impaired. Finally, he managed to put his fascination on hold and kept his gaze locked above her neck. Mostly above the neck.

"The Kraj have stated they want me—not your salvage," he pointed out.

She frowned. "You believe they're trying to stop your mission?"

She caught on fast, even if she was eyeing him as if he had three brains. He shrugged and kept his tone unconcerned. "They seemed quite determined. That's why we can't simply outwait them in the dust clouds."

She drummed her fingers on the console and then, as if she realized what she was doing, she clenched her hands. "What do you suggest?"

He respected that she was willing to listen. During his vast travels he'd found those with that ability rare. "What if we continue on to Dakmar as you'd originally planned?"

She eyed him, but spoke to Petroy. "Status?"

"Exiting hyperspace." The engines slowed, the webbing raised. The stars that had been appearing in space as streaking ribbons changed to stationary pinpoints. They'd popped out of hyperspace in a completely different quadrant—one that appeared empty of other spacecraft. "We've lost them, for now. But they may again appear right on our tail when we exit the clouds."

"Keep me informed." She eyed Kirek, her eyes glinting with speculation. While he couldn't read her well, he didn't believe her interest was hostile as much as curious. He could work with curious—especially when encased in a package as attractive as Angel's. She gestured for him to follow her. "We will be in my work room, having a private chat."

"Understood." Petroy didn't look up or change facial expression, but Kirek noted a tension in his shoulders that hadn't been there before. And Petroy'd had plenty of time to research Kirek's background. While many of his activities and abilities had been kept secret, enough had made it into the public databases to make Petroy uncomfortable.

Beings who didn't understand Kirek often feared him. Long ago he'd decided he could do nothing to change the short-sighted perceptions of others. As a child, and then later—before the wormhole blast had weakened his psi— he'd often wondered if being normal and accepted would be worth giving up his rare gifts. But now that he could no longer astral extend, he realized just how valuable his differences had been.

The freedom of leaving behind his body to soar with his mind through the universe at the speed of thought had been exhilarating. And yet for much of the time that he'd been separated from his body, he'd feared he wouldn't make it back. Or if he did return, that his body would have died and he'd have been left alone to roam forever—as a spirit.

But after he'd reintegrated his mind with his body, he missed the freedom of astral extension. How human that was—always wanting to be in a state that he couldn't have. But he would adjust to his new handicap. He would find out if—and *why*—Angel was important to his future, and he would succeed in his mission.

Angel's workroom was tiny, organized with a vidscreen along one entire wall and bulkheads of dull gray *bendar* everywhere else. He saw no holopics of family, but personal items were shoved into cubbyholes and attached to shelves along the walls. A case of expensive *frelle* perched in a corner. Assorted bottles of Terran and Dellarin wine hung on a rack beside a painting from Scartar of an exotic green-skinned woman. Iridescent aqua seashells of a shape he'd never seen shared shelf space with rare books in a language he couldn't read.

When a scruffy orange-and-white-striped animal tipped over a casket of glittering beads and lunged straight at Angel, Kirek used his psi to activate his suit. Moving at the speed of thought, placing his body between her and the menacing creature, he shielded her, his protective instincts and Rystani reflexes on automatic.

The creature slammed into his chest, all claws and hissing, the fur on its back rising. If not for the protection of the shield in his suit, the animal might have shredded his flesh.

Unhurt, Kirek grabbed the animal by the scruff of its furry neck. The creature screeched and hissed in protest.

"Don't hurt Lion." Angel barreled around him and reached for the feline.

Kirek frowned at her in confusion. "You keep a lion aboard your ship?"

He'd heard of the Earth animals that could be man-killers, with a nickname King of the Beasts, but he'd thought lions were larger. However, not even zoologists could be familiar with every life form on every world and its small size didn't mean it wasn't dangerous. Many animals with high metabolisms could consume their own body weight a hundred times over in just a few hours. And the way the creature had just attacked, Kirek suspected he was famished. Although this one didn't seem large enough to consume a human, he was taking no chances with her life and lifted the spitting creature out of Angel's reach.

" 'Lion' is my *pet cat's* name." She used null grav in her suit to float her to the beast and gently took him into her hands. The animal immediately settled into her arms, but the hair on its neck still stood straight up.

She had a pet. A living, breathing cat.

"I thought he was attacking you."

"He was." Angel grinned and cuddled the cat against her chest and under her chin. Clearly, she was in no danger. She threaded her fingers through the animal's coat—his fur flattened and he purred. If she'd held him against her chest and stroked him like that, Kirek would have purred, too.

Shoving aside his jealousy, he eyed the cat curiously. "You keep a pet on the ship?"

"I have his suit adjusted to automatic and he likes it in space." Her voice softened as she held Lion. "We've been together a long time. I rescued him from the streets about ten years ago. When I took off in the *Raven*, I tried to leave him behind with a friend, but the rascal stowed aboard."

Her cat had a suit? He'd never heard of such a thing. "I've never had the luxury of owning a pet."

"Cats aren't a luxury. On Earth, you can pick one up for free at any animal center."

"On Rystan, it was difficult enough to keep people fed. And after my family moved to Mystique, I made one journey after another."

He'd never had time to make friends with other children, but the lack of others his own age hadn't bothered him since he'd had so little in common with them. He'd preferred the company of adults. However, a pet would have been a wonderful companion and his heart lifted at the prospect of spending time with a domesticated animal. He broke into a wide smile of pleasure. "May I pet . . ."

"Lion?" She plucked the cat from her chest and let him look at Kirek. "He may not forget your rough treatment. He doesn't like being held by the neck." She spoke softly to her pet as if he was an intelligent being. "Lion, this is Kirek, a Rystani warrior who is on a mission to save the galaxy from the Zin."

"You weren't supposed to tell him that." Kirek admonished, grin widening. "My mission's a secret."

"Lion can't talk."

"Sure he can."

He let the animal sniff his hand, then gently took the furry feline who gazed back at him, his yellow eyes wary, his back arched and stiff. He let out another sharp hiss.

Angel snorted, but played along. "What's he saying? That he doesn't like you?"

Kirek stroked the soft fur, but the animal didn't purr for him like it had for Angel. However, his fur finally lay down and Kirek figured that was at least some progress. Lion's stomach growled and he wriggled to get down. Kirek wanted to hold him but wouldn't force his will on a pet. "He says he's hungry."

"He's always hungry." She plucked a container out of a

drawer and placed a handful of pellets into a fired clay bowl that was attached to an automatic watering device. "Cats are supposed to be picky. But Lion will eat anything."

He expected the cat to gobble the food, but it ate daintily, chewing one piece thoroughly before going on to the next. The dry food didn't look too appetizing but as Angel had predicted, Lion didn't mind.

Angel rested her hands on her hips and her tone became guarded. "I suppose since you thought Lion was a threat and that you might be risking life and limb to protect me that I should thank you."

He shrugged and tried to keep the sheepish expression from his face. "I've never seen a cat."

Her eyes flashed with indignation. "Did you think I'd allow a dangerous creature on board?"

"You let *me* aboard." He stepped closer and crowded her just a little. "And we are now alone. In my book, that's a lot of trust."

Didn't she understand how tempting she was? What a vulnerable position she'd placed herself in by relying on his honor?

She rolled her eyes at the bulkhead. "You aren't dangerous . . . to me."

He allowed a measure of heat to enter his gaze. "I wouldn't be so certain. You have no inkling of my intentions."

She laughed and her words turned bold. "So then tell me, Mr. I'm-so-noble-and-I'm-on-a-quest-to-save-the-galaxy-from-the-Zin, what are your intentions?"

Angel didn't have a clue that Kirek found her sassy sense of humor attractive. While Kirek loved his mother, Miri, and accepted her traditional choice to tend hearth and home, he'd always enjoyed the company of independent women like his Aunt Tessa, who ran Mystique, and Alara, an Endekian scientist trying to discover secrets within her people's biology who'd married Xander, another male of his family. But that he was attracted to Angel on a physical level as well as a mental one struck him like a sucker punch to the jaw. If he had his full psi, would he feel the same way? He had no idea.

Until now, he'd never believed in chemistry, or in that special zing of awareness that others claimed slammed them when they met the right person. But Kirek was fighting his attraction to her on every level. In that unguarded moment when he'd held her during the Kraj attack, he'd opened his suit's filters and her citrus scent had invaded his lungs, seared his brain, and now haunted him. Just the sound of her voice contradictorily relaxed *and* stimulated him.

Looking at her was a treat. Her tall and slender body had plenty of female curves to draw his eyes to places they had no right to go. Her face might not have been beautiful in a traditional sense, but her animated expression and the brazen challenge in her eyes fired his imagination.

And he wasn't averse to enjoying a woman during his mission. The only question was how direct should he be? Because damaged psi or not, he most definitely intended to pursue her. But he sensed she didn't need to know that yet.

However, he had just the item to attract her interest. "What would you say about going after the biggest salvage haul in Federation history?"

Lion licked his paw. Angel sucked in her breath and her eyes brightened. "You do know how to tempt a girl. Tell me more."

"We're talking about an entire world of metal—solid *bendar,* millions of miles of wiring, the latest in electronics, circuitry, and mechanical systems."

She crossed her arms over her chest, as if bracing herself against falling for a trick. "A world of metal?"

"An entire planet that is about the size of Jupiter."

"Jupiter? How do you know about Earth's solar system?" Suspicion clouded her eyes.

"I was on Earth to stop the Zin virus from coming through the wormhole."

"You were on Earth, but you've never seen a cat?" she scoffed.

"We were in the desert. A remote area on the southern continent of Africa. All I saw was sand and sky and more sand."

She drummed her fingers on the counter. "An entire planet of metal?"

"Yes." He kept back his grin. He'd used the right bait. Despite her disbelief, he read the thrill of the chase in her eyes.

"How come I've never heard of such a world?"

"The information isn't readily available."

"Then how did you hear about it? How do you know your data is accurate?"

"I've seen the world."

She arched a skeptical brow. "What's the catch?"

"To reach the world of metal, we have to find an ancient portal left behind by the Perceptive Ones. And to find the portal, we have to go to Dakmar."

"I don't understand."

"On Dakmar, I'm meeting someone who will give me the coordinates of the portal."

"Why not just head straight for the metal planet?"

Here came the tricky part. "It's in another galaxy."

"How did you see it?"

"That's a long story—and a long trip." Before she could tell him that he was out of his mind, he quickly added, "However, with the portal, we can get there in a . . . timely fashion."

Her eyes widened. "A portal that sends ships to another galaxy? That's how you got there?"

"No," he admitted, his hope rising that she really might come with him. Kirek had never planned to complete this mission alone. After he arrived on Dakmar, he'd always intended to purchase a ship and find a crew. While he didn't know if the portal would send an entire ship or just him alone into the Andromeda Galaxy, his plan required human backup. And his approach had to be done by stealth, so he couldn't accept any help from those at home on Mystique, who would be watched closely by Zin spies.

"And how would we get back with an entire planet?"

He liked her use of the word "we." As if she was already thinking of them as a team, she'd moved right to the practical aspects of the journey. "Once I sneak in and defeat the Zin, you can slice up the planet and return through the portal in the other galaxy." He hoped. He didn't know for certain exactly how the portal worked.

She heaved a sigh of aggravation. "You're insane. You have no idea if there's even a portal in this galaxy, never mind one in the next. Or if it's big enough to send through an entire planet."

"I'm not *guessing*. My mathematics are accurate."

"I suppose you have a math degree from MIT?"

He grinned. His credentials weren't from the best college on Earth, but the most elite university in the Federation. "Actually I possess dual degrees in physics and math from the Zenon Institute."

Her eyes widened in surprise but his extraordinary education didn't throw her. "You said you saw this Zin world?"

"Yes."

"If you didn't use the portal, how did you get there to see it?"

"When the Zin opened the wormhole on Earth to send through a virus, I astral extended."

"You went inside a wormhole?"

"Not physically. Only with my mind."

"You're insane."

"My presence and that of others was necessary to stabilize the structure while we initiated an explosion."

"Yeah, right."

"I was caught in the blast, which swept my mind into the Zin galaxy. My friends kept my body alive with machines. It took over eight years for me to get back."

"And now you plan to return?"

"I need my body to destroy the Zin. In the astral state, I could only scout for weakness."

"Let me get this straight. You astral extended into another galaxy?"

"I was caught by mistake in the blast."

She eyed him with skepticism. "If you can astral extend . . . Go down to engineering with your mind, leave your body here, and come back and tell me what color the main thruster is."

"I can no longer astral project." He tried to keep the sorrow from his tone. Daily, he automatically reached to use his psi only to find it wasn't there anymore. Since birth, his psi had set him apart, but to him, using his psi came as naturally as most humans used their eyes. And without his psi, he often felt . . . unbalanced. Vulnerable. Uncertain if he could rely on his judgment. "The doctors say the total reintegration of my body and mind will take time."

"And you expect me to believe your wild story without one shred of proof?"

Showing off a bit was one thing, bragging went against his moral upbringing. His father Etru had taught him that any man who used his skill to support his family should be proud—even if he did something simple, like digging ditches.

Yet, Angel didn't know him. He couldn't expect a reasonable person to take his admittedly far-fetched tale on faith. "I can still do some things . . ."

"Like?" She cocked her head to one side and folded her arms across her chest.

"I have hunches—like when I believed the Kraj would return."

"What else?"

"I seem to break down time into smaller pieces than you might do."

"Yeah, and you're good at math. But there are lots of brainy people in the Federation—and lots of them are right on the edge of crazy." Her tone suggested she was including him in that group. "Give me something concrete," she said in challenge.

"You can't pick up my body on your sensor scans unless I want you to."

She nodded and moved to her console and ran several tests. Her eyes watched the readings, giving him an opportunity to study her. Her skin tone looked pale and yet her cheeks flushed pink with excitement. "The first scan says I'm alone."

"Run another test. This time your sensors will see me."

Her nostrils flared. Her eyes widened. "Hide yourself again."

After he did as she asked, she ran a computer diagnostic. "Sensors are all functioning properly."

"So do you believe me?" he asked, knowing that she didn't, not yet.

"Who are you?"

He grinned, hoping to lighten the moment. "I'm the man who's come to make you rich."

"Get me killed by the Kraj sounds much more likely."

"Don't worry. I'll protect you."

"Like you did from my cat?"

He chuckled. "Aren't you still safe?"

"I was never in danger," she protested, "but if I accept your crazy offer . . ."

He shrugged as if her agreement didn't matter, as if his heart weren't pounding in his chest. He didn't expect her to answer right away. After all, they barely knew one another. But he understood her better than she realized. And they were both explorers, travelers, and he was betting she wouldn't want to miss out on the fun.

That he intended to have fun with her—he kept to himself.

Chapter Four

ANGEL STARED AT the Rystani who took up more than his share of available space in the central cabin the crew used for meetings. He was larger than any Terran she'd ever met, but his size and warrior abilities only served to remind her that he was suggesting she go on a dangerous mission. While the ultimate prize might be worth the risk, while every cell in her body vibrated at the excitement of the adventure, eight years as captain on the *Raven* had taught her that offers that appeared too good to be true often were exactly that—too good to be true.

So she'd called her crew and Kirek to a meeting in the only cabin big enough to hold everyone. She'd explained the situation to Frie, Leval, and Petroy, and then Kirek answered their questions before departing for the dining area—leaving her alone with her crew in the lounge.

Frie, an even-tempered engineer from a Terran colony, gazed at her husband, Leval, who served as copilot when she and Petroy slept. The husband-and-wife team had been with her since the beginning. Most captains were reluctant to take on a married couple, fearing that a marital spat could hurt ship efficiency. But Angel had found the opposite to be true. The couple had been married for years and often seemed to read one another's minds.

Frie, tiny and chunky, with a round face and big brown eyes, seemed a perfect match for Leval. Leval wasn't much taller than his wife, and he'd gone bald years ago and made up for the lack of hair on his head with a bushy mustache.

Petroy, the Juvanian pessimist in her group, never spoke about his home world. Angel had yet to comprehend how one creature could be so full of contradictions. Although he always pointed out every problem, he was often the most gung-ho member of her crew and he'd saved her life twice, so she trusted him to cover her back.

"So, what do you think?" Angel asked Frie and Leval.

Frie took her husband's hand. "This could be the opportunity we've been waiting for."

"Or it could get us killed." Petroy frowned. "Kirek intends to go after the Zin, the most dangerous foe known to the Federation—single-handedly. According to him, even the Perceptive Ones couldn't defeat the Zin."

"Kirek has special powers, he's proven that." Frie spoke softly, her numerous rings sparkling, as she waved her hands enthusiastically in the air. "And he's already scouted the territory during his astral journey."

"He wouldn't risk his life," Leval added as if completing his wife's thought, "unless he believed he could accomplish his mission." Whatever the couple decided, they always seemed to agree—even if they came at a solution from different vectors.

"By his own words, Kirek claimed he almost died in that wormhole blast," Petroy reminded them. "Perhaps the man has a death wish."

Angel shook her head. "There's too much life in him for that."

"What do you mean?" Frie asked, her brown eyes curious.

Angel thought carefully before she explained. Although on Earth people no longer went hungry and all received medical care, she'd grown up in one of the poorest and meanest areas of Jersey. Her mother had been sick for a long time before she'd died and family and neighbors had been kind, sharing what they could. And yet, Angel recognized despair. She'd lived with the emotion too frequently not to recognize it in others.

Angel spoke slowly. "I've seen the downtrodden and the hopeless. Some people sink into their misery, using booze and stims to get through their days. Others are workaholics. Some turn to crime or join the military, recklessly take any risk at all. But all of them have a defeated air about them. Kirek is full of optimism and hope."

Petroy rolled his eyes. "Maybe he's *hoping* for death."

"Kirek's brimming with exuberance and life," Angel insisted.

When Kirek had spoken about his mission, she'd seen undeniable sparks in his eyes as well as obvious heat, revealing his interest in her as a woman. And it had been a long time since any man had caused her to be so aware of him on so many levels. Usually, she settled for good sex and moved on before complications had an opportunity to arise. But Kirek's self-confidence made him as enticing as his marvelous body and she actually found herself considering what it would be like to have a fling. He had a certain way about him that suggested experience around women. And her imagination had no difficulty envisioning hot kisses, a powerful embrace, a sexual joining that would last for an entire night and leave her totally reinvigorated.

Petroy stared, his gray eyes locking with Angel's. "How can you trust him when we know so little about him?"

In truth, Angel didn't have a trusting nature. As much as she wanted to see the good in others, in her short lifetime, she'd noted that when people gave they expected to receive in return. And along with charity, she'd seen too much greed, disloyalty, and betrayal to blindly place her trust in a stranger.

But she wasn't so jaded that she wouldn't consider that Kirek might be a rarity in the Federation—a good guy— out for the betterment of them all. While he could be martyr material and that scared her, he didn't seem fanatical, but *determined*.

She could put her personal interest on hold, taking a wait-and-see attitude. But whether or not to join Kirek on his quest required an immediate decision. Going with him appealed to her for financial reasons. Staying just ahead of the *Raven*'s next mechanical failure had grown tiresome. She could spend centuries hunting salvage and never again hear about a prize so rich. Yet, she couldn't ignore the danger attached to the prize.

Already, Kirek's presence aboard her ship had caused the Kraj to attack. And because of Kirek she and her crew were now hiding in a dust cloud, instead of selling the Vogan ship on Dakmar and rehauling her engines.

And the Zin were a complete unknown. Did Kirek really stand a chance of defeating them?

If she wanted to play life safe, she should have stayed on Earth. But, the opportunity he offered, an entire world of metal—the mother lode—would set her up for life. If they succeeded, she could buy the most expensive ship with the best technology, spend the rest of her days doing whatever she liked. She'd never have to worry about a repair or fuel bill again.

"I haven't seen you think this hard," Petroy muttered, "since we fought off the Besali for that broken-down luxury liner off Kendor V."

Angel usually made decisions without hesitation. "Throwing in with Kirek is a big decision."

"An exciting decision," Frie added. "It's the opportunity of the century."

Leval gazed at his wife, his mustache emphasizing his knowing smile. "You want to salvage the Zin planet, don't you?"

Frie's face had a dreamy expression. "Do you suppose the Andromeda Galaxy will look the same as this one?"

"We might not make it out of this dust cloud, never mind all the way to Andromeda," Petroy predicted with gloomy-eyed discouragement.

"If Frie wants to go," said Leval, squeezing his wife's hand lovingly, "count me in."

"Frie?" Angel asked.

"I came into space as much to explore as anything else. And going to the Andromeda Galaxy is an opportunity so extraordinary that if I said no, I'd regret it."

Petroy snorted. "You'd follow Angel anywhere."

"That I would," Frie agreed and turned to Angel with a cheerful smile.

"Petroy?" Angel prodded.

The gray-skinned Juvanian shrugged. "Someone has to keep you out of trouble."

"Then it's decided." Angel spun around, her heart happy that her friends supported what she'd known in her heart all along. "I'll tell Kirek."

* * *

"WE'RE ALL SET to join you." Angel strode into the dining area to find Kirek on his hands and knees.

"Great." He held out a sweetmeat to her pet in an obvious attempt to bribe Lion into approaching. But her cat crouched, wary of his peace offering, refusing to come near him. At her announcement, Kirek disgustedly tossed Lion the sweetmeat. Lion pounced on it, daintily lifted the delicacy into his mouth, and carried it away to Angel's quarters.

Kirek stood and gestured to the table. "Are you hungry?"

He'd prepared a meal from their supplies and when she altered her filters and sniffed, the savory scents made her mouth water. He'd mixed a salad of leafy vegetables with an aromatic ginger dressing, cooked potatoes and topped them with a creamy cheese, and had added several other dishes she couldn't name. "Were we talking that long?"

"Not that long. My mom taught me how to whip together a meal. She insisted I learn to cook, saying no man should have to depend on a woman to eat well."

"You didn't need to do this, but I'm glad you did." She grinned and adjusted her suit to float her into a sitting position at the table. "Too bad your mom didn't train my first husband."

Kirek paused in the middle of handing her a soft-grained roll. Although he did his best to cover up his surprise, she could tell she'd shocked him.

He spoke carefully, removing all intonation and judgment from his expression and tone. "You have more than one husband?"

"I've had two." At her admission, he clearly lost the battle with his face. His lower jaw dropped and she refrained from laughing. "Not both at the same time."

"I see."

"No, you don't. After my mom died, I was eager to get away from Earth and her rules."

"What kind of rules?"

"My mom didn't want me to repeat all her mistakes and was strict. But all her rules simply caused me to become very good at rebellion. And after she died, a relative took me in, but I was done listening to what others wanted for my life. I married the day I turned eighteen—when by law I no longer required an adult's permission."

"Why not just leave home? Why marry?"

"Because I was a dumb kid, who thought I knew what I wanted." She placed a napkin on her lap. "I really had no idea what I was letting myself in for."

He leaned forward, his eyes intense. "What do you mean?"

"I confused lust for love."

"You had no mother to guide you."

"True. However, my aunts told me I was making a mistake. But I was eager to prove I was grown up and knew everything." She took the proffered roll and split it in half. He'd actually gone to the trouble to warm the bread and she used her knife to spread honey butter over the crust. "We didn't last a year."

"And your second husband?"

"I was determined not to make the same mistake."

"What happened?"

"I married . . . a friend."

"Why didn't this marriage work?"

"There was no passion. We didn't fight. We enjoyed one another's company—but there was no spark. When I won the *Raven,* he wanted to remain on Earth. I left him behind." She'd always have fond memories of Alan, but she had never been sorry she'd said goodbye.

"And since then? Have you been lonely?"

She shook her head. "I have friends, Frie and Leval and Petroy, and when the need arises, I take a lover. But never again will I marry."

"Why not?" His tone was casual, interested, yet his eyes burned, giving away his disapproval. She had to give Kirek credit. Her life probably sounded decadent and wild to a Rystani. His people chose once and mated for life. However, it seemed as if he wasn't condemning her culture, her failure, or her morals, and that upped her estimation of him.

"I like my freedom and my life too much to change." She sipped her drink. "What of you? Are you married?"

He shook his head and forked salad into his mouth, chewed and swallowed. "You mentioned after your mother died that you wanted to move away from your relatives. What of your father?"

Kirek was a good listener. Angel shrugged as if what she was about to say didn't matter. But it still hurt. "My mom was never sure who my father was. And after she was pregnant none of her lovers stayed around long enough to take a DNA test."

Although single motherhood was accepted on a social level, she'd always been jealous of the kids who'd had fathers. She and her mother hadn't shared much in common—and then her mother had gotten sick. They'd lived mostly on government welfare and charity from relatives. Her mother had expected Angel to be perfect, to not upset the delicate balance that was their life. And she'd always felt guilty that she'd been more interested in sports and space and business than the handmade pottery her artistic mother had sold to help make ends meet.

"I'm sorry." Kirek's warm gaze found hers and she had the feeling he wanted to wrap her in a giant bear hug. "I was very lucky. On Rystan, we have family units. One wife to each husband, but couples live together and bring up children together. My parents are wonderful."

"Tell me about them." She liked the way he spoke so freely about his family. And she appreciated how much he obviously cared about them and didn't mind letting her see his affection. Kirek was one self-assured man. But it was already quite clear to her that he wanted a marriage like the one his parents had for himself. Clearly, he was not "fling" material.

"Dad taught me to hunt. Mom always fusses over me. And although they always worry about my voyages, they never hold me back."

"And what of the others in your family unit?" she asked, curious. One of the reasons she enjoyed her work was the interesting people she met. And learning about other cultures fascinated her.

"We're getting to be a very diverse group."

"Really?"

"Tessa is from Earth."

Tessa? Surely there couldn't be that many Tessas on his world from Earth.

"Tessa Caymen?" Angel stopped chewing. Tessa had become a living legend ever since she'd won the Challenge and had been responsible for Earth joining the Federation. "You know her?"

"She's my aunt. Her husband, Kahn—"

"Is your uncle," she finished, more impressed than she could have imagined. Tessa and Kahn were famous for surviving a particularly difficult Challenge, and their love story had been made into holovids. It seemed strange that Kirek could be from such a famous family and that she hadn't recognized him. Although Kirek was a common Rystani name, why hadn't his face also been plastered on the holovids? "How do I know you aren't lying to impress me?"

Kirek appeared genuinely puzzled. "Why would my family impress you?"

"Tessa and Kahn are legends." She wouldn't have been as impressed by royalty or presidents. But she admired adventurers and explorers. People who soared into the unknown and blazed trails. Perhaps she was romanticizing the Challenge, but she'd grown up reading the story in her history books.

He shrugged. "Dora and Zical are legends, too. They reprogrammed the Sentinels which guard the galaxy against the Zin. And Xander and Alara saved the Federation from the virus. Everyone did their duty."

"But they succeeded where others could not and in spectacular fashion. Why haven't you asked them to help you with the Zin?"

"Zin spies are always watching. I have a better chance of slipping through their defenses alone, on a small ship, with strangers." He spoke easily. "I'm just as proud of my mother's cooking as I am of the rest of the family."

As she bit into the salad and the tangy sweet taste spread over her tongue, she grinned. "She taught you well."

"Thank you. Since I've been gone so much, she's been cooking for Dora's twins and Tessa and Kahn's two boys." His mouth softened as he spoke about his family, sending warning signals straight to her brain.

She knew Rystani valued their families. She'd read about their old-fashioned values. And she realized that as sure as old Sol kept shining, Kirek would want a family of his own one day. The need was stamped all over his handsome face. For his sake, she should maintain a distance. Because clearly, he was interested in her. There could be no mistaking the heat in his eyes. But she valued her independence way too much to hook up with a Rystani male, one who took his "hooking up" way too seriously.

"How does Tessa find time to be a mom and run a planet?" she asked as she dug into a potato.

"My mother and Shaloma help. So does Alara. Tessa still frequently sneaks away for lunchtime picnics with Kahn and the boys." Kirek made their life sound practically idyllic.

"Do you think Tessa is bored with her life?" she asked.

Kirek laughed. "She adores those boys. She's trying to talk Kahn into another child. She wants a girl. And I'm sure Tessa will get her way—she usually does when it comes to her husband. He loves her with his whole heart—even when they're fighting. Maybe *especially* when they are fighting."

"Now, that I would like to see."

"Come to Mystique and I'll introduce—"

"Captain." Leval interrupted their meal over the com.

"Yes?"

"If we maintain this heading, we'll exit the cloud within twenty Federation minutes. Already our sensors are picking up indications the Kraj ship is waiting for us."

So Kirek's assessment of the Kraj tactics had been correct. They hadn't given up. And neither would she. "Change direction, twenty degrees to starboard."

"Aye, Captain." He paused. "The Kraj ship is turning with us."

"I'm on my way to the bridge. Find an option to get us to Dakmar without confronting the Kraj ship." She stood and took a potato with her as Kirek cleaned away their implements. "Thanks for the meal."

On the bridge, Angel discovered the situation to be exactly as Leval had described it. The Kraj ship hadn't entered the cloud and remained on the fringe of their sensor readings. While her first officer piloted, Frie monitored the data and shook her head in disgust.

"Kraj sensors must be more sensitive than ours. They

seem to know exactly which way we're heading but are
no doubt afraid to follow us into this dust storm. With the
Raven towing the Vogan ship, the Kraj are much faster.
They can wait in safety and cut us off when we emerge."

Since they'd used up the *Raven*'s booster fuel to secure
their salvage, Angel's options were dwindling. "Can we
lose them if we go a little farther into the clouds?"

"I don't know." Frie's hands flew over the console. "If
you plan to go in deeper, let me increase the shields
first."

"Do it."

Apparently Kirek had finished his kitchen duties because he appeared on the bridge. He glanced over Frie's
shoulder at the console, but didn't comment. He looked
like he wanted to make a suggestion, but pressed his lips
together and remained silent.

"Shields will drain power a little. Nothing we can't
handle," Leval reported.

Angel nodded. "Understood."

"Shields are now at full strength," Frie said.

Leval kept a steady tone. "Captain, the Kraj ship is
closing fast."

As if determined to hold back a comment, Kirek now
had his lips pressed together so tight, they'd turned white.
With every muscle taut, it was obvious he wanted to say
something, yet he didn't violate her edict to remain quiet
while he was on her bridge.

"Suggestions?" When her crew didn't answer, she included him in her glance.

He didn't hesitate. "Let's cut through the center of the
dust."

Frie gasped. "We can't. Our shields aren't meant to—"

"I can calibrate them to a higher efficiency level."
Kirek looked at her for permission.

"How long will your modifications take?" Angel asked.

He glanced at the vidscreen. "If we steer toward the center cluster now, I should be done before we arrive."

"Should be?" Leval asked.

"It's going to be close," Kirek admitted.

Angel took a deep breath and released it in a whoosh of air. Since she'd decided to follow Kirek into the Andromeda Galaxy, she would have to trust him, his skills and his timing. While she hadn't expected to have to do this so soon, she had few choices open to her. Fighting the Kraj with the Vogan ship in tow was not a viable option. And she wasn't willing to hand Kirek over to his enemy. So they had no choice but to flee.

After she gave her permission to modify the shields, she'd expected to have to unlock the computer codes she'd placed to keep him out of her systems. But Kirek didn't even move to the control panel for direct access to the computer. Instead, he remained still and closed his eyes, as if going into some kind of trance.

Angel exchanged a long glance with Frie, who raised an eyebrow. Then Frie's gaze focused on her monitor and surprise caused her to stare, then blink hard several times.

"Report." Angel requested softly, unwilling to pull Kirek from whatever he was doing. However, later she intended to ask how he so easily bypassed her codes.

Frie rubbed her chin, leaning closer to her vidscreen as if to watch more carefully. "Captain, I've never seen this kind of configuration."

"Will the shields hold?" Leval steered deeper into the thick of the dust cloud.

"I don't know. I don't even know how he's altering the systems without touching the controls." Clearly fascinated, Frie didn't even look up from her systems.

But Angel took a moment to glance at Kirek. He appeared more relaxed than she'd seen him since he'd come aboard. Whatever he was doing, he was right at home with their systems, displaying ultimate confidence in the casual tilt of his head and the squared set of his shoulders, fully assured in his ability to alter her computer.

Leval spared a glance from the vidscreen to Angel. "Ten seconds to contact with the thickest dust."

"Kirek?" Angel asked softly.

"Almost there."

"Five seconds." Leval ticked down the count.

"Shield status?" Angel turned to Frie.

"One hundred and forty percent and climbing." She bit her bottom lip. "We need one sixty."

"One sixty-five point eight three," Kirek corrected.

"Two seconds." Leval kept his tone even as if he had no worries at all and complete faith in Kirek.

Angel held her breath and hoped she looked as calm as her crew. But her heart pounded. And the hull groaned as it withstood enormous bombardment from the stray particles.

"Shields at one fifty. One sixty."

"We're in the center."

"Kirek's extended the *Raven*'s shields around the Vogan ship." Frie's tone rose in awe. "There is no way our computer system could do what the monitor says it's doing. Even if he could force all our power into the shield, we'd be short energy by a factor of two."

Leval piloted through dust so thick, the viewport looked as if they flew through a sandstorm. The hull held. "The energy has to be coming from somewhere or the dust outside would penetrate our shield."

If the shield failed, the hull would be breached, and they'd lose pressure and explode. Angel looked at Frie. "Are you certain?"

"Yes, Captain."

"She's correct." Kirek jumped into the conversation without opening his eyes.

Angel assumed she could now safely ask questions. "Exactly what have you done to my ship?"

"I've tweaked the shields by routing power straight to the drives."

"Tweaked?"

Her chief engineer frowned. "Captain, he's done a lot more than tweak."

Angel could hear the puzzlement in Frie's voice. Obviously more was going on than normal engineering could account for. And the unknown factor was Kirek. She looked to him for answers.

"I added my psi to the force field." He spoke as casually as if he'd adjusted the thermostat.

"But you said your psi was damaged."

"It is."

Frie snorted. "If he's damaged, I'd like to see him at full strength."

"We're shooting out the back side of the dust now," Lavel reported.

"Any sign of the Kraj ship?"

"Nothing."

"Good." Angel forced her gaze off Kirek. "Set a course for Dakmar."

"Course plotted and laid in. Expected arrival . . . late tomorrow morning. You have time for some shut-eye, Captain, but since the spare cabin is filled with cargo, you'll have to find quarters for Kirek."

Chapter Five

Leval was rarely subtle and this time was no different. Usually Angel didn't crowd her copilot's shift, leaving the decisions to him. With a nod, she handed command back to her able first officer, knowing he'd call her if anything else unusual came up.

Angel left the bridge and wasn't a bit surprised when Kirek followed. Space on the *Raven* was at a premium. As husband and wife, Leval and Frie shared the largest cabin. Petroy's quarters were tiny because he was such a loner; he'd insisted on his own private space when he'd joined her crew.

She had much to think about—and not just where to find quarters for her guest. Kirek was such an enigma. He displayed unusual abilities with such casual modesty that he appeared unassuming—yet she suspected he might be manipulating them all like a master puppeteer. Still, she couldn't help wondering what else he could do—and she didn't mean with his psi. Between his saving her ship, and the special heat in his eyes that seemed to warm her straight to her core, he'd succeeded in imprinting his presence on her mind.

She couldn't recall the last time a man had fascinated her like he did. And that made her interested. Too bad he was Rystani—their no-divorce policy was positively uncivilized.

But Angel wasn't accustomed to having good things dumped in her lap. She'd worked hard to scrape together the credits to enter the card game where she'd won the *Raven,* worked harder still to overhaul the ship's systems to keep her running.

So when a perfect man like Kirek—who could have been anywhere in the universe—happened to turn up on her salvage, offering her a prize of all prizes to help him, her wariness increased. It was almost as if she'd been dealt four aces off the top of the deck.

So who'd stacked the cards? She knew enough about his powerful and wealthy family to know the *Raven* must be a slow, uncomfortable tub to him. No doubt, Kirek was accustomed to food materializers, sentient computers, and the best starship designs in the galaxy. Supposedly he needed *her* to help him enter Dakmar undercover, but with his connections, he could have made better arrangements.

She stopped and spun on her heel so suddenly, only his lightning reflexes allowed him to halt in time to prevent him from bumping into her. But she'd wanted to catch him off guard. "Why didn't Tessa arrange for you to go undercover?"

"Due to the family connection, any arrangement she makes might be uncovered by Zin spies." Kirek answered immediately, but not without a sheepish look.

"I'm not sure I follow. I thought the Zin couldn't get past the Sentinels that guard our galaxy."

"The Zin have coveted Federation space for a millennium. But what is not well known is that the Zin once lived here. Before they left, they set traps. One of those was on the Jarn world. They changed the Jarn DNA and made them slaves. While the Jarn are now free, other races like the Kraj may work for them—willing or not."

"That's why you didn't kill the Kraj—they might be unwilling slaves to the Zin?"

"Yes. And if Tessa, Kahn, Dora, Zical, Xander, and Alara came along or helped me, we'd have a much higher chance of being spotted."

"But the Kraj have found you. Why not call in help now?"

"Because it's easier for a small ship like the *Raven* to disappear again in hyperspace after we leave Dakmar."

"Okay. I get it."

"If I asked, they would all help. But I don't want to endanger families. My relatives all have children." His voice softened as he spoke of them.

He came from a big happy family that looked out for one another. She suppressed a stab of jealousy by reminding herself that she was independent and self-sufficient because she'd learned to stand on her own from an early age.

"How do you think the Kraj ship found you?"

His eyes flashed and she could see he'd already considered the problem. "Either someone in my last port or the ship that dropped me on the Vogan ship recognized me, or the Kraj intercepted one of my messages, or I was betrayed by the man who sold you the information about the salvage. For the duration of the mission, I don't plan to make any communications with my home world. I'll have to ask for the same commitment from your people."

"Frie and Leval don't have family except each another. And Petroy is a loner."

"That leaves you."

"It's not a problem."

He slanted a shoulder against a wall, thrusting one hip slightly forward. His tone changed to a husky murmur, increasing the intimacy of his already-suggestive tone. "We'll have to depend on one another for conversation."

Wow. For a warrior, the man knew how to flirt. And while she might be suspicious of drawing four aces, she wasn't about to toss in a winning hand. She'd made it clear to him she wasn't marriage-minded, and now saw no reason not to explore the possibility of knowing him better. She leaned very close to him and enjoyed watching his irises dilate and his nostrils flare. Using her psi to lift her body with null grav, she rose until her lips almost brushed his cheek.

He held perfectly still, watching her with a crooked and pleased grin.

And then she whispered into his ear. "Somehow, I don't think I'll have to worry about a lack of conversation."

Before he had a chance to respond beyond a slight widening of his eyes, with a flick of her psi she dropped to her feet, spun, and started to walk away, making certain to sway her hips just a bit more than necessary—and was quite satisfied with his reaction.

She'd taken two steps when his hand closed over her wrist. With a predatory gleam in his eyes, he tugged her against his chest, and she barely restrained a pleased chuckle. Resisting didn't cross her mind. In fact, she couldn't have been more thrilled that he'd taken the initiative. There was something exciting about a man who

knew what he wanted and wasn't afraid to pursue it, that
got her blood pumping and her pulse racing.

And, the Rystani *did* have a great chest. With his broad
shoulders and powerful arms, he really possessed an incredible physique. She knew Rystani men were all built
like warriors—but Kirek was the only Rystani she'd seen
up close. And as a woman who appreciated well-made engineering and masculine lines, she couldn't help but savor
the contours of his hard muscles beneath her palms. At
her touch, he dropped his psi shield and she could feel the
thump of his heart and the heat that radiated from him,
upping her own temperature.

If the simple act of touching his chest was causing her
mouth to go dry and her pulse to jump into hyperdrive,
she figured a kiss would shoot her straight out of the dust
nebula. His hands closed about her waist, holding her
gently, and she half expected him to lift her to him, but he
didn't. Tilting back her head, she caught his eye and at the
sparks in his, her breath caught. They'd gone from zero to
light speed in less than seconds, and her thoughts swirled.

He'd been hinting that he wanted her almost from the
moment they'd met.

She taken his hint and raised the stakes. Would he fold,
call, or raise the stakes?

Locking his blue gaze on hers, he lowered his head until his lips stopped an inch from hers. And then he
waited . . . waited for her to close the remaining distance.

Oh, yeah. He was tempting, seducing. But not taking
her for granted.

Perfect.

She'd wanted to know if kissing him was as good as
talking to him, as good as looking at him. Past experience
told her his kiss might be nothing but a pair of deuces. But
at the first touch of his lips, she knew he wasn't bluffing.

His kiss was exactly what she liked.

Not too soft. Not too hard. He applied the right amount of pressure to take charge, yet gave her wiggle room. She used it to wrap her arms around his neck and part her lips. While her fingers explored his thick neck and silky hair, she ached to press her breasts against his heat and fire more of her senses, but his hands held her in place, allowing no more than their lips to touch.

She inhaled and he smelled like fresh-mowed grass after a spring rain. And he tasted like ginger—not too tart, not too sweet, but with enough bite to make her want . . . more. Again she attempted to lean into him. But he didn't budge, holding her still. Right where he wanted her.

But his clever mouth kept her too busy to focus on the distance between their bodies. The man knew how to kiss. And he knew how to take control. His lips commanded and then demanded more. She willingly gave and her lips swelled under his attention. Her lungs strained for air, and she had no idea when she'd closed her eyes, allowing her to focus on the scalding rush of heat that boiled through her veins and elicited a whimper that sounded close to a plea.

If Kirek's kiss had been a tide, he would have rushed in and swept her away. If his kiss had been a drink, it would have been the rarest champagne, bubbly and effervescent and lingering. If his kiss had been a fire, it would have been smoke and flames that sparked and flared into an inferno that burned away to leave white hot embers.

And if they'd been playing poker, he'd just won the entire pot.

Stunned by her reaction, shocked by the pleasure he gave, she had no idea how much time had passed. She only knew that the connection between them ran like molten lava, burning hot, dangerously thrilling, totally awesome.

Explosive.

She had no doubts that together they would ignite. Yet despite the rushing in her ears, despite the hammering of her heart, she knew that while lust would be enough for her, it wouldn't be enough for him. A man like Kirek wouldn't settle for less than long-term potential.

"I'm not looking for more than a fling."

"I am."

His words reminded her that Kirek was all about home and hearth and babies. And then she opened her eyes and looked at him . . . and swallowed back the tightness in her throat at his fierce hunger.

Before he'd been imposing, but now he dominated the space around him. With his passion firing on all cylinders, he had a reckless heat in his eyes, a swarthy swagger in the curl of his lips that reminded her of a man who could deliver more pleasure than she'd ever dreamed. From the cocky tilt of his hip, to the flex of his powerful shoulders, he brimmed with a magnificent command of sexuality.

His gaze flared with wild need. A muscle in his neck rippled. And yet he held perfectly still—all that power perfectly contained—just waiting for her to unleash.

He would be delicious. She knew it. He knew it—she could tell by the utter confidence in his eyes.

So it took every measure of her control not to forge ahead. After all, if they became lovers and it didn't work out, they still had a mission to finish and on a small ship, there was no room for a lovers' quarrel. "We aren't right for each other."

"If you say so."

"We shouldn't . . ."

He grinned. "We won't." And then as if she'd said nothing at all, he kissed her forehead, her nose, and once again found her lips.

And she practically melted. Her bones seemed to go liquid. She had difficulty breathing, standing, reasoning.

"I can't think when you do that."

"Thinking isn't required."

"But—" It took all her self-control to yank her lips away from him and what she craved. "I said *no*."

"But you meant *yes*." He raised one hand and slowly traced a finger down her cheek, her jaw, her neck. She yearned for him to go lower, to explore her collarbone, her breasts, and the moisture between her thighs.

She tried to put resentment and attitude into her tone. "Don't tell me what I mean."

"Someone needs to." Amusement lit his dark blue eyes. As if reading her body's demands, his hands slid up from her waist to gently cup her breasts. "Are you denying that you don't like this?"

He looked her straight in the eyes. His thumbs flicked over her nipples, his touch rough and perfect. Electric heat shocked her and she moaned. She had the urge to bite him, claw him, throw herself at him, take him right there in the corridor up against the bulkhead.

Her tone came out sassy and bold. "I don't do relationships."

"Okay."

"You don't want me."

He flicked her nipples again. "You're exactly what I want. Look how well you fill my hands."

Ah, his hands felt like heaven. It had been much too long since anyone had made her feel so good. And Kirek seemed to know what her body was craving. She craved him. His touch. His kisses. His flesh against hers.

Yet, despite her hunger, despite how much she savored his skillful teasing, she resisted. "Are you sure you won't want more than I can give?"

He chuckled. "That's not your concern. Rystani warriors take what we want."

Oh God. Moisture trickled between her thighs. She wanted him to take.

And take.

And take.

Yet . . . that was lust talking. They'd still have to work together. She should keep the relationship simple and became true friends. "Just so you know I'm not cut out for long term—"

"Long term didn't work for you before because you chose the wrong men for the wrong reasons."

Damn him for turning her words against her, though his logic was faulty. It didn't matter who the man was, she simply didn't do long-term relationships. Period. She liked her freedom too much to compromise. She craved her independence as much as she craved air in her lungs.

While he played with her breasts in the most delightful manner, she cocked her head and challenged him. "And what makes you think I'm doing a better job of choosing this time?"

She expected him to tell her that he was different. Special. But no . . . he shot her a wicked grin. "Because this time, you aren't making the decision."

"I'm not?"

"*I* am choosing *you*. And my judgment is always sound."

"And you're always right, too," she teased, but then grew serious. "But—"

"I won't take no for an answer." His eyes darkened with desire, sparkled with interest.

Stars! Lust ripped through her.

And he read her as clearly as a holopic. He slid his hands down to her waist. Immediately her breasts missed his touch. Her nipples hungered for more. This time he lifted her by her waist. She yielded and wrapped her legs around his hips. No way could she fight her own needs and him, too.

Placing her hands around his neck, she leaned back and mock-scowled at him. "Who put you in charge?"

"Rystani don't require permission to take over." His hands cupped her bottom and squeezed. "In fact, during our marriage ceremony husbands place bands on their wives, bands that allow them to control their partners' suits."

She'd never heard of such a practice and yet the idea excited her. She liked sex toys and playful experimentation: "Too bad we'll never marry."

"My psi can take control without the bands."

All of a sudden, he tweaked her nipples and the feeling was just as wonderful as before. But his hands remained on her bottom. He'd adjusted her suit to give her pleasure. And the idea of such power and confidence and skill mixed with passion excited her.

Angel had gone into space for new experiences. She'd always enjoyed the thrill of stepping onto a new planet, meeting beings with other customs. But never had she imagined meeting anyone as intoxicating as Kirek.

In awe of his psi and the wondrous things he was doing to her breasts, she started to squirm and learned that she couldn't move. He'd taken total control of her suit and their lovemaking, placing himself in charge of giving her pleasure.

"Yes." Her muscles quivered and her breath hitched.

"There's more pleasure to come." He sounded so pleased with himself.

"Bring it on."

He tweaked her nipples again and while she bit back a moan, he slanted his mouth over hers, cutting off any more words. Her lips parted of her own accord and when next she noticed her surroundings, they were in her quarters. Lion hissed at Kirek for interrupting his nap, but then with an arrogant flick of his tail, her cat disappeared around the corner, leaving them alone.

The Rystani didn't bother looking around at her desk or her rock collection. He didn't glance at her cheery curtains that framed the portal. He looked only at her.

Kirek turned her suit transparent, leaving her wonderfully naked.

But he was frowning at her breasts.

Damn. Now was not the time for him to become picky about her body. "What's wrong?"

"You use your suit to compress them."

"So?"

With a psi thought he gently lifted her breasts. No longer confined by the parameters she'd set in her suit, her breasts looked perkier, larger. Her waist smaller. And when she glimpsed her reflection in her mirror, her nipples appeared tight from his attention, her lips swollen from his kisses. She looked softer. Willing. Eager.

He fluffed her hair from her face, the pads of his fingertips soothing her scalp. Although his hands no longer supported her bottom, she remained locked in place by her suit and his will.

"Tell me what you like."

"I like my men naked."

At her wish, he turned his suit transparent. And if she'd thought him awesome before, the nude Kirek stole her breath. His well-proportioned body sported magnificent bronzed skin—and a multitude of thin scars across his shoulders, back, and hips. She had the urge to kiss away the memory of every hurt he'd ever suffered and wondered what kind of accident he'd been in.

As if reading her mind, he answered her unspoken question. "The scars are from a whip. From my stay on Endeki."

His tone may have been light, as if he'd put the incident

behind him long ago, but she was outraged for him. Someone had deliberately marred his beautiful skin. And yet she instinctively understood that he didn't want pity. "The scars give you character. Otherwise you might be too pretty."

He winked at her. "If that's a compliment, then thank you. Now tell me what else you like."

"Hmmm." She eyed him, making her expression sassy. "With you—I think I'll like just about everything."

"Captain." Leval's voice came over the com. "The clutch beam just went down."

"The Vogan ship?" Angel asked, her mind snapping back to business.

"We've lost her."

AT THE BAD news, Kirek had immediately released Angel. They'd rushed to the bridge and Angel acted as though she had never kissed him—and Kirek expected no less. He appreciated a woman who took her work seriously—even if his loins ached and his skin still tingled. At first her revelations about her past husbands and the taking of lovers had thrown him. Luckily, Kirek had been exposed to other cultures and understood that he had no right to judge Angel by the morality of his world. Kahn had taught his Terran wife to fight like a warrior in order to win the Challenge. Zical had learned to love a woman that had been born as a computer and due to their love, they'd kept the Sentinels on guard at the galaxy's rim. Extraordinary tasks required adaptation. If these great Rystani leaders could alter their morality and beliefs to serve their people, then so could he. Kirek could accept that her past was not the normal one man, one woman relationship of his people, and still take her as a lover. Obviously, she'd grown up without the guidance of a loving family. And he still believed Angel was special enough for him to disregard her scandalous past when she had so much to offer. While he was on board, she would take no other lovers. They would spend enough time together for him to discover whether his attraction rang true. So he bit back his disappointment over the interruption and told himself the delay would sharpen his appetite. Meanwhile, he watched her handle the emergency.

"Frie. How long until you fix the clutch beam?"

"Not until we reach Dakmar. I need spare parts."

"What's the status of the Kraj ship?" Angel asked.

"Still out of sensor range."

Angel nodded. "Leval. Turn us around. Place the *Raven* alongside our salvage—as close as possible without endangering us."

"Aye, Captain. But without our clutch beam—"

"Frie. Get the chain out of storage and into the shuttle bay. I'll be down there shortly. If you think we need more brawn, wake up Petroy."

"I can help," Kirek offered.

"Thanks." Angel didn't hesitate to accept and that pleased him. While working, he wanted her to think of him as one of her crew. During his many trips around the galaxy, he'd seen how a crew could gel, forming friendships that lasted a lifetime. When people put their lives on the line for one another, the bonds forged could be as strong as those of blood kinship.

But when they weren't working, when she wanted to talk, or kiss or make love, he wanted her to think of him as a man. She was intelligent, determined, and independent—all traits he admired. He'd recognized almost immediately that she was special and meant to be his. The memory of his vision and his powerful response to her told him that Angel was the woman for him, despite her protestations. Had he been a gambling man, he'd have bet all his credits that Tessa would never have imagined she'd end up in love with Kahn. And Zical had protested strongly against a love match with Dora, not to mention the fact that Alara and Xander had come from enemy races. She could protest, but Kirek would prevail. Rystani warriors always did. And after one sizzling kiss, he couldn't ever imagine being with another.

"Coming?" Angel feistily tossed the question over her shoulder as she left the bridge.

Kirek happily trailed after her, enjoying the sway of her hips as much as her determined stride. "I'm right behind you."

"Stop staring at my butt," she ordered as if she had eyes in the back of her head.

"You ask the impossible," he said, enjoying the view.

With a scowl, she stopped, turned, and gestured for him to go first. "Behave. And turn right at the end of the corridor."

He laughed and took the lead. A few steps later, he glanced back, and caught her watching him. "And now who's enjoying the view?"

"Captain's prerogative." When she didn't even try to deny her interest or her irritation that he'd caught her, he began to whistle happily.

His mission might require personal sacrifices but at the moment there was nowhere in the galaxy he'd rather be than on the *Raven*. During his life, Kirek had been in enough dire circumstances to appreciate the good times. He didn't mind that Angel wanted to remain independent. In fact, he was going to enjoy overcoming every single one of her doubts.

When he turned the corner, he found Frie and an antiquated bot struggling to remove a giant ball of chain they'd salvaged and stored in a cabin. Obviously space on the Raven was tight and they used the extra room for cargo.

Frie had turned off the artificial gravity and the chain floated, but managing the mass in such tight quarters was tricky.

A careless mistake could set hundreds of tons of metal into motion with little effort, but to stop that kind of mass once it was in motion required enormous forces. And so Frie and the bot were moving with extreme care.

"How long did it take to stow the chain in this cabin?" Angel asked.

"Hours," Frie told her. "I wouldn't have bothered if I'd known we would find the Vogan ship, but at the time . . ."

"We needed every credit," Angel finished her sentence. She surveyed the chain, the doorway opening, and the corridor. "Let's unroll it."

Frie shook her head. "There's no room."

Angel lifted one end of the chain. "If you took this end to the shuttle bay, we could unwind—"

"Even if I could handle this end by myself, not even you, Kirek, and the bot would be able to stabilize the spinning mass." Frie shook her head. "And if you lose control, the ball of chain could crash straight through the hull."

"Ladies," Kirek interrupted, "I can control this end by myself."

Frie eyed him. "Not even Rystani muscles are up to—"

"I will place a psi force field around the mass. It will spin but stay in place." He could do that much with a damaged psi. If he'd been healed, he could have moved the entire mass with his mind.

"Let's do it." Angel attached the end of the chain to the bot, and then she and Frie guided the chain down the corridor, around a bend, and into the shuttle bay. Kirek kept the mass steady and allowed the chain to unwind slowly.

One Federation hour later, they had the entire chain in the shuttle bay. Angel had rewound and rolled the chain into another ball and was busy welding the end of the chain to the *Raven*'s outer hull. Frie was gone.

The hatch to deep space was open. In her suit, Angel had enough air to breathe for several hours. Angel obviously planned to secure the other end of the chain to the Vogan ship. But if they ran into trouble, she had no way to cut the salvage loose.

Kirek used his psi to float outside and joined her, appreciating the straight and even weld. "Nice work."

"Thanks."

Kirek didn't want to criticize and yet . . . he couldn't stop from suggesting. "What about a quick release?"

"Since I won't be releasing the salvage, there no need for a safety mechanism."

"You're risking our lives for salvage?"

She winced, but her steady hand didn't waver. "We need the salvage credits to pay for supplies and fuel. I'm not stranding my crew on Dakmar without the means to leave." Finished, she turned off the welder. "Besides, I gathered your mission to defeat the Zin was important."

"I have funds on Dakmar."

"No." Her tone was tight.

"The credits were transferred months ago. It's unlikely they have been traced."

"No."

"I don't understand." He'd thought she was concerned about the danger of being traced. The Kraj had already tried to kill him. And if they found them, they'd try again. So what was the harm in him giving her credits so they didn't have to risk their lives to save her salvage?

"I don't use credit. I don't want to owe anyone," she huffed, refusing to meet his gaze. Instead she examined the chain.

"The funds would be payment for my transportation."

"Look, we already made a bargain." Her tone was

prickly. "I agreed to help you on the mission. In exchange, I have salvage rights on the Zin world. Anything that goes beyond that—then I'd owe you."

"And why would that be so terrible?" he asked. But he finally understood her reluctance.

She didn't want to owe him because she didn't want any permanent ties.

Chapter Six

"I'LL BRING EXTRA air with us," Kirek told Angel in a matter-of-fact tone.

"How?" Although she didn't doubt him, she was unwilling to accept a statement—that risked her life—on trust. Just because he'd had the good judgment to turn her suit's control back over to her when their lovemaking had been interrupted didn't mean that his judgment was *always* sound. Just because he had a powerful psi—even when damaged—didn't mean he never made mistakes. With her life on the line, she was entitled to an explanation.

They'd returned to the bridge and were discussing the next step to transport the salvage, but her body still yearned for more of his touch. But she was also annoyed that Kirek had affected her to the extent that her body would dare to distract her from business that required immediate attention. Yet, no matter how much she yearned to be back in Kirek's arms and wished for his skilled hands on her body, the *Raven* and her salvage came first.

With one end of the chain already attached to the *Raven*, they needed to make a space walk to weld the other end to the Vogan ship to tow it. And their equipment was limited.

Leval frowned at his monitor. "Captain, I can only fly so close to the rotating Vogan ship without placing the *Raven* in danger. If she wasn't wildly spinning out of control—"

Angel peered at the vidscreen. "I'll fly the shuttle—"

Frie shook her head. "The Vogan ship is revolving way too fast to fly the shuttle into her bay. Her flight path is unstable and unpredictable. You can't even place the shuttle in a nearby orbit without risk."

Angel wasn't about to give up. "I'll use a booster to close the remaining distance." Boosters strapped onto the back required fuel to propel a body through space. Angel didn't like to leave the safety of her ship for what would be a space walk with a primitive rocket on her back, but she would do what must be done to re-secure the salvage.

Again Frie shook her head, her eyes full of concern. "According to my calculation, even using a booster, the amount of air you can bring within your suit will likely run out before you complete the weld and return."

Kirek looked at Frie. "Don't you have extra oxygen tanks?"

"We did." Angel sighed. "But since we don't use them often, I traded the tanks for fuel. I'll have to fly the shuttle."

"Captain. I really don't recommend it." Frie peered at her monitor. "Your chance of success is less than five percent."

"Any other suggestions?" Angel asked.

Kirek spoke up as if he'd been waiting for her to ask. "We use the boosters and I'll extend my psi around us both."

Angel appreciated that he wanted to contribute, but his offer sounded incredible—and impossible—until she recalled how he'd used his psi to enhance the *Raven*'s shields to keep them safe through the dust cloud's center and how he'd held the chain ball with his psi. "How will that help?"

Kirek explained without a wisp of condescension in his tone. "Your psi runs your suit and holds a force field full of air around you. I simply make us a bigger force field, so our air will last longer."

"You've done this before?" she asked, her doubts subsiding even though she'd never heard of anyone who could expand his psi shield around another. But Kirek had already exhibited unusual psi power. He'd held the spinning mass of chain without any problem, exhibiting more psi strength than she'd thought possible. And while she didn't know how much of his psi and how much of his upgrading her computer had been responsible for reinforcing the *Raven*'s shields, she had to accept that his psi was unusual.

But then he shook his head, revealing he hadn't attempted such a task before, and her stomach flip-flopped. And no doubt he read her renewed doubts because he spoke swiftly, confidently. "I would not risk your life if I wasn't certain of my ability."

"But earlier you said that your psi was weakened from your long journey. And you just used up a lot of energy to get the Raven through the dust—"

"That was mostly your computer."

"And holding the ball of chain," she reminded him.

Kirek seemed to go inward for a moment, as if he was checking some internal gauges. "I'm healing. Even faster than the doctors' best estimates."

"But after we go out there, how do you know that you won't suffer an unpredictable setback? That the force field around us won't collapse?"

"Do you fear your hands won't be strong enough to hold the weld?"

"That's different. I'm not . . . injured. And if my hands fail, our lives won't be in jeopardy. But if you can't hold the force field, we won't have enough air—"

"It's not a problem." Kirek's expression remained calm, his gaze sincere. His confident attitude reassured her as much as his words. And so far he'd done exactly what he claimed he could do. Or perhaps it was the memory of his wondrous kisses that compelled her to believe him.

He headed for the door as if a decision had already been made. "I will go alone."

She appreciated his offer, his willingness to put his life on the line. And she also appreciated how he hadn't made suggestions until she'd asked for them. But welding was a specialized task. "You know how to weld?"

Her words stopped his forward progress. He glanced over his shoulder, his mouth curling into an impish grin. "I watched you."

"Welding is not that simple. Different metals require different heat and pressure."

"We could always give up on the salvage." Kirek's eyes drilled into hers, yet twinkled mischievously as if suggesting they return to her quarters and continue their former activities. "I will arrange for a credit transfer to—"

"No." Angel made up her mind. She could accept that she found Kirek attractive. She could accept that she wanted to make love. But she did not accept favors that would place her in anyone's debt. "We'll both go."

In the shuttle bay, Kirek helped Angel into her booster pack and then she did the same for him. The mechanical device was the equivalent of strapping on unstable rocket fuel. While space holovids often showed explosions erupting into flames, due to the lack of oxygen in space, combustion was not a factor. However, the compressed fuel was packed into tanks and remained under enormous pressure, and if a valve failed, the brain would never have the time to realize there was a leak. The unlucky wearer would become a fatality.

"Turn around." He held a meter to the booster, checking fuel, compression, and the last safety inspection date. "It's been two Federation years since the last inspection?"

She shrugged. "The *Raven* isn't a military vessel funded by governments and taxes. When we don't find enough salvage, I have to compromise on equipment."

Not acceptable. If Kirek had been prone to cursing, he would have let loose several profanities. Instead he suppressed his irritation with her for taking such risks with her life. However, right then he made up his mind to correct the situation. The *Raven* wasn't up to Kirek's standards, and he refused to take the ship to the galaxy's rim without some major upgrades. But how was he going to get the proud captain to accept?

Angel tossed her hair over her shoulder and peered at him. "Since the boosters have never been used, I consider them brand new."

Kirek pressed his lips together. They should abort the mission. The salvage wasn't worth gambling their lives. He had an important mission before him—and yet, he required Angel's help on Dakmar. And even if she was more stubborn than a *masdon* over accepting credit, she knew the beings in charge of Dakmar. She could get him into the quasi-legal areas of the moon.

Arguing wouldn't change her mind. And he was too

much a warrior to stay behind and allow her to take all the
risk. Telling himself he would have made the same decision if she didn't have skin so soft that he felt compelled
to brush her hair from her cheek just for the opportunity
to touch her flesh again was a prevarication. There was
much he would do to know Angel better. She'd been an
eager and enthusiastic lover and he looked forward to being with her again with impatient anticipation.

He'd risked his life many times—but never for a hunk of
metal. And yet, to her, selling the salvage meant self-
respect. Independence. If she weren't an experienced captain, he'd secretly arrange to buy the salvage from her for
an outrageous price so she could properly outfit the *Raven*.
But he'd bet the mission she would know what the ship
would bring on the Dakmar market down to a quarter
credit.

"We're good to go." Angel finished checking his equipment and set the gauges aside. Without waiting to see if
he would join her, she slung the welding equipment over
her back and leaped from the safety of the *Raven*'s bay
doors and the protective force fields that trapped the air
inside. Like a fearless warrior about to face her enemy,
she didn't look back.

After clearing the *Raven*, she turned on the booster and
soared directly toward the Vogan ship. Kirek stopped admiring her lovely long legs, adjusted his psi to take in a
large bubble of air, and followed her outside. "Don't get
too far ahead."

"Then catch up. We only have a limited air supply."
She spoke in official captain mode, her tone reminding
him that her crew was monitoring all communications.

"We have plenty of air if we don't make any mistakes,"
he agreed.

Kirek had been born in hyperspace and he'd traveled
across the galaxy, but he never tired of the view. To some

beings, space was a big black empty region—cold and harsh and unforgiving. To him space was just as much home as Mystique or Rystan. He enjoyed the lack of gravity and the liberty of movement. He loved the unlimited freedom, the sense of adventure. And besides, deep space was nature's most awesome spectacle.

Stars strung out around them like glistening Devallian diagems on black matte. Through holes in the dust clouds, even with the naked eye, he could see neighboring galaxies, colorful nebulae, and star clusters. Nearby tumbling asteroids spun around each other in a fragile gravity mix. Even the dust clouds had their own special aura, a hint of cinnabar amid thicker sunbursts of rusty orange.

As much as he appreciated the sweeping vistas, he enjoyed the sight of Angel even more. Accustomed to null grav, she soared with the grace of the weightless dancers of Zenon Prime. Her hair floated in a halo around her head, and though he couldn't see her face, his last glimpse of her expression had told him she was in her natural element. She might have been born on Earth, but like a salmon born upstream, she was meant to spend her life swimming in the ocean where she had room to roam.

He followed, keeping hold of the end of the chain, letting it unwind behind him, and enjoying the sight of her soaring through space with only the booster rocket pack to mar her feminine lines. He never figured when he'd stranded himself on the Vogan ship that of all the beings in the universe, he'd be so attracted to the one who picked him up.

Was their meeting an accident? During his journey from Endeki to Earth to close the Zin wormhole, Kirek had met Clarie and Delo, two Perceptive Ones. And he'd sensed the beings' interest in him. Had they orchestrated his birth in hyperspace? Had they manipulated his genes and his destiny? Kirek didn't know.

He joined Angel, accepting with pleasure and satisfaction that fate had brought him to this place, this time, this woman. As they secured themselves to the hull of the spinning ship, he removed the welder from her back, handed it to her, and shot her his most charming grin.

"Need any help, or did you bring me along to admire the view?"

"WE CAME TO work." Angel thrust a U-shaped piece of metal into Kirek's hand and extracted a welding rod from the pack on her back, refusing to acknowledge his flirtation. "Hold the tow hook steady against the hull, please."

"Why not weld the end of the chain directly to the hull?" he asked.

Next, she removed her torch and fired it up, taking care to keep her eyes focused on the hull, but darkening her suit's filter to protect her vision. With the ship spinning end-over-end like some wild carnival ride, she didn't want to risk disorientation or blindness. "Salvage with this much mass should be anchored in several places."

With one hand he placed the tow hook directly onto the flat metal plating. Angel held the rod with one hand, the torch with the other, and welded a seam of straight metal, fusing the hook to the hull.

Although she worked as quickly as she could, the air inside her suit was growing stale. While the plan for Kirek to share oxygen with her had been to wait until after they finished the welds, she was growing light-headed. "I need more air."

"Captain," Leval interrupted. "Sensors have picked up the Kraj ship."

"Damn." If she'd once doubted Kirek's importance to the Zin, she'd changed her mind. The Kraj persistence had led her to believe Kirek had told her the truth—that he was a direct threat to the Zin.

"How long until the Kraj arrive?" Heart racing, air giving out, the Kraj looming ever closer, Angel turned in search of another place to weld while Kirek ran the chain through the hook she'd just made.

"Ten minutes."

"Explain."

They should have had more warning. But she wouldn't waste oxygen asking detailed questions or again cursing the timing. They had to finish and return to the *Raven,* but by her calculations, they wouldn't finish. They would die here where they were so vulnerable to Kraj attacks.

Kirek joined her, expanded his shield, and suddenly she had plenty of air again. And with the air, she redoubled her efforts. "Thanks."

"There's a flat spot over there." Kirek pointed to a location on the hull that would balance the load—assuming they could attach the chain before the Kraj arrived.

"Captain. Dust clouds are limiting sensor range," Leval explained.

"Give me a five-minute countdown." Angel headed toward the spot Kirek had indicated. Keeping his psi wrapped around her suit's force field, he followed, pulling the chain behind. She handed him another tow hook and he attached the end of the chain, then held it so she could weld.

Angel gestured for Kirek to leave. If the Kraj showed up and fired on them before she was done, there was no reason for both their lives to be at risk. "I'll finish. Return to the *Raven.*"

Kirek didn't budge. "We're sharing air."

"And I have taken enough inside my shield to return on my own. Go."

"I'm not leaving you. And may I point out that you're wasting time by arguing."

Furious that he was right, annoyed that he was going back on his word, and nonetheless pleased that he didn't want to leave without her, she welded and reminded him, "You agreed to obey my orders."

"Five minutes." Leval's calm voice came over the com.

"I'll obey your orders while on the bridge." Kirek grinned, and by the heat in his gaze she suspected he was remembering exactly who had been in charge in her quarters. And that would most definitely have been him. He'd been determined to have his way, determined to give her pleasure. She hadn't minded then, but that was play and this was work.

"Just on the bridge isn't good enough," she complained.

He cocked a brow haughtily, then spoiled his scowl by winking at her. "You can always fire me."

She glared at him over the weld. "I never hired you."

"Three minutes," Leval reported.

Kirek gave the chain a yank. "Looks good."

Angel began to repack the welding gear. "This conversation isn't over."

"There's no time." Kirek grabbed her wrist and the welding gear tumbled into space. Before she could grab it, he blasted them toward the Raven with his booster.

"Hey. Welders cost credits."

"I'll buy you a new welder."

She snorted, turned on her booster, and recalled how he would only obey her on the bridge. "As if I can rely on you to keep your word."

"You just insulted me." Shock and amusement entered Kirek's tone and she had the feeling that he hadn't been insulted often, revealing just how loving a childhood he had. He'd grown up so differently from her. She'd been insulted on a daily basis, and kids could be cruel—especially those whose parents doled out charity.

With both boosters blasting on full, they sped back to the *Raven*.

"One minute." Leval counted down. "Captain. You aren't going to make it."

"Bring the *Raven* to us," Kirek suggested, this time not waiting for her to ask his opinion. But as the Kraj ship in the black sky grew from a glinting dot to a shiny streak and then braked in a flashing glow, she didn't argue over who was in charge.

Frie's worried tone joined the conversation. "If the *Raven* advances, you won't be able to calculate the proper vectors to fly into a moving ship's cargo bay."

"Yes. I can. Do it." Kirek's voice snapped with authority.

God. Were they going to die out here? She didn't know which was more likely, the *Raven* running them down or the Kraj shooting them out of space. Tension grabbed her by the throat as they soared into what appeared to be the wrong direction.

The *Raven*'s engines kicked in. But it appeared at first that her ship was about to abandon them. But then Leval turned starboard, leaving the bay doors open so they could aim for them.

Kirek had to factor their speed, their trajectory, the *Raven*'s velocity and direction, and make them all come together. If he erred on the side of caution, they wouldn't reach the ship before the Kraj arrived. If Kirek erred the other way, they'd end up like bugs splattered against the bay's far bulkhead. Or they could simply miss the *Raven* altogether and the engine's flare could burn them, or they could tumble away into space, easy targets for the Kraj.

Angel broke into a sweat, held her breath, and kept her doubts to herself. If there was any chance Kirek could perform the complicated calculations in his head, she didn't want to distract him.

That his brain could work as well as a computer was awesome. To get her pilot's license, she'd had to perform simple calculations with a computer to back her up. Not even her professors could perform such complex calculations in their heads. And in under a minute, with their lives on the line, the task seemed impossible. Crazy.

And yet, Kirek adjusted their boosters and they finally aimed straight toward the bay, wobbling only once, which he corrected with a steady hand and a slow grin. Her heart was pounding, her mouth was dry and he was . . . smiling. The big Rystani warrior was showing off.

And then the Kraj fired a shot.

Chapter Seven

ANGEL AND KIREK jetted into the shuttle bay. Leval tried to raise the shields behind them, slicing off a burst of Kraj fire aimed at the *Raven*. But part of the burst came through with them. Kirek placed a hand on her back and propelled her forward, taking the tail end of the enemy fire. She turned to see an energy surge surround Kirek like a halo.

Stars. He had just saved her life and taken the blast himself, and at the sight of his slumped head and closed eyes, her gut knotted.

Barely keeping her panic at bay, Angel grabbed his wrist and began to reel him closer. "Kirek's hit. He looks unconscious."

"On my way." Frie served as unofficial healer.

But Leval needed Frie at engineering and communications to help deal with the Kraj. "Stay on the bridge," Angel ordered while she spun, tugged Kirek's wrist, snagged his pack, and turned off his booster.

She couldn't have maneuvered the Rystani's bulk without null grav. But after slowing his speed and ensuring they wouldn't slam into the bulkhead, she removed her booster and then eased his from his shoulders.

Kirek's bronze skin had paled. His eyes remained closed, his breathing was shallow. But at least he was still breathing. Placing a hand over his heart, she was pleased to hear a steady, rhythmic beat. Without knowing how much of the blast had struck him, she wasn't sure what to do next.

If he'd been stunned by a hand blaster, he would come around in pain, nerves twitching. While he'd only suffered a partial hit, and most of the force had been cut off by first the *Raven*'s shields and then his psi, he'd nevertheless absorbed part of a shot meant to take out a starship.

After easing him onto the deck on his back, Angel leaned over him, her concern escalating with every passing second. The longer he remained unconscious, the worse the injury. She wanted to consult the computer for instructions but at the same time she didn't want to leave his side.

"Captain." Frie's worried voice broke in through the com. "The Kraj have broken off their attack."

"Did they sustain damage?" Angel asked.

"Yes. We fired several shots, but only one locked on target. We've scored a direct hit to their port engine."

Leval spoke through the com. "Captain, the other ship appears to be retreating."

"Let me know if there's a change." If the Kraj ship attacked again, she had every confidence that her crew could hold their own until she made her way to the bridge, so she had no guilt over staying with the injured Kirek.

He'd told her his psi had been damaged during his long journey. Yet despite his injury, he'd placed himself in danger, at the same time protecting her. And she feared he'd burned out, short-circuited his mental pathways.

She had no idea if he was in a deep coma or a lighter stage of unconsciousness. And as she realized she didn't know how to help him, panic stole down her spine and froze her.

Do something.

What?

She'd spent time in hospitals—too much time. *Think.* She had to help him. If not for Kirek's last-second push, the blast would have hit her, too. Now his fate might be in her hands and she could do nothing except rock on her heels helplessly and shiver.

Injuries scared the good sense out of her. All her young life, she'd been around doctors, hospitals, and the injured and sick and infirm. In her experience, the doctors had been good only at sending bills. They hadn't cured her mother or alleviated her pain or even eased her death. And the years of disappointment now returned to swamp her.

Once again she suffered the frustration of not knowing what to do. And this time she also had to deal with guilt. She'd allowed Kirek to help her. She'd allowed him to stay after she'd ordered him back to the ship. She'd been responsible for his well-being.

What if she'd gotten him killed, the only man who could save the Federation from the Zin? Stars. Sorrow, responsibility, and despair weighed on her shoulders, made her heart heavy.

Gently, Angel opened Kirek's eyelid. His pupil was

large and black, so dilated that only a blue rim showed. And he didn't focus on her. But the white of his eye was bright and clear and her hopes rose.

She'd recalled some doctor saying that bright white was good, yellowed or bloodshot was bad. Then again, the doctors had mostly been talking about sickness—not injuries—and she could be mistaken.

"Come on, Kirek. Wake up." She spoke gently but was unable to hold back a thread of anger. She would not have his death on her soul. She'd sat at her mother's bedside and held her hand as she'd died and all the hopelessness and fury from that moment rose up to choke her. Hopelessness that there was nothing she could do. Fury that her mother's last words hadn't been ones of love. "Are you listening to me? Damn it. Wake up right this minute."

When Kirek didn't move, she grabbed his shoulder and shook him. "Don't do this to me. Don't you dare go and die on me."

"Okay."

She blinked. He hadn't moved. Hadn't opened his eyes. Had he really spoken? Or was she so desperate to hear his voice that she was hearing things?

"Kirek. Talk to me, again. Please. Say something. Anything."

She didn't shake him again but instead carefully watched his lips. He said nothing. He didn't move. But perhaps a tinge of color had returned—or was that wishful thinking?

"If you dare go and die on me, I'll have to shove your body out an airlock. No one will ever know what happened to you."

"Liar."

His lips *had* moved. He was talking.

And insulting her. Damn the man. He was arguing with her, but she was actually relieved to hear his teasing. He might be only half conscious but he still knew how to irritate the hell out of her. She didn't know why a tear escaped her eye but she swiped it away with the back of her hand, then glared at him for putting her through an emotional scare.

He opened his blue eyes and they fixed on her with amusement. "Are you going to spend your entire life pretending that you don't have a heart?"

He wasn't making sense. Or perhaps he was making way too much sense. "Thank the stars. You're alive."

"You won't get rid of me that easily."

"I don't want to get rid of you at all. At least not until after you lead me to that planet full of metal."

He frowned at her. "So your show of concern is all about salvage?"

"Absolutely." She shrugged as if she didn't think about his big hands holding her, his full lips kissing her, his teasing voice riling and heating her.

Kirek laughed. "And here I thought you wanted me for my body."

She grinned. "Oh, I'm a greedy woman. I want that, too."

When he began to shove to a sitting position and he winced as if in pain, she placed a hand on his arm and let him see her genuine concern. "What hurts?"

"Mostly . . . my ego."

She didn't buy it. "Don't get up yet."

"You want me on my back?" he teased.

Her worry and upset should have dissipated when she realized he was all right, but along with relief, her frustrated feelings were still swirling in her system. "I need to make sure you don't topple over and hit your thick skull. I don't want to have to scrub your blood off my deck."

He crossed his hands behind his head. "You're welcome."

"Huh? I didn't thank you." Perhaps his brains were more scrambled than she'd first thought. He wasn't making sense and her gaze locked with his.

But his stare was knowing, lucid, and he watched her closely. "Sooner or later you'd get around to thanking me for pushing you out of the way of the blast. Rather than let it eat away at you, I figured we'd get it over with now . . . so we could move on to more important things like you inviting me back to your quarters and—"

"Don't you ever think about anything else?"

ANGEL HOPED THE Kraj ship was too damaged to bother them again. Although the other ship had followed the *Raven* from the dust cloud, the Kraj had maintained radio silence and had kept just on the edge of their sensor scans. While the Kraj actions made sense if the ship had sustained minor damage, she ordered her crew to keep a wary eye out for trouble. After docking she had arrangements to make. First she'd sell her salvage, then decide which repairs on the *Raven* required immediate attention—not an easy decision. She reminded herself to also add new welding equipment to the list of supplies she needed.

In addition, she required a cover story for Kirek. Although he could fool Dakmar's machines into letting him past security, Dakmar was a rogue moon where many people were wary of strangers. Virtually no one trusted the computer systems to verify identity. And live guards manned many of the sensitive areas.

To complicate her problem, she saw no way to hide his massive physique in a disguise. Rystani warriors were the largest humanoids in the Federation and their bronze skin was distinctive and well-known. While she could alter his hair, eye, and skin color, she couldn't hide his massive shoulders or his height.

"Perhaps instead of trying to hide me, you should flaunt me," Kirek suggested during the evening meal.

Drawn from her thoughts, Angel swallowed a bite of sweetmeat, washed it down with a cola—one of her favorite drinks from Earth—and considered Kirek's suggestion. But it was difficult to be rational when he refused to give her a straight answer about his injured psi. When questioned, all he would say was that he was healing. And while he'd revealed nothing to indicate if he'd suffered a setback during the Kraj attack, his silence made her suspect he was more wounded than he wanted to admit.

"Flaunt you?" she asked.

"Why not claim I'm your bodyguard?"

She had to admit the idea held appeal. She liked the thought of Kirek staying close. His cover would even provide an excuse for them to share quarters during their stay and at the thought, her pulse accelerated. The more time she spent with Kirek, the better he looked. And she was more than ready to let off some sexual frustration that had been building up since their interrupted encounter in her quarters.

She cocked her head, considering his idea. "And where did I find my Rystani bodyguard?"

"Let's stick to the truth. My crew stranded me on the Vogan ship and you picked me up. We made a deal. I'd protect you in exchange for . . . sanctuary."

"Sanctuary from what?"

"Deep space. Without your help, I would have perished on the salvage."

She drummed her fingers on the table. "That story might work—except for one thing."

"What?"

"Are you capable of acting as a bodyguard?"

He glared at her.

"You'll be tested on Dakmar. And the beings here don't fight with honor. You might be expected to kill."

He glared at her so hard a shiver of apprehension slid down her spine. But when he remained silent, she didn't stop prodding. "And there's the matter of your injury."

He raised one brow but maintained the scowl.

"Your psi." She said the words softly. "How badly are you hurt?"

Kirek folded his massive forearms across his chest. His blue eyes shot angry sparks, his lips tightened, and if she hadn't known him better, she would have thought he might have lost control.

"Don't even try your intimidation tactics on me." Angel pushed aside her food and stood, glaring right back at him and poking his chest with her index finger. "If we're in this together, I'm entitled to answers."

"WE'RE ABOUT TO jump into hyperspace. You should be concerned whether the Kraj will follow," Kirek said to distract her from her concern over his condition. He would heal—eventually. At least he hoped so. "You should be worrying about—"

"Captain." Leval interrupted, "Per your instructions to warn you, we're jumping into hyperspace. On my mark. Now."

The *Raven,* with the salvage in tow, left normal space. Without webbing to hold them, Kirek automatically tried to use his psi to activate his suit to lock him to the deck. Webbing was a security measure in case of engine trouble or a collision with another ship—like a seat belt on a skimmer. So the lack of webbing in the dining area shouldn't have mattered. Except for the first time in his memory, his psi failed. The Kraj discharge had burned out his already weakened mental capacity, and since he'd refused to admit that weakness out of pride, he would now suffer physical consequences. The extraordinary gravity changes began to play havoc with his body mass, picking him up. In less than a second, he'd slam into the bulkhead.

But Angel reached out and locked her arms and her psi around him, anchoring him. She'd known. And she was risking her own safety to help him. Embarrassed that he required protection like a baby, Kirek closed his eyes. The logic of telling himself there was no shame in temporary weakness couldn't overcome his Rystani training that warriors didn't accept help from women. Intellectually, he knew differently, but not even his vast experience with other cultures and moralities could overcome the deep conditioning of his youth.

Each second seemed to last a minute, and the minute lasted for an hour. All the while, he kept trying to engage a psi he no longer controlled. And Angel seeing him helpless made his infirmity worse.

If not for Angel's quick thinking, he wouldn't have had air to breathe. Hyperspace acceleration or the lack of pressure in space would squash him. He would be naked.

Enforced nudity brought back flashes he'd hoped to repress forever.

During a mission to Endeki, as a hostage he'd had to remain naked, available to any woman who wanted him as a plaything. Kept as the Endekian woman's sexual play toy, he'd been used and whipped. At the time, he'd born the pain, refusing to activate his psi to protect himself in order to keep her unaware of his special abilities that allowed him to carry out his mission to spy on the household. But choosing not to activate his psi was a different matter from not having the choice. At any time on Endeki he could have ended his mission, so even though he had been living in the heart of enemy territory, he hadn't felt as exposed as he did right now.

"Are you all right?" Concern filled Angel's tone. And as if sensing his distress, the moment the jump into hyperspace ended, she released him from her arms.

He forced open his eyes. Saw he was clothed and drew in a deep breath of air. Obviously, she must have adjusted his suit to an automatic setting—like she had for her pet, Lion. Disgusted by how much the loss of his psi affected how he thought of himself, Kirek nodded. "If I'd known losing my psi would cause you to take me into your arms, I'd have lost it sooner," he jested.

"Why are you joking about something so serious?"

He shrugged. "I will heal. I always do."

He felt Angel steady his suit as if she feared he was about to topple over. Damn it. He had muscles. He didn't need her to keep him upright. At the moment, he should have been grateful to Tessa for forcing him to go beyond normal Rystani training. Since she'd been born on Earth in a time where Terrans didn't have suits, she'd insisted her family learn to fight without their psi. Because Kirek respected her, he'd obeyed her wishes. So even as anger flooded him, he was far from helpless. He had muscle skills—lots of them.

However, like any man going into battle, he wished he could be fully armed with both muscle and psi. He was on the most important mission of his life.

But he would find a way to cope. While he hadn't expected it to be so difficult, he also had never planned to have someone like Angel at his side.

He would look at this setback as a . . . test. A test of patience, of willpower, and of intelligence. Then he could move beyond the loss.

"How long will it take you to heal?" She gazed at him, her eyes steady and sharing strength. If he'd seen a trace of repugnance in her expression, he might not have answered. That he was willing to share showed him that her opinion mattered to him, more than he'd thought possible.

"That might depend on you." He made his voice confident.

"Me?"

"Lovemaking is supposed to help the psi heal."

She rolled her eyes at the ceiling, but he caught a sparkle of interest. "Obviously you aren't too badly hurt. You still seem to have only one thing on your mind."

"Do you know how good your skin feels against mine?" He answered a question she thought rhetorical. "It's smooth as *siltie* silk, softer than *collez* cotton, and intoxicates like Debubian brandy."

"Now is not the time—"

"And your scent. Your hair always has a citrus scent that reminds me of Rystani *esby* berries and your female scent teases with hints of cinnabar."

She snorted, but her mouth curled in a pleased smile. "Some men will say anything to seduce a girl."

"And you think I would say anything to seduce you?" He shook his head, wanting to be very clear that he was after so much more. Right now, without a shred of psi, he wanted her. And he suspected that when he healed, he would want her all the more. The challenge to convince her had already begun and like any goal he set for himself, he was not about to give up until he got what he wanted. "It's not just your body I'm interested in."

"Too bad." She fisted one hand on a cocked hip, her eyes honest, her expression sassy and confident. "Because my body is all I will offer you."

And what a body—she was pleasing to him in shape. He

recalled her bountiful breasts, her nipped-in waist, her long legs. But it was the boldness in her heart that attracted him most.

He grinned, knowing full well that she meant every word—that she was willing to share only her body. For now, he would take what she would give.

And he enjoyed letting her know how much he wanted her. "Then we really should retire to your—"

"I'm all for lovemaking at the appropriate time." His pulse skyrocketed at her brazen words. A Rystani woman would never declare her intentions so boldly, but Angel had told him what he wanted to hear.

He leaned forward and kissed her, his sudden move taking her by surprise. Her lips parted immediately, though, and she pressed herself against him. Ah, she fit perfectly against him. He caressed her back, trailing his fingers up and down her spine.

He wasn't surprised that after heating him up, after his blood simmered and his heart warmed, she pulled away.

Eyes dilated, slightly breathless, she still managed to harden her tone. "You need to remember that when this mission is over, I will go my way and you will go yours." And then she totally changed the subject. "How good are you with a blaster?"

"Worse than average." He tamped down his desire and focused on the mission. During fights, he'd always depended on his psi. His hand-to-hand skills were a fallback, and he hated using a weapon—so he didn't practice shooting often enough to have much skill with a blaster.

"If you're going to be my bodyguard, you should put in some time at target practice."

He nodded. "Good idea." And with the idea of honing his skill, his determination renewed. If Tessa had lived over half her life without psi, he could certainly manage. He refrained from dwelling too closely on the fact that

Tessa had lived in a world where no one else had psi, either. Instead he preferred to think about making love to Angel. She'd certainly responded to him, when his psi was healed and when it wasn't, and that pleased him.

Kirek's past had included women who'd wanted to make love to him—but he'd never known if they were attracted to his power, or to *him*. With Angel, after sharing that searing kiss, he had no doubts.

Chapter Eight

EXHAUSTED, KIREK TOOK over the now empty cabin where the ball of chain had once been stored. Before he could rest, he sent several encrypted messages to Dakmar. The first went to the bank to ensure his previous transfer of funds awaited him as requested. The second message went to see if the equipment he'd sent ahead had arrived. The third was to see if his contact had arrived— he hadn't. And the fourth was to arrange for a place where he and Angel could share some private time.

Never had Kirek needed sleep so badly. But after he closed his eyes, he couldn't find a comfortable position. All his life Kirek had used his psi to sleep on a cushion of air. But now he rested on his back, his shoulder blades and hip bones in full contact with the hard deck. And thinking about Angel didn't help. He couldn't help wishing she was with him now and that he didn't have to always put the mission first.

He should be thinking about his mission, about how he was going to pose as a psi-less bodyguard, about how he would meet his contact who possessed the portal coordinates that would take them to the Zin. Apparently, his contact traveled regularly to the moon and had no difficulty getting in, and he'd offered to help Kirek. But Kirek refused—the less people who knew about his disguise the better. While accomplishing his objective came first, his thoughts nevertheless drifted to Angel. Her soft skin. Her hot kisses. Her brazen heat and the enigma of her vulnerabilities.

He suspected the scars from her failed marriages ran deep, and while the surface wounds had healed, her prickly behavior warned him that she still bled. Yet, she lived with a courage that drew him. He liked her independent spirit. He liked the way she pretended to make decisions based on logic and facts when she was clearly such a creature of instinct.

He warned himself not to let his fascination with Angel get them both killed. And some time between dreaming about holding her in his arms again and fantasizing about exploring her breasts with his tongue and driving her into a frenzy of need, he fell asleep.

He awakened with a groan, every muscle in his body stiff from sleeping on the deck during the ship's exit from hyperspace. Shoving to his feet, he ignored the painful prickles caused by blood recirculation into areas that had gone numb. Peering out the porthole, he took in his first glimpse of Dakmar. The moon loomed bright reddish-silver. Alien ships in a variety of sizes—from one-man shuttles to huge passenger liners—landed, departed, and docked in bays. Satellite buoys marked space lanes for the traffic.

From their position, it appeared they were in orbit waiting in line for the dock master to assign them a slot. Kirek stretched the kink from his neck, but his back and torso remained stiff. Since the *Raven* was in a holding pattern, he would use his free time to limber up for his bodyguard role, ease his sore muscles and practice with the blaster.

In the empty dining area that doubled as an exercise room, he began with simple stretches and twisting motions. Kirek rotated and extended his limbs and torso slowly, taking care to flex all his joints before proceeding to *kata*—an ancient series of exact movements that martial artists on Earth had used to fight imaginary opponents before psi powers had been developed. Tessa had taught him *kata* as a boy. But he hadn't practiced for years, instead preferring to work out with sophisticated bots that moved at the speed of thought.

However, the *Raven* didn't come equipped with such luxuries—maybe a good thing considering his condition. The bots expected an individual to have rudimentary psi and he wasn't certain they could be programmed to match his sluggish pace. Although his head no longer ached from the blowout, his temples remained tender, a serious reminder of the loss of his psi and a warning not to try to find it again so soon.

Kirek's recollections of the childhood exercises might be rusty, but his muscle memory took over and the skill returned. But now he had the power and focus of a full-grown warrior. Finding his balance, he began to move with more and more confidence, appreciating the beauty of the punches, spins, and jabs that had evolved in two dimensions, before psi made it possible to levitate into the air with null grav. The simple, efficient, and economical combinations could be deadly when performed correctly or if an opponent with psi could be taken unawares.

After fifteen Federation minutes, Kirek's skin was coated in a light sweat, and by thirty, his muscles had warmed up and he'd left his former aches behind. He furrowed his brow in concentration, Tessa's instructions drilled into his head as if she'd said them yesterday.

"The mind is the engine that drives the hands and feet."

He kicked, he elbowed, he performed a series of blocks and followed through with a combination that struck at pressure points meant to stun, then delivered a quiet imaginary death blow. The sound of flesh clapping flesh caused him to jerk his eyes to the portal.

Angel stood there, a heated look in her eyes which were outlined with dark liner and green sparkles in a diamond shape that rose partway up her forehead and down over her cheeks. Her lips were colored in a soft berry color lined in a darker red, making them look even more lush than usual. "You have some interesting moves."

"And you're wearing an interesting outfit." He should have been upset that he hadn't noticed her presence sooner. So much for his supposedly keen powers of observation, but he promptly forgot his concern as he stared.

She wore her psi-suit in a provocative leather that emphasized her chest and narrow waist and long legs. Twin *bendar* blasters that looked fully functional hung from holsters suspended from a shiny silver belt.

Flashy earrings dangled down to her neck and matching stones shimmered in her hair, which she'd swept atop her head. Several locks had escaped and artfully curled over one eye. Armbands encrusted with gleaming crystals entwined her toned forearms. Through the cutouts that allowed him to view her cleavage, flashing green glitter dusted her flesh, creating enticing shadows that danced over her skin. She taunted him with every breath.

She shrugged as if she didn't know she was dressed for

seduction. "To be taken seriously on Dakmar, frosting is necessary."

"Frosting?"

"Sparkle. Bling. A show of wealth."

She intended to walk around in public dressed like that? Disappointment that she hadn't fixed herself for him warred with possessiveness he had no right to feel. But stars, he didn't want other men to see her on display. He swallowed hard. "Protecting you just became twice as difficult."

"Why?" Her eyes widened as if she had no notion of how provocatively she'd dressed.

"No man could possibly look at you and not want you."

"Wow. Thanks."

His tone hardened. "It wasn't a compliment. We don't need a fight over you."

"On Dakmar, a man can buy a willing woman. There's no need for one to attempt—"

"Men often want what they can't have."

Her hands went to her blasters at her hips. "I have these."

"Keeping a low profile is preferable to shooting—"

"A low profile is not an option on Dakmar."

He bristled. Knowing that she was likely following the local customs didn't prevent his annoyance. Not only would she attract trouble, but Kirek would be distracted. He wouldn't be male if he weren't.

The cutouts at her chest alone could drive a man mad. But her sassy attitude combined with that sleek black leather made his heart pound. His palms itched to touch, to run his hands over her. Right now he wanted nothing more than to strip her slowly, then have her right there, up against the wall.

He used superhuman control and still barely kept his

irritation in check. However, without his psi control over his suit, he had to turn toward the portal so she wouldn't see the growing bulge between his legs as his *tavis* grew erect.

Angry at his loss of control, he snapped his next words. "We're entering a criminal sanctuary. You'll become a target."

Angel rolled her eyes. "On Dakmar, the weak are targeted. Wealth shows that I have the power to protect what is mine." She wriggled her fingers in the air to show off several rings, and the leather stretched across her chest, the peephole widening to show additional cleavage. "These are glorious fakes. I have better things to do than spend my credits on genuine frosting." She glared at him and changed the subject. "Besides, the only enemies I have here are your enemies."

"What do you mean?"

"The Kraj ship just docked."

It was a measure of how much psi he'd lost that he'd temporarily forgotten about the Kraj. The lapse could not happen again—no matter what Angel chose to wear . . . or not wear. "I'd planned to get a feel for Dakmar before my contact arrives, but if we can wait to insert and then extract quickly—"

"We can't. First off, we must sell the salvage. Second, I need to order parts for the *Raven*'s repairs—and until the mechanics tear her down, I won't even know what we need."

"How long do you intend to stay?" he asked, keeping his tone casual, pleased that his *tavis* was back under control for now, but worrying how the Kraj had found them, and exactly what they knew about his mission. Perhaps he could find time to spy, or pay for some intel.

"We'll stay in port long enough to complete the engine

overhaul and bring supplies on board. The good part about Dakmar is that they are quick and efficient. Everything I need is here, including the best mechanics in the Federation."

"And the bad part?" He raised an eyebrow.

"Prices are outrageous." She looked over his suit, then altered his automatic setting. "And you must be dressed properly, too."

In the blink of an eye she changed his suit. His shirt no longer had sleeves. A large V cutout revealed his chest, and instead of the plain matte material he normally wore, she'd turned the fabric to shiny black. His pants hung low on his hips but allowed plenty of freedom to move. She handed him a heavy satchel filled with "frosting" and he chose from a wide assortment, picking out matching silver armbands and clasping them over his biceps.

"Nice." With appreciation, he slid a set of four connected rings over his fingers. When he clenched his fist, the heft turned his knuckles into a solid weapon. "Where did you acquire all this paraphernalia?"

"If you hadn't shown up, I'd have hired a bodyguard. And he would wear my emblems." Relieved that the armor didn't belong to one of her former husbands, he searched through his choices. "Each piece has the *Raven* logo stamped into the metal. While you wear these items, Dakmar's citizens will know you ship out with me. And that I vouch for you."

He jerked his eyes from the frosting to her. "What does that mean? That you vouch for me?"

"It means you must behave according to Dakmar customs."

"And if I don't?"

"*I* won't be welcome here anymore. The next time I try to dock, they'll simply shoot me out of space."

Obviously, she was risking a port and contacts, perhaps her life, by bringing him here. He'd try not to ruin it for her. "So what are the rules?"

"Don't piss off the people in power."

He would have preferred she didn't use coarse language, but now when she was risking so much for him didn't seem the time to voice his objections. "And I will recognize those in power by their frosting?"

"You catch on quick."

"What offends them?"

"Looking them in the eye. Not looking them in the eye."

"What?" He narrowed his eyes, searching to see if she was jesting.

"Being rude or being courteous can cause difficulties. Asking questions. Asking the wrong questions. Not paying attention. Paying too much attention." When he cocked his head, obviously puzzled by her contradictory instructions, she spoke plainly. "Dakmar isn't like other places with written laws. It's more like a jungle. You have to go with your gut."

He buckled metal guards over his forearms and others over his knees, adjusting the straps to fit. Whoever had worn them last had been of smaller stature, but no doubt their psi had been in working order.

She strode to a bulkhead. "Ready to choose your poison?"

"Poison?"

Angel laughed, her tone throaty and sexy, and then she pressed a panel in the wall. A compartment opened to reveal a large assortment of hand weapons. She displayed throwing knives, tiny derringers, fully automatic signature heat blasters, laser cannons, hyperspace distorters, and even a crossbow with arrows in a quiver.

Kirek grinned in pleasure, removing a shiny cluster

shooter with a solid *bendar* handle. "Please don't tell me that these are also frosting?"

"Of course they are. But unlike the gewgaws, these are genuine."

For a Rystani, Kirek possessed an unusual aversion to killing, but he appreciated fine weapons as much as any warrior. To him, life was sacred and he'd gotten by in the past by using his intelligence to avoid violence—if he didn't count what the wormhole blast had done to the Zin. That blast had wiped out millions of beings and although they were the enemy, although the blast had been an accident, he carried that burden on his soul.

He took a portable force field inhibitor, an illegal device on most worlds that shut down psi forces and would make a fight more even. "Now, this . . . I like."

"I picked up that little item in card game off Helvar Beta II, but I've never had occasion to use it," Angel admitted.

He recalled that she'd won the *Raven* in a card game, too. "Sounds as if you could gamble as a profession."

"I've had my share of luck—both good and bad. I prefer to depend on skill." As he slipped a knife under his shin guard, she nodded her approval and placed a dagger into the top of her own boot. "But the best place for gossip is a card game. Players are so focused on winning credits that they often reveal more than they should. That's how I first heard about the Vogan ship, as a rumor during a game."

"You took my bait." He'd planted the rumor, knowing a salvager would pick him up and take him to Dakmar. What he hadn't know was that the *Raven* and Angel would be the ship to arrive first.

Angel nodded. "My first stop in port, after selling salvage and ordering repairs, is always a casino."

Before his burnout, Kirek had been able to use his psi

to alter gambling machines in his favor. He'd used the skill only once, on Kwadii, in order to save the lives of his crewmates. However, knowing he could drop onto any Federation planet and survive was another in the growing list of abilities he no longer possessed.

Reminding himself that he was a whiz at figuring odds reassured him only a little. He was landing on an alien moon, among strangers and enemies, and his jobs were to protect Angel, meet his contact, and avoid the Kraj. He should be better prepared.

Kirek was as accustomed to using his psi to accomplish his missions as the fish on Endacron used their tails to swim upstream. If he forgot his new circumstances and hesitated during a critical moment, he could jeopardize the mission. He'd prefer Angel was stepping onto a more civilized moon, especially when she'd dressed to call attention to her delectable female shape.

"Are Petroy and Leval accompanying us?" He placed a stunner into the waistband at the small of his back. Since Angel hadn't bothered to hide most of her weapons, he didn't either.

"Petroy will remain here to oversee the repairs and make sure the supplies I've ordered are loaded. Leval and Frie never leave the *Raven*."

"Never?" He glanced at her and she hesitated, clearly torn about whether to say more.

Finally she asked, "Ever heard of agoraphobia?"

"The fear of leaving home?"

She nodded. "The *Raven* is their home. When I won the ship, they were already aboard."

"And before that?"

She shrugged. "Frie once mentioned a communal Terran colony that didn't take kindly to the practice of marriage. They escaped on the *Raven*. If I even mention them taking a vacation, Frie breaks into a sweat and Leval curses."

She glanced at him, as if sensing his unease. "Is there a problem?"

He shot her a wicked grin, deliberately provoking her. "In my experience, females are always a problem."

She chuckled. "Then you obviously haven't had the right experiences."

"A situation I'm more than willing to rectify."

DESPITE THE HEAT in Kirek's eyes which had given her a warm glow, Angel felt a chill at the knowledge that while Dakmar's premier bank might appear civilized, the moon was run by the most powerful tyrant in the quadrant. There might be a ruling council and police, but corruption was rampant. With enough credits, one could arrange for murder or slavery or spacejacking or just about any crime one could dream up. While the Federation occasionally sent inspectors, the moon had remained a hotbed of criminal activity for hundreds of years.

With her salvage parked in orbit, estimators from several firms had already inspected the Vogan ship by the time the *Raven* had docked. Angel merely had to accept the highest bid and inform her bank, and the buyer transferred credits into her account. She'd stopped by the bank to pick up her credit chip, fully intending to put almost all of her proceeds back in the *Raven*.

Her bank transaction took only moments and Kirek's dealings as he appeared to open his own account didn't take much longer. He joined her with a quiet glance at the guard, the lobby, and the other customers. "Banks here are most efficient."

Kirek's demeanor might be all business, but she kept catching his gaze on her chest. Tonight, she had plans for him and she fully intended to enjoy teasing him all day. She didn't even mind that when another male approached too closely into her space, Kirek bristled. But when they entered the repair bay and he stepped forward to take charge, she signaled that she would take over. When it came to repairs of the *Raven*, no one knew her ship as well as she did. And she was mighty particular about parts and labor.

Caught up in her instructions and haggling over price, she noted Kirek talking with the chief mechanic while she dealt with the owner. She supposed men would be men and paid little attention as he walked around several ships in progress, checked out an engine repair, hovered over a vidscreen with a mechanic, and appeared to admire one of the latest trade ships out of Zenon.

However, she also noted that he never strayed far, always keeping her in his line of sight. And when she wrapped up her business and took back her credit chip which was now worth considerably less, he appeared at her side. "All set?"

"I would have liked to purchase heavier hull plating but the cost was prohibitive."

"We should be fine."

Kirek seemed oddly unconcerned about her preparations for the journey. Yet he intended for her to take the *Raven* through an alien portal into another galaxy. From there she wasn't certain of his plans. While she wanted to prepare for every contingency, he hadn't even asked her how much fuel she could carry, never mind weapons, oxygen, food, or extra parts.

Perhaps Kirek trusted her. Or perhaps the scenery had distracted him. More likely, he was in protective mode.

He might appear relaxed, but his gaze kept moving, scanning not only ahead, behind, and to their sides, but also above them—as if he expected the Kraj to drop out of the ceiling panels and attack. They left the repair facility and proceeded onto one of the many moving walkways.

She kept her voice low so the couple behind them couldn't overhear. "Are you concerned about the Kraj?"

His gaze sparkled. "They've been . . . detained for questioning."

She frowned at him. "Did you arrange—"

"Dakmar's computer has them owing some back-port taxes. No doubt they'll clear up the mistake soon."

She'd underestimated Kirek. He had been busy. No wonder he hadn't been concerned with the *Raven*'s repairs. He'd been taking care of delaying the enemy—but how?

"Has your psi healed?"

"One of the mechanics and I hacked into the system." She'd thought she'd seen him hand over his credit chip when he'd been talking to the mechanic. Now she understood he'd paid the hacker.

Kirek gazed curiously at a woman posing for business in an upstairs window who wore nothing but a veil and thigh-high boots. Her expression bored, her body sculpted to perfection, she performed an erotic dance. "I've never seen a place quite like Dakmar. Even on Endeki, the sex isn't advertised on the street."

"Enjoying the scenery?"

"Very much." His stare drilled her, then flicked down to her chest, then back to her eyes, leaving no doubt about which scenery he was enjoying.

They exited the hangar bay through a portal and entered a rolling sidewalk, joining humanoids and several sentient birds that couldn't fly since their wingspan was longer than the corridor. Although the space on Dakmar was much larger than on the *Raven*, the moon was crowded and always made her feel slightly claustrophobic. Even with her suit's filtration set on full, she felt as though the air was stale.

"Now what?" Kirek asked.

"We find a card game."

"And then?"

"Food."

"And then?"

"I thought we'd have a party." She leaned forward and let the side of her breast press against his arm.

"A private party? Just for the two of us?" He jerked, she laughed, and then he glared at her as if he was about to burn up right on the sidewalk. My, oh my, her big Rystani warrior was edgy.

"Actually, I thought maybe you'd want to take me dancing," she teased.

"Dancing is not what I have in mind."

Chapter Nine

ANGEL SIDLED CLOSER to Kirek, enjoying that she could adjust the filters of her suit, and his, to allow her to breathe in his appetizing scent and touch his awesome heat.

She shot him a brazen look. "What *do* you have in mind?"

"Not a card game."

He caught her gaze and from the deep violet sparks, she saw he wanted her. His patience had oh so obviously almost run out, and she wondered if making love with Kirek would excite her as much as the anticipation. She couldn't recall ever being this on-edge, all her nerves dancing, her stomach fluttery and jittery, her veins bubbling with glossy desire. She suspected it wouldn't take a whole lot of stimulation to arouse her past a point of no return.

With a grin of satisfaction that indicated he seemed to be right there on the edge with her, she snuggled even closer against his hard muscles. "With the right enticement, I could be tempted to play other kinds of games."

"Good." He closed a hand over her arm. "I've planned a little surprise."

Angel didn't normally like surprises, but at his words, a pitter-patter of tingling seeped down her spine in a delicious tickle of heat. And when he stepped from the moving sidewalk and guided her toward an establishment with two unmarked platinum double doors, she realized he wasn't thinking fast on his feet but had made prior arrangements.

Interesting. She shouldn't have been surprised, but she was. It wasn't necessarily logical that if he'd lost his psi he would also lose his take-charge attitude, but losing one's psi might be as disturbing as losing one's sight and she'd expected Kirek to display a certain amount of disorientation. But he seemed to have adjusted almost effortlessly, revealing that confidence that made him so damn attractive.

The building had no sign. No portals. Just a discrete address—*Deck 52, Quadrant 4*—carved into the sparkling marbalite steps leading to the imposing front doors.

Angel was delighted that under his difficult circumstances, he wanted her enough to strategize a seduction. They approached and the doors opened with a hiss, inviting them into a lush foyer that widened into an opulent living area. The enormous building appeared to be more like a private home than a hotel, and she stared in open-eyed wonder. Plush white carpeting, billowing white floor-to-ceiling curtains, and a magnificent crystal chandelier showed off exquisite sculptures and precious art that hung from walls decorated with silken tapestries woven from shimmering star silk.

"What is this place?" She expected security to arrive at any moment and ask them to leave, but they appeared to be alone. "I've been to Dakmar many times, but I had no idea this building existed right in the heart of the merchant district."

Kirek seemed completely at home, as if accustomed to vast wealth. Either that or luxury didn't impress him—but if not, then why had he chosen this place?

"A government official keeps the apartment for his off-world mistress. She's visiting her home world and he's currently on Zenon Prime and isn't due back for—"

"You broke in?" Her voice rose in awe of the magnitude of his thinking. "But those doors outside opened after recognizing our identities."

"Security is run by computer." Kirek grinned, took her hand, and led her farther into the building.

The way he avoided a direct answer to her questions made her wonder if he'd also paid the mechanic to hack in and make these arrangements. But Angel decided that for once, she was going to try to go with the flow. She owed herself a vacation and had no intention of using their limited time in arguments. Besides, his silence about his methods added a bit of a thrill to their rendezvous.

They strode past a miniature waterfall and a cascade of scented blooming plants, dozens of varieties of white flowers from many different worlds. And in the great room, music and mist gathered around them creating an exotic atmosphere.

Beside her Kirek gave her an innocent look and she sighed. As much as she wanted to relax and trust him, she didn't believe a mechanic had hacked into such an elaborate mansion. She hadn't wanted to spoil the mood by questioning him, yet she simply couldn't let it go and changed her mind about questioning him. She disengaged her hand from his. "Are we here illegally?"

"Have a little trust."

She supposed he could know the owner, or perhaps he'd rented the place for the night—but she didn't believe that wealthy people rented out their residences like a hotel. Thinking aloud, she narrowed her gaze on him. "Why are you refusing to tell me how you arranged all this, unless . . ." She frowned. "What else have you done?"

"Come and see." Kirek didn't appear the least bit perturbed that she was suspicious. Instead, he kept walking and she followed him into a large dome that appeared empty. A materializer, a toy for the wealthy, stood by the domed wall. The materializers could create food from their memory banks or create simple objects. "I programmed the entertainment area. I hope you don't have any water phobias."

While she eyed the expensive materializer, wishing she could afford one for the *Raven,* she worried that he still hadn't answered her question about how he'd arranged for them to stay at this beautiful estate. "No, but—"

He threw a switch. The dome disappeared and holograms now presented them with a gorgeous blue sky, powder-fine white sand, and a turquoise bathing pool. Water cascaded over a rock wall into the inviting rock pool, creating a pleasant roaring in her ears. And a thudding in her pulse.

Kirek had gone to a lot of trouble and yet, it disturbed her that he wouldn't answer her questions. Worry niggled through her bones that she should be thinking long and hard about why he hadn't been up front with her.

And yet, he may simply have wanted to surprise her. She didn't like secrets and reminded herself that since she had no intention of becoming involved, his methods shouldn't matter.

She wanted no more than a fling and hoped her attraction to him might even last for the duration of the mission. So she shouldn't be worrying about how he'd arranged this surprise without her knowledge—not with such a magnificent setting, not with such a fine specimen of a man to share the beach. Besides, they probably wouldn't be caught.

And she *so* needed a few hours of glorious sex.

"Ready for a swim?" Bronzed skin gleaming in the sunlight, he took her hand and tugged her toward the water.

Determined to have a good time, she cast aside her suspicions. They were about to begin a dangerous mission and she owed herself a good time. And while she still didn't know if she could trust Kirek's arrangements, she had no doubts about trusting him with her body that was already clamoring for his attention.

She shot him her sexiest grin. "First one in the water gets to touch the other first—for as long as they like," she challenged him, turning both their suits transparent.

Angel had vowed never to let herself grow bored with her sexuality. She loved adventure and experimentation. And a little creativity could go a long way toward adding to the excitement. And right now she couldn't think of anything better than a new man to ease her ratcheting arousal.

Sensing she and Kirek were about to make memories that she'd cherish for a long time, she unbuckled her holsters. But instead of gracefully flinging the weapons aside in a sexy movement, the strap caught on her ankle. She hopped awkwardly on one foot and her jerky movements caused her breasts to bounce. Kirek's eyes blazed bright with interest, and she realized with this man she could be herself and he would appreciate her. The idea that he found her naturally sexy caused her heart to thud.

"Am I distracting you?" she teased, racing to remove the rest of her flash so she could beat him into the water.

"You're cheating," he accused, his tone a gruff growl of impatience. And hot interest.

"Can't blame a girl for wanting to stroke all those hard Rystani muscles."

Flinging him a mischievous pout, she grazed her finger over the top of her breast and flicked off an imaginary speck of sand. But taunting him wasn't as easy as she'd have liked. He was quite good at giving her back some of her own teasing. When he bent to remove his leg shields, she got a great look at his fantastic butt, and then he straightened to his full height. His powerful chest narrowed to a very flat stomach causing her gaze to roam . . . and go lower.

Yum.

Kirek's proportions could have served as a model for a Greek god. His muscular calves and thighs were strong without being massive. And his buns—all tight and hard and coiled as if to pounce.

With her squeal of glee and his roar of approval, they bolted toward the water. The race was on. She couldn't quite get over her luck that Kirek would be all hers for the next few hours. And she eagerly awaited having so much of his attention directed only on her.

They sprinted step for step across the sand. When she reached the water first, winning the foot race, her shorter legs splashing into the cool pool before his longer ones, she laughed knowingly. "You let me win."

"It's I who has won."

Angel suspected there would be no losers here. He waded out, then dived head-first into the water. Knowing his suit could hold at least enough air for what he had in mind, when he didn't surface immediately, she plunged in after him.

She'd assumed the pool would be . . . empty. But assorted neon-colored sea creatures swam, scooted, and dived past her. One sea snake lit up with a pink phosphorescent glow. Angel had no fear that any artificial creatures in the tank could hurt her. Kirek had set this scene with pleasure in mind—she enjoyed the surprise of a rainbow-hued coral reef near the bottom. But even as the coral beckoned to be explored, she wanted Kirek.

Where was he? The water was so clear she could have seen him if he was below.

Flipping onto her back, she found him directly above her and reached out with her psi to claim her prize. While she couldn't extend her psi bubble like Kirek had done in space, hers was large enough to bring him inside hers, where they could share air and talk, yet still have the sensation of water everywhere but on their faces. She set both suits to automatically keep their mouths, noses, and ears in the air with water everywhere else and the resulting sensation was indescribably intimate.

Looking savage and bronzed and huge as he floated above her, his golden flesh tempted her. She placed a hand on his shoulder, loving the combination of his slick, hard flesh at her fingertips. "I'm very ready to claim my—"

"Not just . . . yet."

Surrounded by blue water, yet able to breathe and talk, they had created the perfect cocoon in which to make love. Or so she thought until he grinned and swam them slightly closer to the surface . . . where the waterfall cascaded down into the water, creating an erotic tattoo on her skin.

"This is so awesome." Even if they'd inadvertently set

off a silent alarm, she doubted anyone would find them down here.

"*You* are awesome." He wriggled a bit, causing her palm on his shoulder to slide down his back. And his flesh was warm, wet, and pleasingly supple.

"So where should I touch you first?" She trailed her fingers up and down his back, leaned forward and demanded he give her a kiss.

He parted his mouth and she pulled back from the kiss, nipping his bottom lip with a gentle tug. Then she let him see the desire in her eyes. "I've never made love while under water. Thank you."

"You still haven't made love under water," he pointed out with a gruff impatience.

"But it's going to be good, isn't it?" She barely knew what she was saying as she trailed her tongue over his earlobe down his neck to his collarbone. His skin tasted slightly salty, with a bite of tang and a hint of exotic spice.

He leaned his head down to capture her lips, and impudently, she flipped him over so his back was to her stomach. He took one surprised stroke of the water with his hand, then settled into an easy float, letting her position him between her and the surface the way she wished.

And now without his flaming eyes watching her every move, she could explore his nape, his shoulder blades, his waist. As her hand grazed his buttocks, his muscles tightened and he let out a ragged hiss. Between the water cascading onto his chest from above and her fingers trailing wherever she wished and her mouth skimming down his back, she sensed he might be having difficulty holding still, but he allowed her to do as she wished . . . and it was her wish to see how far she could push him.

Ever so slowly, she worked her way down his back with her lips. She enjoyed the dimpled hollows at his waist, the curve of his spine, the arc of his tight buns. Damn, he had a fine butt. And she explored the curve of his cheeks, quite pleased when his balls drew up tight against his body as she teased her way over.

She occasionally allowed the tips of her breasts to graze along his back or butt, and a nearby muscle would spasm, proving he was most definitely paying attention. And when she reached between his legs and took his balls into her hands, then squeezed gently, he gasped.

With a grin of satisfaction, she didn't let go but held on tight. Then she bit his butt and licked away the sting, and all the while her hands firmly kept him captive. In the water it was easy to maneuver around his big body and she swam between his legs, maintaining hold of his tight balls with her hands. With a mischievous grin, she took his erection into her mouth in one smooth lunge.

His back arched. His hips bucked. His fingers threaded into her hair.

She used her tongue to flick over his sensitive ridge, then sucked hard, keeping her hands tight on him, letting him know that he was hers to have, hers to stroke, hers to lick.

If she hadn't known before, Kirek was proving now that he had supreme self-control and confidence. Most men wouldn't so easily give a partner the upper hand, but with him, he either had no ego, or his ego was so extremely confident that ceding her power was his way of showing her that he was truly free. Free of any concern but giving or taking pleasure.

And in her view that made Kirek even more powerful, more attractive, more of a turn-on. She couldn't seem to get enough of his smooth flesh under her hands, into her mouth, next to her own skin. And she sensed that no matter what she did right now, he was prepared to let her.

His letting her being the important part.

That trust made her feel honored and shaky and stimulated and aroused and intrigued. Even as he filled her mouth and hands, her head spun with thoughts of him.

"Angel," he gasped.

"Mm?"

"You keep that up . . . and there'll . . . be consequences." His tone was half growl, half promise.

Until he uttered those words, she'd hadn't realized exactly how far she'd been prepared to go . . . but between his raw need and his promise of thrilling and intimidating "consequences," she was determined not to hold back. She tightened her hands, worked her tongue furiously.

In truth, his implied threat aroused her. So did his giving her this power over him. Never had she felt so feminine. Never had she so wanted to give pleasure or been so turned on by the freedom.

She demanded with every squeeze of her hands, every stroke of her lips that he take . . . more and more . . . and just when she sensed that he was about to spill, she released him, swam over his chest and watched his eyes slowly open to reveal deep purple sparks. Watched his gasp from passion denied turn into a fiery groan.

"You okay?" she asked, with an impish lilt.

He locked his hands behind his head, then winked at her. "I'm thinking about the consequences."

"Hmm. Obviously, I haven't given you enough to think about." She leaned down, bit his nipple. The big guy was still entirely sure of himself. She threatened, "You know I could keep you up for hours."

"First, you might want to surface to replenish your air." He spoke carefully, his eyes bright with hungry amusement. "And you might want to consider that eventually . . ."

"Yes?"

"It will be my turn."

She'd been so wrapped up in pleasure and his sensual promises she hadn't remembered the need for air and grinned at him. "Wait right here."

And then she swam for the surface, giving him a good look between her legs as she kicked upward. After requesting several play toys from a materializer, she then ducked back down to Kirek. He remained exactly as she'd left him, hands laced behind his head, erection tight and firm. She merged their suits and replenished his air, keeping her acquisitions hidden from his view.

"Miss me?" she asked.

"Why would you think that?"

She chuckled, leaned forward, sucked hard on his nipple, and when it hardened and accommodated her wishes, she attached a clamp to the dark skin, then repeated her actions on his other side. By now she knew better than to expect him to protest. In fact, she was beginning to think Kirek would make a perfect creature of passion—everything seemed to please him.

And when she set the clamps to pulsing, he smiled, confirming her impression. "That feels wonderful."

"There are other settings."

At her words, his inquisitive gaze found hers. "Do we have time to try them all?"

She held up another device, full of adjustable straps. "Ever tried a ball-breaker?"

Curiosity brightened his eyes. "Is that from Earth?"

"An Earth colony out on the rim makes them. The materializer reproduced it for you." She wrapped the straps around his balls. "Comfy?"

"Very."

With a tug, she tightened the straps, careful not to cause pain, but a feeling of tension. She wasn't done. She placed several bands over his sex, careful to keep them equidistant.

"And the purpose of this device?" he asked.

"Pleasure."

He had yet to move his hands from behind his head. From every indication, he remained willing. As much as she believed her intuition about him to be on target, she needed to be certain.

"What do you think?" She turned on the pulsing that tickled and nipped and aroused his most sensitive places. A device that would tease her just as thoroughly once she took him inside her.

"The sensation is . . . interesting."

"You are pleased?"

"Not yet."

She hesitated, ready to remove the play toy if he objected. "You want me to stop?"

"I meant that to be pleased, we must continue. Finish." He reached for her.

She scooted back. "I'm in no hurry."

His eyes darkened with interest. "You would do well to remember my words."

"I'm looking forward to enjoying the consequences," she practically purred, suspecting this man might be her sensual match in every way. All too often, her partners had tired or lost interest long before she had. Learning that Kirek was into prolonging their mating pleased her. Had she finally found a sexual partner that could equal her own need for adventurous passions?

He spoke, his tone husky with need as the pulses teased and taunted him. "Do you know . . . anything of Rystani . . . mating rituals?"

"Only about the Rystani marriage bands that you mentioned." She skimmed her breasts across his chest and

watched his eyes dilate with hungry lust. She let her
breast touch his lips and he took the tip into his mouth.
Ah . . . he felt . . . too good and she forced herself to
pull back. Right now, she needn't distract herself with
anything except how badly she wanted to drive him into
a wild frenzy of need.

And as if he knew exactly what she wanted to do, he
interrupted her thoughts. "Rystani women like their warriors to take charge."

"Uh huh." She trailed her mouth over his stomach and
increased the pulses another degree.

"Ah . . ." She was pleased to hear the soft moan in his
voice as she began to up the sensations. "We tend . . . to
push our women to experience more pleasure . . . than
they've ever had before."

"Really?" If he was trying to excite her by hinting at
Rystani rituals, the tightening in her gut warned her that
his tactic was working.

"Yeah. I like the idea of you at my mercy, feeling exactly what I . . . ah . . . want you to feel."

She bit the tip of his sex and sucked away the sting.
"Sounds like . . . fun."

She supposed she should focus on his words, but in
truth, she was simply having too much fun with her hands
and her mouth and her toy. Her lips already ached with
sensation. Her breasts wanted more of his attention and
she ached to climb onto him and ride him, but again she
delayed the pleasure.

"There's one more toy to attach." She swam under him,
parted his buttocks, and placed the last pulsar where it
would do the most good. By now she knew he wouldn't
stop her and he didn't.

Pleased that she could control his every sensual quiver,
she swam over him, straddled his waist, and angled her

mouth over his. And then she kissed him, long and hard and deep. And she kicked up the pulses to fire more frequently and in no particular sequence, but never enough to push him over the edge. And the effect soon had him squirming to hold still beneath her hands.

She whispered into his mouth. "How much more do you want?"

"That's your choice." His breathing turned ragged. His lungs sucked in air. But his spirit remained willing and she adored him for it.

If she didn't want him so badly she might have pushed a little harder. But his kiss had been hot enough to light a firecracker and she was burning to climb onto him.

To be certain she didn't lose control too soon, she turned the pulses down. The sensation would be quite intense for her without having had the advantage of a long slow build-up like she'd given him.

When she lowered the sensation, Kirek glared at her. "I'll remember that."

"What?" She swam over him and parted her legs.

"You're a tease."

She took one delicious inch of him inside her. "Are you calling me names?"

"Oh yeah. Brazen. Sexy. Fabulous."

His compliments bought him another inch of heat. The water was cool, but his skin was hot. And as her flesh surrounded his and clamped tight, the pulsars fired, and the tickling sensation caused her to suck in her breath.

She wanted to move slowly. But the cool water on her skin combined with the cascading waterfall that rained over her everywhere, plus the pulses, had her hips pumping in a rhythm all their own. She tried to hold back, but her need for him burned through her like a wild fire.

"Um . . . we have company."

With her ears roaring, she must have understood. But she opened her eyes and saw him staring past her shoulder. Twisting, she saw several gray-skinned creatures hovering above the water.

Even if her mind had commanded her body to stop, she was too far gone to hold back release. She kept pumping her hips. "I'm not stopping unless they swim down here."

Then before she could say another word, he grabbed her hips and thrust into her. Again. And again. Together they churned up the water. And as a delicious orgasm burst through her, she felt him exploding and pulling her deeper.

Chapter Ten

IF KIREK DIDN'T get them away from the Kraj he'd never have the chance to find out why he felt right with Angel, to tell her, or find out if she'd ever feel the same way. Using his arms to swim them deeper, he exploded into Angel's heat, the sexual satisfaction and his new-found emotions surging into one powerful explosion.

While he would have preferred to wallow in the after-math of sexual satiation, the Kraj above the surface were pointing at them. Kirek didn't have time for the luxury of holding and cuddling and thinking about how Angel hadn't wanted to stop their lovemaking—even in the face of danger.

However, if Kirek interpreted the Kraj leader's gestures correctly, he was about to order part of his team into the pool to come after them. Luckily, the Kraj didn't appear to enjoy water and the delay to obey orders gave Kirek extra time to backstroke down to the bottom of the pool.

Aiming toward his escape route, taking Angel with him, Kirek focused on swimming efficiently, not an easy task after a mind-blowing orgasm that had already ramped his pulse into high gear. Although he'd hoped the Kraj wouldn't find them here, after examining the building's original plans, Kirek had chosen this particular mansion for a private tunnel that connected to the moon's central transportation system.

He'd learned war tactics from his father on Rystan when Endekians had invaded his home world. Their people had lived in caves—and every underground facility always had several escape routes.

"Where are we going?" Angel lifted her head and peered at him. With her face flushed from pleasure, her lips swollen from their kisses, her hair slicked back and plastered against her skull, she'd never looked so gorgeous.

"The reef."

"You have weapons down here?"

"An escape hatch." He looked for a seam in the coral and appreciated the skill of the craftsman who'd built the tunnel. He would never have spied the crack if he hadn't known exactly where to search. He and Angel separated and she waited nearby, head tilted back, anxiously watching the Kraj enter the pool.

"They don't know how to swim," she told him.

"But they'll figure it out. With their suits keeping the Kraj supplied with air, they need only sink and walk across the bottom." And Kirek didn't want to stay around to learn if Kraj blasters would still work under water. Pulling a lever disguised to look like a piece of coral, Kirek watched in satisfaction as round panel slid open to reveal a dark and ominous hole. "Go."

Angel didn't ask questions. She didn't even hesitate. She swam into the darkness and he followed, taking care to close and lock the hatch behind him.

Forced to swim single file, they could no longer share air and speak—he couldn't elongate his shield that far—but their presence activated lights along the tunnel showing there was only one direction to swim down the narrow tube. Angel swam strongly, keeping a steady pace that Kirek had difficulty maintaining. Swimming with hunched shoulders and arms at his sides to fit inside the tube reduced him to propelling forward by his kick alone.

According to the plans he'd seen, the tunnel was about two hundred meters long. With their air once again dwindling, it seemed like two miles. But there was no going back, even if they wanted to—they had neither room to turn around within the narrow tube nor enough air to reach the surface.

If Angel panicked, they would drown in this watery grave. But she swam hard, her kicks steady. And Kirek was glad to have her as a partner. Angel was the love he'd always hoped he'd find and he was determined that now he'd finally found a woman to love, he would not lose her to the Kraj.

Eventually Angel stopped at a dead end. A panel on a door before her required a code to open. Kirek knew the code, but didn't have enough room to swim past her to engage the system. And they still couldn't speak. Even if his psi had healed enough for him to elongate his suit that far, he didn't have any extra air beyond what was in his lungs.

"Come on, Angel," he spoke, focusing his mind, even though he knew she couldn't hear him. "I'm giving you the code."

He repeated the code. Over and over, damning his weakened psi, but knowing he wasn't strong enough to send the mental message.

But suddenly she pressed the corresponding panel buttons, and relief flowed through him. He used one of Tessa's Earth phrases: "Way to go."

But his relief was short-lived. Instead of the forward hatch opening, she'd tripped a hatch to close behind him. And his lungs began to burn from lack of oxygen.

Now they were caught underwater, both ends of the tube closed. A ripple of unease shot through him. Had he done what the Kraj could not accomplish? Trapped them? Killed them?

He should have tested the escape route before using it. But he'd been so eager to have Angel alone, so eager to make love with her, that he had failed to take proper precautions. His heart pumped loudly, his ears roared. He ached to pound the tube in frustration but didn't waste the oxygen, knowing he couldn't break the strong material with muscle power alone. And all the while his frustration mounted, he wondered if he had brought her down here to die.

It seemed like a lifetime, but in actuality, likely only seconds passed before drains opened in the tube's bottom to suck out the water. Blessed fresh air vented in from above.

Angel drew air into her lungs in huge gasps. She spoke between shallow pants. "I . . . thought we . . . were going to . . ."

The panel in front of her opened and she crawled through, appearing as eager to be out of the tube as he was. After listening to her hard breathing, Kirek suspected the air in her suit might have been dwindled to dangerous levels, even less than his—and yet, she hadn't panicked. Although he'd always known she was a fighter and possessed a strong will, now he had proof.

"How did you figure out the code?" he asked.

She frowned, looking puzzled. "I . . . don't . . . know."

He pulled himself into an underground chamber and then slammed the door shut to lock out the Kraj. The room was stocked with a materializer, a com, a vidscreen, and a car that used electromagnetic power to propel itself over a track. "From here we can travel anywhere on Dakmar. The mag car ties into the central transportation system."

"Good planning," she complimented him, and then muttered, "Would have been even better if you'd warned me."

"Sorry. I really didn't expect the Kraj to clear up their problem and to find us so quickly. They are clever and persistent."

He headed to the control console, checked his messages, and learned his contact was still delayed. He programmed the car to first head for Dakmar's busiest nexus, then sent the car to stop in random places throughout the moon in hopes of confusing the Kraj.

Angel peered over his shoulder. "Where are we going?"

"Nowhere."

Her eyes narrowed. "Is the system broken?"

He shook his head. "If the Kraj trace the magnetic signature of the car, they'll follow it to hunt us down."

"You're laying a false trail for them to follow?"

He nodded. "Why leave this sanctuary when we have all the comforts of home right here?"

While he worked on the program, Angel reset the suits to dry and warm them. As she headed for the materializer, he realized that they were no longer naked. Once again he wore slacks and a shirt, and she had changed to a dark green V-necked blouse that brought out the color of her eyes and a long full skirt that swayed deliciously as she walked.

"What about your contact?" she asked, as she used her psi on the materializer to order them a meal.

The scent of food made his stomach growl. He shot a

thought at the materializer, a request for *octar* meat with *jarballa* sauce. The materializer didn't have real *octar* meat—the animals could only be found on Rystan, but the machine could process chemicals into a replica of the desired food and neither his taste buds nor his body's digestive system would know the difference.

"How weird," Angel muttered. "I asked for turkey and dressing and instead I got—"

"*Octar* and *jarballa* sauce?" He grinned at the familiar aroma that reminded him of home, his mother stirring the sauce and his father repeatedly entering the kitchen to see if it might be ready ahead of schedule. His mother would pretend she didn't see her husband stealing a spoonful to test and shoo him out of her kitchen before she burned dinner. Miri had never burned anything. Food on Rystan had been a precious commodity and she ran the kitchen like a general, always on schedule.

Angel lifted the food from the machine and carried it over to him, her smile broadening. "It smells scrumptious."

"I used my mom's recipe."

Angel jerked in surprise, almost dropping the food before she steadied her hands. "I thought the machine didn't understand my request. But you used your psi?"

"I suppose I did." Kirek's delight warmed him like the summer sun. "I'm healing."

"That's so awesome. I'm very glad—while undressing you is so much fun, I'd rather you dressed yourself," she teased. "Do you think you used your psi to send me the code?"

"Maybe. I was focusing hard on the numbers . . . but I don't know, either."

She set the food by the console and he picked off a piece of crusty meat, dipped it into the sauce, and offered her the first bite. She opened her mouth, and carefully, he placed the food between her lips.

"Mm."

"Good?" Kirek asked.

"Wow. Better than good. It practically melted in my mouth." She licked her bottom lip. "The flavor is hard to identify. It's a mix of tangy and spice with a hint of cilantro."

She picked up a piece of meat, dipped it into the sauce, and fed him. "So how much psi do you have back?"

"Not enough." He grinned. "But I believe we can remedy that."

"How?"

"Psi power is linked to emotions and sexual activity."

"You made that up." She laughed, accusingly.

"Actually, I didn't. You may have read about Tessa taking the Challenge—an alien test that had to be passed to be accepted into the Federation—but you didn't read about how she learned to use her psi."

"I thought Kahn trained her to fight and her psi developed."

"That's only part of the story. He used sexual frustration to help her activate her psi."

"She must have been furious."

Kirek laughed. "She was. She stole a spaceship and escaped. To save her life, he ended up marrying her." When Angel frowned, he added, "The history books did get one thing right."

"What?"

Kirek's tone softened. "They love each other."

"And you want to be just like them, don't you?" she snapped at him.

He chose his words with care. "What's wrong with love?"

She sighed and rolled her eyes. "Been there. Done that. Love doesn't last. And it sure as hell kills freedom."

Kirek winced. Changing her mind might be a more difficult task than defeating the Zin.

* * *

AFTER EATING, KIREK insisted they nap, but Angel was
too jumpy to sleep. While she wasn't certain that Kirek's
theory about his psi healing being tied to sexual activity
was valid, she certainly didn't mind testing it. Although no
one understood how the suits worked, to develop psi
power, powerful feelings seemed a key. And she'd certainly teased Kirek long enough for him to have had a
healthy frustration level.

They had been good together. Already she wanted him
again . . . right away. But he simply pulled her against his
side, floated them into a reclining position, and told her
she would need rest to prepare for their next encounter.

But Angel didn't want to wait. When Kirek seemed to
immediately drop into a deep sleep, she tried to disen-
gage herself from him. She could use the time to check
on her ship repairs, but Kirek's psi as well as his arms and
legs had wrapped around her and she didn't want to risk
waking him by breaking apart.

If he needed rest to heal, then she would allow him to
sleep—at least for a few hours. Always impatient, Angel
restlessly thought about the rock pool, the Kraj, her ship,
the upcoming mission . . . and Kirek. She'd been aston-
ished when he hadn't taken control about halfway
through their lovemaking and had allowed her to keep the
commanding role for as long as she'd wanted.

Rystani warriors had a reputation for always maintaining
the upper hand. Yet Kirek had exhibited an unusual display
of confidence by letting her have her way. Oh, he'd warned
her of consequences but the teasing light in his gaze had
told her she would enjoy herself—he would see to that.

She'd never met anyone with so much confident control. Kirek didn't pretend. He didn't act. He simply was a
force in and of himself.

She had no doubt that when he awakened he would reverse their roles, and she looked forward to what they would do with a thrill of anticipation. Kirek's experience had been obvious and she wondered if he'd ever been in love. And how many women had loved him? She suspected as he'd traveled across the galaxy, he'd left a line of broken hearts behind. Not that he'd promise women and leave them. He wasn't the kind of man to flirt and make love and then callously walk away, but he would appeal to many women who would set their hearts on having him.

And soon, he would focus all that delicious sensual experience . . . on her.

Between her anticipation and eagerness, she didn't feel the least bit tired, yet after selling the salvage, ordering repairs to the *Raven*, their strenuous underwater lovemaking, and the desperate swim through the tunnel to avoid the Kraj, the day had taxed her emotionally and physically. Eventually, she slept.

And awakened to the scent of . . . coffee? She raised her head and peered at Kirek. He hovered over the console, a mug in hand, but he remained aware enough of her to notice the moment her gaze fell on him.

He lifted the mug in greeting. "Good morning."

"Morning." She stretched and arched her spine, causing her breasts to rise beneath her suit. Kirek stared and she enjoyed his appreciation as much as she enjoyed unkinking the knots. "How long have you been awake?"

"Long enough to check the *Raven*'s repairs. They are right on schedule. With the number of mechanical bots helping the mechanical engineers, the engine overhaul should be finished soon."

She would have preferred to check herself, but it would sound churlish to say so. Since she knew she tended to be overprotective when it came to the *Raven*, she repressed a twinge of discomfort and changed the subject. "Any sign of the Kraj?"

"They seem to have lost track of us." His satisfaction and relaxed demeanor told her that he believed them safe.

"Great. Is that coffee I smell?" She strode over to the console.

He casually cleared the vidscreen, then offered her the mug. "Want some? I like mine black."

"Please." She took a sip, appreciating the caffeine kick, even as she wondered if he hadn't wanted her to see what he'd been working on. She told herself to stop it. She didn't like being so paranoid without reason. He'd probably been done looking at . . . whatever it had been. "Do Rystani drink coffee?"

"Tessa has addicted some of us to her vice," he admitted. "And I have to admit that there's only one better way to wake up in the morning."

From the heat in his tone, she knew he was talking about lovemaking. She peered at him over the mug's brim. "I wouldn't have minded if you'd waked me."

"We both needed rest. Our journey may be long and arduous and we should begin in the best shape possible."

"And now that I'm fully rested . . ." She raised an eyebrow and handed back the cup.

"I've cleared the day to make love to you."

"The day?" Here she'd been suspicious and he'd been up early, trying to make time for them. She really needed relaxation practice, but after their conversation, she'd worried that he might not want to make love to her again. While he'd accepted the idea of having a fling, he clearly wanted more from her.

"Would you like breakfast first or . . ." His eyes flared with heat. His bunched muscles reminded her of Lion, right before he pounced on a tasty morsel. Her mouth went dry as she thought about all those muscles over her, under her, inside her. Her stomach knotted and she felt as though she was balanced on the edge of a black hole, about to be drawn into a gravity well so deep she would never be able to climb her way out.

Yet even as anticipation ratcheted up the tension in her gut, she didn't understand why. They'd already made love. This was Act Two. So she didn't quite comprehend why she felt as though she were stepping into unexplored territory.

It wasn't as though she hadn't been twice married or hadn't taken lovers. She wasn't sexually starved. And Angel had already been naked with this man, made love with him. So why did every taut nerve ending in her body warn her that . . . making love with him might be deliciously different from what she expected?

In the rock pool, Kirek had handed over control to her. And he'd abided by his decision with spectacular command of himself. She knew he expected her to do the same. And she was good with that. He'd already saved her life. She trusted him with her body. And yet . . . the tension in her stomach warned her that she took his warning of "consequences" seriously.

Kirek said what he meant. He didn't issue false threats or boasts. She'd already learned that when he said he could do something he followed through. His hints had teased and tantalized and had her surprisingly . . . on edge. Because she had no idea what to expect.

Her uncertainty about his plans raised the stakes . . . although she couldn't say why. That she didn't even consider backing out but was looking forward to making love to him again this soon told her she'd already let him under her skin a bit farther than she liked.

She placed her arms around his neck and kissed his brow, his nose, his cheek. "I'm not yet hungry for food."

"Good." He drained his coffee and set it aside, placed

both hands on her waist and lifted her onto his lap. "Before we go on . . . I want to set some ground rules."

"You want a safe word?"

His tone conveyed amusement. "I'm unfamiliar with that term."

"When lovers role-play, they choose a safe word so that at any time their partner will know when they choose to stop."

"That won't be necessary."

"Why not?"

His eyes smoked with a tender heat that warned her that wrapped in a calm exterior, his interior pulsed with a smoldering inferno. He spoke gently. "I will know how far you want me to go—even if you don't realize it yourself."

"Do you have any idea how arrogant you sound?"

"That's only because you have no idea what my psi is going to reveal."

Huh? She swallowed hard and stared at him, half awed, half excited, and very certain that she wanted to be on his lap and in his arms. "You can read minds?"

He shook his head and chuckled. "You do have a fanciful. imagination." Tugging her against his chest, he smoothed her hair from her brow and nipped her earlobe. "I was talking about ground rules for afterwards. Whatever happens between us . . . the mission must go on as planned."

"Agreed."

"Even if you hate me."

"You damn well better not give me reason to hate me," she warned him, filled with sudden unease. And yet even as she second-guessed her decision, her nipples hardened and moisture seeped between her thighs. And she turned their suits transparent.

He cupped her breast, his palm warm and solid. His thumb flicked over the tip, shooting an arc of heat into her core. "The mission must go on, even if you hate me."

"I don't work with people I can't trust," she said. "And that's all I will agree to."

"I understand." His words were spoken softly, but a darkness flashed in his eyes that then disappeared so quickly she thought she'd been mistaken. Kirek's Rystani blue irises often flared with purples and reds that she could easily read, but for some reason, he gave away nothing right now.

And he had her questioning herself—something that didn't happen often. Had she made a mistake by telling him more about herself than she should have? Confused, uncertain, she didn't understand why they were talking at all when they could be doing things she found much more pleasurable. Like kissing.

"Are we done discussing the ground rules?"

"Almost."

She raised a brow and waited for him to say more. But he seemed content to caress her breast and she caught herself holding her breath, wondering what he'd say next. But he seemed fascinated with her skin. His palm slid back and forth slowly, creating a delicious friction that made her other breast ache for the same kind of attention.

"This is your last chance to change your mind," he warned.

"What do you mean?"

"Once we begin, I will not stop."

She cocked her head to look at him. "Not even if I ask you to?"

"Especially not then."

"Why not?"

"Because I'm going to push you beyond your normal boundaries."

"Suppose I don't—"

"And you will enjoy much pleasure."

"Sounds good to me." She frowned at him. "It's almost as if you're trying to warn me that you harbor some deep, mysterious, kinky need."

He laughed, his tone warm and open and cheerful. "I assure you. I'm into pleasure. Yours and mine."

"Then . . . why are we talking?"

"Stroking you pleases me. Your breast is so silky smooth. I don't think I'd ever tire of stroking such lovely skin."

She tilted her head back and upward to steal a kiss. But he shook his head. "It's my turn to touch."

"All right." She supposed fair was fair. "But my other breast could use some attention, too."

He turned her so her back rested against his chest. Until that moment, she hadn't realized that opposite them was a floor-to-ceiling mirror that spanned an entire wall, making the room seem twice its size. But she wasn't interested in the decor. Instead she watched his hands cup her breasts, lifting her, caressing her. And when he tweaked the nipples, shooting pure pleasure straight to her loins . . . something odd happened.

In the mirror, she saw a curious mist of blue begin to curl from his hands, spreading over her breasts and swirling like smoke around her. "Oh . . . my . . . God. What is that?"

"The blue color represents how you feel about my stroking your breasts."

"Huh?"

"You don't have to tell me what you like. We can both see it. Watch." He tweaked her nipples.

"Ah . . ."

He tweaked them again.

"Oh . . . oh."

Blue smoke flared into an exciting orange. And now

she understood how he would know what she wanted. All he had to do was see what color aura she emitted. Oh . . . my . . . god. He was going to read her feelings and the idea made her squirm, even as it excited her.

"You like what I'm doing, don't you?"

"Yes." Fascinated, she stared in the mirror. Her thoughts swirled and she wondered if he'd put a hallucinogen in the coffee, but he'd drunk it, too. And she felt normal—well, as normal as one could feel when sitting naked on a Rystani warrior's lap while he ever-so-gently stroked her breasts, causing delicious blue ripples. He lightly pinched her nipples, shooting orange flares of excitement ripping through her.

"Hmm. If I keep stroking your breasts and only your breasts, what other colors will you create for me?"

"What do you mean?"

He stopped caressing and the orange flickers vanished. He massaged her upper arms and soothing green vapors billowed in the mirror. "Now green tells me you feel safe."

"This is so cool."

"Glad you like it. Now part your legs for me. We aren't stopping until we do all the colors."

She gulped. He'd said colors represented emotions. And she no longer knew if she wanted to do them all.

Chapter Eleven

ALTHOUGH KIREK HAD warned Angel that he wouldn't
stop after she'd agreed to begin—and she didn't want him
to—seeing emotions as colors was an intimacy issue she
hadn't expected to have to deal with. She wasn't any
more comfortable with him reading her emotions as
clearly as Orion's Belt than she was at seeing those colorful emotions for herself.

No wonder he hadn't worried about picking a safe
word. If she didn't like something, he would know the
same moment she knew it by the color she radiated.

He nipped her neck and an orange light flickered, and as
he lightly nibbled, the sting turned to a pink tickle. "How
are you ... oh my ... oh ..." Fascinated, excited, she
watched him elicit feelings and colors from her with every
touch. "How can you ... do this?"

"I was born in hyperspace."

"That's not an explanation." She wriggled her butt against him, hoping he'd take the hint and lower his hands to her parted thighs. Or at least place his hands back over her breasts.

And even as she thought how much she ached for his most intimate touch at her core, dark, ruby red puffs rose around her, telling him exactly how she felt . . . excited, passionate, aroused.

"I've created a psi field around us that manifests feelings as color."

And then it dawned on her. "So the color isn't only how I feel about your touch . . . it's more?"

"Yes. It's how we feel about each other."

"I don't see any color coming from your flesh," she snapped, not too happy that he hadn't explained his ability to create the emotion field—which felt like a mine field—before he'd set it up. God . . . Kirek would literally see her every feeling displayed as they made love. Although he'd promised her pleasure and he hadn't gone back on his word, he'd upped the intimacy level and she twisted inside, feeling as though he'd invaded her privacy.

The red haze darkened around her—matching her glum thoughts.

He didn't seem surprised. "You're having enough trouble dealing with your own feelings and don't need mine to complicate matters. So I'm keeping my colors out of the mix for now."

Who the hell was he to decide what she could and couldn't handle? She glared into the mirror at him and sputtered, "*You* decided that I'm having trouble dealing with *my* feelings, so you're hiding yours?"

"Hmm. That's an odd way of looking at our arrangement."

"There is nothing odd about it to me." Annoyance rising, she tilted back her head to see his expression, tipping her breasts toward his mouth.

He held her firmly by the breasts and tweaked her nipples a bit harder. His voice remained calm and yet she sensed that beneath the cool exterior was a will as strong as *bendar* and he wouldn't be hurried or distracted by her antics. "It's my turn to make the rules . . . for as long as I like. And I've decided you are thinking way too much. I need to give you more pleasure."

And with that pronouncement, even as her irritation spiked, her pulse quickened and flickers of orange burned through the dark red cloud.

He chuckled. "See. You want me in spite of yourself."

"Damn you."

"Ah, you're such a sensual creature and I fully intend to make use of every advantage you give me."

Angel didn't know if his words were a criticism or a compliment or a threat or a promise. But the slow circles he made with his palms over her breasts, plus the very direct stimulation to her nipples, was beginning to make her writhe with a need for more.

She was all for making love. Revealing her feelings was another matter. Even as she enjoyed his touch, she was furious with him for making her choose. But she was even more furious with herself for letting her flesh dictate her decision. Clearly, with orange and red burning away the black mist, she was more than willing to continue and the knowing awareness in his expression only spiked the tension.

Still, pride made her attempt to summon one last shred of protest. "Once we're done," she said as he licked her neck and a shiver of longing stoked tiny red flames, "I . . . ah . . ."

"You were saying?"

His hands slid from her breasts to her parted thighs. She felt his hands smooth over her skin. Saw his fingers tease the inside of her knees. Yet, her breasts still felt as if he held his palms in the same place, and her nipples tightened under the pinch that duplicated his touch. He was using his psi on her suit, perfectly reproducing the pressure and heat and feel of his previous caresses. But unlike when he'd burned out his psi and she'd activated his suit for him, she hadn't turned control of her suit over to him—he'd taken it.

"My suit isn't set on automatic . . . How did you . . . ah . . . ah. How can I talk when you . . ."

"Look how beautiful you are."

Tiny flames of orange and red rippled over her flesh. When his hands caressed the tender insides of her thighs, the reds dominated. She couldn't wait for him to go where she wanted—but he took his time, teasing and taunting.

"Place your hands behind my neck." He snapped the order and she didn't think. Before she knew what she'd done, she'd placed her hands up and behind his neck. "I'm going to lock them in place so you aren't tempted to move."

She didn't mind. Again he used her suit and although she knew it would now be useless to tug her hands free, she tried anyway. She was sitting on his lap, her back to his chest, her hands behind his head and her legs open and dangling over his knees. In the mirror, her reflection showed a wild lock of hair falling saucily over one eyelid half closed in passion, her lips pouting with brazen lust, and her nostrils flaring as if to draw in the enticing scent of her mate. Her chest rose and fell, her breathing shallow and fast. Since he'd adjusted her suit to continue stimulating her breasts, her nipples had darkened and remained pointed.

But what irritated the hell out of her were the red and orange clouds telling her how much she was enjoying his domination. She liked his touch and his slow, sensual caresses that caused her flesh to shiver and ache. She liked his taking control, liked how he slipped into the role with an ease that focused all his interest on her.

In the mirror, he watched her, tested her, taunted her, making her feel cherished. Adored. As if he had all the time in the world to find out exactly what would please her.

And although she couldn't move, she couldn't ignore the genuine pleasure of having all his interest centered on her. The rest of the galaxy had ceased to exist. There was only the two of them, and he appeared quite intent on discovering different ways to change his stroking to give pleasure.

One minute his pace was slow, the next, a bit more urgent. And just when she adjusted and craved a bit more, he maddeningly gentled his touch.

Her bottom felt . . . warm . . . as if he'd turned up the suit temperature, and the heat began to raise a pulsing need between her thighs. "Oh . . . no . . . what are . . . you doing?"

"Rystani men often spank their women during love-play."

"What?" She twisted her head to glare at him.

He didn't seem to notice. "The spanking is given to increase the woman's pleasure. Gradual heat causes blood to flow to the buttocks and increases desire. I refuse to cause you pain, so I simply created the end effect."

Her voice was breathless, amazed, and husky with need. "My butt is hot. Burning." And his hands on the insides of her thighs moved with infuriating slowness. Wild with frustration and anticipation, she panted between words, "I . . . need you to . . ."

"Look at your passion red colors. Are those flickers of purple I see?" He sounded quite proud of himself, as if he were painting a masterpiece of slashing emotion and spiking heat over her flesh.

"Does purple mean I'm finally going to have an orgasm?" she demanded, hating the way she sounded almost as if she was begging.

"Purple is the color of deep-seated feelings."

"Like love?" She scowled at him. "Are you out of your freaking mind?" If there had ever been any purple there, the color was now gone, replaced with hovering black clouds as if he'd doused the flames with water.

"Black is the color of fear."

"You know, I really might grow to hate you if you don't quit playing—"

"You want me to stop touching you?"

"Damn you. I want you to make love to me—not play with my emotions."

"I can't create your emotions."

"Why not—you were born in hyperspace."

He didn't bother answering her rhetorical sarcasm. Instead, his voice remained cool and almost disappointed. "I'm only showing you what you feel."

"Maybe I don't want to see what I feel." She most definitely didn't want *him* seeing what she felt but kept that obvious notion to herself. She closed her eyes.

His calm tone invaded her thoughts, refusing to allow her to shut him out. "When we were in the rock pool, you didn't ask me what I wanted."

"That was different."

"Was it?"

His hands advanced to the very top of her thighs. She sucked in her breath, refusing to answer his question. She didn't want to look at herself or the colors. Didn't want to talk. Didn't want to think.

Damn. Damn. Damn. She had wanted a simple fling and he was making things . . . complex.

"Open your eyes," he coaxed.

She peeked. The black had vanished. So had the purple and red. Yet the yellow and orange flickers remained, signaling her willingness for more of his touch. Oh, yeah. She most definitely wanted his clever hands back on her body. She squeezed her eyes tight again.

"If you hated what we were doing, you wouldn't still want my touch."

"Of course I want your touch. I've never denied it. I like sex."

"If all you wanted was sex, you could have hired a holosim," he pointed out.

"I could have also pleasured myself." She ground the words past her clenched jaw, her tone raspy. "It would have been a hell of a lot more satisfying than you."

"Patience." His hand brushed over her mons, sending hungry licks of heat to her center, until her stomach knotted and her muscles drew tight.

"Wow," she said, breathing out a happy sigh.

"More?" His so-sexy and husky tone, more than the sensation he'd created with his hand, caused her to open her eyes and stare. The wisps of yellow and orange had formed giant reddish clouds that engulfed them both.

"Yes. More."

"Look at us," he demanded.

"We're on fire."

"That's all you, woman." His fingers skimmed her slick flesh. "Your *synthari* is so soft and so welcoming, so in tune with your real needs."

His voice, always deep, had thickened with a passion he couldn't disguise. Through the red cloud in the mirror, his eyes glinted with ferocious hunger. His lips tensed with a wicked tension. His jaws were locked, the cords in his muscular neck were rigid—he clearly was barely keeping his own passion in check.

But seeing how much he wanted her, knowing he was holding back to give them both pleasure, upped her own need. And she no longer cared if she begged. "Please . . . Kirek."

His tone rippled with ferocity. "Tell me what you want."

"To finish."

He growled in her ear. "Wrong answer."

He changed her suit settings and cool water droplets trickled over her skin, followed by warm sluices. And he increased the heat on her bottom. Maddeningly, he caressed the slick folds between her legs ever so slowly, ever so careful to stimulate . . . but not enough.

And as he stoked her into a frenzy, in the mirror an erotic red cloud thickened, broadening in scope, lengthening in depth. Her bottom stung from heat and she could no longer hold back a soft moan of desperate need.

"Tell me what you want," Kirek demanded again.

"Huh?" She couldn't think much beyond the wondrous pleasure he was giving her.

"Look in the mirror."

Once again the red cloud had deepened, this time with vivid purple slashes. Purple meant . . . what? What had he told her exactly? How could she think when his creative fingers keep her right on the edge?

Purple meant . . . purple equated to love. No. That wasn't right. He'd said "deep-seated feelings."

Obviously, she couldn't deny the molten passion bubbling through her veins like fierce lava, and Angel had no difficulty accepting that at the moment she was a creature devoted to lusty pleasure.

But she sensed that her pleasure wasn't enough for him. He wanted her to . . . to . . . what? Say what? Be what? What the hell did he want? No, that was the wrong question. He'd asked her to tell him what she wanted.

Damn. "I can't think when you're doing . . . ah don't stop. Please . . . do . . . not . . . stop."

"I won't," he whispered into her ear.

He drizzled icy droplets over her, tensed her flesh with the hot water that increased her pulse right along with the magical rhythm of his fingers. And he never stopped caressing her breasts or stroking the sensitive folds of her flesh. But his hands and psi were no longer enough. All his carefully applied stimulation had made her receptive nerve endings require more than usual.

"Look at us." His tone might have remained a whisper but pure satisfaction rushed through him and into her.

Purple swirled into the red, mixing, dominating, the colors so vibrant she couldn't tell where one began and the other stopped. "Is that us?"

"Us?"

"In the mirror. You and me?"

He chuckled. "No. That's still all you."

Oh . . . my . . . God. He'd built a thunderstorm of need but the purple flashes now overshadowed the yellow flickers and the red clouds, making her uneasy. Uncertain.

She licked her lip. "I don't think . . . this is such . . . a good idea." As she spoke, black tendrils of smoke once again wiped out the slices of purple, leaving a murky red haze.

"See what happens when you think," he teased.

"What? What just happened?" She felt caged. Frantic. Tight. "Why can't we just have sex?"

"Because I don't want just sex." At the moment she didn't care that he didn't want sex. She'd never ached so badly in her life. He'd aroused her, teased her. Then he spoke slowly, as if to make sure she wouldn't miss one word. "And I take what I need."

She whispered, her tone needy. "You can't take what I don't offer."

"Exactly." He shot her a grin so wicked, so determined, so absolutely resolute that whatever she'd been thinking, whatever she'd been about to say, evaporated like a ray of starlight amidst a thunderstorm. Her throat closed tight. She couldn't breathe.

How could she argue when the damn Rystani had agreed with her? How could she think when he had her so on edge that she had to grit her teeth to prevent a scream of sheer frustration? How could she protest when her body yearned for completion?

"Tell me what you want."

Had he asked again or had his demand kept reverberating in her brain long after he'd ceased saying the words? She was losing control and if he hadn't locked her arms behind his head, if he hadn't physically restrained her with his psi, she would never have been able to sit still, open, allowing him access to all of her.

While it wasn't her flesh she wanted to deny him, but the feelings he so carefully drew from her, she wasn't getting any satisfaction. The purple colors that emerged when she couldn't control her lust—the ones that meant deep-seated feelings, which she wanted to deny with every atom in her body—kept getting in her way when he forced her to look at them.

And she was spitting unnerved that every time the purple showed up, he made her think, ruining all the delicious tension by interrupting her physical sensations. Every damn time she looked in the mirror, black wiped out the purple, denying her completion.

"Let me go. Now." Perhaps he heard the anger in her voice, perhaps he'd decided she'd had enough of his silly games, or perhaps he couldn't hold back any longer himself.

One moment she'd been waiting on him, the next he set her free. She jumped from his lap and spun to face him, hands fisted on her hips. "I should walk away."

All his psi touches ceased. Her flesh ached for his attention to her breasts, yearned for the heat on her bottom. The icy droplets and warm sluicing had also vanished, leaving her feeling empty.

His eyes narrowed to twin slits of blue heat. "Is that what you want?"

"I wanted you . . . before you . . ." She waved her hand at the mirror, confused because she wanted nothing better than to fling herself back into his strong arms and use sex to chase away her chaotic thoughts.

"You wanted me before I what?" he prodded.

Before he'd showed her those colors in the mirror. "Before you showed me that you're a freak of hyperspace." The minute she spoke in anger, she regretted her outburst. Normally she kept her temper under tight control, but he had made her feel vulnerable and that had made her careless. She raised her hand to her mouth wishing that it wasn't too late to recall the hateful words.

At her insult, another man might have winced in pain, but Kirek's eyes revealed only a hint of disappointment before he shut down all expression and went into Rystani-stoic mode. "Sorry," he apologized, "I pushed too hard."

God. After what she'd said, *he* was apologizing to *her.* Could he possibly understand that she'd lashed out because he'd made her confront feelings she didn't want to acknowledge? "I wasn't ready . . . I didn't mean what I said about you being a freak. I'm sorry, too. I was frustrated and confused." She glared at him, still annoyed, still on edge, still unsatisfied.

"I backed you into a corner and you came out swinging, so I can't claim foul if I got punched." A tiny smile curved his lip. "So what do you want?"

Stars.

"How did I end up with the most persistent, most determined, most arrogant male in the galaxy?"

He laughed. "You got lucky."

"Wrong," she muttered as her anger cooled and her repressed passions resurfaced. At his use of the Terran expression for making love, she couldn't help shaking her head and grinning back.

He crossed his arms over his chest. "I'm rarely wrong."

"If you were perfect, you'd know that I need to get lucky again."

"Again? So you still want to finish what we started?" He raised an eyebrow inquisitively.

And her lower jaw dropped. He knew the Earth euphemism. He'd been playing word games with her.

His grin widened. "Just call me Mr. Perfect."

"Mr. Perfectly Annoying would be more accurate." It was about time he realized that she knew how to play, too. "You keep asking me what I want."

"Yes?"

She advanced, her breasts coming within inches of his lips. As his breath fanned her flesh, her nipples pebbled. "Ask me again."

"Tell me what you want."

"I want you to stop burning starlight. I want you—"

"Finally, you're admitting—"

"I want you on your knees with your mouth between my legs."

"Darling." He grinned, as if he'd been expecting those very words, and dropped into position, placing his big hands on her bottom and drawing her toward the heat of his mouth. "I thought you'd never ask."

"I'm . . . not . . ." His tongue found her center. "Your

darling. I'm not ... your ... ah ... ah." His tongue worked magic and her breath came in gasps. Her muscles clenched and her thoughts turned to pleasure but she needed to make him understand. She would never again belong to anyone. Threading her fingers into his thick hair, she steadied her tremors. "I'm ... not ... yourrrrrrrs."

In response he flicked his tongue faster, shooting her right over the edge. She shuddered into his mouth, spasming so hard she would have jerked away if not for his insistent hands holding her in place.

And then to her shock and delight, he didn't stop sucking or licking or nuzzling. He continued as though no orgasm had just ripped through her, as though he was unaware that he had pleasured her so completely that her mind had gone numb and her limbs had lost all strength. If not for her suit holding her up, she might have collapsed in a heap.

As the aftershocks seeped away and awareness returned, she realized that he was priming her all over again. He was using his psi on her breasts and every inch of her skin felt as though he was brushing her with silky feathers, the touch light and almost as provocative as his tongue.

She hadn't known it was possible to feel so satiated, yet at the same time so ravenous for more. It was if Kirek was determined to feed her a fantasy feast and so far she'd only dined on the tantalizing appetizer.

She'd never met a man who was so comfortable with himself. Kirek seemed to equally enjoy bossing her around or acceding to her wishes. And oh my ... stars. What the man could do with his tongue ought to be classified a Federation secret ... or illegal. Because after experiencing his skill, she would be forever spoiled.

Muscles clenching, fingers gripping his shoulders, she

flung back her head and welcomed the spiking tension. So soon, he had her right back at a pivotal moment and like a tide rising with a full moon, she crested, broke, and surged. If her orgasm had been fireworks, it would have been the grand finale. If her pleasure had been an exploding star, she'd have erupted in a supernova. And if she'd been capable of screaming, she would have shouted herself hoarse.

But the intensity caused her throat to close and her heart to race and her center to weep with bliss. She would have gyrated her hips, but his hands on her butt kept her firmly pressed against his sweet mouth.

His lips gentled, but he kept stroking, caressing, lapping her moisture. And as the last spasms splashed through her, he ratcheted up his tempo.

Again?

God. Did the man have no limits? Surely she couldn't . . . not this soon . . . but she could.

If a girl could die of pleasure, she would surely be dead within the hour because Kirek wasn't stopping. And her every nerve ending was already so sensitive that in only moments, he was driving her into another wild frenzy.

Her flesh raw with desire, she moaned as he whipped her to new sensations. She wanted to jump out of her skin. Each breath, each touch, each tiny caress inflamed, excited, and encouraged her to take more than she'd ever believed possible. And then more again.

He kept upping her sensitivity level. And she climbed ever higher, poised on the ultimate leap.

All her thoughts focused on what Kirek was doing with his sensual mouth and his psi. Not for one second did he stop caressing her breasts. But there was no pattern. At times he delicately stroked. Sometimes he pinched or rolled the tips of her nipples, and sometimes, he rained icy droplets over her. And all the while he kept her bottom hot.

At the multitude of cascading sensations, she exploded once more and felt as though every brain cell was blowing out. Incredible heat and tension burst from her in wave after wave.

For certain, she couldn't take more. "Enough."

With a surge of desperate strength, she staggered, her knees weak, her psi weaker. She would have fallen, but he stood and scooped her into his arms.

As he gathered her into his chest, she glanced in the mirror. Purple clouds mocked her. She looked at Kirek and found him watching her with wary enjoyment—as if she'd given him exactly what he'd wanted.

"You did that on purpose. Made me forget about the mirror." She spoke softly, so relaxed she couldn't find any anger to put in her words.

"I did what you asked."

"You did more than I asked." She gazed at him, wondering what he really wanted. "I didn't know my body could explode so many times."

"For a twice-married woman who has taken many lovers, it seems there's a lot you don't know."

Confident she was a good lover, she frowned at him. "And what's that supposed to mean?"

"You're a very sensual woman."

Kirek was good at pricking her into thinking one thing, then soothing her. She ran a lazy finger over his lip. "Tell me something I don't know."

"I take great pleasure in pleasing you." His eyes sparkled with intimacy, as if sharing a secret.

She suspected whatever Kirek did, he would do well and to the utmost of his ability. She'd never doubted his ability to please her sexually.

But she hadn't expected that after so many orgasms she would still want to make love to him again.

Chapter Twelve

THE NEWS WAS bad. Horrible. After making love, eating, and sleeping in the mansion, Kirek let the real world back in by flicking on the vidscreen. Gripping pictures of devastation coming from the planet Zenon had both Angel and Kirek putting their own difficulties aside.

Zenon, the pride of the Federation, was a smoking hulk of a planet. The famous architectural cities that resembled masterful works of art had toppled. The giant space port that had been capable of landing thousands of ships simultaneously had melted into a lava sea. One moment billions of beings had been going about their lives, working, loving, and learning—and the next, every facet of civilization had ceased to exist.

Federation scientists speculated that someone had activated a geothermal explosion that had tapped the planet's core heat and melted the crust. Nothing could survive the tremendous heat. Billions had lost their lives and almost every Federation world had lost diplomats, visitors, families. Every planet had suffered horrible losses and the devastation threatened the stability of the galactic organization.

"The Zin are behind the massacre." Sickened by the devastation, Kirek had no doubt who was responsible.

"How do you know? Couldn't this have been a natural disaster?" Angel asked, her face ashen.

Kirek's tone was grim, his emotions bleak as he checked the computer system and collated data. "Just before that geothermal weapon ignited the core, a wormhole opened up, the same kind of wormhole the Zin used to send a virus to Earth less than a decade ago. Besides, who else would want to take out Zenon?"

"Are you certain about the wormhole?" Angel asked.

"Several starships in the area took readings during the attack. Since the first wormhole attack, many planets installed warning buoys to set off alarms to detect wormhole activity. Those alarms went off, but they didn't give enough warning to do any good."

Angel's face paled even further. "They didn't have time. Even ships in the atmosphere melted."

"Who else but the Zin would give no warnings?" Kirek checked his data. "The disaster wasn't natural and no other race in the Federation possesses the kind of technology necessary to open a wormhole and heat up a planetary core until the crust melts."

A news starship flew over Zenon and sent back images. The great cities were no more than smoking slag heaps. Gigantic parks, precious art, a proud people, and their history had been wiped out as if they'd never been.

Angel stared at the vidscreen, her eyes full of shock and anger. "There's nothing left. Why would even the

Zin do such a thing? The crust won't cool for thousands of years. The planet is now just as useless to them as it is to us."

"To the Zin, a thousand years is the blink of an eye. The virus they tried to spread through the galaxy would have killed every living plant and animal. They are relentless, ruthless. If not for the Sentinels—the giant machines the Perceptive Ones built and left behind long ago to keep the Zin from invading—we would not have lasted this long."

Angel's voice dropped to a whisper. "It's hard to comprehend so much destruction. So much evil."

"Zenon may have been a test and now that the Zin have succeeded in taking out a world, they will strike again." Kirek rubbed his jaw. Although his home world was nowhere near Zenon, he ached to contact his parents. He wanted to see his father's face, look into his mother's eyes, and make sure they were safe. He wanted to go over plans with Tessa and Kahn, but now more than ever, he needed to maintain a low profile.

The Kraj were still on Dakmar and after he and Angel left the safety of the mansion, they would once again become targets. In the two days they'd hidden here, they'd slept, made love, and rested. Only the utmost self-restraint had kept him from showing Angel his true feelings. Although she readily came into his arms, she remained touchy about her emotions and he had to face the fact that she might never admit she wanted him for more than just a fling. Obviously, she wasn't ready now. Clearly she didn't feel the same connection to him that he did with her.

Angel needed space and he would give her as much as possible. So he forced himself to curb his natural tendency to pursue, to insist, and to demand that she admit she had feelings for him.

With the Federation capital a slag heap, Kirek might

have to rush his plans. He had most of the pieces in play, but he was still waiting for one item of essential equipment to reach Dakmar.

Kirek had also pulled every string he could to expedite the *Raven*'s repairs. Without Angel's knowledge, crews had worked day and night, with specialized teams on each section, and thanks to skilled workers and the greasing of many palms, the *Raven* was almost ready to go.

Kirek wished that Angel would never find out what he'd done to her ship. So far her crew had assumed the repairs were what she'd ordered and hadn't contacted her. But when she returned to the ship and learned what he'd done, she would see his act as a betrayal. But he'd had no choice. He could not go up against the Zin without every advantage he could muster—even if that meant testing his relationship with Angel to the limit.

That he knew she considered the *Raven* her sole responsibility couldn't alter his decision. However, after she learned that he'd gone behind her back and altered her precious ship, he'd be lucky if she didn't shove him out the nearest airlock and leave him in deep space.

He should have found a way to tell her. But the mission was too critical to take a chance that he'd be able to change her mind. Besides, he hadn't wanted anything to intrude upon their rest until necessary. Their lovemaking meant too much for him to detract from it, and although she might see his choice as dishonesty, he'd seen too much hardship during his life not to want to steal moments of pleasure and happiness when he could. And he'd hoped their lovemaking and time together would bridge the emotional chasm between them.

But his plan hadn't worked. He supposed once she'd learned what he'd done, she'd hold that against him, too.

He would cope by keeping his love for her to himself. Telling her would likely send her running away.

And while this time they'd spent together hadn't turned out as he'd planned, it might have still forged a bond between them that she couldn't so easily break. Although he hadn't again used his psi to show her the emotions she usually repressed, he could see by the gleam in her eyes and the curve of her lips that she was softening toward him.

Angel stared at the news coming out of Zenon, her blond locks messy and adorable in contrast to the tense lines in her shoulders, her eyes narrowed in fierce resolve. Kirek would enjoy nothing better than to place his hands on her shoulders, to rub out the knots of tension and kiss her until they both lost themselves in pleasures of the flesh. Too bad he didn't have a month, or a week, or even a few more days to spend alone with her without other obligations.

Within the hour his contact would land on the darkest quarter of the moon. And as distracted as Kirek had been by Angel's lovemaking, and now by the catastrophic news about Zenon, he made himself focus on his mission and called up three-dimensional holomaps of Dakmar's nightclub region. Residents called the nasty quarter of the moon "The Peel" after one notorious knife fight where the victor had skinned his opponent in the street in front of a mob. No one was safe in The Peel—not without bodyguards, heavy armor, and lots of credit to pay one's way out of trouble.

Angel glanced at his vidscreen. "Why didn't you pick a more reputable place for the meet?"

"It wasn't my decision." Kirek's psi itched at his nape, a sure sign of trouble, but his contact had been reliable until now, and his information credible . . . if expensive. Kirek didn't mind paying for accurate intel, but in this quarter of the moon, a man had to go in with the expectation of encountering attempted murder, robbery, or at the very least, a brawl.

"I'll watch your back." Angel picked up a stunner from a cache left by the mansion's owner and strapped it to her gorgeous thigh, handling the weapon as casually as some women donned jewels.

The leather holster against her shapely legs made his mouth water. He recalled those long legs wrapped around his waist, her nails digging into his back as she urged his hips to move faster. The idea of a beautiful woman like Angel going into that den of misfits caused every protective instinct to flare into the hot zone.

He folded his arms across his chest. "You aren't going anywhere near The Peel."

"Of course I am." Her tone remained matter-of-fact as she shoved a knife into her boot and altered her suit to hide her tan legs with a skintight black that outlined every curve. "You'll need my connections to get past the outer sector."

"You've been in The Peel before?" Kirek frowned at her. The combination of a thigh holster strapped over the too-revealing black pantsuit was an image of feminine curves and lethal weapon that repeatedly drew his gaze. Kirek would have objected to any woman who looked as sexy as hell walking into the grittiest, nastiest section of Dakmar, but Angel had just made love to him, and by all Rystani moral codes that made her his responsibility.

Too bad she wouldn't see it that way. Although he knew she could handle herself, he wouldn't let her go into danger to watch his back.

She strapped a second stunner on her other thigh. "The Peel is not my favorite place for a date. The food bites, the men are slime-sucking slugs, and the women are body-sculpted predators, mercs at their worst."

"Mercs?"

"Mercenaries."

Her somber tone told him The Peel was no place to

bring a women, but Angel could handle herself. However, while she'd draw notice in an upscale establishment, in The Peel, she'd be tempting every bad element. "You're staying. I'll get there on my own."

She lowered her neckline with a psi thought, revealing enough cleavage to make his mouth go dry. "And here I thought you had more intelligence than a sand flea. Didn't you hear the part about the female predators?"

"Excuse me?"

"You need me."

"I don't."

"Fine. Go get yourself killed and let the Zin take over the galaxy because you don't know the secret handshake."

"Secret handshake?"

"You don't know the culture here. You don't know who to pay off and who to slug and who means business. You won't take five steps into The Peel before you're marked for scraping."

"Scraping?"

"A local custom where two gorgeous women pin the mark so a third can take him down. After the scavengers finish with you, there won't be anything left for the bot-cops to scrape off the street."

"I think I can defend myself against a few determined females."

"Oh, really?" She advanced, her hips swaying. "You can't even defend yourself against me."

"I can't?" He raised an intrigued eyebrow.

But Angel wasn't coming on to him—she was challenging him and he didn't understand why. She might be in shape, but her muscles were no match for his. Neither was her psi. But unless she was bluffing, she believed every word she'd spoken. Kirek had known women warriors with extraordinary powers. Skilled in ancient Terran martial arts, Tessa could take on most men with her bare hands and her psi. And there wasn't a man alive who could match Dora when she linked to a computer.

Angel stepped closer and he breathed in her citrus scent. Her chest rose and fell enticingly with every breath, drawing his gaze to her breasts. "I suppose you think these babies are lethal weapons?"

When Angel's hands dropped to caress her gun grips, he realized his mistake. He refocused on her guns and noted they shot projectiles and weren't stunners as he'd first assumed. "What are they?"

"HGLs. Hypnotic Grenade Launchers. All I need to do is pop one off anywhere in your vicinity and you go to la-la land."

"My suit's filters—"

"They don't require air and they only take out *men*. We could both take a hit and you would go down and I wouldn't notice a thing."

"Really?" He'd never heard of such a weapon.

"The techno-geeks have created an electromagnetic wave that fries male neural networks. I don't know exactly how it works, but the major principle has something to do with a male chromosome that makes you vulnerable."

Kirek had faced death many times, but the idea of the grenade damaging his mind made him uneasy. And if the women on Dakmar could so easily render him unconscious, he *would* require Angel's help, although he wasn't quite ready to admit it.

"What exactly would happen to me if a grenade goes off?" he asked with a frown, wishing she'd move her hands away from the weapons.

"Some men dream sweet dreams or wake up with a raging headache and there's no damage. Others don't remember so much as their name or their past, including families and friends. Some don't wake up at all. Appar-

ently, the geeks have yet to fine-tune the grenades, either
that or they react differently on different species."

"What's the detonation radius?"

"Ten to twelve feet. About three meters."

He set his psi shield to register an alarm if a grenade
penetrated the critical area. But while he might evade one
or two grenades, if they encountered trouble, he might
face dozens of HGLs.

He considered her statements. "If I agree to let you ac-
company me, I could still get hit by grenade."

Angel rolled her eyes at the ceiling, then released a
heavy sigh. "Women on Dakmar won't mess with me. If
we're together, they'll leave you alone."

"And why don't they mess with *you*?" he asked, suspecting he really didn't want to hear her answer. As
much as he admired a woman who could take care of
herself, he preferred she'd never have to defend her life.
And Angel had implied quite clearly that she'd placed
herself in dangerous situations, ones that might give him
nightmares.

"The time before the *Raven*'s last landing, a man by the
name of Jaz tried to switch in shoddy materials on the
Raven's repair work for the top-quality *bendar* cannons I'd
commissioned. Petroy and I tracked Jaz into the Peel. He
got word of our arrival and set up an ambush. He lost. I
recovered my cannons. Word got around."

The way she summarized led him to believe Jaz was no
longer alive. She'd left out details—which told Kirek
more than if she'd bragged about her abilities. But what
scared him right down to the marrow in his bones was that
she hadn't hesitated to track Jaz into the Peel. She could
have shrugged off the loss . . . but that wasn't Angel's nature. She defended what was hers and had willingly put
her life at risk to do so.

Obviously, he required her help. But Jaz might have

friends who want revenge. The idea of taking Angel with him into The Peel seemed reckless.

He checked the vidscreen, searching for female mercs to hire to protect him. Angel leaned over and shook her head. "You can't trust them. For a large enough bribe, mercs will turn on one another."

"All right." He flicked off the monitor, knowing he was beaten. "Let's go scout out my contact's meet-and-greet locale. I suppose you'll be happy to hear it's at the Lay Down Easy, a gambling establishment."

"And a house of prostitution." She grinned. "It's known for men who can last for days."

"Days?" He hoped she was teasing him again, but one glance at her hard eyes told him she had a history at Lay Down Easy or another establishment like it.

"The males use stims." Her tone ripped with healthy disapproval.

"And how do you know?" His gaze searched hers and he read loathing in her eyes.

"Petroy makes no secret of his past. He used to be a slave in a place like this."

"On Dakmar?" Slavery was illegal in the Federation, but space was wide and Kirek had heard rumors that authorities on some worlds looked the other way, allowing the slave trade to trickle on.

She shook her head. "Slavers grabbed Petroy from his home world and imprisoned him on Friva, a space station in another sector. The methods to enslave are the same. The men are addicted to the stims."

Kirek had never been a slave, but being a hostage on Endeki was close enough. Women had used him as they wished. One Endekian had been particularly cruel. Although he'd escaped within days, the memory of his own brush with that demeaning life caused a shudder of distaste.

Angel must have misinterpreted his reaction. "I rescued Petroy . . . and before you ask . . . no, we have no personal history." She spoke defensively. "I'd never met him until his stim wore off and some merc toasted him with a grenade. I could hardly leave him twitching at my feet, so I brought him to the *Raven* and helped him recover from his addiction."

"And his fried neurons?"

"He has no memories before his time on the *Raven*."

"You seem to make a habit of rescuing lost souls. Petroy. The singer on your last trip."

"Petroy makes a great first officer. He's loyal and his life is the *Raven*. Merline, the singer, paid me for passage in *frelle*."

That wasn't the story he'd heard. Frie had told him the rare spice had been a gift from a grateful stowaway. His Angel had a soft heart, one which she hid behind a tough exterior.

Kirek didn't fit into the lost-soul category. He had a wonderful family, friends, and a home to return to. Was that why Angel refused to admit she had feelings for him? Kirek wished he understood her better, but now, as they were about to head toward the Lay Down Easy, was not the time for personal concerns.

Instead, still worried about taking Angel with him, he searched the cache of weapons and helped himself to a stunner and a knife. Knowing he required her help increased his concern. Yet, he accepted that she would distract him and that he would have to stay doubly alert and ready for action.

ANDROMEDA GALAXY

"Have you found the Rystani named Kirek?" the Zin demanded, his tone more aggressive and hostile than before.

Clearly the Great Zin was losing patience, but the Kraj captain had no reason to cower. He had good news.

"Yes. I have found him. He hides on an insignificant Dakmar moon."

"You're certain?"

"He and the woman Captain Angel Taylor are together. We saw them copulating in an underwater pool."

"You killed Kirek?"

"He escaped through an underwater tunnel."

"Again you failed?"

"But we will take him soon. Even as we speak, he walks into my trap."

"How do you know he hasn't already fled?"

"He's with the woman and the woman wouldn't leave without her ship, a ship that remains in the repair dock."

"You are making assumptions you cannot prove. He could have left the woman."

"But he didn't. My scanners have located them exiting the mansion's secret entrance. They are on the way to The Peel, where I have set up a plan to ambush him."

"Good. Contact me when you have him."

"Agreed."

Chapter Thirteen

THE LAY DOWN Easy looked and felt like Kirek
expected—with one exception. Dim lighting, dancing
men and women, an assortment of humanoids and beings from other sectors, harsh music, greasy food, and
watered-down drinks seemed standard fare for seedy
gambling establishments. However, usually Kirek could
use his psi to alter the machines to pay out in his favor.
Although his psi might not have recovered enough to
overcome the computer locks' resistance, he was picking up unusual shielding, or dampeners that made his
psi feel as if he were reaching through a dense black
fog. Following their plan, Angel strode in ahead of him,
invited herself into a card game, and proceeded to pretend she didn't know Kirek. One handsome and

dangerous-looking player moved his chips over to make room for her and shot her an engaging smile of welcome. Kirek refrained from bristling and told himself that the sexy grin Angel returned was all for show.

Their walk into the Peel had been so ordinary and free of conflict that he'd wondered if Angel had exaggerated the dangers, but after two gorgeous redheads approached him, and Angel stood and glared until they backed away, he realized she'd been protecting him from robbery by her presence alone, just as she'd claimed.

And Kirek couldn't deny she fit into the card game with an easy camaraderie that suggested she'd played in many places as disreputable as the Lay Down Easy. With a stack of credit chips at one hand, a drink in the other, Angel played with confidence. However, she multi-tasked, her gaze raking the entire scene, conscious of every moment. He had no doubt that if any mercs approached, she would make her presence known.

Leaning back against a wall, Kirek watched the front doors, awaiting the arrival of his contact, Vee. Since Vee typically used a prearranged drop and this was their first meet in the flesh, Kirek shifted impatiently, wondering why the mode of operation had changed. Uninformed if Vee was a man or a woman or even a non-humanoid, he surveyed the occupants with care, wondering if Vee could have arrived even earlier than they had.

Kirek's instruction had been clear—Vee would find him. Kirek felt as if he was wearing a target on his chest as he waited for a stranger to approach. Several did, but they kept walking by, not giving him a second glance.

For a long thirty Federation minutes, no one except the bar bot approached. Angel used the time to chat, to drink, and to play a few hands. She neither won nor lost a huge amount of chips, playing patiently. Her gaze frequently slid over him but never stopped.

Kirek didn't like meeting Vee in person in such a shady establishment. His psi itched near his nape and as he reached up to knead out some tension a curtain behind the stage moved. He narrowed his gaze, tightened his muscles, and held his breath, waiting to see who might suddenly appear—because the comic performer wasn't due to start his gig for another hour.

Lights dimmed even further and the music changed to an upbeat drum tempo. A hush fell over the room.

The curtains parted and women, men, and several tiny sequined birds gyrated and flew across the stage in a swirling array of sparkling costumes, toned flesh, gliding feet, and flapping wings. Far from the stage, in the darkness, Kirek tensed at the unscheduled performance. And as the dancers made a side exit and left the stage, zigzagging across the room and into the audience, he merged deeper into the shadows and kept his eyes away from the bright spotlights.

Under the cover of the commotion, he spied a humanoid shadow approaching and wondered if his contact had arranged the distraction to divert any curious eyes from his own entrance.

A raspy voice whispered out of the darkness. "Kirek?"

"Vee?"

"You have the credits?" The stranger kept his head down and Kirek couldn't see his face.

"You have the information?" he countered.

Vee reached into his jacket. "Let's do this fast. I may have been followed."

"Followed by whom?" Kirek asked.

Before Vee answered or withdrew his hand, dancers lunged toward them, their speed quick due to their athletic limbs and the coordinated manipulation of their suits. At the same time, exterior doors opened and several Kraj entered, their stunners drawn.

Kirek's muscles tensed, ready for action as he assessed his options. He heard metal clunk and roll, and out of his peripheral vision he spied a grenade rolling toward him. Then a second grenade launched his way, signaling a full-fledged, coordinated attack. One grenade popped early, its flare inciting a riot.

Amid screams and shouts, those patrons who weren't caught in the grenade's devastating blast bolted for the exits. In their panic, they shoved into the Kraj, pushing them backward, delaying their arrival and preventing their shots from hitting their target—him. Random shooting broke out. Blasters, stunners, and projectile weapons flashed, flared, and roared. Terrified customers stampeded for every exit, knocking over other beings, tables, and gambling machines.

With Kraj obstructing the egress, and grenades rolling his way, Kirek glanced toward Angel. She was already halfway across the room, lunging toward him, but there were lots of bodies in her way. An overhead stage light caught her face in its sweeping beam and showed her mask of concentration and fear as she shoved between patrons.

Kirek couldn't remain where he was without risking his brain cells to the effects of the grenades. He grabbed Vee, his intention to employ his psi's null grav to lift them over the heads of the oncoming dancers. But his psi didn't work. The dampeners that he'd noted earlier seemed to blanket and dull his energy. He tried to use his com to contact Angel and wasn't surprised to find it jammed.

Kirek cursed and kicked a grenade toward the Kraj. Beside him, Vee yelped and then shuddered to the floor. And he didn't move again.

Ducking, Kirek kneeled beside the fallen man, whose face was lit up by the fire of nearby stunners. Blank eyes stared unseeingly at the ceiling.

Just to be certain Vee was dead, Kirek placed his fingers on Vee's neck in search of a pulse, and found none. He swore softly. Had Vee taken a hit meant for him? Or did he have enemies of his own?

Either way, Kirek needed the location of the portal that could sling the *Raven* into the Andromeda Galaxy. Without the intel, he couldn't stop the Zin.

He picked up another grenade and lobbed it toward the empty stage, then took precious seconds to search Vee's jacket. When his fingers found an intel disc, he shoved it into his own suit, praying it contained the portal's location. Kirek was about to stand when Angel rolled toward him.

"You okay?" he asked.

"I had to toss in a royal flush," she muttered.

"I'll make it up to you."

"Damn right you will." She took cover behind an up-ended table. "We need to find a way out the back."

Kirek raised his stunner. "I'll cover you. Go."

Angel ducked right, left, and slammed right into a Kraj. Fearful that the alien would kill her, Kirek's heart jammed up into his throat. Kirek took the only shot open to him, a head shot. He hit his target and the big alien almost fell on top of her, but she dodged and squirmed forward through the mass of bodies, not wasting a moment, or even waiting until the stunned Kraj struck the floor.

Adrenaline surging, Kirek hurried to follow, his feet kicking away another grenade even as he shifted left and used a knife-hand strike against a female attacker's throat. He'd never downed a woman before, but she'd given him no choice.

And he had no time for regrets, not with the Kraj advancing and Angel sprinting backstage. With her slender frame, she'd woven through the crowd more easily than he could. He barely kept up as he avoided another attack, this time from a tiny bird that seemed intent on aiming for his eyes.

And Angel had moved so fast, she was now out of sight. Taking four steps at a time, Kirek raced behind the curtain to catch sight of Angel at the far end of the building—in hand-to-hand combat with two redheads. Heart ramming in his chest, sweat pouring from his cells, he lunged forward and simultaneously tried to steady his blaster, waiting for a clear shot. But the women were too close together for him to risk shooting.

As he neared, he watched Angel pull her blaster, jam it against one woman's stomach. Her other opponent attempted to knock away the weapon, but Angel got off a shot. Then she spun and drop-kicked the second woman in the chest, and Angel's attacker collapsed into a moan.

"Nice move." He finally caught up with her and assessed her injuries. She sported a bruise by one eye and a few scratches on her forearm but otherwise, she looked good. Better than good. Her eyes danced and sparkled as if she was having the time of her life. He wanted to scoop her into his arms and tell her she'd better not scare him like that again anytime soon.

Angel glanced at him, barely breathing hard, and gestured toward a rear exit where a Kraj guarded the door. "Try to keep up."

"Don't run," he ordered.

"Excuse me?"

"Running out of this building will attract attention."

"Kirek, a hundred people must have just fled this building. We're hardly going to stick out—"

"The crowd's gone. Kraj are hunting. We need to sneak out without the Kraj spotting and shooting us. And I'd like to find a com that works."

Angel grabbed his hand and tugged him toward the side wall and behind some props. "What do you mean a com that works?"

"A jamming device is blocking my com and my psi. Can't you feel it?"

"I do have a headache. I thought it was from the smoke." Angel changed a setting on her grenade launcher. "Stand back and use your vision filters."

A second later, she blew a hole in the side of the building big enough for them to crawl through. Outside, a corridor led past garbage into an alley with several locked doors. From the alley he could see that it eventually widened into a larger passageway. From the shouts and screams behind and ahead, he suspected the Kraj were shooting bystanders.

They had to get off public roads and sidewalks. Angel tried the first door on the right. "Locked."

He tried the next. "Locked again."

By the last door, he heard a skimmer hovering at the end of the alley. Time was running out. Kirek used his foot to break the lock. Luckily the old rusty hinge broke on his third kick.

He stepped into the rear of a store filled with baskets, plants, and herbs. A pink-skinned man, a terrified blue-haired woman, and an equally frightened child stared at him. The tiny woman screamed and grabbed her toddler, who burst into tears. Angel stepped past the broken door and Kirek held it open to keep it from falling on her, then propped it back in place as best he could.

When he turned around, the man held a shaking blaster aimed at Kirek's chest. Advancing, Angel bumped into Kirek's back but he braced, keeping her behind him.

The man gestured for his wife to take the child to another room, but didn't take his gaze from Kirek. "Don't move."

Kirek strengthened his psi shield, noting the dampening had dissipated, but was not yet gone. "We mean you no harm. If you hide us, I'll pay you well."

"I'll call the authorities," the woman whined. Her child continued to scream. "Stun them so they can't run away. Maybe we can collect a reward for their capture."

Outside the skimmer roared to a stop. Booted feet marched down the corridor.

"Please." Angel stepped out from behind Kirek and pointed at him. "This man wants to make me his slave. If you turn us over to the botcops, he'll pay a fine and I'll disappear forever."

Kirek's jaw almost dropped to the floor. Where did she come up with such stories? Was she trying to make the man shoot him? Already frightened, now doubly suspicious, the man's shocked gaze scowled at Kirek.

Angel sidled over to the woman. "Please, let me scoot out the front door and be on my way."

The man held the gun on Kirek. He paid no attention at all to Angel. With her swollen eye and the way she hunched her shoulders, she looked harmless, beaten, scared. She slipped behind the woman. In one swift move, she pulled her blaster and placed it to the woman's temple.

"Drop your weapon," she ordered the man. Stunned by the sudden turn of events, the man dropped the gun. Kirek scooped it up.

Angel pulled the woman and crying child with her toward a closet while instructing the husband, "Tell anyone who asks that we ran through the store and you want to know who is going to pay for the damage. Do you understand?"

"Yes."

"Do as she says and your wife and child will come to no harm," Kirek's tone was kind.

Angel glared. "One wrong word and I'll roast them both. Got it?"

"Yes."

Kirek didn't approve of Angel's tactics. The man shook so hard, Kirek doubted he could stammer a cohesive sentence. The woman kept screaming and the kid cried, too.

Angel dragged them into the closet. "Shut up, lady. And keep the kid quiet or I'll stun you both."

Boots outside skidded to a halt. Rough voices shouted. "They blasted through this wall. Kicked open that door. Let's go."

Heart pounding, Kirek hid behind a pallet of crates. He didn't like putting an innocent family in danger, and yet he understood that during war, civilians often got hurt. Reminding himself that the Zin had killed billions of beings on Zenon didn't make it right for them to terrorize this family . . . and yet, if they didn't survive to confront the Zin, the fate of the galaxy could be at stake.

However, the terror in the mother's eyes stabbed him with guilt. While Angel wouldn't hurt the mother or the baby, she'd played her part well, looking fierce and angry and desperate.

And she'd been right to use force. They hadn't had the luxury of time to bribe them, or better yet, to convince the family to help. However, if the ruse worked, Kirek suspected the trauma of having their home invaded might cause years of nightmares.

The woman quieted and the child's screams softened to muffled cries. Was the mother holding her hand over the little boy's mouth?

Kirek shut out his concerns and focused on the father and husband. Angrily, the shopkeeper brushed a stray tear from his eye, then faced the broken door with squared shoulders. Several botcops and Kraj kicked down the broken door and entered the back room. Kirek wondered how they'd come to be working together.

"Bless the stars, you have arrived," the man cried out,

his voice wracked with terror. He pointed to the front of his establishment. "Go quick. Catch them. I want them to pay for the damage."

The botcops zoomed out the front. Several Kraj followed but one stayed behind. "Once they left out the front, which way did they go?"

The man wrung his hands. "I don't know."

"What do you mean, you don't know?"

"I hid behind the counter so they wouldn't shoot me."

"Are you very certain you didn't see them leave?" the Kraj demanded.

"I was hiding."

"Did they see you?"

"I don't know."

"I want access to your vidrecorder." A replay of the vidrecorder would show that Kirek and Angel had never fled out the front. It might even reveal where they now hid.

Kirek had to give the man credit. He tried to come up with a convincing lie. "I'm a poor man. The vidrecorder is . . . broken."

The Kraj raised his gun to the store owner's head. "You are lying."

Kirek couldn't let the man die. He had no choice. He stunned the Kraj in the back.

Angel burst out of the closet, pushing the woman who was still holding the child toward her husband. Angel frowned at the downed-but-still-breathing Kraj. "You didn't kill the Kraj?"

"Why?" Kirek didn't like killing, but he hated admitting it since his morals contradicted his Rystani warrior culture. "The Kraj is probably just a soldier following orders. He may have a wife, kids, parents."

Angel eyed him as if he'd lost his mind. "Leaving him behind will cause problems."

"We won't be here."

"What about them?" She glanced at the family, hugging in a tearful reunion. "We need to ruin their vidrecorder or when the Kraj recovers, he might punish them—even if they didn't want to help us."

The man pointed to a lens cover. "It's there."

Angel zapped it. "That should protect you. And I really am sorry for the trouble we've caused."

Kirek made a mental note of the man's name on the store license. "You will soon find a large deposit has been added to your credit account at the local bank. Now, do you have a skimmer?"

The man pointed to the roof.

STUNNER IN HAND, Angel sprinted up the stairs to the roof. With their psi at diminished capacity, she used muscle-power to race to the skimmer. At least everyone, including their pursuers, seemed to be equally affected. Kirek had taken the lead and his longer legs took the stairs four or five at a time, but he stayed protectively close.

He'd already surprised her twice today. Once when he'd stunned the Kraj instead of killing him. And the second time when he hadn't tried to admonish her about the tactics she'd used on the family. Although they'd had little choice, she'd seen disapproval in his eyes. She'd expected him to criticize her but he hadn't.

So when he took the pilot's seat and handed her his weapon to cover them if necessary, she didn't suggest that they should switch places. However, once he lifted off at a cautious speed, she wondered if she'd made a mistake.

"This skimmer can make it to the *Raven*'s docking bay in less than five minutes if you'd—"

"I don't want to draw attention to us. And I'm certainly not going to flee straight to the ship."

"So where are we heading?"

"You're in the navigator's seat," he teased.

Below them, the Kraj and botcops had established a perimeter. They were busy doing a door-to-door search and rounding up the populace. Hopefully, by the time they thought to check the skimmers, they would be long gone.

Kirek was right. Merging with the regular traffic patterns would lose their pursuers better than a frantic flight.

She turned on the nav controls and pulled up a map of Dakmar. "I never use a skimmer while I'm here."

"You don't like turning the flying over to a bot or taxi driver?"

Sometimes he knew her better than she knew herself. She really didn't like being a passenger. She hunched over the map. "I'm searching for a popular place to set down, one that won't be too far from public transportation back to the *Raven*."

"We can't return to the ship yet."

"Why not?"

"For one thing, it's not ready. And second, I need to find a reader"—he reached into his suit—"for this disk."

She glanced at the strange shape. Unlike most Federation disks, which were round, the disk was an oval. "I've never seen anything like it."

"I took it from Vee after he died. I'm hoping the disk contains the coordinates we need."

She handed the disk back to him. "And if it doesn't?"

"We'll have to backtrack to Vee's contacts, friends, and family. And since I don't know what planet he's from, it's not going to be easy."

"It could take months . . ." Angel kept her most negative thoughts to herself. The Zin could wipe out another Federation planet any time they fired up the next wormhole and ignited another planetary core. Shoving the pessimistic reflections to the back of her mind, she perused the map. "What about setting down by the public library? It's not far from the *Raven*, public sidewalks could take us there in minutes, and maybe a research specialist can help us with the disk."

He turned the skimmer in a broad, even sweep. "Good idea. What are the exact coordinates?"

She punched them into the nav system, then peered behind them. "I don't see any sign of pursuit." She flicked on Dakmar's only radio station but when screeching techno music hurt her ears, she snapped it off.

Kirek landed in a public parking area, erased their flight information, and then set the control to automatically return the skimmer to its owner. They exited the skimmer and she led the way toward the library.

"Some park," she muttered. "There's not one green plant to be seen." Instead of the greenery she'd expected, she steered past kids playing bots and robbers amid a bunch of stacked shipping crates. They had no difficulty finding the library. The huge building had a sign over it stating visiting hours and warning patrons not to bring weapons inside or to cause a disturbance.

Angel made certain her weapons weren't in sight and noted Kirek doing the same. Just as they reached the double front doors with a skimmer-load of joking and shoving students, a formation of skimmers landed with precision in the park. She stepped into the building, her gaze focused over her shoulder at the official-looking skimmer. Botcops and Kraj emerged.

Kirek kept his voice low. "It didn't take them long to find us."

"Our skimmer may have had an anti-theft tracker on board."

Swept forward with the group of chattering students,

Angel searched for the research desk. Or a computer vid-screen. But the enormous entryway was packed with children. Little ones holding their mothers' hands. Older ones that chased one another and pulled each other's hair and pushed. Teens wearing day-glow colors and too much eye makeup.

Angel stopped to ask a question of an adult, but Kirek grabbed her hand and tugged her forward. "Don't stop. Don't look back."

Angel did as Kirek requested, but she braced against the stunner blast that would take her out. Luckily the crowds of children and teens hid her. Beside her Kirek had folded himself over, bending his knees and hunching his back to hide his height.

Around them the children shouted, played ear-splitting music, told jokes, trampled on one another, and acted oblivious to their presence. Angel told herself she should be grateful, but she didn't like crowds. Or children. The creatures were always whining, their noses running, demanding attention and crying.

They blended into a group of teens that flowed down a hallway. Bells rang. And the students emptied from the hallways through doorways. Kirek opened a storeroom door and pulled her inside. The room was filled with balls, bats, nets, and assorted sports toys.

"What kind of library is this?" she asked, frowning at the equipment in the tiny room. "I haven't seen one vidscreen."

"I suspect this isn't a library anymore."

"But the map—"

"Was outdated. This is a school."

"We need to get out of here."

Kirek shook his head. "I don't like using the kids to hide us, either. But no matter how badly the Kraj want us, the botcops won't let the Kraj endanger children."

She gaped at him. Of all the places to hide out, a school had to be at the bottom of her list. "We can't blend in here."

"Why not?" Kirek's gazed searched hers as if she was being unreasonable.

"Because . . . the school is full of kids. We obviously aren't children." She tried to give him a logical reason, but in truth, she was too unnerved by the rowdy screaming and yelling coming through the walls. Her pounding brain wasn't functioning properly and her headache seemed worse.

Kirek remained patient. "The school is also full of adult teachers and caretakers." He plucked identification tags off two jackets hanging on hooks on the back of the door and handed her a badge. "There's no reason we can't impersonate substitute or guest teachers."

"You want to stay here?" She struggled to keep her voice calm.

"The school is so large that I'm betting administration can't keep up with substitute employees."

"But . . . I don't know anything about kids," she admitted.

"Think of them as smaller versions of yourself. They like to talk and laugh and—"

"This is a bad idea." She'd rather face half a dozen Kraj that spend time with a bunch of kids.

Before Kirek could say more, the door opened. Angel aimed her stunner.

Chapter Fourteen

THE BOY COMING through the storage closet door could
have been anywhere between eight and eleven Federation
years old. With big brown eyes, curly hair the color of
sand, and freckles across the bridge of his nose, he was in
a gangly awkward stage. He took one look at Angel's
blaster pointed at him, turned white, and opened his
mouth to scream.

"Put away the stunner," Kirek snapped. Then he turned
to the kid with a friendly smile. "She's just practicing the
self-defense moves we're going to teach your class."

"She is? You are?" The kid looked from Kirek to Angel, who holstered her stunner, and then back to Kirek,
suspicion in his eyes. "But Ma'am Holly, our teacher, told
me to come here for catch and bats." He gestured to long
sticks with netting attached.

"She probably didn't get the admin notice. But we've been on the schedule since the semester started," Kirek improvised. "I'm Kirek and this is Angel. What's your name?"

"Hax."

She wondered if it was foolish to use their real names, but it was too late now. And if Kirek wanted to go teach a bunch of kids self-defense to blend in until the Kraj left, he'd best not include her. Perhaps because she'd never had the opportunity to play with other children, or perhaps because she simply wasn't wired with a nurturing gene, children always made her uncomfortable. She really didn't understand why people wanted to perpetuate the species. Parents spent the first months listening to the kids cry, then had to answer a million questions as they grew up. As teens, they ate too much and rebelled and mostly ended up hating their parents. Really, she just didn't see the point. And the idea of spending the next few hours with an entire class of kids made her skin crawl.

Hax gave Kirek a lopsided grin. He grabbed the equipment he'd come for and shoved open the door. "Guess I'll take you to Ma'am Holly. Will you really show us how to fight?"

Kirek slung a hand comfortably on the boy's shoulder. "Every being should know how to defend themselves."

"Not Kel, she's my twin and meaner than spit."

Kirek winked at Hax as if they were old friends. "We don't have to teach Kel *all* the self-defense moves. We'll keep some for just us men."

"Oh, really?" Angel trailed the corridor, keeping her eyes peeled for botcops and Kraj. "Seems to me in this universe females have just as much need for defensive skills."

Over Hax's head, Kirek frowned. No doubt he didn't want her interfering with the male bonding. She snapped her mouth shut, vowing not to say another word.

"Kel's mean. She bites and pinches and spies on me," Hax complained. "And I'm not allowed to hit her—because she's my sister."

"I can see where that would be a problem." Kirek spoke to the kid so easily, replying as if Hax's childish concerns were important. "Maybe we can find a way for you to defend yourself without causing her any injury."

Hax grinned, revealing a missing tooth. "That would be impressive."

They strolled down an empty corridor, passing classes filled with noisy children. Angel didn't know how they could learn anything with all the commotion around them. Teachers looked up as they passed, but no one stepped into the hall to question their presence in the school.

They rounded a corner and Hax's feet picked up the pace. He appeared quite eager to introduce them to his teacher. Of all the contingencies she'd planned for during this op, ending up in a school with a bunch of kids hadn't been one of them.

She glanced at Kirek who appeared relaxed, at ease, and to be thoroughly enjoying himself. It figured. He'd grown up in a loving family. He'd probably been the teacher's star pupil and had had a wonderful childhood.

Angel's own schooling had been hit-and-miss. Her mother had gotten sick when she'd entered primary school. Someone had to stay home and care for her and often that job had fallen to Angel. Sometimes her aunt or her mother's cousin would come over and then her mother would insist Angel attend school. But she'd always been the outsider, often skipping classes, and never spending enough time in one classroom to make real friends.

Most of Angel's education had been acquired at home on an old computer. She'd been an avid reader and had adored stories about space, aliens, and new worlds. Even back then, exploring the unknown and seeing new sights and cultures had called to her. To escape from the sickness and smelly medicines at home along with the dreary job of being her mother's caretaker, she'd dreamed of adventure.

She expected Hax to lead them into one of the classrooms, but he opened the door to a giant gymnasium filled with not just thirty students, but maybe a hundred. The noise level was deafening and Angel's head ached. Kids ran around yelling and shouting, totally out of control of Ma'am Holly, a tiny woman with a pinched face who was blowing a whistle, trying and failing to get the kids' attention.

Angel would have liked to use her suit to lower the noise level, but if the Kraj suddenly arrived, impaired hearing might hurt their chances of escaping. So she put up with the irritation, all the while wishing to be back on the *Raven*'s quiet bridge.

Hax wriggled past some kids, jumped over a bot, and ducked past a group of boys playing tag and using their suits and the wall like a trampoline to boost their speed. Kirek and Angel did their best to follow Hax through the chaos.

Kirek stepped forward and introduced them to the teacher. "Ma'am Holly, I'm Kirek and this is Angel. We're scheduled to teach a self-defense class."

Angel shook her head at him when he again used their real names, but then supposed it didn't matter. If the Kraj came, they'd recognize and shoot them on sight.

"The class is all yours." Ma'am Holly handed him her whistle, took a seat under a hooped net, pulled out yarn and a device that twisted the yarn into tiny squares, and proceeded with her crafting.

Angel's jaw almost hit the floor. The woman hadn't even questioned their authority. Amazing. Then again, she was probably so happy not to have to deal with the

out-of-control kids that she didn't think of questioning
her good luck.

Angel turned to Kirek to give him a "now-what" scowl.
But he was placing two fingers into his mouth, and he let
out a sharp whistle. The kids actually stopped making
noise and gathered around them.

"Look at his muscles." A tiny girl with bright pink eyes
admired Kirek. "When I grow up I'm going to pair with a
man like him."

"He's not my type" said another girl, sizing him up, a
knowing look in her eyes. "He's too—"

"Kel—shut your lips." Hax glared at his twin.

"Make me." Kel glowered right back.

"I could if I wanted to."

"All right," Kirek interrupted. "How would each one of
you like to learn to defend yourselves from attack?"

Kids jumped up and down, raising their hands. "I
would."

"Teach me." A teen with a wide smile and a very curvy
body sidled up to Kirek and placed a hand on his arm.

Either the class was a mix of age groups or the kids
here were different humanoid races and grew at different
rates. Some seemed innocent and trusting, but others
seemed to have too much space-smarts for kids.

Kirek gently disengaged from the teen. "Females to
the right. Males to the left." he directed. "All others," he
continued, speaking to several species that might not have
male and female traits, "choose which side fits you best."

Surprisingly, the children separated with very few arguments, obeying Kirek without question. He hadn't
raised his voice. But he spoke with an authority they automatically responded to, and Angel could easily imagine
an entire fleet of Rystani ships following him into battle
against the Zin, or the Kwadii people believing he was
their Oracle.

But when she thought of Kirek, the image that came to mind was the two of them making love in front of that mirror, his psi showing her more than she'd wanted to see. She was done with marriage. She wasn't cut out for long-term relationships. She didn't want to have feelings beyond friendship and lust for the Rystani warrior. But apparently she couldn't control her feelings. They were incontrovertibly and inconveniently there, simmering below the surface.

She planned to ignore them—not a rational decision but one of self-preservation. As Kirek began to teach the children basic blocks, first with their psi shields and then with their arms; she could see another glaring reminder that this was a fling. She wasn't cut out for family life. Stars. She hadn't been able to keep either of her marriages alive, never mind deal with children. A shame really . . . not only was he the best lover she'd ever had, he intrigued her.

At the moment, he appeared to be having fun. His contact was dead. The Kraj were hunting them. And he was lying on the mat and the smallest children were crawling over him. A wide grin was on his face, and his laughter filled the gym.

As if hearing her thoughts, his gaze found hers and he held out a hand, motioning her to join in the fray. He had to be out of his mind. She didn't want to crawl on a mat with all those tiny bodies with grubby hands. She shook her head, preferring to stand guard. Her gaze swept the exits, expecting the doors to crash open any moment. One of them had to be prepared to defend them.

A teenage girl joined her. Overweight, with untidy dark-brown hair and a sad slump to her shoulders, she didn't say anything, just stood there staring at a group of pretty girls who clearly considered her an outcast.

"I never fit in, either," Angel told her.

The teen eyed her with equal parts hostility and curiosity. "Why not? You're thin and pretty."

Angel recalled the taunts. Kids could be cruel. "It's more like they knew I was different . . . inside."

"So what did you do?"

"First chance I got . . . I ran away." Angel wondered if she was still running.

"Did it help?"

"If I went home now . . . I still wouldn't fit in." Angel couldn't imagine going back to Earth, sitting on one piece of dirt for the rest of her life, living next to the same people for years and years. But she did fit in on the *Raven*. Petroy and Frie and Leval were her family. "But I made a new home and yes, it's better. When you grow up you have more choices. You decide. Not parents. Not teachers."

"I want to farm."

Yuck. Angel couldn't imagine a more boring life. But when she glanced at the kid's face, her eyes looked dreamy. "Why do you want to farm?"

"I've lived on Dakmar my whole life. I want to live with fresh air and surrounded by green plants. Go back to nature. When I'm legal, I plan to ship out to a colony world. In the meantime, I'm learning what I can about agriculture."

"What do your parents think?"

"They say I'll grow out of my childish idea." The girl paused. "But I won't. And I wish I could go now."

"It's a tough world out there. An education can help you get ahead."

"The stuff they teach me in school is useless. What I need is a way to build capital to buy some land."

Angel suppressed a grin. Those words could have come out of her mouth. "I have a friend Merline who lives on a world called Siraz where they produce the spice *frelle*. If you are interested in apprenticing, she might give you work—when you're old enough."

"Frelle?" The girl's eyes lit up as if Angel were talking about the extraordinary wealth of salvaging the Zin home world, instead of a simple job. "I'd . . . that . . . would be . . . so incredible."

Angel tapped Merline's com link into the girl's wrist pad. "Tell her Angel told you to contact her. I'm sure Merline will tell you what you need to study."

"Thank you. Thank you."

Kirek had recovered from the mass of bodies and joined her just as the girl ran off. He looked at Angel curiously. "Who was she?"

Angel shrugged. "I don't know much about kids. I didn't ask her name."

"She seemed to like you." Kirek motioned for a boy to raise his arm higher to block.

"What happens when class is over?" Angel asked, changing the subject. "Because if you plan to stay here all day—"

"I don't."

"Good." Relief washed over her. Not only did she want to retreat from the noise and the kids, she didn't want to risk their safety if the Kraj showed up and started shooting.

"I thought we could volunteer as library monitors next."

"What?" She wanted to depart the school.

Kirek kept his voice low and reasonable. "I'd like to find out more about the disk I took off my contact. With some research, maybe I can find a reader for it in the school library, or at least figure out which planet might have one."

"All right."

"What's wrong?"

"I won't be happy until we're back on the *Raven*. She's home. Aboard her, I know what to expect and how best to handle attacks. We're too exposed here."

Kirek's expression turned grave. "If we find the salvage you want, would you trade in the *Raven* for a bigger ship?"

She couldn't believe he'd suggested such a thing. "I'd rather trade in my right arm."

Bells rang, signifying the end of class. The kids raced, walked, shoved, and pushed their way from the gymnasium. Caught in the mass exodus, the kids swept them back out into the hallways. Kirek asked one child for directions to the library and after walking for several minutes, they entered the quiet refuge from noise.

Each vidscreen was housed in a private cubicle. Before Kirek could talk to any more kids or volunteer for any other teaching activities, she appropriated a computer terminal and shut the door behind them. With two adults cramped into an area meant for one child, she had to flatten her back against the door to make room for the holodisplay.

Kirek took the disk from his suit and held it up. "Please scan and identify."

The computer spoke in a teacher's voice, lecturing slowly, as if its circuits were jammed. "The hand and arm are Rystani DNA with—"

"Computer." Kirek interrupted. "I'm only interested in the fabricated disk."

"Compliance. The material is a polylaminate of the type used by modern computers."

"Can you identify the planet of origin from the composition?"

"Cross-checking components with natural resources. This may take some time."

"How much time?" Angel asked.

The computer didn't answer, but flashed a message saying their request was being processed off-site since the data they required wasn't available locally.

Angel shifted impatiently from foot to foot. It was only a matter of time until the kids from that class talked to an adult who would realize that she and Kirek hadn't belonged there. A report would arrive downtown and a computer collating data would connect their appearance at the school and inform the botcops searching for them.

Every moment they wasted here narrowed their chances of escape. And yet, without knowing the location of the portal, they couldn't continue their journey. Unfortunately, this library-turned-school's antiquated system didn't seem up to the task.

"Perhaps we should find a university."

"Have you forgotten the Kraj that are outside and searching for us?"

The computer hummed, then spoke. "It is impossible to fulfill your request. There are over one thousand planets which have the necessary resources to manufacture the disk—and that's not counting interplanetary imports."

"Scan the disk for DNA," Angel requested. "Ignore Rystani genetic material." Since she hadn't touched the disk, she didn't mention her own Terran biology. "Perhaps the contact left a few cells behind."

The computer clicked. "There is a short hair, the length of an eyelash, which may have DNA. I'm processing."

Kirek squeezed her hand. "That was a good idea. Alara would be proud of you."

"Alara?"

Kirek rarely mentioned anyone in his past, but his fond tone made her curious, even as she noted she also had to suppress a twinge of jealousy.

"I met her during my last mission. Alara's a brilliant Endekian physiologist, and with her help, Xander found two Perceptive Ones and a cure for the Zin virus." Kirek cast Angel a teasing glance, as if he sensed her curiosity about his exact relationship with Alara, a relationship that shouldn't have bothered her. "Xander fell in love and married her."

"The eyelash is Numan," the computer informed them, and a map formed on the holovid. "The planet is located here."

A Federation quadrant showed a map of star systems and planets. The computer had marked Numan with a flashing purple light. Their current location on Dakmar pulsed orange, with a yellow line of light connecting the two locations via the best route.

Kirek required a cross check. "Does Numan have the necessary natural resources to manufacture the disk?"

"Negative." The computer hummed. "But one of its moons mines the primary missing Numan metal and there is frequent trade between the planet and the moon's colonists."

Angel leaned over the screen. "Computer, can you find a Numan disk reader on Dakmar or any closer systems?"

"Your inquiry requires an extensive search. This may take a Federation hour. Shall I continue?" Again the computer hummed, no doubt searching mercantile inventories, as well as private sales.

Angel glanced at Kirek. He grinned. "Computer, please continue."

"What are you so happy about?"

"We shouldn't leave until school is out, when we can depart with the teachers without attracting attention."

"And this makes you happy because . . . ?"

His eyes brightened with heat. "We have an hour. Alone. You and me."

Her mouth went dry and her gut tightened. She hadn't

even been considering making love. The idea of having him right now, right here, excited her, even as she protested. "The Kraj could break in here at any moment."

"And if they find us talking instead of making love, do you think it will lessen their determination to shoot us?" Kirek's tone teased. He reached over and placed a warm hand on her thigh.

Desire angled up her leg. "What if some kid wanders into the library?"

His hand inched higher. "The walls are insulated to prevent sound from interrupting the students' concentration. I've locked the door."

She couldn't think past the warmth of his hand and her need to touch him back. "But—"

"We only have an hour. Let's not waste a moment arguing when we could be enjoying ourselves." He slid his hand up her thigh to her bottom and drew her into his arms.

One minute ago, sex hadn't been on her mind. But with just his touch to her leg, she was suddenly on fire for him.

Stars . . . She wanted him with a lust that coursed through her with amazing strength, took away her breath, made thinking almost impossible.

"What . . . is . . . happening?" she gasped.

She didn't expect an answer. She hadn't been specific enough for him to understand her question . . . and yet, even as her legs quivered and her breasts ached for attention, her mind knew that her body didn't normally start this fast, or burn with this much need.

"Remember when you wanted to see my feelings?" he asked, his tone serious, his hands busily stroking up her back and down over her bottom.

"So?" She frowned. Thankfully they didn't have a mirror in the tiny cubicle. They didn't even have a window that could show a partial reflection of her aura.

"You are feeling what I feel."

"What?" She jerked back, her gaze searching his.

"The burning, the need, the hunger you feel is what I feel for you."

God . . . Her feelings weren't her own . . . they were his. She'd never heard of such a thing, and didn't know what she thought. Thinking was next to impossible as she rubbed up against him, her mouth hungering for his.

Awash in a sea of roaring lust, she wanted his hands all over her, everywhere. Her lips pulsed with the need to meet his. And she was so damp and slick with the moisture creaming between her legs that all she craved was for him to have her. Now. Up against the wall. On the desk. Against the door.

And yet, those desires weren't hers—they were his. She had no idea why he wasn't kissing her, but somehow he held back and kept the ripping need from turning him into a savage.

"You understand what I'm saying?" he asked.

"Yes."

"Tell me," he demanded.

"I'm feeling how much you want me." She gulped, wondering if all men had such strong sexual desires and if so, how any of them ever managed to think about anything else. Stars. She was ready to melt. To explode. And they had barely touched. "How do you stand it?"

He shot her a wolfish grin that sent a shiver of anticipation down her spine. "I'm not giving you a choice to say no."

"Bastard." She licked her bottom lip, knowing he was right and that later she might be annoyed with herself. But at the moment she couldn't muster any clear thoughts—not with the overwhelming lust coursing through her.

Angel couldn't think past the longing to place her hands around his neck, tug his head down, and lift her mouth to his. Usually when he kissed her, she adored the strength of his mouth, loved the way their tongues danced, but now as she yielded to his lips on hers, she also felt him rejoice.

And his happy intensity fed her, until her yearning matched his own.

There was no skill to their lovemaking. No subtlety.

She couldn't wait that long. Her mind screamed with the need to have him now. Now. Right now.

He kissed her deep and hard. And when he broke the kiss to turn her and bend her over the desk, she noted that both of them were naked. He parted her legs, bit her shoulder.

"Yes." She threw back her head, lifted her hips, giving in to his wild demand.

He didn't make her wait. In one fierce stroke he slammed into her and she arched her spine, meeting him more than halfway. And when he reached around her hips and slid a finger into her slick folds, she might have burst right them. But his psi clamped down over her, preventing her release, holding her right on the edge.

Her hips gyrated in a frenzy of need. Her arms barely supported her as her breath came in long gasps.

Razor-sharp delight mixed with a lusty burning for completion.

She couldn't wait. Her mind spun. Her heart pounded her ribs. She was going to lose herself in a massive explosion. Her psi reached out to him and shoved hard, asking for what her body required.

And again, his psi demanded that she wait for him, even as his fingers centered on the tip of her core, driving her in a frenzy.

Stars . . . The man was torturing her with sweet pleasure and she could barely stand the tension building,

growing, burning with a ferocity that had her mind reeling, her muscles clenching.

And then he exploded, taking her with him in a storm
so fierce, she couldn't tell where his pleasure began and
hers started. And with the physical blast came a mental
one. Of domination. Of possession. Of determination.
Of . . . bliss.

Chapter Fifteen

"There is a Numan disk reader on Abacore Prime."

The computer coughed up the information before Kirek's breathing had returned to normal. "The reader on Abacore Prime is not for sale." The computer had given them more than basic facts, revealing itself to be a more advanced model than the *Raven*'s primitive system.

"Does that mean we're going to Numan?" Angel asked, her eyes focusing on Kirek with a wariness he didn't like. Had he pushed too soon and too hard once again? For a Rystani male, he was patient, but would Angel think so?

Kirek memorized the information on Numan, then wiped the computer history clean. If the Kraj followed their trail to this vidscreen, he didn't want his enemies to discover what he was interested in or why. "Once we're back on board the *Raven*, maybe I can arrange for the reader to be brought to us."

"It's not even for sale," Angel argued.

Kirek grinned. "So I'll make the owner an offer he cannot refuse."

"Like you did with me?" She boldly arched an eyebrow. But the wariness didn't leave her eyes.

He kept his tone light. "Exactly." She needed time and space to come to grips with what was happening between them. During their lovemaking, she'd startled him. For several minutes, her psi had shoved against his, seeming almost as strong as his own. Perhaps his own psi had reflected back—he couldn't be certain. However, a conversation about his actions would not be in his best interests right now.

Oh, no. She lifted her chin and locked gazes, clearly in I-want-to-talk mode. "You should have asked me if I wanted you to—"

"I did ask."

"You waited until I couldn't say no."

"As I recall you were perfectly capable of speaking."

"You transferred your lust to me . . . so your asking became rhetorical. No woman could have said no."

He sighed, wishing he could have avoided this conversation. But since he couldn't, he answered directly from the heart. "My feelings aren't for any woman. They are for you."

She swallowed hard, clearly uncomfortable. Good. Maybe now he could change the subject. And then the bell rang, signaling the end of the school day and saving him from saying more.

He opened the door and slipped out. They walked down a corridor filled with children and adults, all exiting the building.

"Don't do that again," she warned. He should have known she wouldn't drop the subject.

But even with all the noise and chaos around them, he felt compelled to argue. "You don't like the closeness we shared."

"You made me want you."

He chuckled. "I can't make you feel anything you don't want to feel."

"Damn you."

"Come on, Angel. Think. You were amenable to sex from the moment I mentioned it. I just hastened the process along a little faster than you were comfortable with."

"What you did was the difference between accelerating a skimmer and jumping into hyperdrive."

"So? You aren't angry at the speed at which I got you hot and bothered."

She rolled her eyes. "How dare you tell me why I'm angry."

"You're angry because I upped the level of intimacy between us beyond your comfort zone."

She glared at him. "You know, sometimes I really don't like you."

He laughed again, trying to keep his tone teasing. "Yeah, it's a bitch to be me because I'm never wrong."

"Correction. Sometimes I really hate you."

"Because I'm right . . . you hate me?"

"Yes." She spat at him through gritted teeth.

Kirek could see her trying to sort through her feelings and work past her confusion. He didn't know if she was succeeding, and though he was utterly certain of his take on her reservations, he wasn't at all certain she would forgive him. Not because of what he'd done, but because she didn't want to feel anything for him. Anger was her best defensive move to shut him out. And once they returned to the ship, he was about to give her another reason, several reasons, to stifle whatever feelings she had. That's why he'd risked pushing her so hard and he accepted that his plan may have alienated her instead of bringing them closer.

"Something's wrong." She stiffened, yanked him into the threshold of an empty classroom, halting them for no good reason he could see. But he was for any change at all in the subject.

"What is it?" In front of them, behind them, and to both sides kids walked, ran, and danced down the corridor. He refused to pull a weapon without a direct threat in sight, not with all the children still exiting the school.

"They know we're here."

"How do you know?" Kirek peered ahead and saw nothing alarming. No botcops. No Kraj.

"I can practically feel the malicious vibrations." At his curious glance, she shrugged. "If you were a botcop and hostiles had hidden in a school full of kids, wouldn't you surround the place and wait for them to walk out rather than take a chance of shooting a student?"

"Yes, but—"

"Trust doesn't go just one way, Kirek." Her tone remained firm, reasonable, and certain. "You have your-born-in-hyperspace psi, I sense . . . trouble. And right now, it's out there. We need to find an alternate escape route."

Angel was so strong and determined. And so was her psi. When Kirek thought back to how strong her psi had been during lovemaking, he surmised it might be possible that she had a much stronger psi than he knew.

Again he wondered if it was fate that they had met. Several times during his lifetime the Perceptive Ones had interfered in the course of history. During his last mission Kirek had learned the Perceptive Ones wanted beings to evolve to a new level of evolution to fight the Zin—but would they go so far as to arrange for his path and Angel's to meet? He didn't know. All he was certain of was his knowledge—almost from the first time he'd seen her—that fate had played a hand in their meeting.

But those were questions for the Perceptive Ones—if and when they ever met again.

Kirek nodded toward the stairs. "Let's try the basement. If that doesn't work, we'll go up to the roof."

"Thanks."

"For what?"

"Believing me."

He grinned. "Who said I believe you?"

She socked him in the arm. His psi shield protected him but he pretended it hurt.

"Ouch. That's going to leave a mark." He took her hand as they headed into a dank and dark basement. "But I've heard there's an old Earth custom that requires kissing an ache to heal it."

She shook her hand loose and flipped on a light. "You are impossible."

"Persistent." He placed a hand on her shoulder.

"Reckless." She smirked, slipped away from his touch with a casual shrug.

"I prefer to think I'm daring."

Janitorial supplies, a mop, cleaning materials, and a bucket stood in a corner with broken desks and outdated vidscreens. Electric wires jutted into central circuitry. Water dripped from pipes.

"There." He pointed. "Those water pipes in the tunnel must come in from outside this building. If we follow them to an exterior wall, we can blast our way out."

This was one of those times he really missed his astral power to extend his psi beyond his body and he had to tamp down his frustration. If he'd been fully healed, he could have zapped to the end of the pipes to see whether they should try this route or another. Now he wouldn't know what awaited them until he went to the trouble of physically moving his body there.

He consoled himself with the thought he'd be following Angel, and he never tired of watching her. "You go first. That way if I get stuck—"

"I won't be able to get back out."

"We aren't coming back this way."

She frowned but slid into the tunnel. "Ever since I've met you, you keep sending me into tight spaces."

"Hey, I wanted to walk out the front door. This was your idea." He squeezed sideways, turned his head, and sidestepped after her.

"I've probably saved your life."

He lowered his voice to a sexy whisper. "I'd be more than happy to show you how grateful I am . . . later."

"Don't you ever think about anything else?"

"Than how sexy you are?" At his words, she snorted, muttered a curse, but kept advancing.

He grinned, knowing it would irritate her if he didn't let her have the last word. "Let's see, would I rather think about your cute bottom scooting along in front of me, or the Kraj outside ready to shoot us? I'll take your hot little body anytime over—"

"Stop."

"Don't you want to hear how much I like—"

"I meant stop advancing, not making advances. I'm at a dead end."

"Already? Can you hear anything?"

"Not hardly. Not past all the hot air coming out of your big—"

"Shh." He heard the roar of an engine cycling. "Listen." Pumps? The whoosh of a generator or some kind of motor? The sound stopped. Then, nothing. But they were underground . . . then he recalled the public transportation system.

"What is it?" Angel asked.

"There's probably a mag tunnel on the other side of this wall."

"One way to find out. Give me a little room."

He scooted back and so did she. "Ready?" Without waiting for his reply, Angel raised the blaster and fired. The wall crumbled.

She advanced and knocked over rocks and crumbling foundation with her boot, then leaped out of sight. A moment later he jumped free of the tunnel onto a mag track.

"Seems like you were right." Angel spoke with no hostility and he took that as a hopeful sign. He'd found being right too often grated on some people's egos, but she was all business, turning toward the tunnel and blasting it again, causing the ceiling to cave in on the pipes. "If anyone comes looking for us, maybe they'll conclude that's a natural cave-in."

He doubted it. Close examination would reveal the blaster burn. But anything that slowed pursuit might give them an edge. He turned in the direction of the space port and began walking along the mag track.

They covered a quarter mile before Angel spoke, her voice tight. "What happens if a mag car comes through while we're in this tunnel?"

"It depends on how much room the engineers left around the vehicle. Why?"

"A mag car is coming."

"You hear it?" he asked, because his hearing seemed keener than hers and he could only hear their footsteps on rock and her breath as they hurried down the tunnel, lit by emergency lighting.

"More like I feel it."

"Vibrations through your feet?"

She shook her head. But he didn't doubt her. How could he—when he also now heard the loud-and-clear roar of the oncoming mag car bearing down on them. "You don't see a convenient cranny to hide in?"

"Not since we blasted in here." Her eyes widened with fear but she didn't panic in the face of what appeared to be imminent death. The cars sped on electromagnetic tracks, and their incredible speeds were lethal.

"All right." Time for an alternate plan. "Jump on my back."

He had to give her credit. She didn't waste time asking why. She simply leaped and locked her legs around his hips and her arms around his neck, careful not to choke him. "What now?"

"There's not enough room to flatten ourselves to the sides, above, or below. So we might as well catch a ride." He turned and faced the oncoming mag car, a silver streak, growing larger by the second.

The mag car's roar rushed into their ears. The blast of air buffeted him.

"Stars," she swore. "That's your brilliant plan. You're going to jump on?"

"Yes." The mag car appeared to be maintaining a constant speed, making his calculations a bit easier. Equations balanced in his head, matching his internal clock. He tensed his muscles, readied his psi.

"You're going to get us both killed."

"Hang on." Kirek stood, knowing the timing would be critical. With his partially healed psi, he could still manage null grav. The tricky part would be timing his wild vault against the front of the vehicle while keeping his shields tight enough to prevent the deadly force from striking them—all while finding and maintaining a grip.

"You're insane."

His heart pounded. "That's why you love me."

"I don't—"

As if they could get out of the way, the mag car's automatic warning system's siren blasted and cut off Angel's words—words he didn't need to hear. He knew she didn't love him, but if he got her killed, she might not even live long enough to yell at him, nevermind fall for him.

For Kirek, time slowed, stretched, altered. The shrieking mag car seemed to alter its velocity, but in reality, his perception changed, allowing him to time the jump with computer accuracy. One moment they stood on the electromagnetic car tracks, the next, he used his psi and muscle to jump up and angle forward.

He slammed the psi shield up, preventing them from splatting like bugs on a skimmer's windshield, then spread his arms, praying he'd find a handle, an edge of metal, anything to cling to.

But the metal was sleek, slippery. And he could only hold them with null grav for so long before he fell. He poured on more psi, his brain cells burning.

"Lower us four inches," Angel shouted into his ear, her voice tearing against the wind.

His psi already weakened, he did as she asked. His fingers found no handhold, but his toes levered onto a perch of protruding bumper. It wasn't enough. His psi drained quickly.

Angel used her own, picking up the slack as he weakened. His legs strained, his toes ached. His lungs gasped and he gulped in huge breaths.

"Hold on." He felt Angel turning her head. "There's a station up ahead."

Kirek didn't have the spare energy to nod. Or speak. He focused every psi cell on maintaining his precarious balance, not easy as the string of cars decelerated. He had to match his null grav and maintain focus on his abused toes. Sweat trickled under his arms and down his chest, his suit unable to keep up with his body's efforts.

When the cars finally stopped, Angel leaped off his back and had to pry him down. His toes were cramped and frozen. But she forced him to exit with the crowd, giving him no time to recover. If she was trying to kill him, she was succeeding, but he focused on putting one cramped foot in front of the other and couldn't spare the breath to complain.

The terminal was like any on a hundred worlds, long, shimmering gray corridors filled with crowds and bot-cops. Vendors sold snacks, meals, and drinks. Just as one botcop headed their way, Angel yanked Kirek around a corner and into a diner, found a booth near the back by an exit, and shoved him into it.

He collapsed, knowing he couldn't have gone another five steps without a rest. His pulse rate had yet to recover and his legs still shook. But even though his mind had yet to return to proper functionality, he sensed that his psi had strengthened again before he'd drained it and hopefully, he hadn't done any more damage. But he alone hadn't held them in null grav for so long. Angel had helped—a lot, and once again he wondered just how powerful her psi truly was.

Without asking what he wanted, Angel ordered from the materializer. Food and drink appeared instantly.

Kirek realized he was starving. He couldn't recall the last time they'd eaten. He'd used a tremendous amount of energy to prevent them from dying in front of that on-coming vehicle and his body demanded food as if every cell required refueling.

Kirek downed an entire packet of water, then ordered another before touching his food. While he ate, Angel pulled up their table's vidscreen and turned on the news. Dakmar only had twenty channels—and half of them were focused on the school. As they stopped on one, an announcer stated that fugitives were inside the building, and that botcops expected to apprehend the suspects for the deaths at the Lay Down Easy within moments.

The perimeter was tight with troops. The Kraj had either paid off the officials or pulled all sorts of behind-the-scenes strings to find them.

Kirek swallowed his food, his mind recovering from their ordeal. "So you were correct. If we'd tried to walk out the front doors, they'd have shot us."

"I've always had this sense of anticipating trouble. Mom used to say that trouble found me . . . but I have a knack for getting out of it."

"I'm glad." When he placed his hand over hers and squeezed, the hardness in her eyes softened.

Angel had spoken as if her ability had been a source of difficulty between her and her mother. But her special psi sense had saved them, and he thought it useful, wonderful.

He was about to say more when their images suddenly flashed on the vidscreen. The botcops had pulled their likenesses off the vidrecorders in the Lay Down Easy. Someone had altered the recording to make it appear as if he and Angel had drawn weapons, killed his contact, and then everyone else in the bar who'd tried to stop them. They were accused of a dozen crimes, from stealing a skimmer to murder.

Angel snapped off the vidscreen. "We need to return to the *Raven.*"

"She should be done by now. Let's hope they haven't confiscated her."

"I'll check."

Kirek stopped her. "Now that we're fugitives from the law, the authorities may have a reverse trace on all transmissions to and from your ship. It'll be difficult enough sneaking back without letting them know from which direction we're coming."

Angel slid deeper into their booth, then adjusted her suit to form a hood to cover her blonde hair. She also added padding around her middle. And she changed her suit to match a maintenance worker's dull tan. Following up on her idea, Kirek did the same. However, his height and the width of his shoulders tended to get noticed, no matter what he wore.

"You done?" Angel asked. She hadn't touched her food but had sipped some water.

Despite the quantity of food he'd eaten, he was far from full but they could delay no longer. He ordered a sandwich and another drink to take with him and planned to eat on the run. "All right, keep your head down, shuffle, and hunch your shoulders."

"Anything else?"

"Turn your face away from the street vidrecorders."

AN HOUR LATER after walking through the city with surprising ease, they'd arrived to find the Kraj and botcops watching her ship, and locks on the landing gear to prevent takeoff. Kirek had cleverly rerouted a smelly sanitation offloader to secretly bring them aboard. The ride hadn't been pleasant, but their suits had filtered the terrible smell and shielded them from the filth. Angel had never been so glad to be back home.

Lion spotted her where he'd been exploring in the ship's belly. He hissed at Kirek, then leapt into her arms. She hugged her cat and he placed two feet against her chest, sniffed her neck, welcomed her with a lick, then began to purr. She petted him and he settled into the crook of her arm. Normally she didn't bring him onto the bridge, but she couldn't bear to put him down so soon and kept him with her.

They'd climbed from the ship's hold through engineering and she'd made her way to the next deck. Angel's mind was full of the problem of taking the *Raven* off Dakmar when she strode onto her bridge and almost dropped Lion.

Stars. She barely recognized the ship she'd retrofitted by hand when she'd left Earth almost a decade ago.

If Lion hadn't greeted her, if Petroy hadn't been on the bridge, if she hadn't just strode down familiar passages, she would have thought that the sanitation device had delivered them to the wrong ship. Her old and reliable vidscreen was gone, replaced by a new and unaffordable model. Her com station had had a total upgrade, and the same went for weapons, engineering, and navigation. Her old gray *bendar* ship sparkled and shimmered as if it had a new coating, some kind of peculiar force field spread along the interior walls, ceiling, and floor.

A man's voice she didn't recognize greeted her. "Welcome aboard, Captain."

"Who the hell are you?" Angel spun, searching for a new crew member. But only Kirek and Petroy were on the bridge. Lion hissed and jumped from her arms, the fur on his back raising before he sprinted away. Smart animal.

"I'm Ranth, your new computer system."

"I didn't order a new computer system. Or new nav and com controls." Head reeling from the unauthorized alterations—especially the new technology she didn't understand—she turned and glared at Petroy. "I could barely afford fuel and the engine overhaul. How did this happen?"

Petroy frowned and met her gaze, but his voice remained cheerful. "Captain, I merely followed your requisition requests."

"Who paid for this?" she demanded.

"You did," Petroy replied, his gaze puzzled.

Stars. She hadn't the funds for a ship of this caliber.

She doubted anyone did. Either the computer had mixed up her order with a military or government vessel or . . . there had been some other huge mistake. And even if the old systems hadn't been scrapped, now with the botcops and Kraj after them, she didn't have the time to spend in dry dock to take out the new systems and put back in the old ones—or have the credits to put everything right.

She didn't understand how even a computer foul-up could have created such a disaster. Because the funds simply weren't . . . or were they?

She fought past her shock and spun around to face Kirek. He met her gaze, nodded at her suspicion.

And then she knew.

Kirek had taken care of the overhaul. Kirek had gone into the computer and altered her orders. Kirek had done this to the *Raven*.

Her rage boiled over. This was her ship. Her home. And he'd changed every system without telling her. How dare he put her in debt? How dare he go behind her back and counter her orders? Fury so white-hot that she could barely see caused her to have trouble speaking and breathing. "You . . . you did all this to my ship?"

He kept his tone calm and even. "We can't go after the Zin without every advantage at our disposal."

She'd be in debt for ten lifetimes—even with a lifetime one thousand years long, thanks to the life-extending properties of the suit. She closed her eyes and reopened them, hoping it was all a dream. But the shiny new instrumentation mocked her. "How . . . much . . . do I owe?"

"Consider the alterations payment for my passage."

Her eyes narrowed, her temper so out of control, she shook with the need to slap him. "We already agreed that the Zin salvage would pay for your passage."

"Then consider the ship's overhaul advance payment from a grateful Federation for your help."

He was lying to her. Again. Damn the man. "The Federation paid you to overhaul my ship? I don't think so."

"It's a . . . bonus."

"A bonus." How dare he counter her orders, lie to her, and betray her like this? She felt like a fool. Because the ship was a dream. The best and latest equipment. He'd spared no expense. She'd never seen such advanced technology. The force field on the inside walls baffled her and she had no conception of the new computer's capabilities.

And no one could accept a gift like this without there being strings and consequences attached. Without her knowledge or permission, he'd changed the balance in their relationship. He'd paid for the upgrades, and sure he could *say* she didn't owe him—just like the neighbors and family who had given her mother charity always *said* they didn't owe anything, either. Each time Angel had taken charity, she'd lost a piece of herself. She'd had to be grateful to people she didn't necessarily like. She'd had to adjust her behavior to what they found acceptable. And she'd been forced to be something she wasn't.

Nothing was free. She'd learned that as a child. Charity came with expectations—ones she might not wish to fulfill.

When she'd left Earth, she'd vowed never again. And now Kirek had gone behind her back and placed her in debt up to her eyeballs for technology she'd neither wanted nor understood. The debt might not be in credits, but it was there. Even if he never collected the debt, she would carry it with her until she paid back every credit— an absolutely impossible task.

She wanted to order Kirek off her ship. She wanted to tell him to take it all back. She wanted to pound her fists on his chest and swear at him.

Her mind spun and she couldn't think past her outrage. Her stomach churned and acid rose up her throat to choke her. Her eyes burned hot—but tears didn't come. She was too hurt to cry, too stunned to think beyond how vulnerable she now felt. She'd always avoided debt and she didn't want to owe this man who had such strong feelings for her.

Never since her childhood had she felt so trapped.

After years of freedom and happy adventures on this bridge, the *Raven*'s walls seemed to close in on her. She no longer felt as if the ship was hers. She didn't know how fast it could go. She didn't know how the computer worked, but suspected it was one of the latest models that came with a complete personality and a living neural network.

Her entire world had spun totally out of control. She was the captain of a ship that possessed technology she couldn't maintain or repair due to lack of knowledge and funds. And now she was supposed to take them all onto a mission to another galaxy when she didn't even know how to start the engines?

Her fingers itched to draw her blaster and shoot him. She wouldn't, of course. But at the moment, she wished they'd never met.

Damn him. How the hell had she let Kirek do this to her?

Chapter Sixteen

"CAPTAIN TAYLOR." RANTH'S smoothly modulated voice startled her. Angel wasn't accustomed to a computer speaking on her bridge, never mind interrupting the conversation. "The Kraj and botcops have discovered your escape route into the mag system. They've also found vidrecordings of you and Kirek in the restaurant. Soon they will extrapolate from this data that you are aboard the *Raven*. I would advise we depart."

"So now you're giving me advice?" Angel's mind worked at warp speed. She had no idea how Ranth knew what he did but clearly he'd tied into local botcop communications—which wasn't legal. The computer's vast resources excited her, but also sent a shiver of apprehension down her spine. Having a sophisticated machine that she didn't trust feeding her data and running her ship made her distinctly uncomfortable. However, that discomfort didn't stop her from seeing marvelous possibilities—ones that might save their lives.

"My function is to advise and aide your mission," Ranth stated.

Angel was certain that Kirek had programmed the computer's mission and that made her more uneasy. "Our landing gear is locked. We can't leave."

"My new technology will allow us to break the locks," Ranth disagreed.

"Do it."

"Compliance."

"Landing gear is free," Petroy confirmed. "The gear contracted and the locks fell off."

Angel should have felt relief, but instead her suspicions increased. "Who's in change of this ship?" Angel asked Ranth.

"Angel Taylor is the *Raven*'s captain."

"Suppose Kirek countermands my orders?" Angel asked, without expecting an answer. Her question was complicated by protocol and most computers would simply ignore it. But apparently Ranth followed human syntax and could infer her meaning in a human-like manner.

"My ethics program allows me to decide what to do. For example if the captain orders me to self-destruct—for no logical reason—and if Kirek countermands your order, I would obey him."

Wow. Not only had the computer not avoided answering, as she had expected, it had given her an example. Despite her mistrust, she was growing to like Ranth the more she knew about him.

"Can I lock Kirek out of your systems?" she asked.

"No, Captain."

"Why not?" She glared at Kirek who shrugged.

"Kirek has the ability to override even my will with his psi. No computer specialist has yet figured a way to stop him, but my experience has shown that he won't interfere unless the mission or lives are in jeopardy."

"How comforting." She scowled at Kirek, who had had the good sense to remain silent, but she was far from over her anger. Obviously Ranth and Kirek had a history and she suspected they'd gone on other missions together. That didn't mean she had to accept his interference. She continued to glare at Kirek. "Get off my bridge."

"You need me." Kirek didn't budge and spoke softly, but she heard the grave edge of determination in his tone. "I know how to run the special technology on this ship."

"Terrific. You alter the technology, then tell me I need you to run it?" Angel supposed she could use Ranth to teach her the *Raven*'s new capabilities, but even she could see beyond her anger and realized that escape from the Kraj was the first priority. "Ranth, start engines, get us far enough out of Dakmar space to jump to hyperdrive." She scowled at Kirek. "We still have a hyperdrive?"

He nodded and changed the subject. "Captain, I'd like your permission to send an encrypted message to Numan."

Encrypted? Angel supposed that meant the Kraj couldn't track their communications, which was another useful tool and a very expensive gadget that Kirek had added, which only served to increase her anger all over again. Her debt reminded her of Kirek's lack of trust in her. She also wondered what would happen if she refused his "request" and suspected he'd send the message anyway. "What kind of message?"

"I'd like to cut time off our journey."

"How?"

"I'll arrange to purchase the reader and arrange for a ship to transport it to meet us halfway."

"Fine." She might be furious with Kirek, but she

wouldn't shoot down a good idea just because of her seething emotions. Just because she was still shaking with the need to scream at him and pound the walls with her fists. Just because she knew that their personal relationship was over.

Done.

He'd lied to her because he hadn't trusted her enough to talk about the *Raven*'s upgrades and he'd ruined their fling, squashing any chance for enjoying the mission in his arms. She shuddered, wondering how anyone so likeable could be so secretive, so insensitive. He couldn't have wounded her more if he'd stolen her ship and shot her. Pain radiated out of every tense nerve and pounded her brain. Her head ached and her stomach twisted with nausea.

Petroy stared at his vidscreen. "Captain, the Dakmar officials are refusing to give us permission to depart."

"Damn." Angel wondered if they'd have to shoot their way free and was about to punch up their weapons' capability when the computer made a suggestion, startling her once again.

"Do you wish the *Raven* to employ shapeshifting mode?" Ranth asked.

"Shapeshifting mode?" She'd never heard of such a thing, but suspected that the new modification had a lot to do with the shimmering *bendar* walls.

"I can change the *Raven*'s hull shape so it will appear to the officials that we are a transport ship—one that has permission to depart."

"Do it." Angel hung onto her console as before her eyes, the hull expanded, as if it were a balloon taking in more air. The bridge lengthened, widened, and deepened, tripling in volume.

"Captain, isn't this new technology amazing?" Petroy's face glowed with excitement.

"Amazing," she repeated, her mind trying to take it all in and failing. She'd thought the shielding would reflect a new size on only the Dakmar officials' vidscreens. She didn't expect the *Raven*'s hull to actually change shape and enlarge, which it did until her ship was three to four times larger than the original.

"Ranth, do we have permission to leave?" Angel asked as she strode around her new bridge, trying to take in the ambiance. "And what are these new stations for?" The *Raven* now possessed several consoles whose purpose she didn't even recognize. Obviously, she had room for more crew to run the new technology, but since she hadn't known about the changes, she hadn't thought to take on crew for tasks she was ignorant about.

"The authorities are arguing with the Kraj," Ranth told her. "The Kraj are asking them to stop all ships from leaving until you are caught."

"You're intercepting Kraj transmissions?" she asked.

"Affirmative."

"Can you make the Dakmar authorities believe that the Kraj have changed their minds and are allowing us to leave?"

Looking relieved at her question, Kirek moved in front of one of the new consoles. His hands danced over the controls. "I'll take care of it."

No doubt he'd wanted to make the suggestion several minutes ago but had restrained himself from taking over, likely sensing she couldn't have coped with more insubordination, disobedience—defiance? She didn't even know the right words for what he'd done. The irony was that she trusted no one at those new controls more than Kirek. Kirek would get them out of here because his mission required it. And stars help her if she ever stood between him and his mission, because he could be secretive and ruthless when necessary. But he wrapped those traits in a man who at first and second and maybe even third glance, seemed easygoing and laid-back. It was still hard for her to believe that the same man who had made love to her with such gentleness and sensitivity could have gone behind her back and stomped all over her trust.

"The consoles have many purposes," Ranth explained. "They allow access to my new systems, the shapeshifting mode, the new weapons, and a tracking system for inventory."

"Inventory?"

"The cargo hold is full."

The *Raven* didn't have a cargo hold. Or it hadn't until Kirek had . . . She called up the cargo manifest on her vidscreen and bit back a gasp. Their entrance through engineering had bypassed the cargo bay which now held spare parts, spare engines, tools of every kind and description, welding machines, spacesuits, extra shuttles, enough food for years, entertainment for children and babies . . . What was Kirek thinking? In the last hour he'd thrown shock after shock at her, but of one thing she was certain: There would be no babies on the *Raven*.

"It appears as if this mission is to colonize the Andromeda Galaxy, not fight the Zin."

Kirek appeared to be in deep communication but he heard her and broke off from his work. "I like to be prepared."

"For children?"

He shrugged. "When Tessa and Kahn lived on Rystan, they didn't know the Endekians would invade and force them to abandon Mystique in a ship—the one I was born on. My mother told me there were no toys."

"Even I know a baby doesn't need toys," she snapped.

"We brought every child we could save with us." His voice filled with pain, as if he *remembered* crying children, worried parents, and the catastrophe that had caused his parents to lose their home world—but he'd only been a baby. Could his mind have already been so developed as an infant that he possessed genuine memories?

At the time, the Rystani had believed their world had been invaded by the Endekians who wanted glow stones, a natural atomic rock indigenous to Rystan. What they found out over a decade later was that the Zin had opened a wormhole to Endeki, and the only way to stop the Zin from sending a deadly virus through the wormhole had been to use Rystani glow stones to blow it up.

So the Zin had cost him his homeland. The Zin were the reason Kirek had been born in hyperspace. The Zin were responsible for Kirek's being caught in a blast to protect Earth that had robbed him of the use of his body for almost a decade. And now the Zin had destroyed the Federation capital planet Zenon, killing billions.

She supposed that her beef with him seemed petty in comparison. And yet, she could no more stop her feelings of betrayal than she could have talked him out of his mission. He'd hurt her because of who he was and who she was. While she understood on a logical level that saving the galaxy from the Zin was more important than his being honest with her, on an emotional level she held back disappointment and anger.

"We have permission to leave." Kirek's tone was official and cool, as if knowing that one more surprise might cause her to unleash her rage.

"Take us out of here," Angel ordered Petroy.

"I've purchased the reader," Kirek informed them, and she realized he'd been simultaneously speaking to her, changing the Kraj communications, and continuing to maintain contact with Numan, all without showing any strain.

"That was fast work," Angel muttered.

"More like hyperspeed," Petroy added.

"He probably paid ten times too much for the reader," Angel speculated.

Kirek sighed, his tone defensive and irritated. "I can't worry about saving a few credits when we must focus on the Zin."

Angel folded her arms across her chest. "You never told me how you earned the credits to pay for renovating my ship."

"Tessa shares her wealth."

"So you were born with a giant trust fund?" Angel asked.

"Something like that," Kirek admitted.

She'd never known anyone wealthy. She'd scratched and saved for every credit. And she couldn't help thinking that Kirek's personality was so set, so strong, that the amount in his bank account had little to do with who he was.

"I've also hired a transport to meet us at these coordinates." He shot them over to Petroy.

Angel nodded at her first officer. "Once we're free to jump into hyperspace, set our course to meet the other ship." She hoped all this effort would be worth going through and that the disk would produce the coordinates Kirek sought.

"There's news . . ." Kirek hesitated and looked up from his vidscreen, his eyes bleak, as if he had just been sucker punched. Mouth tight, jaw clenched, face fierce, he look like a warrior about to go into battle.

"What?"

"Ever since the wormhole destroyed Zenon, Federation scientists have been monitoring the core temperatures of their worlds."

Oh . . . no. She didn't want to hear whatever he was about to say. Her hands clenched.

As Petroy and Ranth flew the ship away from Dakmar,

Kirek spoke through gritted teeth. "Mystique has become the temporary new Federation capital and the core temperature there is heating."

Kirek's parents, his family, his friends—all of them lived on Mystique. His eyes shadowed with worry.

Despite her anger with him, no one should have to bear such pain. "Maybe the core temperature changes are normal fluctuations."

"Federation scientists don't think so. While the core temperature is rising slowly, they still have time to evacuate."

"But?"

"There's nowhere to go."

"What do you mean? The Federation is made up of over two million planets."

"And the planetary cores are heating on all of them. Even the uninhabited worlds."

Stars. She stared at him, so stunned she could barely think.

"How long . . . do we have?"

"No one knows. Since we didn't monitor the process on Zenon, we don't know if the core temperature increases slowly or exponentially."

Angel had no words. The magnitude of the coming disaster was so overwhelming. "Surely the Federation can do something?"

"They are. They're sending us to stop the Zin."

"WHY JUST US?" Angel shot Kirek a look of despair when he followed her to her quarters. She floated in her cabin, stroking Lion, barely looking at him. As Kirek's frustration with his circumstances mounted, he supposed he should consider it a victory that she had yet to order him to leave.

He'd hated the necessity of secretly altering her ship

without her permission, but he refused to face the Zin without every technological device he could assemble in their favor. Ever since Earth's exploding wormhole had pulled Kirek into the Andromeda Galaxy and he'd figured out a way to end the Zin threat, he'd known he would have to return in his body to accomplish his mission. Unfortunately the same encounter that had showed him how to destroy the Zin had made them aware he was determined to return.

After encountering one psi touch from Kirek, the Zin recognized he was dangerous to them and would never allow him to return to their home world. The Zin had psi of their own and they'd identified and tagged him as a threat. One psi touch had told Kirek that the Zin would hunt him with ruthless efficiency, and that's why he'd tried to hide his tracks by secretly going to Dakmar on a salvage vessel, instead of one of Mystique's newest ships.

And that's why he'd shipped a device to Dakmar that sat in the cargo hold, waiting for him to unpack and test. A portable computer neural net made to hold his psi—without it, he'd never sneak past the Zin.

When Kirek didn't answer right away, Angel demanded, "Kirek. Why doesn't the Federation send a fleet of ships?"

Surely Angel understood the terrible choice he'd had to make? He'd been caught between a marbalite rock and *bendar* glass, with no wriggle room. "The Zin have advanced weapons far beyond our ability to counter, and a fleet would warn them I'm coming. One lone ship has the best chance of sneaking through their defenses."

"So what would you have done if I hadn't agreed to transport you?"

"I'd intended to buy the most advanced ship I could find." He hesitated. There was more she needed to know, but not yet. He couldn't allow his frustration to override his good sense. She'd been so angry over his alterations to her ship, he didn't want to put more of the burden on her any sooner than he must. "The Zin know I'm coming and they recognize my psi. Our best advantage is that they don't know how or when I'll arrive in the Andromeda Galaxy."

"Why don't I find that comforting?"

"This ship's shapeshifting technology also has shields that mask my psi. It will allow us to get close enough to surprise them. I wanted to tell you . . ."

"But you didn't trust me. So you went behind my back."

"I wanted to tell you." Aggravation at himself and at his mission boiled through him as he realized he'd given her the perfect reason to pull back from him on a personal level. "If there was one chance in a hundred that you wouldn't let me renovate the *Raven* I couldn't risk it. I was afraid you'd say no and I wanted you with me. The mission stands a better chance of success with your help."

She lifted her head and stared at him. "So you needed my piloting skills?"

He nodded. "The *Raven* can sneak past Zin defenses—when I astral projected there, I scoped out their operation. I know what kind of traps they have, where they are and how they work. It's a one-ship job."

"And then?"

"I turn them off."

"Just like that? You walk into the deadliest enemy the Federation has ever known and just turn them off?"

He couldn't help noting that she was avoiding the personal aspects of his decision to focus on the mission—a bad sign. "The Zin are a combination of machines and live beings. If I kill the power switch to the machinery, the living beings all die."

She quirked an eyebrow at him, seemingly quite aware

he wasn't telling her how he planned to get to the Zin.
"And you, the Rystani warrior who doesn't like to kill, are
going to single-handedly destroy an entire race?"

"I must." So she'd discovered his idiosyncrasy. Kirek
objected to killing. She knew him too well, this woman he
cared for. This woman who wouldn't admit that the reason
he'd hurt her so badly was because she had feelings for
him, too.

If she'd been Tessa, she would have happily accepted
the new upgrades. Tessa was a pure business woman. But
to Angel, the *Raven* was home and carried emotional at-
tachments. He should have taken her feelings into account, understood her better—because she certainly
seemed to understand him.

She spoke evenly, her eyes giving away nothing. "To
kill in self-defense is morally acceptable to most races."

"I've always been able to find another way, but with the
Zin . . . I may have no choice." He stepped forward and
saw her eyes soften for an instant.

"The Zin are threatening everything in the Federation.
They have made this a confrontation to the death. It is not
your fault that they've forced you to kill or be killed." Her
lower jaw dropped. "Why am I trying to make you feel
better when I'm still so mad at you?"

"Because you have a good heart." She snorted. "Because
you know I needed to alter the *Raven*." Angel rolled her
eyes at the ceiling as if he were a test of her patience. "Because you know that if I had asked, you might have said no.
Our mission is simply too important for me to risk when
I might not have been able to change your mind."

"You should have asked me."

"I was wrong." He advanced another step, aching to
draw her into his arms, wishing he'd trusted her, wishing
he hadn't hurt her, hoping she wasn't going to pull back
because he'd screwed up big-time.

"Don't come any closer."

His heart ached. He should have trusted her. He should have told her the truth. He might have made the biggest mistake of his life. He'd violated her trust and the damage might be irreparable. "I am sorry."

"But that's not good enough." She bit her lower lip. "You didn't trust me and so you lied. Go away." Her tone was hard, her words abrupt.

He leaned against the threshold, trying to tamp down his frustration, wishing he could undo the damage and ease her hurt. She'd believed in him, and his error had ruined her faith.

Although he was so certain she was the only woman for him, he had gone behind her back. He couldn't even console himself that he might find another. Angel Taylor was the woman he wanted and her rejection . . . hurt.

But Kirek wasn't giving up on her or himself. "No matter how long it takes for you to forgive me, I'll still be here. Still wanting you."

"I understand what you did and why. But forgiveness isn't the issue."

Sometimes she surprised him. He'd expected her to shout at him about her ship, but she hadn't released any of her rage at him. And if she could forgive him, maybe there was yet hope for them, maybe he hadn't damaged their relationship so badly that they could not make up. "You can forgive me?"

"You claim you want a relationship but your mission is so freakin' important, and you're so driven that I always come second. And I don't trust you not to betray me again. Trust must be earned and how can I ever . . ." Her voice broke and turned raw with anger and pain. "Get out."

Her pain clawed at his innards and shredded him. "Are you sure?"

Kirek didn't like leaving her looking drawn and pale and on-edge. He especially didn't like leaving her when he knew he was responsible for her unhappiness. And he had no plan to make things right again. No idea what he could do—and that multiplied his frustration tenfold.

"I need to be alone."

Stars. She was withdrawing, rejecting . . . him. "I don't want to leave you. Not like this."

She drilled him with a hard and bitter look. "We aren't making up."

He tried a half-charming, half-sheepish smile. "You'll miss me."

She wasn't buying anything he had to sell. "I missed both my husbands after the marriages were over, but that didn't stop me from divorcing them." She glared at him. "You and I, we weren't that involved. I'll get over you."

"I'd hoped you'd be happier with me," he tried again.

He should have known better. She was too upset for him to mention anything to do with contentment.

She squared her shoulders with a dignity that knifed him. "Actually, I believe I'll be happier without you."

"Then I'll simply have to change your mind."

"Out." She pointed to her door.

"I was wrong not to talk to you. It was a mistake. A huge one. I'm so sorry."

"It doesn't matter." Then she looked away, dismissing him. But as he turned to leave, a tear brimmed in her eye, and although she shook, she stubbornly refused to allow it to fall, closing her eyes and denying herself even the relief of tears.

Kirek would have preferred she shout, hit him, or cry than receive this stiff silent treatment that he no doubt deserved. He had abused her trust. Yet she couldn't quite master the indifference she was trying to project to shut him out, and when he saw the tiny crack in her armor, he used his psi and moved at the speed of thought, so she wouldn't have time to protest.

One moment he stood in the door, the next he had gathered her against his chest. For one moment, he buried his nose in her hair and inhaled her scent. For one moment, he allowed himself the pleasure of once again touching her silky skin, hoping he could find a way to make up for what he'd done. Then Lion hissed and leaped away. Angel stiffened and cranked her neck to glower at Kirek.

"Let me hold you. Let me show you how much I care about you."

"No." She clenched her jaw stubbornly and pulled away with such determination that he let her go.

"Then I suppose you really don't want to see how much you care about me?" he suggested, making his voice gentle.

"I'm done with you. From now on—"

"If you were done with your feelings for me, you wouldn't be hurting right now."

"I'm not a fool. I won't make the same mistake twice. I trusted you. You betrayed my trust. Now I don't trust you anymore. It's that simple."

"Come on, Angel." He failed to keep the growl of frustration out of his voice, but he still managed to keep his tone gentle. "There were mitigating factors. Don't you think I wanted to tell you about the *Raven*'s overhaul? Don't you think I wished I didn't have to repair the ship in secret? But if I'd asked and if you'd told me no, there was no longer time to purchase another ship and you wouldn't be making this journey with me. I couldn't bear to lose you."

"You made your choice. And now, you've lost me anyway."

"That's harsh."

She shrugged, picked up Lion and stroked him. "That's life."

Chapter Seventeen

DURING THE NEXT few days, Angel buried her hurt in work. Every waking minute she spent either on the bridge or learning about the *Raven*'s new capabilities. She required the crew to learn, too. Frie spent all her time in engineering, Petroy at navigation, and Leval studied battle capabilities at the com. But as captain, Angel had to know everything from how long it took to jump to hyperspace to the limits of the shapeshifting mechanism to the nutrients required for the food materializers.

Keeping her mind active on the marvelous new technology was the best way to cope. However, while checking the inventory in the cargo hold, she found another terrific device to use to let off steam.

Ranth, a marvel of efficiency who had the capacity to carry on thousands of tasks, including many conversations at once, informed her, "The holosim will allow you to practice warrior skills against a programmed opponent."

Angel spent at least an hour a day honing her skills with her favorite weapon—her blaster. But she also drilled in hand-to-hand combat, and since she'd given Ranth strict orders to make sure she didn't run into Kirek, she'd successfully avoided him.

She programmed the holosim to allow her to punch and kick her imaginary opponent, and slowly she warmed up, then began a sweat. She jabbed with her left, punched with her right, and rolled left, appreciating the extra room and the new toy.

The larger *Raven* had so many advantages she could have doubled as a luxury cruiser. There was an arboretum filled with plants that grew fresh fruits and herbs, a gym, and a kitchen with a materializer that could create any food she desired out of nutrients, as well as a sophisticated medical center that could heal bones or perform surgery.

The *Raven*'s new shapeshifting mode was a spectacular mix of engineering and technology that she didn't understand and probably never would. When the ship changed shape, nanotechnology expanded or contracted matter and the special shielding made the hull five times stronger. And the weapons . . . a girl could drool over the laser cannons, never mind the fleet busters and the fire dousers. Her new hyperdrive engines were a marvel— and the systems were in triplicate, so that even if *two* failed, the third could still carry on alone.

Angel stopped the combat program for a moment, rubbed her overheated brow, and gave her suit a moment to cool her. Her thoughts kept roaming and if she wasn't careful, they always circled around to Kirek. Angel required a higher level of difficulty to make herself focus. "Ranth, change the holosim level to six, please."

"Compliance."

A new holosim formed, bigger, stronger, and faster than the last. But despite the necessity of increasing her physical efforts along with her psi energy, her mind refused to concentrate.

With different decks and several passages to the bridge, she'd avoided Kirek, so far. But a few days hadn't been enough time to heal the open wound. She might need weeks or months to stop feeling battered by what had occurred. And it didn't help that she totally understood his point of view.

She kicked, spun, placed a back-hand slice to a throat. In turn she walked right into a jab, which stung, but she knew a real one would have snapped her neck. Damn. She shifted and punched, knowing that in a real situation she couldn't count on her opponents to pull their punches.

For a few moments she pummeled the holosim, pretending he was Kirek. She'd only wanted a fling. And it shouldn't have been so painful to end, but she seemed to be hurting as badly as when her marriages ended. She told herself she hurt because sex had turned into a relationship, and the end of her relationship meant a failure, a failure in judgment. All along she'd known Kirek would do whatever he must to complete his mission. She just hadn't ever thought that her own desires would stand in the way of his . . . or that he would trample her wishes with the same determination that he'd dealt with the Kraj.

Ranth interrupted her session with a warning. "Your heart is racing faster than the program recommends. Your blood pressure is—"

"I'm fine." She jammed an elbow into her opponent's gut and he hooked her foot, taking her to the mat. She curled, fell, and rolled.

By now she knew Kirek well enough to understand that beneath his charming, laid-back attitude was another facet. He was much more complicated than the man he showed to the world and also possibly to her.

He'd avoided talking about how he intended to get to the Zin. Oh, when they'd spoken, he'd smoothly led the subject in a different direction, telling her how the ship's new shielding hid his psi, but she'd still sensed his evasive tactics with an instinct that had yet to let her down.

And if she wasn't in such debt, she could have given up the idea of salvaging the Zin world and parted ways with Kirek. However, now there was so much more at stake than her own wants and needs—like all of Earth, and the entire Federation. If she turned her back on Kirek, it would be like turning her back on everyone and everything she knew. And she couldn't just give up. It was no more in her nature to turn around and run away than it was for her to stay home and make babies.

So she had to pull herself together. When she saw Kirek again, she wanted no feelings attached. She didn't want anger or hurt or aggression to cloud her judgment, but she didn't know if denying her emotions was possible.

She'd rolled on the mat, but her opponent came in, using superior strength to pin her. Rotating one hip, she tried to topple him, but he countered with a shift to the side.

Out of breath, lungs burning, she yielded. "Ranth, I've had enough."

The holosim vanished, and she slowly shoved to her feet to find Kirek watching her, his eyes calm and blue, his face full of lively interest. Ah, she'd missed looking at the way light reflected off his cheekbones, missed talking to him, missed making love. With just his appearance, he'd managed to demolish every barrier she'd spent the last three days building and it annoyed the hell out of her.

She used the excuse of shoving a lock of hair from her eyes to break her eager stare. "Ranth, I should fry your circuits."

"Don't blame him," Kirek said.

"I'll blame whoever I want," she practically growled, and forced herself to take a deep breath.

"I overrode his program that allowed you to avoid me," he admitted without even a hint of regret.

"Why?" She placed one hand on her hip, straightened her spine, and raised her chin. And held her anger in check that he could so easily outmaneuver her. No doubt he had a good reason and that aggravated her all over again. But she refused to throw a temper tantrum only to feel stupid after he told her some galaxy-shattering reason.

"We're about to jump out of hyperspace to meet the Numan ship." He paused and she said nothing. "I'm planning to visit the other ship to retrieve the reader."

"I'm not letting you out of my sight."

"Why?"

"I've already told you, I don't trust you. For all I know, you plan to leave in the other ship and I'll never recover the salvage you promised me."

"You won't get rid of me that easily." His tone was mild but his eyes stirred with shadows. "Besides, why would I overhaul the *Raven* if I intended to leave it behind?"

"Maybe you need two ships. Perhaps the *Raven* is a decoy so you can slip past the Zin by yourself in another ship."

"I wouldn't do that."

"Not even if it meant saving the entire Federation?" When she threw the accusation at him, he flinched, and she shook her head. "Someone's got to look out for the *Raven* and my crew, so if you go to the other ship to pick up the reader, I'm going with you."

Kirek turned to leave, but spoke as he did so. "Fine. Let's go."

*   *   *

KIREK DIDN'T LIKE thinking he may have lost all hope
with this woman and hoped he could repair the damage
he'd done. But he had no idea how to fix things. Words
wouldn't work when she didn't believe them. And after
she'd asked Ranth to ensure they avoided one another,
he'd tried to accept she needed some time to think. But
the days apart didn't appear to have done him any good—
she was clearly still furious.

And he was so far gone, he wanted her anyway. Even if
she didn't trust him—he loved her still. Even if she didn't
want to be around him—he loved her.

To make things worse, he'd carefully unpacked the neural net computer chip—the one he'd had manufactured to
his specifications to hold his psi. Once he entered the Andromeda Galaxy and left the *Raven*'s heavy-duty protective shielding, the Zin would recognize his psi. In order to
stay alive, Kirek planned to place his psi into the chip—a
chip that would mask his true essence.

But it didn't work. And although he'd spent the last few
days trying to fix it with Ranth's help, the device
wouldn't shield his psi. And they couldn't find a way to
increase the shielding without increasing power—and
then the device became way too large to be portable.

Stymied, he spent almost as much time thinking about
her—like a lovesick teenager—as he did the chip. Even
as they left in the shuttle and she piloted the tiny vessel
for the Numan ship, his focus was on her. How good she
smelled. How he wanted to thread his fingers through her
long hair, massage the anxiety from her tense shoulders,
and kiss away her distrust.

During his time on Endeki as a sexual hostage, Kirek
had been with many beautiful woman, but none of them
had had Angel's independent spirit, or her generous heart
that she tried to hide in practicality, or her enthusiasm to
try new things. He understood that even though she

hadn't wanted to enjoy the *Raven*'s upgrades, she couldn't stop herself from appreciating them.

"Space to Kirek." Angel snapped her fingers in his face as she turned off the shuttle's engines after docking inside the Numan ship's bay. He'd been so deep in thought, he'd barely noticed how easily she flew the new shuttle or set it down softly with the ease of an experienced pilot. "Open the hatch."

The Numan crew waited in their shuttle bay with a reader that Kirek hoped would reveal the coordinates to the portal. The bay was about the same size as the *Raven*'s but the low ceiling made the space feel cramped, especially with a party of three there to greet them.

He popped the hatch and followed Angel out, noting she was fully armed. Kirek rarely went unarmed either, but he'd hidden his weapons in the loose flow of his suit's fabric. The group waiting for them appeared harmless and eager to meet, their stances relaxed, their faces set in amiable expressions.

"Welcome to the *Teardrop of Numan*." A petite woman stepped forward from between two of her accompanying crew. She had no hair on her head and wore a multi-colored bandanna. Huge gold loops hung from her ears and smaller ones pierced her nose and brow. "I would offer refreshments but my orders are to deliver the reader immediately." She held out the reader, which fit in her palm.

"Something's wrong." Angel spoke in an urgent voice, but had used privacy mode, so only he could hear. Her hand dropped to her blaster.

"What is it?" Kirek asked.

Since Kirek had hired this ship, he'd been concerned about Angel and the chip to transfer his psi. Although he'd automatically done background checks of the entire crew before sending them on such an important mission, he knew that even the best background checks could fail. He'd been so busy thinking about the chip and Angel he hadn't given security much thought.

"Trouble's coming." Angel's tone was clipped.

Kirek accepted the reader. "Thank you. Time is short. We must leave immediately for—" The moment he took possession of the reader, a dozen Kraj dropped from the ceiling.

Angel's hand was already on the blaster. She drew her weapon and started shooting. Expert shots took out two Kraj before they hit the deck.

The Numan captain looked shocked, but she pulled her weapon and fired at the Kraj alongside Angel. So they hadn't been betrayed. The Kraj had sneaked aboard.

Even as he analyzed, Kirek stuffed the reader inside his suit and drew his own weapon. Before he could shoot, three Kraj locked their sights on him. And fired. Beams of radiant red light caught Kirek in their direct path and knocked him to his knees. Worse, the light slammed his psi and pain erupted in every nerve ending.

He couldn't move. Or draw breath. Or gasp out one word. It felt as if the red light had gathered up his psi and seared it with fire. Kirek hadn't known a being could withstand such agonizing pain and remain conscious.

Agony wracked him as the fight around him continued. The Numan captain was down, along with both officers. While the three Kraj held him tight in the deadly red beams, another had Angel pinned behind the shuttle where she'd dived to take cover.

With Angel unable to change position, the three Kraj holding him in the scorching red lights advanced. The light became more focused and burned so hot he was certain his skin would char.

Angel peered at him from behind the shuttle, but kept firing at the Kraj. "Kirek, I'll cover you. Get over here."

Kirek couldn't so much as turn his head. His flesh felt as if the sun itself consumed him from the inside out. His brain pulsated with cramps and wave after wave of nausea left him too incapacitated to move.

Kirek wanted to tell her to flee before the Kraj turned the red weapon on her. But the scream stuck in his lungs. Stars. Agony twisted his limbs and he tumbled, slammed into the ground, too weak to even put out a hand out to prevent his head from slamming into the deck.

With relentless precision, the Kraj advanced. One of them lifted a blaster to finish Kirek. Angel fired and the Kraj crashed to the deck.

Twisted in pain, Kirek saw Angel lunge toward him at the speed of thought. He shouted, "Don't."

But the red light caught her. Agonizing pain clawed at him. The excruciating red light hit Angel, too. But she landed on her feet and didn't so much as whimper. Sparking, crackling silver light bounced and popped off her, light so bright it hurt his eyes. Fear gnawed at him that she was about to be consumed in the paralyzing, punishing pain and he couldn't move to help her.

Then his suit's filters adjusted and a silver spherical ball of light popped into place around Angel. Around him. Was this the Kraj's diabolical plan to kill them both?

Wrong. Wrong. He was missing something critical.

The silver sphere wasn't another Kraj weapon. It was a shield—a shield that Angel had somehow constructed with her psi. The intensity of his pain lessened, but his nerves still twitched with the aftereffects.

Angel shot the last two Kraj. The red beams of their weapons disappeared and Angel kneeled beside him. "Kirek?"

Pain still held him in its clutches. "Hurt."

"I'll take you back to our new medical bay. Just hold on."

* * *

ANGEL HAD USED null grav to carry Kirek and one of the
the red-beaming weapons back to the shuttle. She figured
they needed to know how it worked so they could counter
it next time. With Kirek unconscious in the new medical
bay, all beeping machines and ticking sounds that she
didn't understand, she paced, stopped, then started.

"Ranth, what's his prognosis?"

"The damage to his nervous system is extensive."

"Can you fix it?"

"I'm attempting to do so, but I can give no guarantees
how the nerve grafts will take."

She swallowed hard and forced words past her despair.
"Will he live?"

"I'm uncertain. The same as the last time you asked."
Ranth paused. "I will inform you the moment there's any
change."

Angel went back to pacing. Frie had used the reader on
the disk and they now had the coordinates of the world on
the rim that possessed the portal. Even as Kirek remained
unconscious, she'd jumped the *Raven* into hyperspace,
hoping that by the time they arrived at the portal, Kirek
would have recovered.

And now she had nothing to do but worry. Nothing left
to do except wonder why she wanted to cry—every time
she looked at Kirek. Somehow, she'd managed to ignore
her feelings for him when he'd been healthy. But now that
he might die, she was so upset that she'd only spent a few
minutes on the bridge in the last six days.

She couldn't sleep. She wasn't hungry. She had to
force herself to take in liquids. The consuming worry
wasn't because without Kirek, the mission couldn't succeed. Her concern was personal. If he died on her . . .
Stars.

When had he become more than the fling she'd wanted? When had he become more to her than someone she could easily walk away from? Was it the first time he'd smiled at her or teased her or made love to her? She didn't know.

Just seeing him lying in that chamber, with nanoprobes going into and out his nose and throat, made her nauseated. The thought of him never again waking up, of him never again teasing her, of him never again making her angry or making love to her was forcing her to realize how much she cared about him.

She should have engaged the psi shield earlier. The Kraj had had him in the red beams for almost a minute. A few seconds longer and not even the medical equipment would have had a chance to save him. But, since Angel had never before activated a psi shield and didn't know exactly how she'd engaged it, she was lucky to have done so at all. She'd been so upset. Kirek's face had been twisted into a horrific mask of agony. And she'd just wanted to help him and then the shield had been there.

She didn't understand what had happened. And the one person who might be able to explain it to her was beside her in the medical bay—unconscious.

"Ranth?" she called the computer.

"Yes?"

Kirek looked pale and much too large for the medical bed. She'd give anything for him to be back on his feet. "Surely there is something else you can try?"

"There isn't."

"Perhaps a doctor, a specialist we can consult?"

"My medical library is the most extensive in the Federation. If there is a better way, it's not known by—"

"Ranth." Angel stopped pacing. "Kirek just moved his hand."

"It's a reflex."

Angel placed her hand in his. Kirek squeezed. "That was no reflex." She peered over at him. "Kirek. You are in the medical bay. Ranth says you're going to be fine."

"I did not," Ranth argued.

"All those medical books and you don't have a shred of bedside manner," she chided the computer.

Ranth almost sounded insulted. "What is bedside manner?"

"It means that thinking positive thoughts might help him heal."

"That is not logical, but it is sometimes true. The mind can help healing—even though we don't understand how or why. In the future I'll try to maintain a more upbeat attitude."

Angel ignored the computer and leaned over Kirek. "Kirek, can you hear me? It's time to wake up."

His eyes fluttered open. At first they rolled and didn't focus. Angel kept talking softly. "We were attacked by the Kraj. You were caught in the beam of a weapon and I brought you back to the *Raven* to heal. The new medical facility is making you well, repairing damaged nerves. And I'm grateful to have it, because it gives you a chance to live, gives us a chance for . . ." She trailed off and bit her lip, uncomfortable with saying more.

"What?" Kirek asked.

Angel's heart lightened. He was conscious. "How do you feel?"

"Gives us a chance for what?" Kirek asked and she realized he'd been listening to her, understanding her.

A reconciliation? A chance to be together? She didn't say what she was thinking. "Gives us a chance to fight the Zin."

"Is that all?" His gaze probed hers, and she didn't need a prognosis from Ranth to see that mentally, Kirek was as sharp as ever.

"I'm so glad you didn't die." Happiness suffused her and if she'd had the energy, she would have danced around the room. She settled for squeezing his hand.

"Were you only worried about how you would find the salvage without me?" he pressed, his gaze searching her eyes as if he could force her to say what he wanted.

Stars. Leave it to the man to awaken from a coma, know exactly what was going on, and use the knowledge against her when she was exhausted, sick with worry, and at her weakest emotional point ever. And despite his query, she still was so happy to see him that she grinned and smoothed his hair away from his forehead.

"You need to concentrate on getting well."

"I'd feel much better if you'd give me a hug." He edged over to make room for her beside him.

"Now I know you're going to be fine. No doubt while I've been worried about you, you've been resting and thinking up ways to irritate me."

"Sweetheart,"—*Sweetheart,* he'd called her *sweetheart*— "if I'd been awake, I would have been thinking about much better things to do than irritate you."

She snorted.

"Better things, like talking," he continued.

"And going behind my back?"

"Like holding hands."

"And reprogramming my ship?"

"Like kissing."

Lion leapt onto the bed, right onto Kirek's chest. He curiously sniffed the nanotubes, arched his back. Kirek reached up to pet him and Lion peeled off and sprinted away.

"The cat has good instincts," Angel teased.

"Yeah, he couldn't resist coming to see if I was all right either." Gently Kirek tugged her next to him in the bed and she couldn't resist, not when she wanted to hold him so badly. "But he might have gotten a bit more sleep than you have. You look like hell."

She sighed. "You sure know how to compliment a woman and make her fall in love with you."

Kirek chuckled. "It's so good to hear you tell me that you love me."

"I did not—"

"Hush." He kissed the top of her head, drew her against his side, and the stubborn man went back to sleep as suddenly as he'd awakened. Only this time she could relax too because his sleep was natural and healing. Somehow, she'd come to care for him and she would have to accept it. The idea should have worried her. But in no time at all, Angel was sleeping deeply—without nightmares—for the first time in almost a week.

Chapter Eighteen

"How DID YOU make that shield to protect us?" Kirek asked Angel from his medical bed, one day after he'd awakened from his coma. To his dismay, he had needed to continue to hold still so the nanoprobes could finish repairing the nerve damage. But as he healed, his impatience to be up and around was checked by Angel's almost continuous presence. She'd only left him once, to retrieve the chip, so he could work on the faulty shielding for his psi while he recovered.

"I'm not sure." Angel's brow furrowed. "One moment the red beams were on you, the next, I'd moved to your side and the shield popped up." She frowned. "When I brought you back, I also recovered the Kraj weapon that caused your nerve damage. Frie took it apart to see how it worked. She's attempting to make a shield for you."

"Give her my thanks." Kirek placed the chip aside for a moment. "Do you think you could form your shield again?"

She shrugged and looked reluctant to try. "Why?"

"I was barely conscious when you did it and I'm curious." He'd tried to keep his voice casual but she knew him so well.

She narrowed her eyes, her expression thoughtful. "Why are you curious?"

"Your shield saved my life."

"So now we're even. I haven't forgotten how you pushed me out of the way of the Kraj blast in the shuttle bay. But I still think you owe me a truthful answer about your psi shield."

"I *am* curious." He turned onto his side, bent his elbow, and propped his chin on his palm. "While I appreciate Frie's efforts on my behalf, I'd like to try and replicate the shield, so I can protect myself. Since I can't make a shield like that," Kirek admitted, "and I don't know anyone else who can, I thought . . ."

Her eyes widened, as if she hadn't realized that she'd done something extraordinary. "What are you saying?"

"I have a theory I'd like to test. If you would build the shield for me, I could give you better answers."

"Fine." She closed her eyes and appeared to focus inward. And the silver shield again popped into place around them, shimmering and crackling.

Wow. She'd created the shield with apparently much ease and little effort.

During his time in the coma, Kirek's psi had healed along with his damaged nerves. Perhaps the nerves had helped generate his psi, no one really knew for sure. But he'd recovered enough of his own powers to examine her shield. And it was pure energy. Dazzling.

Tight, controlled, and yet immeasurably powerful, Angel was generating a psi field he'd never seen before. Woven, spinning, it appeared to reflect back anything that touched it—air, light, dust, or psi thought.

"How long can you maintain it?" he asked, trying and failing to erect such a shield. But he'd suspected as much. He couldn't teach someone to see or hear or to slow time in a crisis or calculate complex equations in their heads, either. It was simply a skill he had due to a fluke in his DNA. Sure, he'd learned to use the skill, but he couldn't teach someone to mimic his abilities since they didn't possess the proper genetic makeup.

"Most of the effort is in building the shield," she answered, awe in her own voice at what she'd done. Angel snapped it off and stared at him. "All right. You had a chance to examine it. Can you do it?"

"No. Whatever you are doing, I can't replicate it."

"So . . . what . . . does that mean?"

"It means that your psi is much more powerful than you . . . or I thought." Kirek debated how much to tell her and decided to come clean. She deserved to know. "During my last mission, I met two Perceptive Ones, members of the ancient race who built the machines that make our suits and who created the Sentinels."

"I thought they'd vanished eons ago?"

"The Perceptive Ones left their bodies behind eons ago. They are beings of pure energy and thought."

"Are they immortal?"

"I don't know. But they hinted they are trying to help us evolve."

"Evolve?"

"It's generally thought throughout the Federation that because I was born in hyperspace, my psi is more powerful than other beings. But the truth is that I had a powerful psi before I was born."

She didn't look surprised by his revelation. "When you

told me about the Endekian invasion and when your parents had to leave Rystan, you sounded as if you remembered it yourself. But you were only a baby."

"I was born with almost adult mental awareness and maturity. Even when I was in the womb, during a healing circle—which is when a group of Rystani merge their psi—I could speak with my mind and had vast psi power."

She honed in on the important point. "So if being born in hyperspace can't account for your psi, then what made your psi so strong?"

"I don't know. Perhaps it was simple genetics. But I now believe the Perceptive Ones helped alter my chromosomes on an electromagnetic level. And it simply cannot be a coincidence that I've just happened to meet you, the one other woman in the galaxy with a psi as unusual as mine."

She snorted. "Maybe other women can also make a shield. But even if what you say is true about my psi, I'd think the Perceptive Ones would have better things to do than pick me and you as partners. It's likely lots of people have a strong psi but don't use it. I mean I've gone an entire lifetime without suspecting I was any different from others."

"What about the way you sense trouble? And the way you always happen to be in the right place? Right *before* the Kraj swooped out of the ceiling, you rolled into the best position in the shuttle bay to take them out."

"So I have good instincts."

"What you have are extraordinary psi powers."

She grimaced. "You make me sound like a holovid superhero."

"Your psi has probably kept you alive and allowed you to leave Earth behind. Perhaps your luck at cards isn't luck at all."

"Do you know how outrageous you sound?"

"My theory isn't so far-fetched." He searched her face and could see that what he'd told her about her psi hadn't sunk in yet, not on an intellectual or emotional level. "The Perceptive Ones need us to keep the Zin out, so they are helping us evolve so we'll be strong enough."

She gave him one of those do-you-really-think-I'm-going-to-believe-you-looks. "The Perceptive Ones told you they are making us evolve?"

"They mostly told Xander and Alara, and I heard enough directly from the Perceptive Ones to guess the rest. And the moment I saw you, I felt as if you were my destiny."

She threw up both hands into the air, clearly aggravated with him. "You're scaring me. Ranth, is his brain healing okay?" Angel quipped, but her eyes looked uneasy as the implications of what he'd been telling her began to sink in.

"Kirek's brain is functioning at his usual efficiency," Ranth replied.

Kirek could only hope she'd embrace her newfound abilities—not run from them.

Being different wasn't always easy. Being very different, set one apart. And those who didn't know Kirek well tended to treat him as an oddity. If he hadn't come from such a loving family, he could have easily resented how his psi caused others to be wary of him. Friendships and trust took a long time to build. And for Angel, who didn't have loving parents or a stable childhood, it might be hard for her to accept what she was, and how much potential she had because of her psi.

He suspected she wasn't using but ten percent of her capacity. When she fully explored her psi, she might be more powerful than him. He only hoped she would appreciate the gift.

Kirek spoke openly, telling her much of what she must

have already realized on her own. "With my psi burned, I didn't trust my judgment, but I never changed my initial impression. It's almost as if I'm compelled to want you. I can't imagine ever being with anyone else. Ever."

He knew his words would frighten her. She stiffened, refused to look at him. "Are you saying you have no choice? Because I do. And I'm not going to make babies with you because you think some ancient race wants us to combine our DNA. Forget it."

"Hey. I didn't say they want us to make babies." Kirek hesitated. "Maybe they saw to it that we have what we need to defeat the Zin. Or maybe they saw to it that we would meet and hoped we'd work together. Or maybe our meeting is a cosmic coincidence. Maybe everyone has our psi potential—"

"You don't believe that."

"That doesn't mean I'm not right."

She rolled her eyes. "Very likely it's the first time you've ever been wrong."

He shrugged. But he sensed the fine hand of the Perceptive Ones. They'd been a presence in his life for a long time. He'd ridden on one of the galaxy-guarding Sentinels they'd built. He'd had the Perceptive Ones place the formulas in his head that had helped blow up the Zin wormholes and rid the Federation of a deadly virus. He was accustomed to them messing with his life.

Angel wasn't. And clearly she didn't like the idea of possibly being created and used by an ancient alien race. Once again Kirek tried to give her time to adapt and adjust to what he'd just revealed.

He turned his attention to the psi device and tried to reconfigure the power to enhance energy. And all the while, he told himself that he had to have faith in Angel to accept what she was—what she could become. And he fervently hoped that future included him.

ANGEL HAD SO much to think about, when the *Raven* jumped out of hyperspace, she was still learning her new systems and mulling over all Kirek had told her. While she now admitted that she cared a great deal for the Rystani warrior, she wasn't accepting his we-are-fated-to-be-together story.

After Kirek had healed she'd made it clear she'd welcome him back into her quarters. Almost losing him had made her realize how strong a bond they had, and although she was still upset every time she thought about what he'd done to her ship, she'd forgiven him. And she missed making love. But he'd been working almost 'round the clock on his psi device with Ranth and Frie, trying to finish before they arrived at the portal. And when he staggered bleary-eyed to his quarters, she feared he'd suffer a relapse if she interrupted his sleep.

So she was on the bridge with Petroy when they exited hyperspace into the K-5 Solar System. She peered at the small orange sun and the five planets, which all had moons. "Any sign of the Kraj?"

"None, Captain." Petroy checked his sensors. "The northernmost continent of Jurl, the second planet, is our target. Should I set a course?"

"Proceed. And inform Kirek of our estimated time of arrival in orbit. We'll take the shuttle down to explore before attempting to bring the *Raven* through the portal." She turned from Petroy to her own vidscreen. Jurl was comprised of mostly salty oceans. There were only two continents and the southern one was swampy and appeared to flood in the low-lying areas. Extreme weather systems, hurricanes, swirled around the southern continent but the north seemed oddly stable. "Ranth, scan both continents and the oceans for life."

"There are no life forms with advanced intelligence."

"Anything dangerous?"

"Not unless you eat one of the poisonous plants."

"Any sign of the portal?" she asked.

"There are ancient ruins and an interesting irregularity near the northern pole."

"What kind of irregularity?"

"I'm uncertain. There appears to be a large fissure between two *marbalite* mountains. The fissure sucks in light and air, even dust particles. Even at extreme magnification I can't see much."

Had they found the portal? "Is anything coming out of the fissure?"

"Not at this time."

"And there's only the one anomaly?"

"That's correct."

Kirek joined them on the bridge, greeted her and Petroy with a nod, and flicked on the science vidscreen. "Ranth, does the anomaly contain technology that works on the same principles as the Perceptive Ones' technology?"

"Clarify, please."

Kirek responded with a mathematical equation that she suspected had something to do with the space-time continuum and wormhole theory. Since she didn't understand theoretical physics, she stopped listening and focused on Jurl. The world looked old. Barren.

She wondered if the Perceptive Ones had once thrived on the planet or had simply used it as an outpost. She wondered if the anomaly was the portal, and if it still worked, and who had originally constructed it and why. Had wars been fought over the portal? Was it a technology that had altered the course of civilizations and the entire future of the Perceptive Ones? Or had it been abandoned and considered useless?

And if they entered the portal was their trip a one-way voyage to Andromeda? Because nothing was coming out.

And when they landed on Jurl, would they find and comprehend the instructions or the controls that they needed to steer them to Andromeda? Because otherwise they could end up anywhere. Like in a black hole. Or a parallel universe.

The unknown should have been frightening. Instead, excitement and adrenalin had her eager. She couldn't wait to go through to see where they ended up.

She caught Kirek's gaze and he didn't smile as she expected. "What's wrong?"

"We couldn't power the psi device with enough energy for it to be reliable."

"You don't need it until we go through the portal, right? The *Raven*'s new shields will prevent the Zin from detecting your psi. So you have more time to . . ." And that's when it hit her. "Damn you. You intended to go through the portal alone. Without the *Raven*."

"Just to check things out. To make sure it was safe and that we could return."

She swore and drilled him with a fierce stare. "Did you ever consider that I'd want to go?"

"Did you ever consider that it's dangerous and you might get killed?"

"Do you think I'm stupid enough to believe there's a fairy-tale world just sitting there waiting for us to salvage? With no risk? No work? Do you see stupid written on my forehead?"

"Stupid? No. Reckless, yes."

She rolled her eyes. "I'll take that as a compliment." And she took immense pleasure in tossing words he'd used on her back at him. "You need me."

He raised an eyebrow. "I do?"

"If your device doesn't work, I can engage my shield to mask your psi."

"You're not that strong."

"We don't know how strong I am," she countered.

He shook his head. "I'm not risking the fate of the Federation on—"

"You may not have a choice."

His tone remained gentle and very certain. "I appreciate your offer, but it's not an option." He held up his hand to delay her protest. "The passageways I must go through are very narrow. You wouldn't be able to stay close enough to me to maintain the shield."

"So if you don't fix the chip—"

"I'll make it work."

"—Then we aren't going?"

"I'll make it work," he repeated.

"And if you don't succeed?" she asked, her pulse racing.

"Let's worry about that later." Their gazes locked.

Angel could see he still had another plan if his original didn't work. But before his gaze dropped, she read fear there—whether for him or her or the Federation she didn't know. But Kirek was a man who'd survived astral extension and a wormhole blast into the Andromeda Galaxy. He'd seen what was waiting for them. And the Zin were obviously formidable.

So if he was frightened by his alterative plan, she supposed she should be shaking—but Angel couldn't manage to even worry much. Right now Jurl waited for them and she couldn't wait to explore the new world.

KIREK SLEPT DURING the shuttle ride down to Jurl. He awakened when Angel landed near the anomaly they'd noted from space. The brief nap had revived him and allowed him to recover from some of his exhaustion, but he remained irritable. Lack of sleep and sex tended to do that to him, especially when he still hadn't found a workable, portable power device to hold his psi.

But he put aside the problem and hoped his unconscious mind would come up with a solution as they explored the surface. Millions of years of weather had eroded what had probably once been high mountains, leaving gently rolling hills. And sharp edges from volcanic action were now rounded and smooth.

To reach the fissure in the bottom of a canyon was an easy walk over moderately sloping dull brown rock.

Overhead, the sky was blue, the atmosphere too thin for clouds. Without their suits, the temperature would have caused hypothermia to set in. But the lack of life and the cold didn't bother him as much as the silence. Kirek was accustomed to birds in the sky, insects chirping, rivers running, a gentle breeze rustling the trees, and this part of Jurl was flat and dry and dead.

They strode past ancient ruins, the *bendar* foundations of giant buildings long gone. If the planet's dwellers had once possessed a superior level of technology, there was little evidence left behind. Then again, this was a very old world.

They followed a path that had been carved by the erosion of wind, ever so slowly treading down toward the fissure. Their steps echoed oddly in his ears, their breaths somehow a violation of this dead world.

Kirek wasn't usually given to a fanciful imagination but between the ancient barren hills, the failing orange sun that barely heated Jurl, and the lack of life, he was reminded that failure to complete his mission might allow the Zin to destroy every world in the Federation, burning all life out of the galaxy, leaving not so much as a grave behind to mark the passing of billions.

Kirek wished he could check in and find out how the Federations' planet cores were doing. Had more worlds exploded? Yet, he didn't dare. Communications could be traced and he didn't want the Zin to find his location.

"Is that the portal?" Angel spoke, her tone soft, almost reverent.

Kirek peered at the strange sight. Two thick *marbalite* columns rose toward the sky and abutted stone cliffs. Their view of the valley, a stone floor between two cliffs, ended at the columns. Kirek had never seen anything like what stretched between those columns. The atmosphere appeared to fold in on itself, like an out of focus vidstream. Shadows and indiscriminate shapes kept changing, the edges blurring, preventing his eyes from discerning a pattern. And the entire portal rippled, like gray waves of water, only vertically and without reflecting light.

"It's some kind of space distortion," Kirek finally answered. "We'll have to go closer to see if we can find the mechanism to operate it."

"It's wide and high enough to easily fit the entire *Raven* through it." Angel sounded irritatingly curious and cheerful, as if the dying world had no effect on her. "Do you think we can fly around the back?"

"Let's check out this side first."

As they walked closer, the air around them seemed to go dead, as if a giant filter sucked the life out of the atmosphere. Kirek knew his notion had no scientific merit but the portal felt very alien, and his nape itched.

Beside him, Angel was practically bouncing with enthusiasm. Only his slower pace seemed to be keeping her from running fearlessly up to the portal and throwing herself against it. Clearly where she sensed opportunity and adventure, he sensed danger and menace—but perhaps that was because he'd already been to the Andromeda Galaxy and seen the ominous Zin world they must defeat.

They walked right up to the giant columns. He saw no instructions, no engravings, no control panel. The columns remained smooth shimmering gray *bendar* and the rippling, shadowed portal stretched between them.

Kirek picked up a loose pebble and rolled it toward the portal. The pebble clearly stopped rolling, halted. But then it whooshed inside, sucked into the opening, but it had no more effect on the field than a rain droplet's splash in the ocean.

"How do we operate this portal?" Angel asked, her tone light and inquisitive and a bit awed.

Where do you wish to go? A voice boomed from the rock's face, but Kirek knew that no sound had come through his suit. The message was telepathic.

Kirek and Angel exchanged a long glance. Then Kirek spoke for them both. "We wish to use the portal to go to the Andromeda Galaxy."

Understood.

"You can send us there?"

Affirmative.

"Can we return through this portal?" Kirek asked. The portal remained silent.

Angel tried again. "Can you tell us who built the portal?"

Again there was silence.

"I have coordinates for our destination." Kirek read off a string of numbers. "Now what should we do?"

The portal's voice remained steady and clear. *Step through the portal.*

"We wish to go in my space ship," Angel said.

Affirmative.

"If we fly my ship through the portal, you will send us to the coordinates I gave you?" Angel asked.

Affirmative.

"Will we still be alive when we get there?" Kirek asked, but the portal didn't answer. He turned to Angel. "I'd love to know how the portal works."

"Maybe it's better if we don't know." Awe in her voice, she turned away from the portal.

"Why?"

"Well if the damn thing is going to dematerialize us, scramble our brains, and then squeeze our atoms through a wormhole before reconstituting us later, I'd rather not know."

Kirek tried one more question. "Does traveling through the portal affect time?"

But the portal didn't deign to answer.

Angel frowned at him. "What kind of question is that?"

"It's possible we could go through, complete our mission, and return to find a millennia has passed."

"Now there's a cheery thought. We save the Federation and return only to find everyone but us has evolved." She frowned harder at him. "Sometimes you think too much."

"My mother used to tell me that." Kirek took her hand and they headed back to the shuttle.

Chapter Nineteen

"KIREK." ANGEL STALKED into the room on the ship that he'd appropriated for his workroom. Parts, wiring, chips, and diagrams, along with tools and fuel cells, surrounded Kirek. He'd been working steadily for two days to solve his power problem with the chip, but from the number of miscellaneous components, he appeared to have been moved in for weeks.

"Over here," he answered and she followed the sound of his voice to spot him and Frie behind a roll of *bendar* plating. He didn't look up from screwing a wire onto a plate, but his voice greeted her warmly. "Have you come to watch our latest test?"

"Yes," she lied, hoping he and Frie would succeed. Ever since Kirek had learned that the original device he'd ordered had failed, his mood had been brooding. Last night, she'd brought him dinner and she could see from the leftovers he hadn't touched it. She'd bet the *Raven* he hadn't slept, either.

Kirek now had the chip enclosed in a box, connected to wires that led to Frie's contraption, a sphere that would fit in the palm of her hand. Angel prayed the experiment would work, but her hopes weren't high. This was the fifth prototype they'd made in as many hours. The first four had failed.

"Throw the power switch," Kirek directed.

Frie complied. Something hummed. The sphere cracked, then popped open. A fire erupted and the scent of burned wiring singed Angel's nostrils.

Frie swore. Kirek's shoulders slumped. But his voice remained steady. "We'll try again. Maybe if we increase the diameter of the wiring—"

"There's no time." Angel hated to tell him the real reason she'd interrupted, but Kirek needed to know. She delayed by dumping his uneaten food into the recycler, but that only gained her a moment. "I've picked up encrypted news. Volcanic activity on several small planets has already led to core overheating. Federation scientists estimate that the temperatures of many smaller planets will rise enough to cause massive explosions within hours."

Kirek's eyes sparked with angry reddish-violet embers. "Take the *Raven* through the portal, but we'll keep working here."

"Leval." Angel opened a com to the bridge. "Set a course through the portal."

"Setting course, captain."

Angel peered into a vidscreen, a new and convenient upgrade that allowed her to see and hear everything Leval did on the bridge from almost any position on the *Raven*.

She could even watch their approach to the portal from here. While she'd have preferred to be on the bridge, she needed to talk to Kirek.

He'd been working 'round the clock, but it was now time for him to tell her the backup plan. The one that had caused his eyes to cloud over with such worry. And her stomach curled in dread.

While Frie cleared the smoking ruins of their failed experiment from the counter and Leval piloted the ship toward the portal, Angel approached Kirek. "If you can't fix the power problem in time, what's your backup plan?"

He avoided looking at her. "I have to fix it. The device was supposed to store my psi and hide it from the Zin. If I try to go into their labyrinth with my psi still a part of me, they'll recognize and stop me before I can even land a shuttle anywhere near the home planet."

Since he hadn't answered her question, she suggested, "Suppose we take the *Raven* in close? With the hull's shapeshifting mode we can disguise her as a Zin ship."

Kirek nodded and started to sketch a new design. "That was always part of the plan. But eventually I have to exit the *Raven* and make my way through the Zin labyrinth."

"How long will it take you to leave the ship and navigate through the labyrinth?" she asked.

"Longer than you can hold a shield over us both." He obviously understood where she was taking this line of questioning.

"What if you separate your psi from your mind, but instead of placing it in the chip, you put it inside Ranth?" Angel suggested. After all, Ranth had a massive storage capacity and plenty of power to run it.

"That won't work. I need my body to physically enter the Zin's inner sanctum where they are vulnerable—the Zin core, the inmost circuitry and programming that drives them all—and after I arrive physically, I need my psi to merge with their circuitry and turn them off."

Oh . . . God. He intended to merge his mind with the Zin? Suppose he merged and never came out? Suppose he became locked inside the Zin world? She swallowed back her fear of losing him. If he lost, they all lost. Kirek would die. She would die. The entire Federation would die.

And part of her admitted that she would have hated living without him anyway, but she shoved that terrifying thought aside.

"So what's your backup plan?" she asked again, totally out of ideas.

He hesitated.

"Come on," she prodded, "I know you have a backup plan. Preparation is your middle name."

"If I gave my psi to you—"

"What?" She hadn't thought that was possible. "You can transfer your psi?"

"Dora figured out how to do it when she became human."

Angel knew all about the computer who'd wanted to become human so she could fall in love. Yet she'd never been interested in the technical details. But Ranth needed a psi to operate this ship—so computers had them. "Dora was a computer who transferred her mind into a living body."

"The transfer process is the same whether it's machine-to-human or human-to-human or human-to-machine."

"You've transferred your psi before?" she asked.

He shook his head. "The process isn't that complex."

Kirek sounded certain he could do it. But the idea of holding his psi inside her head—that was his grand plan? "Surely, even if you could transfer your ability to me, my mind couldn't hold it."

"I believe your psi may be as strong, if not stronger, than mine."

"That's ridiculous."

"You can make the shield to protect us."

"That's one little trick."

"You may be the only person in the Federation who can do it. It's likely you have the potential to do so much more but haven't developed it."

"Great. Now you sound like one of my teachers who always complained that I didn't work up to my potential."

He chuckled. "You may have the raw capacity to do more than me."

"And I may not. Even if what you say is true, won't the Zin recognize your psi in my head?" Oh, she finally saw where he was going. "You think I can shield my mind and your psi, hiding it from the Zin, until you need it."

"In theory." Kirek frowned and gestured to the burnt experiments. "This is why I've been working so hard. I didn't want to experiment on your brain. Because if we fail, if you can't hold all that I need to transfer, then you could burn out . . ."

"We have no choice," she whispered, excited and frightened and wondering what it would feel like to have his psi rattling around in her head. Would it fit? Would her brain cells fry? Would the link be intimate? Would they share all their memories and feelings and secrets? Could they really do such a thing? "You once told me that it was destiny for us to meet. Maybe you were right."

"Yeah, and maybe I'm just a frustrated Rystani male who craves your luscious self."

Frie laughed. Angel scowled. Although Frie, Leval, and Petroy were all aware that she and Kirek had a relationship, she remained uncomfortable talking about it openly when she'd only so recently admitted it to herself.

But even she realized that forming an attachment to Kirek frightened her more than confronting the Zin. The possibility of death didn't scare her as much as the idea of being trapped by her feelings. Love for her mother at a tender age had confined her world, limiting her life to their impoverished home. Two failed marriages had done further damage, proving to her that she wasn't cut out for a life of emotional entanglements. To be happy, Angel needed the freedom to roam and explore and while she and Kirek were on this mission together, if they succeeded the mission would end. And he'd eventually go home to family and friends.

She would stay to salvage the Zin world. So emotional entanglements that had to end would only bring her additional pain, and she prayed that if she carried Kirek's psi, it would not increase her feelings for him. Already, she'd almost lost him several times and she knew that it would take a long time for her to get over him after they parted ways.

THE *RAVEN* FLEW into the portal and Angel held her breath. Even Kirek had stopped working on his device to place an arm over her shoulders and watch the vidscreen. Right up until the moment they entered, everything seemed normal. But then the portal sucked the *Raven* into the gray shadows.

Angel had braced for the heightened sensitivities of hyperspace, but the p-space—short for portal space—which connected the two galaxies was spectacularly dull. No stars. No planets. No matter showed on their sensors. It was as if they'd entered a giant void.

"How long do you think it will be until we come out?" Angel asked.

Kirek sighed. "I'm not sure. We may not know until we return."

"You don't have an equation to predict—"

"I have lots of theories and equations. But I can't solve them," Kirek admitted.

"Ran—"

"Don't ask him," Kirek instructed. "I don't want his logic loops twisted into a puzzle and using up too much of his brain when he should be focusing on the power problem."

"I appreciate that you are worried about me," Angel told him, looking away from the boring grayness on the vidscreen into Kirek's warm gaze. "But if you don't succeed, we're all going to die anyway."

As if sensing they needed a private conversation, Frie left the room. A muscle in Kirek's neck throbbed and his jaw tightened. "Remember when I told you that Dora had worked out a way to transfer my psi into you?"

"Yes?"

"Well, we aren't sure if you'll be able to separate your psi from mine and transfer it back."

"You mean you might have to live the rest of your life without your psi?" For Kirek, it would be like living with half his mind. He would have no more ability than Lion and he'd forever be dependent on others to survive.

"You're missing the important point. If I can't merge with the Zin, then you will have to do it."

She swallowed hard. "How?"

"You would have to secretly link with the Zin, find the circuitry that turns them off, flip the switch, then get out before it dies—or you might be trapped in the Zin mind and die with them."

"Show me what I'd have to do."

He turned on the vidscreen and she saw a three-dimensional representation of what looked like a maze. He pointed. "We go in here." A blinking light zigzagged through the three-dimensional maze and mapped out the route. "When you reach the nucleus, you shut them down."

The idea of entering a machine with her mind and getting trapped inside it was a notion that made her grow cold. She shivered. "I'm confused. Are the Zin a hive mentality?"

"Not exactly." Kirek drew her against his chest and into his arms. "The Zin are half machine, half intelligent life form. Each unit is capable of independent thought to complete its task, but they take their orders from the Zin home world."

"So why do you have to go at all? If I can hold your psi behind my shield and do what must be done, then there's no reason to put yourself at risk."

"You may not be physically strong enough to get past the obstacles." He wrapped his arms around her and held her tight. "Besides, there's no way in the Seven Hells of Daragon I'd let you face them alone."

She didn't argue. His tone was determined, final, and very certain. Besides, she wanted him there to steady her.

"But we're getting way ahead of ourselves. We still may find a way to make the power work with the chip. And in theory there's no reason that you won't be able to separate my psi and give it back when it's time. Most likely, I'll be the one going in. I just want to prepare for every contingency." He tipped up her chin. "What's making you tremble?"

Of all the things he'd told her, one stood out and bothered her above the rest. For much of her adult life, she'd run from intimacy and emotional entanglements and now he was asking her to take his psi inside her head. And it seemed petty to mention that she feared she'd never be free again, when he had to face losing his psi forever.

But fear made her ask another question. "What's it going to feel like, if I hold your psi in my head?"

"I don't know." Kirek must have known that she desperately needed reassurance, but he'd told her the truth—she could hear it in his sad tone.

When he kissed her, she clung to him, appreciating how he wrapped her in gentle strength. It seemed like forever since he'd held her in his arms and enveloped her in his heat. But the moment was cut all too short when they exited p-space.

And every alarm in the *Raven* sounded at once. Purple lights flashed. Sirens rang.

Ranth's voice warned, "Zin battleships have locked on the *Raven* and are preparing to fire."

"Alarms off," Angel ordered, pulling away from his arms. "Shields up. Shapeshift to mimic Zin battleship mode."

Changing the *Raven*'s shape to match the Zin ships had been impossible until Ranth had scanned their shape. And while Kirek had scouted this area almost a decade ago, apparently the Zin had upgraded their ship designs after the wormhole explosion had wiped out most of their fleet.

Angel held her breath as the *Raven*'s hull altered. "Status?"

Ranth answered, "Zin ships are standing down. They believe they had a hiccup in their system. We've been ordered by the Zin home world to enter the solar system and maintain an orbit until we can come in for resupply."

"How long do we have?" Kirek asked, already heading back to his diagrams.

"One hour."

"What?" Angel consulted her vidscreen. "Ranth, we can't make it to the home world in an hour."

"A Zin ship can."

"Send a communication to the home world that we've suffered damage and will have to limp in. That should buy us a day."

"Three hours," Ranth corrected. "Otherwise a faulty delay will cause them to send out repair technicians."

*   *   *

THREE HOURS HADN'T been enough time for Frie, Kirek, and Ranth to fix the power supply. So Leval brought the *Raven* into orbit and Angel and Kirek flew the shuttle toward the Zin world. Since he had been here before and knew the route, she took the copilot seat.

And oh . . . my. Kirek had been correct about the value of the metal. Salvaging the Zin home world would keep a fleet of ships busy for years. About the size of Jupiter, the surface appeared to be almost solid metal cities and complexes composed of *bendar* plus a shimmering green metal she didn't recognize. According to her sensor readings the circuitry and metal surface layer was several miles thick. In addition, the Zin had huge space stations, orbiting satellites, and a busy spaceport filled with exotic ships designed in everything from insectoid shapes to giant ovules that were several miles long.

"If you feel as if you can't maintain the shield, try and give me some warning," Kirek instructed, calmly joining a line of ships that appeared to be flying into and landing on one tiny section of the spaceport.

"Understood." They'd decided not to transfer his psi to her until the last possible moment. That way she could focus solely on keeping up the shield.

"What happens after we land?"

"The Zin have many humanoids that are part machine. We will enter the complex with them."

"Will we be questioned?"

"One of the weaknesses of the Zin is their superiority complex. They believe they are so powerful that no one would dare attack their home world."

Angel frowned through the vidscreen. "If they've existed for millions of years, they must have strong survival instincts."

"We won't have to worry until we go deeper into the complex."

"I can't believe we will be able to just walk in."

"Think of the Zin world like a bank. Anyone can walk through the front door. To transact business at a teller, you need ID. To get to the vault, you must pass more involved security checks. But you're right, the Zin are wary. Last time I was here, I was able to modify their computer system. I left myself a back door."

Kirek sounded confident, but as she took in the complexity of the busy planet from orbit—a giant space port, huge manufacturing complexes, and extensive warehouses with no greenery between buildings or cities, she had doubts. "You were here eight years ago. You think the back door is still open?"

Kirek grinned, almost like a kid. Despite the danger, he was clearly excited and enjoying the mission as much as she was. "We'll soon find out. Any problems holding the shield?"

"None." She still felt strong and confident that she could keep them from being seen or sensed by machine or humanoid. But holding the shield while they remained seated and in constant positions relative to one another would be very different from once they exited and had to move through the complex.

They planned to stay close together while avoiding others who might accidentally come into contact with the shield. And as Kirek landed in the busy spaceport, she wondered if that was going to be possible.

This world was crawling with machines, ones that rolled, others which moved on tracks. Some flew. Some walked. And others snaked while a few jumped. And the variations in limbs, heads, eyes, and torsos was mind-boggling. Each Zin seemed to be uniquely specialized for its work. One giant had a cart-like body that rolled up to their shuttle. When Kirek popped the hatch, the body extended upward to meet the hull, stretching and unbending.

Angel wanted to grab Kirek's hand. But since none of the Zin touched and they needed to blend in, she didn't touch him, either. For all the activity of hundreds of ships, thousands of mechanics, and more Zin than she could comprehend, it was a strangely silent world. The motors hummed with silent efficiency and no one communicated with verbal language.

Kirek had planned ahead to have Ranth tap into the communications system for him. In suit privacy mode, the Zin couldn't hear them talking—if they even had ears. Kirek kept monitoring the com and kept her informed. "The Zin are taking no special notice of us."

"Good." Angel didn't mind that she wasn't hooked into the com network. She had enough distractions and now had to refocus her efforts to maintain the shield. One lapse and the Zin would sense Kirek's psi.

"We need to catch a tram." Kirek led her toward a tunnel where machines loaded and unloaded ship supplies. "It's too far to walk."

"Just find us a spot close together," she reminded him. But it wasn't necessary. Kirek never seemed to forget anything. And he understood that the farther they separated the more difficult it became for her to maintain the shield around them both.

"Will that do?" Kirek tipped his chin toward a fuel tank. "We can ride on top."

"All right." She moved closer to Kirek. The tank towered above their heads. And she wasn't certain how they would get up there. Maintaining their shield while they employed null grav would be tricky.

He lifted her into his arms. "Can you maintain the shield while I boost us?"

"Do it slowly."

The machines around them paid no attention to the fact that she was now in his arms. She'd worried the Zin would notice their touching but apparently, she'd been wrong. She supposed that to a Zin, their touching was no different than the lift that had linked with their shuttle. Machines linked and disengaged all around them.

Kirek engaged his null grav and she concentrated on raising the shield with them at the same rate. He looked down at her with concern. "Are you all right?"

She nodded but didn't speak until he had them on top of the fuel tank. As the tram began to move, she tried to relax. For some odd reason maintaining her shield while they sat on a moving object was no problem. However when they moved themselves, she had to move the shield with them.

"Whew. That was tricky, but I'm getting the hang of it. How long are we riding?"

"Need a rest?"

"I'm okay." But Kirek could hear her breathing hard from the effort. Although the work had been mental, she'd tensed her muscles and held her breath. Now she had to force her body to relax.

She'd hoped the tram would give them a look at the Zin world and it did. They traveled through giant dark buildings filled with goods. They passed through cities of lights. They rode underground and over a bridge that spanned a manufacturing plant. And everywhere she saw Zin, some as tiny as her cat, others as large as a battleship.

The Zin didn't rest. They didn't play. Angel leaned against Kirek, allowing him to anchor them into position with his psi. "They seem much more machine than human."

"These are the workers. They are designed to service the others and don't need higher thought patterns. As we approach the core, the Zin have a higher level of intelligence."

"Won't they notice that we don't belong?"

"The back door was open and that allowed me to change the parameters of what belongs. When the Zin see us, they see more Zin going about their tasks."

She realized that while she'd been sightseeing, Kirek had used his psi. And while he likely thought in computer code, he had given her simplistic analogies so she could understand his explanation. She liked that about Kirek. He neither tried to impress anyone with his immense intelligence, nor spoke in a condescending manner. "Why didn't they recognize your psi when you used it?"

"That was part of the back door I left open the first time I was here. Unfortunately, that little trick won't work near the core. The deeper inside we go, the more sophisticated the Zin system becomes."

"So why am I holding this shield—if we don't need it yet?"

"Because when I made the back door, I expected to come back alone. I've now modified it to include us both, but this tram has already taken us deep enough that if you failed to hold the shield, we'd have to do some fast maneuvering."

"Like what?"

"I'd use my psi to take out their weapons in the immediate areas. Then we'd have to escape, give you time to recover, and employ the shield once more."

So that's why he'd asked her to warn him if she was about to lose the shield. It would give him time to attack. As they again descended a level and the air around them cooled and the lights dimmed to glowing red, she realized that not even Kirek's body heat was keeping her warm.

Her initial excitement at the tram ride and her wonder at this Zin world was changing as they rode the vehicle deeper into the planet. As the facts sunk in that she and Kirek were alone and trying to wipe out billions of the most technologically advanced beings she'd ever seen, she wondered if they stood any chance of all of succeeding.

Chapter Twenty

KIREK HAD TRAVELED to the Zin home world in the astral state. And while much of the complex remained exactly the same as it was eight years ago, being in his body now gave him access to sights, sounds, and smells—making the experience different. The Zin had no use for growing plants so the air seemed stale. They communicated by mental links—a combination of telepathy from their animal DNA and enhanced mechanical devices. The eerie lack of noise plus the pulsing red lights on the walls gave the buildings a ghostly and menacing aura as he and Angel rode the tram downward into the bowels of the planet.

Some changes had been made. But none disturbed him as much as the need to bring Angel with him. Bringing the woman he loved into this kind of danger and knowing the likelihood they might not survive clawed at his gut and sliced deep. If he'd had any other choice, any other viable option—Kirek would have insisted she stay on the *Raven*.

In addition to the menace from the Zin, he worried about his psi transfer. He would cope the way he always did, feeling as if he'd lost one of his senses, but he would remain able to go on.

His concern was all for her. He had absolutely no idea what would happen or how Angel would cope after he gave his psi to her. Could she hold the force shield and his psi? And what kind of strain would it place on her? Would there be damage? Would they be able to reverse the process? Kirek simply didn't know—and yet, he also believed that more than fate had caused them to meet.

He strongly suspected that the Perceptive Ones had arranged for him and Angel to come together—possibly with the purpose of defeating the Zin. For a long time the Perceptive Ones had been attempting to encourage humanity to evolve, to help them win their fight against the Zin. And so perhaps their destiny had been planned by the capable Perceptive Ones.

The thought gave Kirek hope. And as they rode the tram, he slowly began to cage his psi power, compressing and focusing inward. The smaller and tighter he could condense it, the less room it would take up in Angel's mind.

After setting his suit on automatic, he retracted his psi from the portions of his brain that allowed him to interact with his suit. Carefully withdrawing his psi from his eyes, he lost the ability to see others move at the speed of thought. Soon, his psi tired of holding the null grav and that forced him to use his hands to hold onto the tram.

As the tram descended another level, he spoke above the rush of air going by. "Are you ready to take my psi?"

Angel stiffened, then nodded. "What do I do?"

Although she'd clearly known the moment would come, he read panic in her eyes. "Don't fight it. Let the energy flow freely through you."

"Okay."

"We'll transfer as slowly as I can manage." He leaned over and kissed her. "Try to relax."

She kissed him back with a ferocity that revealed great fear. And he hesitated, looking deep into her eyes, his stomach twisting at what he was asking from her and wishing he could avoid it. "Are you sure?"

She squared her shoulders and lifted her chin. "I've never been this scared in my life. Not even when my mother died. But we have no choice. You know that." She breathed in and exhaled a giant breath. "I'm ready."

Kirek thought of his psi as a round, glowing ball about the size of a heart. With the very last of his psi that he'd kept for himself until the end of the transfer, he edged the ball from his mind toward Angel, allowing only the outermost corona to touch her. "How does it feel?"

"Bright. Hot."

Kirek tried to turn down the glow and the heat but he couldn't. He'd left himself only enough energy to complete the transfer. If she was having difficulty handling the first ten percent, he doubted she could cope with it all. Maybe he should retreat before he did real damage . . . and yet perhaps she merely needed time to adjust. "Don't forget to hold the shield," he reminded her.

At his words, she strengthened the shield. At the same time she managed to dim the brightness and decrease the heat on her own. Not certain she was aware of what she'd done, he waited, allowing her to become accustomed to the feel of him.

Beads of sweat broke out on her forehead and bottom lip before her suit mopped it away. "Okay. I've got you. I think I can do this."

Apparently Angel thought she had all his psi. Kirek had to tell her the truth. "Sweetheart, I've only given you part of my psi. There's more."

"Let me make room." She proceeded to squeeze her own psi down, going through much the same process he'd just finished, but she didn't sever the connections from her brain to the rest of her body. "All right."

He eased in a bit.

"I'm okay." Her voice was tight, straining. "More."

He gave her half and waited for her to adjust. It took several minutes and a few deep breaths but finally she spoke. "How much is left?"

"We're halfway there."

She groaned. "There's not enough room. I've retreated as far as I can go."

Disappointment washed over him. "You're certain?"

Her fists clenched. "I'm stuffed. Overstuffed. My brain cells are pounding the walls of my skull for relief."

They were going to fail. Despair and helplessness kicked him in the gut, but Kirek couldn't botch this transfer. If they didn't succeed, millions of worlds and billions of beings would die as the Zin heated planetary cores and worlds exploded. Yet they couldn't do the impossible and force more psi into her mind than her brain had room for. And they couldn't make more room . . . unless . . .

"Tell me exactly where you put your psi," he asked as they rushed forward and downward through buildings, mines, factories, and warehouses filled with spare parts and electronics and raw materials.

"Here." She tapped her forehead.

"And where did you put my psi?"

"Everywhere else." Her voice tightened with pain.

"The pressure's incredible. Enormous. My head feels like a ripe tomato in a press."

"In theory, there's no reason why you can't merge our psi and allow them to occupy the same space at the same time."

"Oh . . . God." Her face paled and he suspected she'd lost control. "I didn't . . . do . . . anything and they are already combining."

"Is the pressure easing?"

She grabbed his hand and squeezed so tight, if he hadn't strong bones, she might have crushed his fingers. Her voice rose in terror. "Your psi is taking over. I'm losing . . . my identity."

"No you aren't. We are just merging. You're still there. Don't fight the merge. Please. Angel. Let me in." He understood that he was asking her to let down every barrier that make her unique and her own person. The invasion had to be total and for someone as independent as Angel, her instinct was to fight, to hold on to her self.

"I'm disappearing," she wailed, but she courageously made more room.

"This is only for a little while," he reminded her and gave her more psi, then more again. "We're almost there. Just a little bit more."

She steadied. "You have no idea. Your memories are in my head. But there's no order. It's madness."

"Open your eyes," he ordered, fearing she could become mentally unbalanced. "Focus on me. I'm here, Angel. Right next to you. Think about what we have to do—not the psi. Not the stray thoughts. We must defeat the Zin. Can you do that? Look at my face. We only have a few more minutes and then we'll be close to where we need to be. Only a few minutes. Hang on."

"I'm not sure I can." Her face tightened in fright and

agony. Kirek ached to help her. Instinctively, he gathered her into his arms and held on tight.

ANGEL TRIED TO ignore Kirek's memory fragments swirling in her brain and to instead focus on their situation, but stark images invaded her mind—potent images from Kirek's past. And the images often made no sense. How could a male baby ask to take on the pain of childbirth? Why would Kirek feel hurt when his father refused to allow him to participate in an intimate family ceremony?

Oh . . . God. The memory of a father/son hunting trip and Kirek's violent reaction to his first kill. Nausea. Pain. Dread. And the image of a child sickened by the blood on his hands, a child who adored his father, looking up into his father's face and seeing approval and love when the child felt nothing but horror, and using his psi to conceal his disgust.

Kirek's fierce determination not to kill conflicted with the foundation of the society from which he came. At an early age, he'd developed a code of ethics against killing . . . all life. Kirek didn't even eat real meat—in a society that considered hunting a necessity.

Images of invasion bombarded her. People screaming. Dying.

And in the center of chaos stood a calm woman, his mother, baking over an old-fashioned hearth, the aroma wondrous, the kitchen lit by glowing stones and the laughter of other women as they fed Kirek warm tarts and tousled his hair, clearly all of them loving him.

Flashes of strolling though a serene garden. Mating with a beautiful woman. But there had been no love. Only lust. Knowing that the woman meant nothing to Kirek eased any jealousy Angel might have felt.

Haunting years of loneliness without a body. And the guilt from killing so many Zin during the wormhole blast. Stabbing, searing, agonizing guilt at the deaths he'd caused.

Stars . . . And Kirek's secret determination to now stop the Zin to save those he loved—even if the cost broke him. Killing went against his every moral fiber, yet he was determined to act against his own beliefs to save his parents.

So much love.

And pain.

Plus guilt.

Kirek was a man torn. A man at war with himself. She'd guessed at the strange duality of his nature, but hadn't comprehended his passions and beliefs raged like a hurricane. Caught between love for his people and his conscience, he was a warrior with scruples so set into his heart that killing was always his absolute last recourse, even if it risked his own life.

The agonizing torment of knowing he might have to become the most efficient killer the universe had ever seen in order to protect his family, his home, and his world ate away at him like acid. At times she'd thought Kirek had had it easy. His family loved him. His people adored him. He was handsome, charming, intelligent, and wealthy. Yet, he had withstood torture at the hands of a sadist without flinching, and he'd suffered more from his gentle conscience than anyone she'd ever known.

Knowing his unique psi made him the only candidate that could defeat the Zin, he'd taken it upon himself to finish a warrior's quest—even when the task sickened him.

And then his vision of Angel flashed into her mind, allowing her to see herself the way he did. Oh . . . my. She sucked in her breath. In Kirek's eyes, she glowed with a spirit that made her appear much more beautiful than she was. Surely her walk wasn't so lively? Or her lips that expressive? And did she really roll her eyes with that much sarcasm?

His images of their lovemaking brought heat to her face. Surely, her skin couldn't taste as sweet as nectar? Her breasts couldn't be that responsive. And . . . no man . . . could be that certain of his love.

But his love for her was as bright as the stars in the sky—splendid and sparkling, laden with an all-encompassing passion and sustaining his belief that she was the one for him. His love for her powered him, boosted his confidence in the mission, and for the first time she understood how much she really meant to him. His love was inspiring and scary, wondrous, and so intense she gulped and trembled.

Kirek's arms held her but were ready to let her go free—if freedom was what would make her happy. Because his was not the kind of love that stifled, but a love that accepted her for who she was. That he could open himself to a love so mighty, when he fully knew that she might very well walk away, awed and humbled her.

Angel didn't have that kind of courage. And she didn't think she could love so broadly, so deeply, or allow herself to want someone else so completely. Totally impressed, yet petrified and reeling, she hugged Kirek, hoping and praying she wouldn't disappoint him, but unable to stop the tears from brimming over her eyes.

"Is it the pain?" he asked, tenderly stroking her hair.

"I'll be all right. Give me a second." But she really needed years. Knowing how much he loved her scared her to the bone. She could only cope with her roiling stomach and her roller-coaster emotions by building a wall around them, partitioning off her feelings until she had time to deal with them.

"The shield?" he asked.

She shook her head. "Your psi is giving me energy. Now that I don't have to surround you in the shield, I don't have to extend so much." And it was also boosting her confidence, evening out her surging emotions. The psi he lent her steadied her from the shock. From the revelations.

"Good. Because we have to jump off this moving tram. Can you manage?"

"I guess we'll find out." She had to maintain the shield around her, jump from the tram, and adjust their null grav, all at the same time. But with Kirek's psi merged with hers, she had extraordinary power and focus, allowing her to make the necessary adjustments as they stood on the tram's roof and prepared to leap. And she finally understood how Kirek employed such perfect timing. His psi could break time into the most minute increments. Each second had many, many beats, and she reacted to the smallest change in balance, correcting so quickly they landed lightly and safely on a platform between two cargo pallets.

With no hesitation, Kirek pulled her along the platform to a doorway and pushed hard on the door, bracing his feet and throwing his entire body into the effort. She would have added her meager strength to his, but there wasn't room for them both. Alone, she would have never have been able to budge the thick metal door.

With a grunt, Kirek finally opened the door and she stepped through, keeping close to him in case of sudden attack. She expected a room or a hallway. Instead she saw a long chute that descended so far into the darkness that she couldn't see the end. The tunnel's diameter equaled Kirek's body length plus about three feet. If he intended to travel through the tunnel, their only means to slow their plummet was to employ their psi.

"What is this place?"

"A garbage chute."

"You take me to the nicest places." She crinkled her nose but even when she breathed in some air, she didn't smell anything foul, except the faint scent of fuel. "What's at the bottom?"

"An oil lake, but we aren't going down that far."

"Good." Unwilling to risk falling and leaving him behind without psi, she slipped one leg over the lip and waited for him to do the same.

He joined her and she took his hand. And then they both slipped over the edge. Angel used null grav to keep them from descending too rapidly as well as to prevent them from crashing into the sides of the chute. "How long did it take you to figure out a way past the Zin defenses?"

"I stayed almost a year. Even though the wormhole blast had badly damaged the Zin and this world's security had been temporarily burned out, they knew I was here and observing them. And they worked feverishly on their systems to lock me out. But as they worked, I built in the back door. Luckily for us, they never plugged my hole in their security."

The year had been long and lonely and agonizing for the man who'd caused such destruction. And yet, with his psi in her mind, she knew he'd never entertained the idea of leaving before he'd taken full advantage of the opportunity. While she admired his determination, she couldn't help wondering how he'd eventually reconcile his warlike actions with his peaceful beliefs.

"Stop there." Kirek pointed below them to a hatch in the chute. "That's where we exit."

Angel made the adjustments and kept them hovering in midair while he removed a tool from his suit and drilled out four bolts. Then he lifted the lid and crawled through the opening. She hoped they weren't in another narrow tunnel, and after she followed, was relieved to find herself standing in a room full of machinery. And Zin.

Her pulse raced. But the Zin took no notice of them. She employed private mode on her suit and adjusted his as well. "I thought they would be paying more attention to us down here."

"The Zin are extremely specialized."

She watched them sort parts and bring them to other machines, not one motion wasted. "That's why they're so efficient."

"If we encounter a Zin security specialist, we'll be in trouble. But these Zin are trained only to run the factories."

"The chute took us past security?" she asked, starting to relax.

Kirek frowned. "We've bypassed where they placed their security eight years ago."

And at his words, her muscles tightened again. "What's wrong?"

He nudged his chin at a towering crane. "Where that crane is sitting, there's supposed to be another tram. I'd planned for us to ride the tram down five more levels."

She didn't bother asking if there was another route or if he could have misjudged. He'd spent a year here, planning to return. His memory was excellent and if he knew of another route, he likely wouldn't be hesitating.

So she remained silent and observed. The crane unloaded finished products onto a moving beltway that would pass a wiring station and a plastic capping station. She didn't recognize the merchandise. "Maybe they rerouted the tram. And when the product is done, it has to go somewhere . . ."

"What are you suggesting?"

"Let's see where these supplies are going."

"All right." Despite what Kirek had told her about Zin specialization, when he led them right through the Zin workers with boldness, her mouth dried and her palms sweated. All around them Zin of varying shapes and sizes worked on the assembly line. She finally decided that the sole purpose of this factory was to make more Zin.

And when they passed the neuro tanks, filled with growing brain cells, she shivered. It was easier to think of the Zin as programmed machines. But they weren't. They were alive.

And they could reproduce by the billions. In fact, she was beginning to think that this entire world's purpose was to create more Zin.

If they succeeded, the *Raven* would need several years to complete a salvage of this magnitude. The electronics alone, never mind the metals, would make her and her crew wealthy—no, more than wealthy: they would be fabulously rich. And yet, she also was beginning to understand Kirek's loathing of killing. These efficient creatures were very much live beings and for the first time, profiting from their deaths bothered her. Reminding herself that the Zin had wiped out Zenon Prime and had ruthlessly killed billions, she shoved aside her conscience. They had to find a way to descend several more levels to get to where the Zin were vulnerable.

They never found the end of the assembly line. Some of the Zin parts, perhaps the rejects, were placed on a chain-belted, ramp-like escalator that descended at a constant speed. Kirek moved several spare parts aside and cleared a place for them to ride between the rejected components.

They leaped off the belt before they ended up dumped in a vat of melted metal the size of a small lake. To her, all that metal was like finding a treasure. But she had to keep her mind on the main goal. Using Kirek's psi, she knew they only had to proceed down one more level before winding through a complex maze that he'd memorized.

"Look for a floor vent," he instructed. This level was dark and although the rejected parts had no life to them, she had to stop from shuddering every time a Zin reject splashed into the metal vat and melted down. Her reaction was odd. She should be glad of every Zin death that added more metal to the lake, and she wondered if Kirek's psi could be influencing her emotions.

"How much longer until I can give you back your psi?" she asked, watching her steps. "There." She pointed to a vent. "Is that it?"

"Yes, and I don't want you to transfer my psi back until we reach the end of the maze." He used the drill to open the floor vent. "Is the shield—"

"It's fine."

He watched her face with obvious concern. "And what about you? Are you all right?"

"I'll be better once your morality is out of my head."

He winced. "Sorry."

"I always wondered why you refused to shoot the Kraj back on Dakmar. I didn't understand that a Rystani warrior could be so squeamish about . . . killing."

His tone hardened. "Don't worry. My beliefs won't stop me from completing the mission. I'm not weak."

"Sorry. *Squeamish* was the wrong word. I should have said that I didn't understand your morals." She placed a hand on his tense shoulder. "And you are the strongest man I've ever known. I just wish you didn't have to—"

"Kill billions." He gestured to the vent. "The Zin have given me no choice. They are destroying worlds and billions of innocent lives are at stake. Come on. Now is not the time for an ethical discussion."

"Right." She slipped through the vent and dropped through the ceiling into a very strange room. About the size of her quarters on the old *Raven,* the room had no light, no windows, no doors. In fact she was about to tell Kirek they'd stumbled into a dead end when he dropped down beside her with catlike grace.

He strode to the corner, found a spot halfway between the ceiling and floor and pressed his palm against the wall. A secret panel slid open and a burst of laser light shot at them.

She extended her shield around Kirek. The laser burst reflected back onto the weapon that had fired it, melting the metal into hot slag. "Next time, you might want to warn me before you trigger—"

"The laser weapon wasn't here eight years ago. They've set traps in the maze."

Terrific. "Can we bypass the maze?"

Kirek shook his head. "To program a Zin to install the hatch and the floor vent to allow us to enter took me four months. To erase the memory of the hatch's existence from their systems took two more. Since their new systems are now up and running, even if I could cut the time, I can't use my psi from behind your shield or they'll recognize me."

"So we go on?"

Before he could answer, the walls of the room began to glow a bright yellow-orange. Searing heat approached their suits' meltdown temperature.

With her psi, Angel grabbed Kirek and propelled them both directly toward the melted laser.

Chapter Twenty-One

THEY LANDED IN a tumbling heap. Angel had barely managed to maintain the shield and keep them alive. Shaky, she called on Kirek's psi to help her shove to her feet to look around. Kirek was already on his feet and after he saw she was unhurt, he immediately began to survey their surroundings.

The heat had incinerated the room they'd just escaped, leaving charred walls and the stench of burnt metal. Before them metal bars blocked their route. The entire floor suddenly shook, rattling her teeth.

"Now what?" she asked, tamping down her adrenaline rush. There was no place to run forward and they weren't going back until they'd accomplished their mission.

"I'm worried the laser may have warned them we are

here." Kirek pulled his blaster and shot a hole in the ceiling.

"If they are aware of us, let me give back your psi."

"No. We need to disappear and hope the fire will have cleaned out the evidence of our presence. If we're lucky, they'll believe a faulty circuit triggered the laser." He reholstered his blaster. "Let's go."

Angel used null grav to lift them out. "Surely if they investigate they'll realize this hole was blasted?"

Kirek was already way ahead of her. Once they reached the next chamber, full of spare parts and crates, he shoved them into the hole, blocking and hopefully hiding their exit. Taking her hand, they ran through the warehouse.

"We may be able to bypass most of the maze and the traps if we stay on this level," Kirek spoke as they ran past several forklifts.

Their footsteps echoed in the huge warehouse, but no Zin worked here and Angel was grateful. His pace was brutal and a stitch formed in her side but she ignored it, worrying that the Zin might be closing in. But the warehouse must have taken up several square miles.

Despite the overhead lights, she couldn't see walls or a roof and her breath began to come in gasps. Worse, her weariness began to make holding up the shield more difficult. Her physical efforts made concentration on her psi much harder to maintain. "How . . . much . . . farther?"

"Almost there."

Kirek redoubled his efforts, pulling her along. Her feet barely skimmed the floor before she was airborne. She would have used her psi to help her muscles but she couldn't spare the brain power. Her mind ached. Her lungs burned and the stitch in her side began to slide down into her thighs, cramping her muscles.

As if sensing her distress, Kirek suddenly slowed. "Wait here."

Grateful at stopping, Angel bent forward, gasping for air and taking huge gulps. Kirek had leapt onto one of the many forklifts, and now powered it up and drove it straight toward the wall, using the machine's two steel prongs as a battering ram.

She barely had the strength to lift her head and watch him smash into metal plating and then slam through the wall. Then he revved the engine, and backed the forklift against the wall, tipping the forks downward. With a jarring shift, he jammed his foot on the fuel and stabbed the floor with the two prongs.

The floor gave. The metal beneath her own feet quivered. And the entire machine and Kirek fell to the level below. And she was too far away to use her psi to lift him to safety.

Horrified at watching Kirek and the machine disappear in a roaring cloud of dust, Angel ran to the edge. She peered down to see Kirek hanging onto an exposed beam with one hand. He must have leapt to safety at the very last moment.

With a gentle psi thrust of null grav, she lowered both of them to the undamaged floor, far from where he'd crashed the forklift. "That was crazy."

"Necessary." He again took her hand and pulled her forward and to the right down a hallway.

"You should have taken me with you. I couldn't use my psi from that far away."

"You were too tired. And I need you rested for what's to come next."

She wasn't sure she was up for any more running. Or null grav. Her head was pounding. Maintaining the shield was making her sweat, even with the use of Kirek's psi. "I might need . . . more rest."

"Can you hold on two more minutes?"

She nodded. "If I don't have to do anything but walk."

He scooped her into his arms. "You don't even have to walk. Now rest."

After all their running and then his wild leap onto the machine, he wasn't even breathing hard. His arms held her as if she weighed nothing. Automatic weapons fired lasers at them from hidden positions set in the ceilings and the walls.

Kirek weaved and ducked between them. Obviously without his psi, he couldn't outrun a laser. He must have memorized the pattern. She was too weak to extend the reflective shield she used before. She was barely keeping the shield around his psi.

So she closed her eyes and focused on breathing, trusting Kirek to get them through the laser blasts. And oddly, even as lasers fired around them, she did trust him. And if she had to be in the Zin stronghold, there was no one she'd rather be there with than Kirek.

He might have issues with killing, but he'd do everything possible to keep them alive. And so she focused on relaxing her muscles, breathing and tuning out what was happening around her. Very soon, he would need her strength and she damn sure wanted to be able to do what he asked.

Kirek zigged and zagged in a crouching run for at least a minute before he gently stopped and set her down. His movements remained soothing, a smooth rocking motion.

When he stopped, she opened her eyes to find him watching her with concern. "Are you—"

"I'm better now." She refrained from mentioning her trembling legs, her aching chest, or the muscles that had barely stopped cramping. If she had enough air in her lungs, she could think clearly, and mental energy was what he needed from her.

"This is the core of the Zin brain. We have to find an access panel."

He'd brought them to the clear window of a control center.

Inside, the medium-sized control center was filled with dials, buttons, knobs, and blinking lights. No vidscreens. No Zin either. The place looked fully automated and empty of life. The clear doors that guarded the only entrance were at least one foot thick. Shooting their way inside didn't appear to be an option, and she saw no handles or manual locks to pick, either.

But as alarms sounded, she pulled her blaster and her gaze shot straight to Kirek. "Now what?"

"IT'S TIME TO transfer my psi." Kirek ignored the blinking red-and-orange swirling alarm lights, the shrieking whistles, and the ominous metal shutters descending from the ceiling to prevent them from seeing through the clear glass doors.

"What should I do?"

"Let me inside your shield. Then push my psi out of your head. Try not to drop the shielding until I'm all back."

He spoke as casually as if he was telling her how to drive a flitter into a garage. And although she understood her goal, the exact process by which she was supposed to follow his directions eluded her. Between the flashing lights and the whistles, her awareness of how much was at stake—including their lives, and her fear of failing, panic started to creep into her.

She clamped her hands over her ears and closed her eyes—not even bothering to use her suit. Angel could only use her psi for so many things and the shield was critical. So was giving Kirek back his psi.

Steady.

First she spread the shield around him. In her weakened state, accomplishing the task was more difficult than when she'd first raised it hours ago, but she managed. "The shield is covering you, but not as strongly as before. I'm not certain how long I can—"

"Do your best."

Easy for him to say. "I'll try."

Angel figured if she expanded her own psi, it might push his out of where it had lodged in her mind. So she gathered her psi from where it had merged with his, then tried to unfurl his, hoping his psi would expand toward him.

Slashing pain ripped through her head.

Gasping, she staggered to her knees.

Kirek grabbed her and stopped her from toppling to the floor. "Angel!"

Gnashing her teeth, she squeezed down hard on her psi. The pain eased, leaving her with a throbbing headache and a great reluctance to try again. But the alarm, now once again loud in her ears, reminded her of the urgency. She didn't have the luxury of time to recover.

Zin might show up at any time. So she tried building a force field around Kirek's psi, then gave it a gentle nudge. Nothing happened, but she didn't feel any pain either. So she pushed a little harder. And it gave way.

"It's moving," she panted.

"Good." Kirek's tone was gentle and encouraging, as if she had all the time in the universe.

Angel shoved his psi with more force, directing it toward Kirek. For some reason, his psi resisted. She pushed harder and when it didn't hurt, she pushed as much as she could, but his psi seemed snagged and stuck. Sweat poured from her body and trickled over her flesh, which the suit cleaned up, but her energy was failing.

"We're halfway there." Kirek held her steady as if he feared she'd collapse. "I can feel my psi pulsing."

"Take it." She had no more strength left. If she used any more the shield would snap.

"Just a few more seconds, sweetheart."

Kirek pulled and his psi zapped from her and into him. With relief and glee, her own psi expanded into her entire mind, but the effort had left her weak and drained.

God . . . the shield. She had to hold the shield. She braced, but she had no more strength. Without Kirek's psi to help, she couldn't hold on. And gasped. "I'm losing it."

"It's okay. You can let go."

Exhausted, Angel wearily opened her eyes to find herself sitting on the floor, her back against a panel where Kirek must have lowered her.

Kirek stood in front of the barred glass, his palms flat on the metal, his face rigid with determination. She heard a creaking groan. And then somehow, Kirek bent the metal and pried opened the doors.

He must have used his psi—although she had no idea how.

"Come on." He leaned down, tugged her hand, but when her weary muscles failed to gather her feet under her, he again scooped her up and set her down inside the control booth.

Then the doors shut behind them.

Had the Zin trapped them? Or had Kirek closed the doors to protect them? Angel didn't know. But several seconds later the blasted alarms stopped ringing and she took a few reviving swigs of water from a supply packet.

Angel didn't bother Kirek with questions. Knowing he had only a short amount of time to insert his psi into the Zin core and take them out, she didn't want to distract him.

Kirek strode to the middle of the controls. He placed his hands on a screen and spoke under his breath, concentrating on his task. With his shoulders squared and his jaw thrust forward, he looked every inch the proud warrior going into battle. Only his battle would be one of the mind—pitting his psi against the entire Zin home world, a planet made up of billions.

She prayed Kirek's psi was powerful enough to do the job. And wished she could do something to help, wondered how long the mental battle would take.

Because the Zin had found them.

Angel stared in horror as machines crawled, scooted, and flew into the metal and glass, pounding and congregating around the doors. Kirek didn't move and she wondered if he was even aware of them. He appeared to be in a trance.

Outside the control center, Zin dropped from the ceiling, rolled, stepped, and careened down the corridors, even drilled upward from the floors, their movements quick and coordinated. Some Zin were so tiny she barely could make out their shapes and those tried to squeeze in through cracks, attempting an attack from every angle to protect the core.

Angel fingered her blaster. One huge Zin began to drill between the bars. Others tried a variety of weapons from torches to cutting lasers. None seemed effective.

Yet, the Zin did not give up.

They tried acids, gases, and concoctions she didn't recognize. They bombarded them with sound, electromagnetic waves, and sonar. They tried searing heat and frigid cold.

But their own system prevented them from getting inside.

If Angel had had the energy, she would have paced. Instead, she broke into her rations and ate an energy bar as she watched the Zin's lack of progress.

As busily as the Zin attacked the control center's

perimeter, Kirek remained still and silent inside at his initial position by the controls. What was taking him so long?

Had the Zin booby-trapped their core—like they had the labyrinth? Were they overpowering Kirek? As he stood there as still as a mountain were they attacking his mind?

She wished there was something she could do besides wait and looked around for other weapons—but saw none. However, the big Zin with the drill seemed to be bearing down hard. White smoke from the drill bit curled into the air outside.

How long would it take the Zin to break through?

At the sound of glass cracking, Angel wearily pushed to her feet and aimed the blaster. To prevent the drill bit from melting, the Zin had poured fluid. The combination of heat and cold was cracking the thick glass. Tiny spiderwebs now extended out from the center.

As if sensing victory, the Zin pressed forward. A replica of the first Zin driller jammed another drill up against the glass, and then another. Angel imagined them creating Zin drillers from the parts room upstairs and sending them down here to attack.

The huge glass held but the cracks spread, deepened. And the only wall separating them from the Zin shattered. Glass fragments blasted inward.

Instinctively Angel stepped in front of Kirek and raised the shield around them both. She'd rested, but had by no means recovered her full strength.

She might have used up all her adrenaline, but fear powered her shield. The Zin advanced right up to the edge of her shield. One tested the force field with his clawlike hand. Her shield sheared off the limb. Another used a flamethrower and when the shield reflected back the heat, the Zin melted. Three others advanced to take its place.

And Angel weakened. Her limbs shook. Her gut tightened. Fear grabbed her by the throat and she drew on it, used it to fuel her psi.

When her shield failed—and it would do so shortly—she'd resort to using her blaster. She hoped she'd still have the strength to hold it; she was determined to protect Kirek. Praying he would finish before she wore down or the Zin found a way to neutralize her shield, she called on every last shred of resolve to hold.

But the shield was failing . . . and even with her blaster, she estimated they had mere seconds left to live.

KIREK HAD INSERTED his psi into the Zin brain with ease. However, once inside, finding his way to one central switch that he could turn off proved frustrating. One link after another led him into dead ends, or areas in which he had no interest. He hadn't expected the brain to have such complexity, with so many duplicate systems.

He was aiming for the core identity, the place where the Zin ego lived. Once he found the Zin essence, he could cut off that part from the rest and the Zin would die, because while each Zin unit was an individual, their resolve came from the core. Without resolve, the Zin would simply stop . . . and die.

Part machine, part neural matter, the brain used the best of both animal and computer to survive and dominate its surroundings. Eons of history were stored in the brain and Kirek followed the link back to the beginnings of the Zin, before their conquest of the Andromeda Galaxy.

He wasn't surprised to discover that the Zin had once lived in the Milky Way. After all, the Zin had altered Jarn DNA and made that race spy for them against their will. But what rocked Kirek was learning that the Perceptive Ones and the Zin had once been the same race. The Perceptive Ones had evolved to a pure energy state and had left their bodies behind. The Zin had chosen a less spiritual evolution, combining living DNA with machines.

The ancient races had clashed. The Perceptive Ones had thrown the Zin out of the Milky Way and had built giant Sentinels out on the rim to stand guard. But the Zin believed the Perceptive Ones had stolen their galaxy, and they'd been trying to invade for a millennium.

While the information fascinated Kirek, his findings didn't help him find the Zin essence he needed. Even as he plunged deeper into the brain, he noted a growing presence in his own. At first, he tried to keep out the presence, fearing the Zin had mounted a counterattack to stop him. But the psi inside his head seemed familiar . . . and panicked.

Kirek. It's Angel.

He shook off the mental communication, fearing a trick.

Damn you. Listen to me. The Zin broke through the glass doors. The only thing standing between us and death is my shield and it's fading.

I haven't found a way to turn them off. I need more time.

There is no more time. Unless . . .

Unless?

Merge our psi. Lend me strength.

Merging will slow my search.

If we don't merge, there will be no search. We'll be dead. Open your eyes. Look at what's going on around us.

He didn't have time. He'd found the core. A neural nexus so tight, so sophisticated that he sped from nerve cell to nerve cell with hyperspeed. But even as he went in, he merged their psi. Immediately, he was inundated with images of Angel's past.

Trapped images of sitting by a sick woman's bed. Guilt

at how badly she wanted to leave. Guilt and sorrow when her mother died.

And the marvelous freedom of space. The *Raven* was the only home Angel ever wanted. She relished the freedom, reveled in the adventure.

As Angel tapped his psi and he felt her growing stronger, he found the Zin "off switch." But as he began to shut down the Zin, he noted an ethics program. An ethics program with a flaw that caused the Zin to believe they never had enough and would always need more. Greedy domination was programmed into the Zin mindset.

If he could change the programming—alter their flaw—he wouldn't have to kill them.

No.

Even as he thought to avoid killing, Angel read his thoughts.

If you are wrong, we will die and they will win.

If I'm right we all win, he countered.

You're betting all our lives. And the Zin have redoubled their efforts to break our shield. You don't have time to mess around. Turn them off.

Kirek didn't heed the logic of her words. As much as he yearned to live, as much as he wanted to save his parents and friends and the Federation, he finally knew why he was here at this moment. Making the right decision . . . was his destiny.

With a psi thrust, Kirek changed the flaw. He rerouted a few chromosomes, altered the DNA that made the Zin invaders, conquerors, warlike creatures who wouldn't be satisfied with anything less than total domination.

Kirek withdrew from the Zin brain. Zin of all sizes and shapes attacked the shield. With no regard for their own safety or lives, the Zin threw themselves at the shield, dying as the force field fried their brains. Relentless, the

Zin paid no attention to the deaths of their comrades. They kept advancing, from above, from below, and from every side.

Kirek poured his strength into the shields, but he didn't have much left.

Why were they still attacking? Had his alteration of the flaw been a mistake? Were they going to die because he abhorred violence and death?

By now the mother brain should have sent out orders for the Zin to cease their attack. But the Zin advanced with a ferocity that didn't let up, throwing their bodies against the shield. And dying. Dying. Dying.

And each death stole some of Kirek and Angel's energy. Growing weak, Kirek grabbed his blaster. Had there been a duplicate strand of DNA that he'd missed?

Suddenly the Zin stopped their attack. "Maybe my adjustment worked."

"I hope you're right," Angel said softly, her blaster aimed at the Zin who began to clear away their dead and drag them away. "Oh . . . Stars. Here they come again."

He'd been wrong. The Zin hadn't stopped their attack. They'd simply had difficulty throwing themselves against the shield with their own dead in the way. After removing the dead, they'd resumed once again—and with more room to work in, it seemed as though they died by the dozens.

Each death depleted Kirek and Angel's psi energy, draining them until Kirek knew they would soon lose the shield. He shouldn't have gambled every life in the Federation against the hope he could cure the Zin of their aggression. He'd had no right to play God. And now everyone would pay for his mistake.

Then their shield failed.

Chapter Twenty-Two

AT THE SHIELD'S failure, Angel braced for death. Determined to go down fighting, she blasted the advancing Zin, who clearly sensed victory and threw themselves into her blaster heat with a frenzy. Metal bodies fell and the Zin behind them climbed over the dead.

A Zin reached for her foot. Angel shot it and stepped back, only to find she had no place to retreat.

Her back against Kirek's, they blasted the Zin, but even if their firepower didn't run out, they couldn't outfight millions of Zin. And with them surrounded, there was no place to run.

When her blaster ran out of juice, she threw it at the Zin, then pulled her knife. Slashing and slicing to keep the Zin at bay, they had just moments to live.

It would have been fitting to say something heroic to Kirek before they died, but she couldn't spare a breath. Her psi exhausted, muscles weary, lungs burning, she was about to keel over.

She shifted to evade a claw and then the Zin—all of them—suddenly stopped advancing, stopped moving. As if rooted into the deck, they ceased rolling, flying, and tracking. Pinchers and claws and hands ceased attacking.

Was it a trick to get them to let down their guard?

Or had Kirek succeeded in turning off the Zin?

But if he'd accomplished his mission, why weren't the Zin dead? Because although they had ceased to advance, their eyes still moved, their limbs twitched.

Baffled, she looked over her shoulder to peer at Kirek. His face flushed from exertion, his eyes sparkled deep violet and red. And his lips relaxed from a feral grimace into a pleased smile.

She slowly lowered her knife. "What's . . . going . . . on?"

Kirek's face glowed with satisfaction. "We will soon reach a peaceful agreement with the Zin."

"What!" He hadn't turned them off, but he'd obviously reprogrammed them. And while relieved to still be breathing, she frowned at Kirek. "What did you do?"

"They possessed a flaw in their programming that made them overly aggressive."

She snorted. "No kidding."

"We eliminated the flaw."

"No—*you* eliminated the flaw. I would have shut them down." So many emotions washed through her that she didn't know how she felt. Distrust of the Zin. Furious that Kirek had taken such a risk with their lives—with everyone's lives.

And the disappointment that she had lost the greatest salvage opportunity of all time paled compared to the fact that Kirek may have lied to her. She spun to face him, but didn't quite turn her back to the Zin. "Was that always your mission—to fix them? Did you lie to me from the start?"

He shook his head. "I didn't even know about the flaw until I entered their brain."

"Let's be clear. You had the chance to shut them down?"

"Yes."

"How do you know you succeeded in reprogramming them?"

"We're still breathing, aren't we?"

He had a point. "Maybe they'll pretend to be our friends for a while, then turn on us again."

"I overloaded the weapons that opened the wormholes to heat planetary cores. All the worlds are now safe. And the Federation will install safeguards to make sure that can't happen again."

"And the Zin will allow your safeguards?"

"Yes."

A mysterious and almost compelling computer voice, the voice of the Zin, answered for Kirek. "The Zin will permit Federation supervision."

"What about us?" Angel asked.

The Zin didn't hesitate. "You are free to go in peace. And we will escort your ship to a portal to speed you on your way home."

And so the Zin treaty was left for the arbitrators of peace to negotiate. Meanwhile, Angel had her own problems.

BACK IN THE Milky Way Galaxy aboard the *Raven*, Angel sat at the helm of her ship, staring out at the stars. Ever since they'd returned to the *Raven*, she'd been out of sorts with the way the mission had ended. She didn't know what to think about the Zin. Or about Kirek's risking their lives for a chance at peace.

She was irritated with herself for feeling annoyed at losing the Zin home world for salvage. Obviously, even she could see that turning the Zin into an ally would benefit the Federation far more than killing them all. And her personal disappointment seemed petty after all that had occurred.

Yet, she still hated her debt to Kirek for the *Raven*'s upgrades. She supposed the new ship systems would allow her to find many more prizes, but still owing him for the upgrades irked her. It wasn't that she didn't want to see him—she simply wanted any relationship between them to be her choice, and without the Zin homeworld to salvage, she might be paying back Kirek for her ship's retrofitting for centuries.

Kirek slipped behind the console beside her. He'd been so busy sending reports back home, they'd had no chance for a private conversation. "The mission didn't turn out as we'd planned."

"No, it didn't," she snapped, not certain she was ready to talk. While brooding hadn't helped her feel any better, she suspected arguing with him wouldn't either. And while she was saddened that their time together was coming to an end, she had to face that soon they would say goodbye.

"Tessa and Kahn have asked me to come home to Mystique. The Federation Council is in an uproar. According to Kahn, Tessa is fed up with politics and she thinks my statements will help the delegates reach a consensus." Kirek spoke as if choosing each word with care.

She didn't understand how the distance between them had grown so quickly. They were talking like two polite strangers—not lovers. And while she wanted to bridge the gap between them, she didn't dare. She already had too many feelings for Kirek.

When she remained silent, he placed his hand on hers. She jumped, but didn't draw away. She'd missed his touch and soon he would be gone. What harm could there be in enjoying a bit more of his affection? "I'd like to show you my home and introduce you to my parents and friends."

Her heart ached. "Why?"

"They wish to thank you for all you've done."

At his words, she did pull her hand away. She'd been inside his mind. She knew the way he felt about her. And while she returned some of those feelings, she would feel just as trapped on his world as any other. "I'll take you. But I . . . won't . . . stay—at least not for long."

"I know." He sighed. "When our psi merged, I realized that the *Raven* will always be your home."

Kirek's sense of duty to his people and his parents was so strong that he'd never leave them to come with her. He'd missed them all terribly during his long years of separation. Deep in his soul he longed to be with those he loved as much as she yearned to stay aboard the *Raven*.

She probably should have refused to take him to Mystique. But she wanted to meet his family and friends. And she wanted to spend more time with him. Just a few more self-indulgent weeks . . . Her heart might break when she said the final goodbye, but the damage was already done. Kirek already meant more to her than she'd ever intended.

So she might as well enjoy him for a bit longer.

AND ENJOY KIREK, she did. They made love repeatedly during the journey to Mystique and she discovered that the *Raven* had many facilities conducive to relaxation. After living in space for so many years, Angel had forgotten how lovely making love could be in a pool of warm water or on a blanket on a hot sand beach. She'd enjoyed every moment she'd shared with Kirek in the recreation facilities that could duplicate the pleasure pools of Lazpar IV or the pink powder sand beaches of Denbub's third moon. But Kirek's lovemaking made every encounter special and poignant as if he too was well aware that they had to live a lifetime of loving during the journey to Mystique.

They'd made an unspoken pact not to discuss the future. Instead they slept and made love and watched old holovids, fed one another delicious meals, and enjoyed their vacation. Angel thought she'd be ready to leave him when they reached Mystique, and hoped she'd tire of his company, that their lust would wear off and she could meet his friends and family and say goodbye with no regrets.

But as she viewed Mystique's green mountains from the vidscreen with trepidation, she realized that all too soon she'd have to share Kirek with those he loved. So many times she'd wanted to ask him to come with her, but as she'd seen the eagerness in his eyes as he spoke to those at home, she knew his heart was with his family. He'd been gone for almost nine long years and asking him to consider leaving before he'd arrived would have been selfish.

Kirek came up behind her, placed his hands around her waist, tugged her against him, and placed his chin on her shoulder. "So what do you think? Isn't Mystique a beautiful world?"

If he was hoping to convince her to stay, it wouldn't work. She was already dreading going down there. "I didn't expect the spaceport to be so busy."

"After the Zin destroyed the Federation capital, Mystique became the temporary home of the ruling council.

Kahn says they want to make it permanent, but Tessa, Mystique's leader, isn't pleased."

"Why not?"

"You can ask her yourself." Kirek nipped her neck, sending a delicious tickle down her back. "Ready to meet everyone?"

She hesitated. "You should go alone. Your parents haven't seen you in years. I'll be in the way."

Kirek's tone was light, eager. "Miri and Etru can't wait to meet you."

"What did you tell them about us?" she asked.

"That you kiss like a sweet dream. That when I hold you, I'm happy. And after we make love, all I can think about is how long until we can do it again."

She turned around and glared at him. "I'm serious."

"Will you relax? My mother and father will be so happy to see me, they won't care who I bring with me."

She raised a brow. "So they won't like me for myself?"

"They'll adore you because you saved my life more times than I can count." He gripped her arms, his eyes searching. "Besides, why do you care what they think? It's not as if you're planning to stick around for very long."

"Planets, homes, and families make me edgy," she admitted.

He grabbed her hand and tugged her toward the shuttle bay. "Since nothing I say is going to change your mind, we might as well get going."

That he'd let her off the hook and hadn't pressed her should have made her feel better. But her stomach knotted. Even piloting the shuttle down to the family's private landing strip did little to calm her nerves. She was about to meet living legends—Tessa Caymen and Kahn of Rystan. Dora—a living computer—and her husband Zical, plus Kirek's parents and cousins and assorted kids.

She should have dropped him off and left immediately. But she would never have forgiven herself for missing this opportunity. And if she didn't like his family she could always make up an excuse to leave. Angel really was comfortable in most social situations—probably because she didn't give a damn what anyone thought. But now . . . she wanted these people to like her and it bothered her that she cared so much.

She set down the shuttle in the middle of a pad that had been surrounded by a verdant garden with blooming flowers. Outside about thirty people had gathered to greet them. Before she unsnapped her safety harness, Kirek leaned over, angled his mouth over hers, and stole a kiss.

Heat suffused her and of their own volition, her fingers threaded into his hair. If only the world wouldn't intrude. If only he didn't have so many obligations. But for one moment, he was all hers and she reveled in his kiss. She didn't think she'd ever tire of him surprising her with those sparks in his eyes, or the mischievous grin she'd spotted before he'd swooped down to ravish her mouth, heating her blood and escalating her pulse.

When he finally pulled back with a satisfied smirk, she was certain her eyes had glazed over with lust. Great. With her lips all puffy from kissing him, her hair a mess, it was the perfect time to meet his parents—whom he hadn't seen in forever.

As usual, he'd known just what she'd needed. She slapped his butt with a playful smack. "Let's go before your parents think we forgot how to use an exit hatch."

Kirek grinned, unnecessarily helped her to her feet, then popped the hatch. "After one look at your swollen lips, they'll more likely believe you've been seducing their son."

Angel swore under her breath, wondering how their

words could have echoed outside—but apparently they
had carried. From outside the spaceship, she heard a
woman chuckle. "Kirek, there are children out here who
can hear you."

A woman laughed. "I'm sure Dora has already cor-
rupted the children."

"More. More," the kids shouted. "We want to hear
more."

"Settle down," an adult male ordered, but apparently
no one took him seriously—Angel and Kirek exited the
shuttle to more shouts of encouragement.

Kirek hadn't taken two steps forward before a woman
broke away from the others to hurry forward and embrace
him. "Mom." Kirek placed his arms around his mother
before Angel got a good look at her. "I've missed you so
much."

The warmth in Kirek's voice twisted Angel's heart.
And then his father joined the family hug and for one moment, she felt like an outsider. But then Kirek reached out
and pulled her forward. "Mom. Dad. This is Angel Taylor.
She's saved my life more times than I . . ."

Miri hugged Angel so hard she stole her breath and Angel didn't even hear what Kirek said—not that it mattered. Kirek's mom smelled like fresh-baked bread and
sweet cinnabar jelly and her crinkled eyes welcomed her
without any reserve whatsoever. It was as if whoever
Kirek brought home to her deserved her friendship. When
Miri finally stepped back to wipe away happy tears, Etru
hugged Angel all over again. With his dark hair and blue
eyes, the family resemblance was unmistakable. Thankfully the huge Rystani warrior knew his own strength, but
his bear hug was just as hospitable as his wife's. "Welcome
to Mystique."

Angel didn't have time to feel the least bit awkward.

Kirek kept an arm draped possessively over her shoulder as he introduced her to Tessa Caymen and Kahn, Dora and Zical, Alara and Xander, and Shaloma and a bunch of intelligent-eyed and happy kids, too many for Angel to even attempt to keep track of. With everyone laughing and talking and hugging at once, she learned that Miri had been cooking for a week to prepare a feast for Kirek's homecoming, that the Federation Council was awarding him the Qudsar Medal of Honor for his efforts, and that endorsement and holovid contracts were awaiting his signature in case he wanted to start a business venture or become a holovid star.

Kahn teased Kirek over the holovid offer, but Angel watched him draw Kirek aside for a serious private moment before they all headed toward a white canopy that draped a buffet laden with food, the enticing scents causing her to salivate. But Angel also noticed the security guards stationed around the picnic area. As Kirek poured her a fruit drink, she wondered if the guards were there for a specific reason or if the political problems Kahn had hinted at were more severe than he'd let on during his ship-to-Mystique conversations with Kirek.

However, the meal was one of celebration and Angel hesitated to bring up politics when everyone was so obviously determined to have a good time. Kids of all ages helped themselves to food and played mock war games. And unlike the kids at the school on Dakmar, these children seemed happy and well-behaved. Adults relaxed in the sunshine, but Angel noted that the men and Tessa's gazes never strayed far from the children and the perimeter.

The men had gathered around a barrel of brew, refilling their glasses as they spoke in low murmurs. The women wandered to the other end of the table. As much as Angel wanted to hear the men's conversation, the women here fascinated her.

"I'd love to see the *Raven*," Dora told Angel. "Kirek nabbed first dibs on the shapeshifting technology and Tessa's outfitting a new ship but it's not finished yet."

"I'd be happy to give you a tour," Angel told the gorgeous woman with holovid looks, finding it hard to believe she'd once been a computer. She seemed so alive, so motherly with her kids, and yet so in love with her husband.

Dora shot Angel a mischievous look. "Did Kirek install the bathing pool I designed?"

"He did." Angel had spent many wonderful hours in the pool with Kirek but the family gathering didn't seem a good time to mention that fact. But Dora seemed to know. Her eyes twinkled.

But before Dora said anything more, Tessa smoothly inserted herself into the conversation. "And the shapeshifting hull fooled the Zin?"

"Tessa, I hadn't finished asking her if the shape of the pool enhanced—"

Tessa rolled her eyes. "After all these years of being human, surely you can think about something else besides lovemaking?"

Dora shrugged. "Why should I have to? Alara's always talking about sex and you don't complain about her topic of conversation."

As Tessa and Dora spoke, their voices teased and there could be no doubting these two women were the best of friends. It was obvious from their tones, their glances, and their ease with one another, making Angel very aware that although she considered Frie a friend, she'd never shared as much with her as these two women seemed to.

Tessa sighed. "Alara is a scientist working on a biological problem."

"A problem no more." Alara's eyes gleamed. "I found a

way to break the link. Endekian women will no longer be forced to make love to regenerate their cells."

"That's incredible." Tessa raised her glass in a toast. "To Alara." They all sipped. Then Tessa eyed the scientist, speculation in her sharp gaze. "You didn't file the patents, did you?"

"The formula is my gift to Endeki."

Tessa grimaced but her tone remained light as she spoke to Angel. "Alara is a brilliant scientist but she has no head for business. I can't imagine working for years on a project only to give the work away."

"It's your fault," Alara teased her, not the least intimidated by the famous former Terran who was now the political backbone of Mystique and one of the foremost Federation leaders.

"Mine?" Tessa's eyes widened.

"You're so successful, none of us have to work."

Tessa sighed. "So my success has spoiled you."

Alara and Dora chuckled. "Your success has given us opportunities to pursue our goals."

"What will you do now?" Angel asked the scientist.

"I'm not certain," Alara admitted.

"I could use your help with the Federation Council," Tessa told her. "The Federation united to fight the Zin, but now that the threat is over, the delegates seem to have nothing better to do than squabble over resources. We have planets where entire populations are starving, a war about to break out over the mining rights in Orion's Belt, and the asteroid city of Halmenica wants independent status."

Dora's eyes narrowed on Tessa. "I've heard rumors about an attempt to overthrow the Federation Council."

Tessa sipped her drink. "They're just rumors. We haven't pinned down—"

"Excuse me," Angel interrupted, the hair on her nape

standing up and practically screaming from an instinct she didn't understand but had learned to trust. "Danger's coming." With a psi thought, she sent an order to her shuttle to lift into an orbit where it would be safe.

"Kahn! We're under attack!" Tessa shouted, almost at the same time Angel had spoken.

Skimmers shot across the previously empty sky. On foot, men charged out of the surrounding woods, weapons firing. The attackers fanned out but kept advancing, their movements coordinated and purposeful.

Security bravely placed themselves between the family and the attackers, but they were outnumbered and many of them died during the initial attack.

With a child in each arm, Dora, Alara, Miri, and Shaloma, with another youngster on her hip, quickly gathered the children into a group and rushed the youngsters toward the cover of the nearest building. None of the kids cried. All obeyed the instructions without panicking, surprising Angel.

Angel, Tessa, and the men retreated more slowly, firing their weapons to cover the retreat of the other women and children. Their defense was almost choreographed, or much practiced. But this was no drill. Men downed by the enemy fire didn't get up. And their shrieks of pain rang in Angel's ears.

"You okay?" she asked Kirek, retreating by his side.

"What the hell is going on?" he muttered. "Those are Federation troops."

"Tessa mentioned political problems." Angel raised her blaster and fired, bringing down a skimmer. Then she ducked into a building that appeared to be an electronics factory. But on closer inspection she realized the building was a control center with a vast security network and information-gathering system from where Tessa likely ran her empire.

Kirek made certain that everyone had retreated inside the building, then barred the doors. "There are always political problems. We are safe, here. The inside of the complex won't be penetrated by anything less than an army. Or a Zin core meltdown. And I wouldn't be surprised if Tessa's engineers have discovered a way to prevent that kind of attack."

Once again, Angel was surprised by the total calm of the children. They had gathered in a corner of the building outfitted with toys for the youngsters and vidscreens for the teens, who seemed just as intent on figuring out what had happened as the adults.

An hour later, the family gathered around a traditional hearth to discuss the situation. Kirek had insisted that Angel join them, his expression grave. She didn't believe she belonged here but since they hadn't had one moment of personal time since she'd arrived, she was reluctant to recall her shuttle from orbit and leave.

The family congregated in a large comfortable room, the hearth filled with Rystani glow stones. Angel was surprised to see that children, from babies to toddlers to the almost-adults, were also included. Once again, she was surprised at their good behavior. Obviously loved, yet not spoiled, the kids seemed happier than many others she'd seen—even after a nerve-wracking day.

Tessa spoke from a position beside her husband. "We've put together the pieces from today's attack and I'm happy to say it was due to a small faction of malcontents who are unhappy with the Zin peace treaty."

"Those responsible have been rounded up and the law will mete out their punishments," Kahn added. "The threat was minor and we believe that after the treaty is ratified, life here will return to normal."

Dora held a baby on her lap. "So why are we here?"

To Angel's surprise, Kirek stepped forward. "I have a proposal I wanted to make to our entire family."

Stunned that he'd said nothing to her about his proposal, Angel watched the family members turn to him, giving him their full attention and respect. And love. But she saw confusion on their faces, too. Apparently, no one had any idea what he was about to say.

Standing straight, shoulders relaxed, chin high, Kirek spoke slowly, as if knowing what he said next was of the utmost importance. "Now that my mission is over, I've been thinking about my future. All of our futures. I understand Alara has finished her task?"

"I have," Alara admitted. "Endekian women are availing themselves of my vaccine."

"And Tessa, you've been totally frustrated with Federation politics. Kahn's hinted that you've been looking for a successor."

"True."

"Kahn and Xander have completed the defense system of Mystique and can now leave the work to others."

Kahn folded his arms across his chest, his amber eyes bright with curiosity. "Are you saying we're no longer needed?"

"Not here on Mystique. Not even in the Federation. Most worlds are settled. It's crowded with political backstabbing, arguments over space lanes and trade routes, and—"

"What are you suggesting?" Tessa asked Kirek.

Angel was shocked that he would speak of these peoples' lives as if they were antiquated, almost as if he were belittling all they were doing. Yet, Kirek had always spoken about his family with love and the utmost respect, so she too wanted to know where he was taking this conversation.

"Angel and I have found a portal out on the rim that would allow us to travel to other galaxies—perhaps we can find one that needs exploration and colonization."

"You want us to leave Mystique?" Miri's lower jaw dropped open.

"I won't go without you. We've been parted long enough." Kirek's words were soft, certain.

Oh . . . God . . . Kirek's plan suddenly struck Angel full force. He'd always known she wouldn't leave the *Raven*. And he wouldn't leave his family. So he'd come up with the solution that they should all leave the galaxy—together.

But surely they wouldn't go? Tessa and Kahn owned an entire world. Within the Federation she wielded more power than almost anyone. They'd made a home here that would become the new capital of the Federation. Why would they want to leave?

And yet, at Kirek's words, she saw excitement bolt like lightning across the room until the very air around them crackled with electricity.

Two young boys separated themselves from the other kids and threw themselves at Kahn. "Dad, can we go? Can we? Please!"

Tessa shook her head, love in her eyes, and chuckled. "You know, the Milky Way is damn crowded. I wouldn't mind shaking down the new shapeshifting ship in a new galaxy."

Kahn hugged his boys and tousled their hair but remained silent.

Dora placed a hand on Tessa's shoulder. "If you're going, then I'm going. You'd get into way too much trouble without me." Then she turned to Zical with a question in her eyes. "Unless—"

"I was getting bored, anyway," Zical agreed. All at

once a dozen conversations broke out across the room as everyone speculated about Kirek's proposal.

"Hold on, before we all get swept away in excitement." Kahn spoke quietly, but everyone settled down. "A trip like this one will be dangerous. I suggest we all get a good night's sleep, maybe take a week, and then return to discuss it again."

Kirek immediately turned to Angel. "Will you stay until we make a decision?"

"Of course."

ENSCONSED IN THE luxurious private quarters of Kirek's home, Angel's emotions vacillated between hope and despair. As much as she wanted to spend more time with Kirek, she wished he'd spoken to her about his idea before he'd presented it to his entire family.

"What's wrong?" Kirek asked.

"Even if your entire family wants to go exploring in another galaxy, it doesn't mean that they won't eventually settle on another world."

"That world can be our base. We'll make the *Raven* our home and build a second home near my family. Seems like a good compromise to me."

He had everything all worked out. She should be happy. She shouldn't feel trapped. She should feel honored that he was willing to go to such lengths for her, and yet, if he was committing to the exploration and journey only for her, she suspected he might end up resenting her for it. And that would ruin what they had together.

"Does exploring the galaxy really appeal to you?"

He eyed her and kissed her neck. "Do you really think I would go just for you?"

Kirek knew her so well. She turned in his arms to look into his eyes. "So why do you want to go?"

"Curiosity. Challenge. Opportunity. Adventure. My work here is done." He lowered his head to nibble her collarbone, sending a delicious shiver of delight through her. "Besides, I can't imagine a life where we can't be together. Can you?"

She couldn't. But she didn't feel like talking about space travel right then. Not when there were so many other more pleasurable things they could be doing.

He lifted his head, whispered into her ear. "I love you with my entire heart and all my soul. Whatever it takes, I'll always find a way for us to be together. For as long as you want me."

Stars. He sure knew how to sneak under a girl's skin and steal into her heart. But would she always return his love? Twice before she'd thought she'd been in love. Twice before she'd been wrong. And yet she didn't want to think how much she would miss him if they weren't together. "I do love you."

"And you always will." He grinned at her. "I'll make sure of that, sweetheart."

His words sounded so good, yet she couldn't still her doubts, not so much in him, but in her own ability to commit to love and a permanent partner. "But—"

He cut off her words, tracing his finger over her lips. "You've been inside my mind. You know me better than anyone else in the universe. Did you see anything there you can't live with?"

"People . . . change."

"We'll change together. We'll grow old together—but not for a long, long time."

Angel bit her lower lip. "You're so certain."

"Certain. And determined to have you. Forever. Perhaps you've heard that Rystani warriors can be very stubborn men."

"Oh, really?" She started to laugh. "Define stubborn."

"We know what we want and we go after it."

She threaded her arms around his neck, arched her back, and pressed her breasts against his chest. "And here I thought you were all talk."

"Take a chance on me, Angel. Marry me?"

She tilted back her head, recognized the love in his eyes, and accepted what was in her head and her heart. Kirek understood her. He loved her. She loved him. She'd found her perfect mate. "Yes. I'll marry you . . . but I'm not promising to have your children."

She expected him to argue. He laughed, instead.

"What's so funny?"

"I was just thinking how much fun we're going to have while I change your mind."

"Rystani warriors aren't the only people who can be stubborn," she muttered, letting a challenge enter her tone. "Now kiss me, please. Before I decide you're all talk and no action."

"Woman, was that an insult?" He pretended to take offense.

"Take my words however you want." She grinned at him. "Take me, however you want."

And he did.

TURN THE PAGE FOR A PREVIEW OF

Island Heat

BY SUSAN KEARNEY

Available from Tor in February, 2007!

Prologue

After a two-year wait, Jamar finally had the opportunity to shoot his brother out of the sky. Now that the slime worm, Cade, had arrived, Jamar's cunning would pay off. Banking his spaceship to lock on his brother's craft, Jamar targeted Cade in his cross hairs. And fired.

"Got you."

Jamar's missile homed in on the ship breaking out of orbit. At this angle, it couldn't miss. But even as a thrill of satisfaction sizzled through Jamar, he noted three discharges and the pilot's ejection from the craft.

He checked the scanner and pounded his fist on the console.

Damn, Cade. The man possessed more tricks than a dock rat. Instead of attempting to return fire, he'd ejected his precious cargo—along with himself. So when Jamar's missile struck and Cade's ship disintegrated into a ball of flames, the stubborn bastard hadn't died.

Jamar swore and brought powerful scopes on line, watching as his brother plunged into the sea. He prayed he'd soon be fish food. Cade should never have been allowed to leave the creche. But that slime sucker had fooled his educators and his taskmasters, hiding his minuscule measure of cunning behind a devious mask. Cade's deception was a blight on all Jamar held sacred—order and discipline. So when the rebel had secretly conspired to foment discontent and disrupt the economy, Jamar had sworn to crush the nuisance.

Yet, his brother still breathed. But not for long.

Chapter One

It wasn't every day that Shara Weston saw a man fall out of an otherwise empty sky. Back in her Hollywood days, she would have assumed coke and booze accounted for the strange sight of a man plummeting toward the sea. But Shara had abandoned her movie career almost five years ago and she hadn't sniffed, injected or drunk herself into oblivion in almost a decade. She couldn't be hallucinating.

The sonic boom's echo that had drawn her attention from the Polynesian coral reef to the sky had been real. Lifting her head from the turquoise water, she'd anxiously thrust back her face mask and searched for the aircraft responsible for disturbing her late afternoon swim in her favorite island cove.

But she couldn't see any aircraft—just a body falling

through clouds too wispy to hide a plane. Shara held her breath, watching him fall, waiting for his parachute to deploy. It didn't.

When the horrifying notion finally sank into her stunned brain that no canopy was about to flare open, Shara's adrenaline revved. Replacing her mask over her eyes, her snorkel into her mouth, she swam for her boat, using her flippers to propel her through the water. Years of swimming made her quick, powerful and efficient.

As her arms churned the water in an effort to reach her boat, her thoughts swirled over the mystery of the man's fall. It didn't matter if he was a downed military pilot or a stuntman or a paparazzi come to spy on her in a plan gone terribly wrong, Shara couldn't survive another death on her conscience. Whatever his circumstances, she was the only person around who could help him. Her home on Haven Island in the South Pacific was wonderfully private, yet sometimes privacy could be damn inconvenient, especially if he required medical care.

He crashed into the ocean about twenty feet from her and struck the surface with enough force for a backlash wave to tug her under. Spinning ninety degrees to the left, she searched for him in the clear water. Bubbles surrounded his body but she made out a golden flight suit and his dark hair.

Please, please let him be alive.

Praying he wasn't a dead body someone had pushed out of a passing plane to dispose of, hoping his limbs would begin to move and he'd swim toward the surface, she hovered a moment. But he remained as still as her heart that seemed to have stopped beating.

She'd heard of freak accidents where people had survived a fall from such heights. So if he was alive and the force of the fall had merely knocked the wind from his lungs, she might yet save him. Shara gulped a large breath of fresh air through her snorkel, then dived downward. He was about four meters below the surface, and with the sea calm and the sun bright, she had no difficulty snagging him. Grabbing his gloved hand, she tugged, kicking them both upward.

She burst back to the surface and gratefully sucked oxygen into her lungs. As she breathed, she turned him unto his back, slung an arm around his neck and shoulder, and staying on her side, swam him toward the stern of her boat.

There was no way from her position in the water that she could shove the man's large body unto the diving platform. Somehow, she tossed her flippers into the boat, then climbed aboard with one hand while preventing him from floating away with her other. With both her feet planted on the decking, she hauled him up, first his powerful chest, then his muscular legs. She tossed aside her mask and snorkel, then wasting no time, she rolled him onto his back, pleased a pulse beat in the strong cords of his neck, but he wasn't breathing.

Tilting back his head, she pinched closed his nostrils, placed her lips over his mouth and blew air into his lungs. "Come on. Come on. Come on."

She exhaled more air into his mouth.

"Breathe. Damn you. Breathe."

Pale as a jellyfish, he didn't so much as flicker one black eyelash. Fierce determination compelled Shara to keep filling his lungs with air. No blood seeped from his nose, mouth or ears. He had a pulse and he was not going to die in her puddle of the ocean. Surely he hadn't been under water long enough to drown.

"Take a breath. Come on, man. Stop being so difficult. One breath."

He coughed, spit out water. With a groan, he opened his eyes, sea green eyes as deep as her lagoon. Bronzed skin tones replaced his former pallor. Relief washed over her, even as she noted his features. A bold nose and a strong jaw complemented his direct stare and made him as handsome as any of her costars, if she discounted the twist of his lips that grimaced in obvious pain.

With another grunt, he clasped one hand over his obviously injured shoulder, while still managing to convey his interest in her with a piercing stare. The reminder that she wore only a minuscule bikini caused a smidgeon of wariness to trickle through her psyche. Now that she was fairly certain he'd live, she wondered if he posed a threat.

Was it simply coincidence that out of the entire Pacific Ocean, he'd crashed in her backyard? She had to consider if he'd deliberately sought her out. While the world hadn't forgotten Shara Weston the movie star, reporters came to Haven much less often now that she was merely a casting consultant. But she remained wary, knowing that one compromising photograph could sell for big bucks. One exclusive scoop could make a reporter's career.

"Easy. Don't sit up yet." Shara placed a hand on his good shoulder, pleased at the warmth that indicated he'd thrown off the chill of the deep.

"I'm fine." Voice tough, but threaded with pain, he ignored her instructions. Shoving his good hand onto the deck, he raised himself to a prone position, shaded his eyes from the sun and searched the empty sky. At his effort, sweat beaded on his brow. "Have you seen anything . . . odd?"

"Other than you falling out of the sky?" she cracked, and when he didn't react, she figured from the way he cradled his arm that he was in more pain that he wanted to admit. "After your swan dive into the ocean, you may have dislocated that shoulder."

He licked his top lip, apparently needing the taste of

salt to believe he'd fallen into the ocean. Glancing sideways at her, he spoke carefully, almost as if he feared he might offend. "You have medical training?"

"You're holding that arm just like my stunt double did after Sweetie Pie bucked her off."

"Sweetie Pie?"

"Finest horse that ever made a movie." She bit her bottom lip. "Maybe you should—"

"I'm fine." The confident timbre in his tone suggested he was accustomed to giving orders.

He obviously wasn't fine. As he clutched his forearm to take the weight off his shoulder, his fingers trembled. Yet, with his gaze once more on the sky, he exuded masculinity, even as he again licked his top lip and a tiny smile of satisfaction curled his lip. The breeze carried his tantalizing scent to her nostrils and sunlight glinted off his reflective gold flight suit that molded to his broad shoulders. His wet dark hair, cut military short, spiked straight up and emphasized his chiseled cheekbones. A chest wider than the Pacific Ocean revealed the guy was in shape, possibly dangerous, reminding her that she had no idea of his intentions.

Shara stepped into her boat, opened a locker and tossed him a towel. Feeling too vulnerable in her skimpy bikini, she thrust her arms into a robe and tugged the belt tight.

Plucking two bottles of ice water from the cooler, she kept one, untwisted the cap of the second and offered it to her guest who had yet to make use of the towel. "Shara Weston."

"Cade Archer."

When Cade held her glance and introduced himself as if he'd never heard of her or the scandal, he raised her impression of him another notch. However, unless he was in too much pain for her name and face to register, or unless he'd grown up under a rock in a third-world country, he'd

undoubtedly read her name and had seen her face plastered on any of a dozen magazine covers during her scandalous heyday.

"Thanks for . . . saving my life." Cade accepted the
water bottle without letting his eyes drop to the open v-
neck of her robe, winning another point in his favor.

"No problem." She twisted off the cap of her bottle,
took a healthy swig, appreciating the cool liquid on her
parched throat. Shara hated personal questions so she
hesitated to ask them. But her curiosity got the better of
her. "You a pilot?"

"It's one of my skills." He downed his water in several
long gulps, then neatly recapped the bottle with only one
hand.

When he didn't volunteer more information, she raised
an eyebrow. "So exactly how did you end up here?"

A muscle clenched along his jaw. "I was shot down."

No kidding. And he'd survived a fall without a parachute. True, he'd landed in the water, but still, he'd fallen
thousands of feet and the crash should have broken every
bone in his body and caused all kinds of internal injuries.
That he'd survived was a miracle.

But why hadn't she seen any burning metal falling into
the ocean? "Where's your plane?"

"When another pilot locked onto me, I ejected before
he got off his shot," he explained with a commanding air
of self-confidence, as if he hadn't questioned his decision
to eject for even a second. "The missile disintegrated my
craft."

She hadn't heard of a war breaking out, especially over
Polynesia. She didn't even believe any nearby islands
possessed a landing strip long enough for military aircraft
either, but she supposed an aircraft carrier could be
nearby.

"Where are you from? Who shot you down?" She

shuddered. She knew all too well about accidents involving weapons. "Were you on a training mission that somehow went wrong?"

"That's classified." He craned his neck to search the sky yet again.

"Did you take off from a—"

"That's classified, too." The words sounded dangerous, menacing, but he delivered them softly, almost with regret.

"You're just full of secrets."

"You have no idea." Cade grinned, his smile all the more charming for his attempt to ignore the pain in his shoulder. It had been so long since she'd allowed a man to talk to her, never mind charm her, that the sudden warming heat in her core took her by surprise.

"Is your wingman coming to rescue you—"

"I'm alone." He had a solitary air about him, as if accustomed to the success or failure of a mission riding solely on his broad shoulders. However, she sensed no violence or threat coming from him and that eased her mind over her own safety. She didn't like the idea of bringing a stranger to Haven, but between his injury and the storm clouds moving in from the west, she saw no other choice.

"Let's get you back to my house and take care of that shoulder."

He turned irritated sea green eyes on her. "You haven't been listening."

"Sure I have. You said that your shoulder's fine." Shara moved to the bow of her boat, pulled up the anchor and secured it on deck. Her sarcasm got the better of her. "In fact, you're in Olympic gold medal form, no doubt able to swim across the ocean back to wherever you came from."

He let out a soft chuckle, then winced. "I wouldn't go that far."

"Your pupils are dilated. When the shock wears off, the pain will likely increase." She started the engine, turned starboard and set a course for her dock. When she noted his keen interest in a gorgeous stand of royal palms, she spoke with pride. "Haven's a tiny island, about one hundred acres of paradise, but I have my own water source and there's a surprising variety of flora and fauna."

"You own all of this?" Cade moved into the copilot's seat, careful to avoid jarring his arm.

She smiled with pride. "I bought Haven from a nervous seller. When the volcano at the south end rumbled and shot ash into the sky, I convinced him to sell the place to me."

Cade's gaze scanned the southern peak and returned to rest on her, his eyes full of curiosity. "You aren't worried the volcano will blow?"

She shrugged. "I had experts look over the place. They figure there's as much chance of an eruption here as there is of an earthquake taking out LA."

As she navigated through the reef and along the shoreline, they passed papaya, mango and breadfruit trees, several varieties of coconut palms and dense tropical plantings full of ferns, palmettos and banana plants. Wild chickens, iguanas, and turtles roamed the island, but Haven housed nothing more dangerous than an occasional mosquito that she could swat away—until now.

As an ex-actress Shara was good at reading people, but she couldn't get a bead on Cade Archer. Composed, intelligent, thoughtful, he kept his feelings checked. And he didn't talk about himself unless she pressed. Although he hadn't given her one solid reason to question his integrity, she sensed a well-hidden determination in the angle of his jaw and the glint in his eyes as he assessed his surroundings and took in the scenery with more than a casual eye.

"Would you consider selling your island?"

She shook her head. The first three years she'd lived here, she'd never left. Although during the last twenty-four months, she'd vacationed and had done some consulting abroad, Haven was not for sale. "This is my home. To me, it's paradise. No press. No trick-or-treaters. No nosy neighbors."

"You live here all alone?"

She hesitated, then nodded, seeing no point in lying when he'd see for himself soon enough.

His eyebrows rose in surprise or disapproval—she couldn't be sure. "Don't you fear pirates? Or storms? Or what if you get sick or hurt or lonely?"

"I have a satellite phone and a shotgun." And a vibrator, but she kept that fact to herself. In all ways important, she could take care of herself. "I also have medical books that will instruct us how to set your shoulder. Unfortunately for you, I don't keep painkillers on hand."

"Why not?" For an extra beat, he studied her face with an enigmatic expression.

"What I don't have, I can't ingest." She kept her tone light, noting a wry but indulgent glint in his eyes as her thoughts veered to the thirty-year-old bottle of scotch she kept on her mantle. Many a night she'd taken that bottle down, played with the seal, but it had yet to be broken.

She'd love a drink right now—to take the edge off a disconcerting day. No longer accustomed to sharing space with another human being, much less entertaining, she couldn't help feeling as if he'd invaded her world, her personal space. She'd moved to Haven in order to heal. And Cade's presence and questions were bringing back painful memories.

The Chevas had been a present from Bruce Langston, her leading man and husband's first-ever gift to her. During their four-year relationship, she'd never opened the bottle, and after his death, she'd kept her promise to him to stop drinking. She'd saved the aged alcohol as a memento, not only of their too-brief marriage but to test her willpower, to prove she was still strong enough to resist temptation.

With the afternoon's sun setting into the west, thunder clouds moved in. The breeze kicked up and the ocean responded by spewing white caps. In deference to her injured guest, she kept the boat speed slow and the bouncing to a minimum. However, by the time she'd entered her tranquil and protected cove on the lee side of the island to dock, Cade's bronzed face had paled to a sickly white and he clenched his teeth against the pain.

After she secured the boat with a line at the bow and another at the stern, he carefully climbed onto her dock, his breath coming in sharp grunts accentuated by a soft hiss. He staggered and two deep lines of worry appeared between his eyes.

Taking a quick step to his good side, she slipped an arm around his waist and tried not to recall how long it had been since she'd last touched another human being. "Think you can make it to the house?"

His knees buckled, and she took the brunt of his weight on her shoulder. If she hadn't supported him, he might have toppled into the water or onto the dock and caused additional injuries. Shoving her shoulder into his armpit, she half-carried, half-dragged him toward her home.

"You can make it to the porch, can't you?" she coaxed. "One step. That's right. Now another."

Between Cade's clammy skin and the shudders that racked his body, she feared he had internal injuries and was about to keel over. But without his help, she'd never make it from the dock and over the stone path along the beach, never mind carry him up her porch stairs. Cade was a big, rugged man. Although she tightly gripped him, her muscles ached and her legs shook from her effort.

She needed him to remain conscious and keep his feet under him.

He spoke with calm and authority. "I must . . . rest."

"Not yet. Soon," she promised. "Soon you can rest." She feared if they collapsed, she might not coax him back onto his feet. Together they covered the last dozen yards but wobbled to a halt at the bottom of the steps. "We have to go up."

"Up," he agreed with a cross between a grunt and a groan and a curse.

Breath coming in pants, muscles quivering with effort, Shara urged him with words and pushed him with as much strength as she could muster to climb one step, then another. The ten steps seemed like ten miles. And when they reached her porch, his legs buckled. She'd barely lowered him onto a chaise lounge before he passed out.

Shara didn't attempt to wake him. If he'd suffered from internal injuries, there was nothing she could do to help him, but if she could find the medical book and figure out how to pop his shoulder back into place before he came to, it would be a blessing. Hurrying into her home, she automatically wiped her sandy feet on a braided throw rug before treading across her wooden floors into the library. This was where she read scripts for A-list actors to help them decide whether to accept or turn down a proffered role. This was where she corresponded with the world, where her satellite cell phone and the occasional mail boat kept her in touch with friends and clients.

She'd stocked her library with hundreds of books and she'd catalogued them by categories. Gardening and food preparation took up one shelf of her bookcase. Engine repair, boating and navigation manuals shared shelving with carpentry and fishing books. Heading straight for the medical section, she removed a text from the top shelf and her first aid kit from her bottom desk drawer. With a scowl, she stopped by the fireplace to pluck the Chevas bottle from the mantle.

She'd vowed never to break the bottle's seal.

But did it count if the hooch wasn't for her?

Shara snatched a glass from her kitchen and returned to her front porch to find Cade once again conscious, but lying in the exact same position in which she'd left him. The sun had set and she flipped on a light. He didn't turn his head, but followed her movements with his eyes. His chest heaved and his breath sounded raspy. His color remained wan.

Pulling up a chair beside him, she opened the Chevas, poured three fingers into a glass. The rich golden color and the savory scent made her mouth water, but she ignored her burning yen for one quick sip.

Instead, she lifted Cade's head with one hand and tipped the rim of the glass to his lips with the other. "Drink."

He sniffed. Took a gulp. And sputtered. "Are you trying to poison me?"

How ironic that he didn't like the taste of the scotch that she had to fight against downing. "Chevas will help ease the pain."

"It's medicine?"

"Sure." His reaction and questions seemed peculiar. She placed a hand on his forehead to check for fever but his flesh felt normal to her. She held the glass to Cade's mouth again. "Drink some more."

He sipped and swallowed, screwing up his eyes but downing the alcohol. She kept the glass to his lips until he'd drained it. And when he lay back, he mumbled, his tone low and husky. "Mmm. That wassssn't ssso baddd."

Wow. The alcohol must have made a beeline from his gut to his brain. She supposed it was too much to hope the booze would work that fast on his pain as well. "How's the shoulder?"

"Goodd 'nuf to hold you." His voice, deep and sensual, sent a ripple of interest through her. A ripple she was determined to ignore. So what if lately she'd been yearning for conversation—one that wasn't by satellite phone. So what if she missed chatting about her day during a walk or over dinner with someone who cared. So what if she missed touching and being touched? Her recent yearnings likely meant she would be all-too susceptible to the first man she'd let set foot on the island in five years.

Annoyed she wasn't immune to his charms, Shara sighed, needing a distraction from the totally hot man on her lounge chair. She picked up the textbook and turned to the back where the appendix listed medical problems.

Cade hiccupped and then spoke slowly to enunciate each word with the excess care of a drunk. "You're reading backwards."

Shara turned to the page she needed, consulted the diagram. Did she possess the strength to pull his arm straight then slowly release it back to the correct position in the socket? The medical text suggested the procedure should only be done by an expert, and her stomach rolled as she read how she could cause more damage. But her closest neighbor was a three-day boat ride away, and by sea, it could take a week to reach a real doctor. The text also said that the sooner the arm returned to the proper position, the sooner it would heal.

"Give me your hand." She moved back her chair to the correct angle.

Jaw thrust forward, Cade shook his head, his profile strong and rigid. "Don't want to."

She didn't argue. Leaning forward, she picked up his long, callused fingers and gently raised his arm. Following the text's directions, she placed her bare foot under his armpit but on his ribs.

Two dimples appearing in his cheeks, Cade grinned at the sight of her foot. "Pretty toes."

"This may hurt." Betraying none of her uncertainty over the procedure, Shara slowly applied tension, tugging on his wrist and implementing pressure with her foot against his ribs to cause the necessary separation between his shoulder and the socket.

In fascination, Cade stared at her toes. Then he jerked up his head, his mouth twisting into a line of discomfort, his eyes hardening. "Ow. That hurts."

"Sorry." She kept right on tugging.

Cade grunted, his arms stiffened. His entire body tensed and bowed.

And something in his joint moved. Very slowly, she lessened the pressure. When she finished, she noted his hand had slipped into hers and his former grimace had relaxed noticeably. "How do you feel?"

Eager affection radiated from him. "Kiss me again."

Again? "We've never kissed." She attempted to draw back her hand.

He refused to release his grip. "You kissed me back to life. I tasted the salt on your lips."

He remembered her artificial respiration? How was that possible? He'd been unconscious. Shara didn't have to be a doctor to know Cade's reactions were all wrong. First he'd survived a fall from a plane without a parachute, without sustaining one broken bone and apparently no internal injuries beyond the dislocated shoulder. Next, he'd recalled memories from when he'd been unconscious, and last, she'd never seen anyone who had gotten drunk that fast.

And his flight suit was composed of a very strange material. She could have sworn when he'd been in the water that the sleeves had covered his arms down to his gloved hands, but now the material was short, hugging impressive biceps.

Shara really could use a drink. She stared at the open Chevas. Licked her bottom lip.

He tugged her closer and she didn't want to risk hurting his shoulder by resisting. She sat beside him, close enough to inhale the scotch on his breath that taunted her, tempted her. If she kissed him, she'd taste the delicious liquor on his lips.

Stop it.

While the alcohol had clearly lowered his inhibitions, she didn't have an excuse for the sudden desire to kiss him that flooded her. She simply craved the booze—not the man.

Attributing her sudden fascination with his mouth and the yearning for him to the overload of leftover adrenaline from her taxing afternoon, she squared her shoulders. "How's your shoulder? Will you let me fix a sling?"

"So pretty." His tone was singsong but pleasant and musical and very powerfully male. "I'll let you do whatever you want with me."

Sheesh. One little drink and Military Man had turned into charming Lover Boy. Wary, but amused, she finally disentangled her hand from his and opened the first aid kit.

Cade raised his head. Catching her by surprise, he brushed back a loose lock of hair from her face and kissed her brow. "Thanks for making the pain go away."

"You're welcome." His eyes held hers, almost as if he knew exactly what he was saying.

Again she thought his reaction odd. She'd seen a lot of drunks. None of them got wasted as fast as he had. None of them recovered as quickly. It was almost as if his system worked at super-human speed.

"I didn't mean for us to meet like this," he mumbled, his tone cagey.

"Really?" She dug through the first aid kit, putting

aside ointment, bandages, scissors. Behind a roll of tape, she found a folded sling.

"I was supposed to . . ."

She shook out the sling and adjusted the neck strap to the roomiest setting. "You were supposed to what?"

"Supposed to seduce you."

He wasn't making any sense. Obviously the alcohol was doing his talking and she took no offense. "You're a pilot and you've been shot down."

"But not in hostile territory." He seemed quite proud of himself and his gaze on her was as soft as a caress. "You like me, right?"

"Sure." She hadn't known him long enough to make a decision, but so far, so good. He'd piqued her interest, made her aware of him as a man. She slipped the material over his head, bent his arm and placed it into the sling. "I'm certain you're a really great guy. But you shouldn't get any wild—"

The roar of an aircraft cut off her words. A roar so loud it sounded as if it the plane was about to crash into her home.

Tilting her head to search the night sky, she saw hellish sparks. Flames. Smoke. Surely two different people couldn't crash into her island on the same day?

Her porch shook as if sprayed with hail that ripped large holes in the deck. Dust from the eaves rained down and her eyes teared.

What the hell was going on?

Cade grabbed her shoulders, tucked her against his chest. A strong, hard chest. "Get down. We're under attack."